_un_ BECOMING

Emma

a novel

KELLY BYRNE

Two Pens Press
Los Angeles

Published by Two Pens Press
6450 Sunset Blvd. #1363
Hollywood, CA 90028

Library of Congress Control Number: 2024905102

First print edition published 2024

Unbecoming emma / Kelly Byrne
ISBN: 979-8-9902931-9-9 (paperback)
ISBN: 979-8-9902931-4-4 (ebook)

To everyone who loves.

*The only person you are destined to become
is the person you decide to be.*

— RALPH WALDO EMERSON

ONE

The morning after my father died, I woke on the cool ground under our backyard willow tree with my golden retriever Bob snuggled by my side. Of course, waking out there surprised me. I'd never been a sleepwalker before. Then I found it fitting, poetic even, given the time Dad and I had spent together under the tree. It was our place to talk, our leafy sanctuary.

But damn. It had been weeks, and I was still pulled nightly to the tree by a force I didn't understand. To hell with poetry, I needed lumbar support and a good night's sleep.

The day things changed, everything began the same. Bob woke me at dawn under the tree, curled up in his usual spot. The tip of his tongue poked out the front of his mouth as he blew warm dog breath in my face. His body shook and his paws twitched, chasing squirrels in his dream.

I reached over to soothe his fuzzy head and he coughed. A dry hacking sound, like he was trying to clear something from his throat.

"It's all right, mister. You're okay." I scratched behind his ears, his favorite spot. He wasn't getting worse, but he wasn't getting better either. I'd have to take him to Dr. Dixon soon if things didn't change. "You have to be okay," I said, massaging his groggy face as he woke.

A swift breeze from Maiden Lake swept across our lawn and up through the tree. Instead of dancing in the wind, the willow branches closed down around us, like a flower unblooming, sheltering Bob and me from the early morning elements. They crept inward, ever closer, reaching in to touch us.

Bob coughed again and the tree released, expanding outward all at once in a rush of rustling branches, back to a leafy bell jar again.

I grabbed the wooden seat of my old swing to pull myself up, and an orange envelope fell to the ground. It was exactly like all the others I'd found and hadn't opened for the last few weeks, since the morning I began using my backyard as a bedroom.

It was smooth and substantial in my hand, upscale stationery. My father loved pricey paper products. But how could I be sure any of these were mine? None of them were addressed to me, there was no writing anywhere on the outside. Maybe someone had put them there by accident. Twenty-three days in a row.

I stared at the tree trunk, looking for answers.

Not for the first time lately, I considered the rumors that used to fly around town about my mother, Cassie McCormack, and whether I was following in her footsteps.

Back then, Calypso Springs buzzed with theories about what happened the night she disappeared. Most of the town thought she'd come unglued after giving birth to me. So my grandparents, Jack and Mary McCormack, kidnapped her and fled the area to avoid the stigma of mental illness in their perfect family. A few said they all ran off to join a cult. And one enthusiastic believer blamed aliens.

However they left, and for whatever reason, my mother and her parents disappeared without a word when I was born forty years ago and no one I knew ever saw them again.

And now my father was a tree.

If they found out, I imagined everyone in town would have a

good laugh and pat themselves on the back for being right all along about Cassie McCormack, because the cheese had flown right off my cracker, too. Must be something in the McCormack genes.

He smiled through the knots and whorls of wood, like it was the most normal thing to do early on a Wednesday morning. It made me miss him even more. When I was little, I believed his laughter could heal the world.

But I wasn't going to talk to him. That might take things to a level I couldn't come back from, *because what if he answered me?*

"Em?"

Oh god, here we go.

He had a high voice for a tree, though.

Bob shot a warning bark across my bow. He didn't stand. Just stared at the trunk of the tree.

"Em, honey, are you out here?"

Bob barked again, toward the outside world this time. He stood next to me in welcome mode with his propeller tail roaring at full speed.

"Oh, thank Christ," I said under my breath to no one because, thank Christ, the tree wasn't talking. It was Tee.

Teresa Potrero, Dad's best friend, was the closest thing I'd ever had to a mother. A beige wall of a woman, she didn't believe in slouching and never took no for an answer. Except from my father.

I wasn't expecting guests and my current situation didn't look good for my sanity, so I turned my back to Tee before she pulled the curtain of willow branches open, and kneeled next to Bob.

"You can't wander off like that, mister. You worried me," I said, loud enough for my neighbors to hear.

"Em?"

"Holy nuggets, Tee! You scared me."

"Sorry, I thought you might have heard me calling you."

"I was looking for this guy," I said, petting Bob. "He sneaked out this morning and I didn't know where he was." *I was going to hell for lying to her. This I knew.* "It's so early. Everything okay?"

"Yeah, sure. Everything's... I just wanted to check in on you. It's been a minute." Bob sat like a good boy and pawed at her leg. "Hi, Mr. Wigglepants, it's good to see you too," she said, wincing as she crouched down to pet him. He eagerly awaited another face to kiss.

"Careful with your back, Tee."

"Oh, I'm fine. Nothing a few shots of cortisone can't fix."

Bob continued his noble mission to give all the kisses until Tee couldn't take any more love. Before she stood, she glanced at the ground where we'd slept the night before and spotted my body-shaped imprint in the matted grass. "Em, were you—"

"I think my phone's ringing." I charged toward the wall of branches. It was so early-morning silent you could hear the wings of my lie flapping like a butterfly in the stillness. Lying to my mother-figure made my stomach burn, but desperate times. I couldn't answer her questions and I had to get her out of there before she saw anything untoward.

"I've got to get to work early today, Tee. Sorry. You caught me on a busy one."

"What's that?" she asked, following me.

"What?" I turned to her, and she pointed to the orange envelope in my hand. I was the proverbial deer in headlights. "Oh, it's nothing." I shrugged and kept moving toward the back door.

"Letter from Dad?" She recognized his stationery.

"Just some old mail I found." I shoved the envelope into my pajama pocket on my way to the house. It would go on the expanding pile of identical orange envelopes in the living room. I had no intention of opening any of them.

I knew, from that deep place that makes the hair on your neck shoot up when you're in danger, if I opened it, things would never be the same. I trusted the goose bumps. I lived by the goose bumps.

Tee's tight-lipped smile told me she didn't buy it, but she

didn't press the issue. Unusual for her, but I appreciated the restraint. I wasn't about to spill the tea to anyone about the strange things happening in my world. Not even Tee. My friends would never engage in town gossip, but what they didn't know couldn't hurt me.

"Feels like we haven't talked in a year, Em. Do you need anything? Are you eating?"

"Yeah, we're good. We're—" I glanced behind me to make sure Bob was following. He wasn't. "Where's my good boy?" He'd actually wandered off now.

Tee and I both scanned the backyard. Then I checked the water. Our house was a hundred feet from Maiden Lake. "Damn it. Not again. No, Bob! Leave it," I yelled, rushing toward the hollowed out tree stump he was tearing into by the shoreline.

He'd become obsessed with the old stump after Dad died, burrowing into the wet, rotting wood for the last couple of weeks, on a mission to find it. I didn't know what *it* was, but Bob knew, and he wasn't about to stop until he found it.

"Sorry, Tee," I yelled, halfway across the lawn. "If you've got to get ready for school..."

"I'm here," she yelled, waving and waiting by the back door for me like she didn't have a full morning to prepare for. So often, it's the little things people do that show how much we're loved. Made me feel like an even bigger jerk for wishing she'd leave.

"Bob, come!" I yelled, still about twenty feet away from him. His fuzzy, rust-colored head sprang up out of the stump. He stared at me, panting, almost daring me to make him move.

"Robert Redford. Now!" I meant business when I used his full name. He raced to me without hesitation. "Good boy—gah!" Spoke too soon. Soaked and dirty, he shook out all over me. Flecks of sand and moldy, wet wood flew everywhere. "No, Bob! No shake!"

I shielded myself and raced toward the house. He chased after me like it was a game. Tee stood next to the back door, staring at my flower garden nestled up against the house.

"Beautiful, right?" I said, out of breath from my quick sprint. She didn't answer. I pressed on, proud of my handiwork. "Look at those snapdragons and peonies. And the hyacinth. I've never seen them like this."

"Em..." Tee surveyed the flowers like she was looking for her words inside them. Then, she slouched. A slight dipping of the shoulders, imperceptible to anyone who didn't know her like I did. She was not a woman who hunched or lost her words, so it was clear she was holding on to something she didn't want to say. Quite the aberration. The thing I admired most about Tee was her enthusiasm for sharing every one of her opinions with us, whether or not we asked for them.

She turned to me and took a breath before she spoke. "How are you, honey? Really."

A lot of weight in that question. So I used my dog as a diversion again. He sat at my feet, that starvation longing in his eyes, dumbfounded because I hadn't fed him yet.

"I'll feed you in a minute. Right now, you go to bed." I pointed inside the house. His ears drooped, but he opened the back screen door with his nose and trotted to his bed inside. "My dog is a superhero." I smiled proudly at Tee.

"Your phone is *actually* ringing now," she said. "Might want to answer it." She smirked, letting me know she was on to me.

My phone was on the island in the kitchen surrounded by several large vases full of blooming yellow daffodils. I ran in to check the caller ID before I answered it. *Cranston & Associates.* Dad's lawyer. He'd called every day since the funeral. I sent it to voicemail.

Why was everyone in such a rush for me to settle things and move on like my father had never existed? I wasn't interested in discussing Dad's will with Lou Cranston, Esq., or anyone else for the foreseeable future. And I was *this close* to filing harassment charges against him.

I turned the phone off and dropped it in my purse, along with the orange envelope. Bob intercepted me on my way back toward

Tee in the living room. He sat at my feet, like a statue, staring up at me. His look was clear. *Immovable until fed.*

"Okay, mister. I've got you."

After he ate, I checked on Tee in the living room. She stood in the middle of it, surveying and silently forming an opinion. "I've got a light morning," she said. "Parent/teacher conferences later this afternoon. I can stay and clean up a bit."

"How's Hopper?" I asked. "Did they let him out of jail yet?"

Hopper Potrero, Tee's father, had been arrested the night after Dad's funeral last month. They caught him driving his neighbor's lawn mower around town in nothing but her stolen lingerie. He said he liked the feel of silk on his skin. He was, of course, driving drunk.

"Yes, he's out," Tee said, roaming around the living room aimlessly. Tee did nothing aimlessly.

"That's great. I mean, he makes a good point about the lingerie."

"Sam said she hasn't talked to you since the funeral. Every time she stops by, you're gone. You haven't returned any of our calls. We're starting to feel like you're avoiding us."

"I know. I'm sorry. I'm not avoiding you, I'm just busy." *Liar liar.*

"Do you have a little time after work tonight? I want to talk. I miss you." It was comforting to see the twinkle in Tee's eyes still. I always felt safe with her, but talking was the last thing I wanted to do.

"They're shorthanded at Connie's this week and I told Agnes and Gerty I'd be there for bath night tonight." *Pants on fire. Why had it become so easy?*

"You're volunteering again? I thought...maybe you'd take time off."

"I took time off. The last six months."

"You've been taking care of Josiah. That's not time off, honey. It's the opposite."

"I promised Dad."

"Promised him what?"

"I'd volunteer."

"Em, you need a break. A real one. Give yourself time to grieve."

"I know that."

"Do you?"

I wasn't sure I did, but there was no way in hell I was going to admit that to her.

"Tomorrow? We could grab lunch."

"Sorry, Tee," I said, checking my watch, "I really do have to to —where are my keys?" I shot around the living room like a pinball let loose, searching. "I'm always losing something." *My keys. My mind.* I felt along the sides of the couch, came up with willow branches—*How did they get there?*—and threw them behind the couch before Tee noticed.

"Nesting?" Tee noticed.

"They're for a project at Connie's." *Lying for sport now.*

"Okay, I'm just going to say it." She surveyed the living room looking for more of her words there. "I'm worried about you, Em. We all are. It's been almost a month now. You need to start moving forward."

"I am moving—"

"Perpetual motion is not...have you even called Cranston back yet?"

"I'll call when I get some time. I've been—"

"Busy, yes, fairly obvious, given..." She gestured around the room.

"Found 'em!" I pulled the keys out from under the couch. Bob must have hidden them there. He always hid his bones and toys under the couch, ready to take to the backyard and bury later.

Tee was unimpressed. I faced her and held her by the shoulders. "I know you're worried, but I wish you wouldn't be."

"We can all come by tomorrow and help you clean up a little."

"I don't need help, Tee."

"Emma, you have a garden of rotting flowers out back and the same in your kitchen. Foot high stacks of unopened cards littering the living room. Piles of laundry, a kitchen full of dirty dishes. Something frightening growing in the sink and somehow also the corner of this room, which, I presume, is hazardous to everyone's health. You haven't even called hospice to come for the bed yet." She glanced over at Dad's bed, still set up in the corner of the living room. "Let us help you."

I surveyed her grievances. Maybe I could tidy up a little. Yes, there were piles of unopened sympathy cards around the living room, because why would I want to revisit my grief over and over?

But the flowers? "My garden is amazing, Tee. Best one I've ever had. And those daffodils in there are...nice," I said, pointing at the vases in the kitchen. "Though I wish the lovely people of this town would stop leaving them on my doorstep every morning. Or at least, mix it up a bit. We all know daffodils aren't my favorite."

Tee gave me *the look*. That look all mothers perfect to let their children know their time for bullshit is up.

"Fine. I'll call. First thing tomorrow." I wasn't about to call anyone tomorrow, but I couldn't bear the weight of that look. "Or, you know, as soon as I can find a minute. Tomorrow's our busiest day at the shop. We're prepping for the Kingston wedding this weekend. So many bouquets, so little time. And I signed up for everyday deliveries with Meals, so—"

"Who are you going to call?" Tee asked, like she was quizzing one of her fifth graders.

"Ghostbusters?" Not even a hint of a smile from her. "Cranston. I'll call Cranston."

"Do you have his number?"

"Of course."

"Want to check?"

I took my phone from my purse in the kitchen, still off, and pretended to search my contact list. "Cranston & Associates. Right here."

"We'll come by, do a little light dusting. Get rid of that thing in the corner. Nothing major. I'll call hospice."

"It'll all get done, Tee. But right now, I've gotta get to work." I headed for the door, hoping she'd follow.

"Casual Wednesday, is it?"

"What?"

She pointed at my clothes. I looked down. Still wearing my mismatched pajamas.

"Clean nothing," I said, wagging my finger at her on my way up the stairs to get dressed.

She couldn't help herself. When I raced back down, properly clothed, she was busy cleaning the living room. Specifically, that thing in the corner, which was too close to the pile of orange envelopes I didn't want her or anyone else to notice.

"I'll take care of it tomorrow," I said, moving her toward the front door. No simple task that, since she stood about three inches above me. A low growl escaped from her as we moved, but we still ended up there.

"Let's go, Bob!" I squawked, heading outside. In my haste, I'd forgotten about the daily flower delivery and almost crushed the fresh bouquet of daffodils waiting on the front porch outside the door.

"Whoa. That was close," I said, picking them up.

Tee gave me a strange, sad look when I did. I tried to cheer her up. "Want a perky bouquet for your classroom? Daffodils are all about new beginnings."

"I believe the new beginning is meant for you, honey." She smiled, but there was still sadness in it.

If chronic sleepwalking, strange multiplying letters, and dad-trees were part of my new beginning, I preferred the same old same old, thank you.

I took the flowers into the kitchen, snipped off an inch from each of their stems, and nestled them into the least crowded vase next to the other daffodils.

"Let's go, mister!" I yelled again. Bob came bounding out the front door after me, skipped all the steps on the porch, and headed straight for the passenger side of my old Chevy pickup truck. He knew the routine.

That truck was fifty years old, reliably unreliable, and the only thing I could afford. I never knew, from one day to the next, if it would start or get me out of my driveway. Kept me on my toes. Just like life.

I opened the heavy door and patted the seat for Bob to jump in. He happily obliged. His fur was almost dry, but I'd need to brush him out later. Goldens are notorious shedders. A tiny burden to bear for the biggest love in the world.

He licked my cheek to show how excited he was to be going for a ride. I kissed the pointy knob on the top of his head before I closed the door.

Tee waited for me on the driver's side.

"You better leave that living room alone. I'll clean when I get home later."

"I'll leave the living room if you call Cranston."

"Yep."

"You'll want to turn your phone back on before you do. Might make the calling part easier." Tee winked, kissed my forehead, and sauntered down the driveway toward the street.

"The jig is up, mister," I said, climbing into the truck with Bob. It finally started on the third try.

The hairs on the back of my neck stood at attention, like I was being watched, so I checked the rearview mirror before I put it in gear to leave.

"No. Not possible. Trees don't *move*."

I inspected the side of the house out the back window of the truck. Bob barked, like he knew what I saw, what I couldn't have seen, peeking out at us.

It was gone. Of course it was. It had never been there.

"It *would* explain the branches in the house, though."

I drove away without looking back again.

TWO

We had visitors when Bob and I pulled into our driveway later that evening. It was still hot and muggy as I hopped down out of the truck, but the evening heat didn't cause the sweat on my hands. I love my friends, but I could feel it. They were there to handle me, and I was never in the mood to be handled.

When I opened the front door, Tee peeked out from behind the blanket she was folding by the couch, but didn't make eye contact with me. Bob whined and wiggled over to greet her. He was always in the mood to be handled.

"Hi, Mr. Wigglepants. Yes, it's good to see you again," Tee said, flinching as she bent down to let Bob have his way with her. His tail clicked into propeller mode.

"You guys," I said, standing in the middle of my house, not knowing which way to go first. "This is so unnecessary."

In the kitchen, Sam stood at the sink washing dirty dishes. I tried to stop the madness.

"Samantha Obermeyer, put that plate down," I said, rushing her.

"Touch me, I'll cut you," Sam said, holding up a sudsy butter knife. A patch of bubbles sparkled and popped on her freckled cheek where she'd swiped it with a glove. It only added to her charm and flawless complexion.

"Make it stop," I said, leaning against the counter.

"No-can-do. Em, there were things growing in there." She pointed to the sink. "Like creatures from another galaxy."

"I was experimenting."

"Experiment over there." She nodded in Tee's direction. "She's worried about you."

"I'm fine."

"Aforementioned creature would indicate otherwise."

I growled at her. She turned to me and we shared a look, all joking aside.

"We all are, Em. Worried."

I was worried about me too, but for very different reasons. Reasons I couldn't share, even with my best friend. That killed me because there wasn't anything I kept from her. Since first grade, Sam always had a way of reading me like nobody else could. She took me in her arms. Warm, sudsy hands embracing me. Her hair smelled like bubble gum and childhood.

"Breathe," she said. "It'll be over soon."

Neither of us knew how wrong she was.

In the living room, Hopper, the great redwood, bent stiffly to collect willow branches one at a time from where I'd tried to hide them from Tee earlier.

"No. Hopper, please stop." I pulled away from Sam and charged toward him. "You're going to throw your back out again, just like Tee," I said, trying to snatch the willow branches from him. I almost threw my own aching back out yanking on them.

"Em, we come to see how you're holding up. And to house keep," he said, playing tug of war with me for the branches.

"Tee, tell your father to give me the branches and stop picking things up off the floor."

"Ha! When has he listened to anything I told him to do?"

"He's here, isn't he?" I said, surrendering the branches to him.

Hopper may have been twice as old as my truck, but he was unreasonably strong.

"Yeah, he's here. That's more about you than it is me, honey," Tee said.

"He is here and he don't appreciate bein' talked about like he ain't. Think I'll have a nap now," Hopper said. Still holding the branches, he lumbered to the corner and flopped down in Dad's recliner to take that nap. His attention span left something to be desired, but at least he wouldn't be rummaging around the living room anymore.

"Thanks for the help, Dad. You go to sleep here, you're staying the night." Tee's face turned red, flustered, as always, with her father. Their relationship had two settings: estranged and nuclear. I never understood where all the tension came from, but this was not the time to defuse that bomb.

"Fine by me. Comfy chair," Hopper said, pushing back in the recliner and closing his eyes.

"Oh, I don't think that's necessary," I said. I glanced at Tee, terrified she was serious about leaving Hopper overnight. That's when I noticed it. Couldn't believe I hadn't seen it before. The big open space in the corner of the living room, full of nothing, where Dad had been living horizontally for the last few months. Tee saw what I was not seeing and approached me, resting her hand on my back. "I called Hospice this morning, after I left."

My fists clenched and unclenched along with my jaw. I didn't know what to do with my frustration. It felt like I might explode and I didn't want to do that on my friends when all they were trying to do was help. So I shot over to Bob and laid down to snuggle with him on his bed. His slobbery kisses calmed me enough to make sense of my thoughts again. He always had a way of bringing me back to myself.

"Honey, I know it's a shit situation, but it was time," Tee said, following me over to Bob.

I took a deep breath before I spoke so my voice wouldn't shake. "I know you want to help, Tee, but I wish you wouldn't."

Sam strolled in from the kitchen, her gloves leaving a soapy trail on my hardwood floor. She and Tee shared a look, each one nodding. What was happening?

They closed in on us like Bob and I were rabid animals they didn't want to spook for fear we'd bolt or bite.

What the hell was this? An intervention?

"You don't need the stress of cleaning up the house, taking care of the will, and everything else all at once," Tee said.

"As usual, you're taking on too much, Em," Sam said.

Holy shit. That's exactly what this was.

"The will?" I stopped petting Bob. Why was everyone so obsessed with the damn will?

"You call Cranston?" Tee sat down in front of Bob and me on the floor, gritting her teeth as she bent down.

I glanced away without answering.

Sam sat next to Tee, still dripping blobs of bubbles onto the floor in front of Bob. He stared at them, like maybe they were his to eat, but he didn't even try to lick them. My brilliant dog.

We squished in around Bob on his bed and Hopper snored from Dad's chair in the corner. My family.

"Let us lighten your load for you," Sam said, rubbing my back with wet rubber gloves.

"But *your* load is heavy enough, Sam. The twins are on summer vacation soon and you're running the paper and dealing with your parent's divorce all at the same time. And I still need to come help you with the garden. I've been promising since last April—"

"Who cares about the garden, Em? I mean, come on. Your plate has been full for the last forty years. It's time to empty it and start over."

"Forty years?" I said. "I wasn't born busy."

"Weren't you? You always take on too much. You can't— you're always—ugh, this is ridiculous. Emma Marie Rosen," Sam said, standing to pull up her tough love pants. She only ever used my full name if she was serious, which she rarely was. "We're going to clean up the house and you're going to go see the lawyer about the will and settle that business so you can move on and start living your life. End of story," she said. "Bam."

Tee winked at Sam, like they'd planned this in advance. She pulled my phone from my purse and offered it to me with a warm smile. "We're here for you, honey. No matter what."

They were keeping something from me. I could feel it.

Wait a minute... "Start living my life?" I said, staring up at Sam.

"Come on, Em." She squatted down to our level. "You're volunteering again." It was almost an accusation.

"And?"

"Have you taken any time for yourself since he died? Have you allowed yourself time to grieve? I'm asking seriously because I haven't seen you, so I have no idea what your life is right now."

There it was. My negligence had wounded her, and for that I felt terrible. I'd never hurt her on purpose. But how the hell could I explain what had been going on for the last month and not sound like they should lock me in a padded room?

I didn't know what to say or how to make her feel better without lying more, so I didn't respond. Just kept petting Bob.

"Em, we wanted to be there for you, but you shut us out," Sam said. "I don't understand why. Maybe you'll explain it someday, but right now, it doesn't even matter. We want to make sure you're taking care of yourself, and by the look of this house, you're not."

"I don't have time to clean. I told you, Tee, I promised Dad I'd go back to volunteering. It gives me purpose."

"Fair enough, honey. But does it make you happy?"

"Helping is good. It's a good thing to do. I don't understand why you're—"

"Yes, but does it make you happy? Is it what you want?"

"It's not about me."

"That's the problem," Sam and Tee both said in unison, as if they'd rehearsed it.

"I don't have a problem." Now I was defensive and delusional.

"Em, when was the last time you went on a date or made plans that had anything to do with something you wanted?" Sam asked.

"I don't know what dating has to do with anything."

"When was the last time you researched shop space? Or land for a flower farm? I haven't heard you talk about your dreams for years," Tee said.

"The medical bills. And the mortgage. I can't afford any—"

"You had a dream, Em, from the minute I met you," Sam said. "Six years old and you knew what you wanted. I wanted Barbies, and you wanted flowers. Then you buried your dream to take care of everybody else. It's time to resurrect it, or at least think about building a new one."

Dream? What dream? It had been so long since I'd let myself consider dreaming I couldn't even remember what it had been. Sam and Tee exchanged another knowing look. It made me feel like the little kid left out of the adult conversation. *The grown-ups are speaking, sweetheart. You hush now.*

"Sam's right, honey." Tee still held my phone in front of me. I didn't take it.

How dare they barge into my emotional world to boss me around? Their hearts were in the right place, but I wasn't about to be bullied into doing something I wasn't ready for.

"What does it matter when I call the lawyer? What's the rush?"

"What are you afraid is gonna happen when you call?" Sam asked.

"I'm not afraid." Another lie. I'd most likely lose the house because I was too many payments behind to catch up. I wasn't ready to deal with that or packing up my father's life like he'd never existed. The idea of me moving forward when he wasn't here to move forward with seemed wrong. Unnatural.

Like he was feeling my agitation, Bob hacked out a choking,

dry cough. Then another. He didn't stop for ten long seconds. We all tended to him like three mother hens around a baby chick. Sam sat back down with us and took off both rubber gloves to pet him.

"That doesn't sound healthy. How long's he had it?" she asked, rubbing his chest, his third favorite spot.

"A bit," I said, not wanting to give away how long it had been. I felt guilty enough for waiting weeks to take him to the vet. "I'm going to take him in soon if it doesn't go away."

Bob calmed with all the attention, but he wasn't done with us. He rolled onto his back for belly rubs. Tongue flopping out the side of his mouth, all goofy, limp, and happy.

We obliged for a few seconds, and then they refocused on me.

"Honey, listen, whatever happens with the will, you've got us," Tee said, as if it should go without saying.

I needed more time to figure out what the hell was happening with the tree and whether I was losing my mind before I dealt with everything else. Though I wasn't sure how to go about doing that.

"I want things to go back to normal," I said, not looking at either of them. If I had, I might not have been able to hold myself together.

"Honey, this *is* your new normal." Tee put her hand on top of mine on top of Bob's belly. "This is your life now."

A simple statement containing the weight of the world.

Was she right? Was this it?

A dad-tree, a grass-stained bad back, magical letters, and flowers I didn't want, every day for my foreseeable future.

An emptiness and constant agitation I couldn't fill or shake. Would I have to remain in perpetual motion to outrun the strange my life had become and the gaping void I felt with the loss of my father? My default setting was already exhaustion, and it had been less than a month.

Damn it. They'd handled me.

Tears streaked down my face and I had to pee and I'd

forgotten to bra up earlier and I was starving like I hadn't eaten in a year and...in an instant, my life was impossible.

"I'm so tired," I said, finally speaking my truth.

"We know, honey," Tee said. They both wrapped their arms around me and we sat, huddled up, until Hopper farted himself awake in the corner. A duck through a bullhorn. He always knew how to punctuate those special moments.

I wiped my tears and, against my better judgment, held my hand out to Tee. She placed the phone in my palm and smiled, like she knew that one act would change the rest of my life.

THREE

M onday morning began the same as all the others in the last month, early under the dad-tree with Bob, but this time I woke full of dread. Everything in me felt heavy. I wondered what my body knew that I didn't.

My appointment with the lawyer was at ten, but Bob's health had deteriorated enough in the last twenty-four hours to worry me. He'd been coughing more frequently and for longer periods. His appetite was low and so was his energy. I had to lift him onto the front seat of the truck when we were leaving for the vet. I tried to focus on one step at a time and not leaning into thoughts of all the devastating illnesses he probably had.

After I got Bob settled, I rounded the driver's side of the truck and noticed a strange little woman with dark hair and black-rimmed glasses crossing the street toward us. She halted in the middle of the lane when I made eye contact with her.

"Hello," I said, smiling to put her at ease. Something seemed off, like she'd been wound too tight. I could relate. "Can I help you?"

She looked older, around Tee and Dad's age, and wore all black. A turtleneck sweater and long pants, which I found odd in the heat. She said nothing to me, but seemed to talk to herself under her breath.

Something behind me drew her attention and her hand flew to her chest, like she was in pain. She scurried back over to the sidewalk without a word and headed toward town, yanking at her sweater.

Odd.

I spun around to survey the house and yard. Had that woman seen him? Did he scare her off? *Was he real?*

Nothing was out of place, not even a leaf on the ground. Just our old garage, the leaning tower of fire hazards, next to the house, and the lake beyond the yard. But I could've sworn I'd heard the rustling of willow branches behind me before she hurried off.

Our vet, Dr. Dixon, saw us as soon as we arrived at the Maiden Lake clinic. He and Dad had been poker pals with a decades-old good-natured rivalry. Anything to do with Bob was a priority, so he took us in before any of his other patients.

He diagnosed Bob with a bacterial lung infection and put him on antibiotics. I must have broadcast my deep concern while I snuggled Bob in the corner, because Dr. Dixon glanced over from his laptop on the counter and smiled.

"He'll be fine, Emma, don't worry. All the normal things, make sure he's eating and drinking. Very little exercise until he's done with his course of antibiotics. Lots of rest. Oh, and make sure he doesn't lie too long on one side or the other. Mix it up so there's no fluid accumulation in his lungs. Don't want it to turn into pneumonia. Overall, not too much excitement."

"No trips to Rainbow House or Connie's or delivering meals with me?"

"Does he get excited?"

"Only with Agnes and Gerty. And Stuart. And Marin. And—"

"Right. I'd say no for now then. Until he's back on his feet."

"He'll be disappointed," I said, scratching Bob's forehead as he stared up at me. He looked concerned, like he knew what we were saying and was not happy about it.

On our way to the front desk, a minor ruckus with a German shepherd, a pug, and a vet tech at the back of the clinic caught my attention. When I turned to see what the trouble was, my knees went sludgy and everything in me stopped working.

I always thought the idea of your breath catching in your chest was silly hyperbole. It wouldn't actually get caught, you could still breathe and everything would be fine. But standing there, in the middle of my vet's waiting room, I stared at the broad back of a stranger in a lab coat as he closed the exam door behind him, remembering how to breathe.

It couldn't be him. Maiden Lake was a small city, a college town, with twenty thousand residents about half an hour from Calypso Springs. We shared the lake they named the town for. With all those people milling about, there was bound to be someone who resembled him, living and working here now. At my vet clinic. It couldn't be him. He'd moved back to Indiana to take care of his mother, like I'd taken care of Dad, when we were in college here. There was no way he'd come back after all this time. It couldn't be him.

I picked up Bob's medication and tried to pay, sweaty and disoriented by the ghost I'd just seen. I kept checking the door to see if it was going to open and reveal the mystery man behind it, but it stayed closed.

The assistant at the front desk shoved her palm at my credit card, pushing it away when I offered it to her. "Dr. Dixon says you're all set."

"What now?"

"He says you're all set."

"I heard that part. I don't understand."

"I guess he owed your father from their last poker night."

"That's very kind of him, but I'm fine paying." Of course, I wasn't fine paying. This bill would almost max out one of my last credit cards, but Rosens did not accept charity. And I knew it was charity because my father's poker night friends all settled their debts on the night they played. It was the one unbreakable rule for them.

"Okay. I'll let him know," she said, lifting the phone receiver to call him.

"No no. Unnecessary. I'll pay like normal and we'll move on with our day."

She took the card and glanced around, like she might get in trouble for letting me use it. I began to sweat more, from the cash flowing out instead of into my life, and from the impossible possibility I'd just seen Jake Benson, the only man I'd ever loved.

Like I said, dread. And it was only getting started.

FOUR

I n all stories, there's a moment that changes everything. That marks the *after* of the before and after timeline. The page in your diary you want to burn because it was the moment your life fell apart.

I thought that page was the day my father died. I thought that was as bad as it could get. *Silly, naïve me.*

My moment began and ended with a set of ears.

Earlier that morning, on our way to the vet, I'd tried to convince Tee she didn't need to come with me to the lawyer's office. I appreciated the moral support, but I didn't need hand holding. She insisted till steam shot from her ears, so I agreed. Hers were not the ears in question. But there would be questions for her ears afterward. If I ever spoke to her again.

Still recovering from my impossible Jake sighting, I was already on edge when she met me downstairs in the lobby of the office building. We rode the elevator in tense silence and as we approached the tenth floor, my stomach churned with appre-hension.

The moment we stepped out, I could feel it. Something wasn't right. We were ten stories up in an architecturally sound high-rise in the middle of Maiden Lake, but the floor felt wobbly under my feet. The air buzzed with ominous energy.

I convinced myself it was just nerves.

Until we entered the conference room.

Two large, suited men, one with a white-gray mustache, one without, sat at the far end of a long conference table that could seat twenty. A tiny woman stood between the two at the end of the table like she was giving a sermon. With raised hands and voice, she seemed impatient and a little unsettled. The sermon was interactive because they all spoke over one another in a cacophony of muddled, angry voices.

The men sitting at the table stopped talking over one another when we entered the room and welcomed us. "Hello, ladies." Lou Cranston, Dad's portly, mustached lawyer stood to greet us. He checked his watch like we were an hour late. "Please, have a seat so we can get started. As you know, this is extremely time sensitive."

As I know? I knew nothing. And I was about to find out how much nothing.

The tiny woman kept talking over Cranston, like we hadn't entered the room, until she made eye contact with Tee. She'd asked something about getting into the house and then I recognized her. She was the strange little woman who ran away from me earlier that morning. My mind spun in circles. What was she doing *here*? Was she an attorney? A spy? Had Cranston hired her for this?

Before I could speak, Tee gasped beside me and grabbed my arm without tearing her gaze away from the mystery woman. Everyone focused on Tee. She went sheet white and stopped breathing.

"Tee?" I said, panic filling my voice. I looked from her face to my forearm, still tight in her grasp. I'd never seen her like this before.

Without a word, she yanked me away, back toward the open door and the hallway.

I resisted. "Tee. What's going on? Are you okay?"

"Teresa, don't run away. I didn't expect to see you either, but cripes' sake, be an adult," the woman said.

Wait, they knew each other?

Tee let out an exasperated gasp. It was a strange sound coming from her. Unexpected, uninhibited. She turned to the woman and spoke with a voice full of venom. "You, of all people, better see the absurd irony of that statement." I'd never seen her seethe before.

I pulled free from Tee's grasp and turned back toward the other woman. Her voice seemed familiar. It was deep and smooth, full of confidence. Not at all what I would have expected after the way she'd acted earlier that morning.

She crossed her arms, studying me, like she was appraising a sculpture or painting, unconvinced she wanted to buy. Stretched end to end, she was five feet tall, but her essence filled the room. Not in a positive way.

"Let's get this over with," she said. I didn't know who she was, but the disdain wrapped in her voice convinced me she wasn't anyone I wanted to know. She smoothed her turtleneck against her torso and sat, imperiously waiting for everyone to follow her.

Cranston exhaled sharply, but followed suit. Who the hell was running this meeting?

"Emma," Tee said in a strangled voice as she reached for me again. She sounded like a scared little girl. It was disturbing.

"What's wrong?" I whispered, turning to her. "Is it your back? Are you having a stroke? What's going on, Tee?"

"We'll come back another time. You don't need to deal with *this* right now, too."

"What are you talking about? I'm here. I'm not leaving. What about your big intervention? You told me to handle it. I'm handling it. This is me moving forward." To show Tee how serious and literal I was, I took a step forward, away from her toward the table.

"Ha! Intervention?" The little woman erupted with sudden vigor. "Not surprising." She narrowed her eyes at Tee. "Things don't change, do they, Teresa?"

"Everything changes," Tee spat back at her. The temperature in the room rose about fifty degrees. This situation was bonkers.

"You're still sticking your nose in places it doesn't belong."

Tee neared her boiling point next to me, all angry waves of heat.

"I don't know what's happening here, but can it wait till after we do the will?" I said. I didn't want to be there any longer than was necessary.

"You should listen to that one, Teresa," the woman said, gesturing in my general direction. "She seems smart enough. What do they call you now?"

"Me?" I said.

"Yes, you. The one I'm looking at."

"Emma."

"Emma," she said, with unwarranted contempt filling her voice. "No. You're Flora. Cannot believe he changed your name. That was the one thing..." she trailed off, speaking more to herself than any of us. Then she refocused her scorn on me again. "Needs substantial assistance in the wardrobe department, but that's not what we're here for."

Before I asked what the hell she was talking about, Tee stepped up. "Her name is Emma and it's always been Emma," she said, like a mama bear would if a mama bear could talk. To my knowledge, Tee was right. She moved forward and positioned herself in front of me, blocking my view of the people at the end of the table. "You would know this if you bothered to come—"

"Blah blah blah. Don't start with me after what you did." The accusation shut Tee up like a slap in the face.

It felt like I'd stepped into an episode of the *Twilight Zone* where nothing was supposed to make sense in the beginning and all would be revealed in the end.

"Ladies, if you could please have a seat?" Cranston pointed to the chairs opposite him at the table. "We do have a lot of ground to cover this morning." He wiped his sweaty brow with the back of his hand.

"Why are you here? Why is she here?" Tee asked both the woman and Cranston at the same time. She sounded almost hysterical. I'd never seen her this frazzled by anyone. Even Dad. Tee was the even keel upon which our ship sailed, holding us all together, especially when things like cancer threatened to capsize us.

"I'm here to take what's mine," the woman said without reservation.

Enough was enough. I stepped out of Tee's shadow, shook hands with Cranston and the other lawyer, and turned to face the woman. When I held my hand out to her, she looked at it like I was proposing an alien custom she did not recognize and would not abide.

"No," she said, as if I'd asked her to eat a handful of earthworms. She was flustered and pushed back away from the table to increase the space between us.

Then she did the thing that broke my world open. It sent everything I knew about my life flailing out the window of that ten-story building.

She reached back with both hands and tucked her straight, dark hair behind her ears. A simple, normal gesture. Who would have noticed what she'd been hiding under there if she hadn't done that?

"Your ears," I whispered, more to myself than anyone else, breathless and lightheaded. I leaned forward and rested on the table because I wasn't sure I could stand on my own at that moment.

I'd spent my entire life being the opposite of what I thought my mother was. She had dark hair. I'd dyed mine blonde for years when I was younger, so Dad wouldn't have to see her in me. I committed my life to selflessness instead of selfishness, filling the void she'd created when she left us.

But short of surgery, the two things I couldn't change were my ears. I never wore my hair up in a ponytail or cut it too short for fear of exposing them. They were the Andy-Rooney-eyebrows of ears. Like Kate Hudson's, only far more pronounced and unruly, flapping about at a conspicuous angle from my head.

I stared at the person across from me. The roundness of her enormous hazel eyes behind black-rimmed glasses, the delicate slope of her nose, even the Mona Lisa curve at the corners of her lips. These things were all foreign to me. If I stared at her for hours, dissecting every part of that face, I wouldn't assume we shared the same DNA.

But those ears.

I'd never seen anyone with ears like mine. They were feral, untamed. They did not sit quietly against the head. They were feisty. Did what they pleased, much like my hair. They said, *I'm here and you're going to notice me.* They were restless and relentless.

They were not docile Rosen ears. Dad had a perfectly boring set that laid against his head like well-behaved pets. They were not unruly.

Like ours.

Ours.

I turned to Tee, searching her face for some kind of answer to contradict the conclusion I'd come to about the person in front of me. "Tee, is she...?"

Tee took a deep breath, stood as tall as she could, and said... nothing. Nothing to tell me I was wrong. Nothing to stop the ugly truth. "I'm so sorry, honey. I didn't know she would be here."

I knew several things for certain at that moment. Those ears, my ears, were McCormack ears. At least one McCormack was still alive to prove it. My father and Tee and everyone else I loved had lied to me for a very long time. And this would not end well.

"She *wouldn't* have been here if this...lawyer hadn't made her fly in from the other side of the country on a moment's notice," the mother-person said, put out. Also, speaking in third person? Never a good sign.

"So what did he want? She'd like to know," she continued, pointing her tiny forefinger at Cranston. She ignored me, like this was just another Monday morning.

Was I losing it altogether now? Shouldn't this be a bigger deal to some of us?

A portal to another time and place opened and all I could hear was the sound of my father's voice saying how this person in front of me had died. Over and over it came, louder and louder, in a loop. All I could see in that moment was Josiah, how sincere he'd looked as he lied to me about the most important thing in my life. The last twenty years we'd spent together inside that lie before he died. All those moments he could have told me the truth but chose not to.

The sound of my friends, my family, deceiving me for half of my life was deafening. And the compassion-free smugness of that mother-person, not considering what this meeting might do to me, was a wrecking ball.

I saw my father's face in a willow tree on the ledge outside, clinging to the window of the conference room ten stories up. He opened his gnarled wooden mouth trying to say something, but I couldn't hear him over the roaring tornado of his past lies in my head.

I turned, shot straight past Tee and out the door, vowing never to speak to any of those people or trees again.

FIVE

The fierce sun streamed in through the cheap motel curtains and woke Cassie McCormack early that morning. Probably gave her wrinkles. Yet another annoyance. Add it to the growing list. The vague, terminal diagnosis she'd received from her doctor. The surly lawyer summoning her back to Calypso Springs for Josiah's will. It had been a week of vexations. But if she could find the cure here, it would be worth the trip.

Standing in front of her old house that morning, she held no fond memories, no memories at all, from that time in her life. It was as if she'd never existed there.

A modest, two-story craftsman, like most of the other houses on Main Street, it was in a desperate state of disrepair. The ancient garage leaned deeply toward the house, the lawn was shabby and overgrown, and the paint peeled over ninety percent of the clapboards. A disgrace. An unmitigated disaster. How could her parents have ever lived here? Had she not been desperate to find the box in the house, she wouldn't have considered putting a toe over the threshold of that calamity.

The desiccated bushes surrounding the front porch were ominous. No matter. She wasn't interested in exploring the grounds or a relationship with the person who lived there now.

She had come for one reason only: to get the lockbox. In it, she would find the cure for whatever scourge had invaded her lungs. At least that's what her father had told her.

It wouldn't take long to find it once she was in. He'd said it was in her old room, under the loose floorboards. She would simply have to figure out which room had been hers.

She stepped off the curb and started across the street, but the daughter-person emerged from the house with a large canine. It seemed quite ill or old. Cassie didn't see the point of dogs. Filthy, slobbering beasts.

When the daughter rounded the truck to the driver's side, she spotted Cassie in the street. This could complicate things. Cassie stopped cold in the middle of the lane. It was after seven in the morning. Why wasn't the woman at work or the gym? She was too soft around the edges, could do with considerable time on a treadmill.

"Hello," the daughter said at Cassie. Like she was talking to just anyone.

Cassie tried to retreat, but stood glued in place. This was her first direct contact with the daughter-person, only twenty feet away, and it threw her concentration.

That was...unexpected.

"Can I help you?"

Cassie wanted to blurt out *yes, open the house and leave,* but the words wouldn't come. She was stuck in place, couldn't move or speak. That had never happened before. She needed to reconnect with her purpose to break this strange magic.

She was there to take her life back. To survive. Nothing to do with that daughter-person who was a stranger and nothing more.

So what was this force keeping her locked in the middle of the street, staring like an idiot? What that daughter-person must have thought.

Something large and green rustled beside the house and broke Cassie free from the spell. She grabbed her chest because that's where it hurt the most.

"Chrissakes. This wasn't supposed to happen again," she said to herself.

There he stood, Josiah Rosen. The one and only love of her life and, hell's bells, he was a willow tree now. How was she supposed to make sense of that?

Even after all these years, tremendous heat, stirring up from her toes, rose like fire into the rest of her body. She nearly ripped her turtleneck off in the middle of the street to get air on her burning skin.

Cassie couldn't tell from his look whether he wanted to hold her or hang her from his highest limb. He rustled his branches and puffed himself out like an aggressive shrub. With that, she guessed it was the latter. Everything in her hurt down to the cells.

It was supposed to be quick, easy, pain-free. Her father had said nothing about Josiah becoming a sentinel tree, guarding his old house.

Being this close to him again almost took her down in the middle of the street. She tugged at her sweater to let air in, turned on her heel, and sped off toward the sidewalk as quickly as her legs would take her.

Unfortunate change of plans. She'd have to find another way in. Who knew what that lawyer wanted with her, maybe he had the box. She'd have to find out now. Because, years ago, Cassie McCormack vowed she would never abide that kind of agony for anyone again.

SIX

I tore into my driveway, still reeling from the meeting with the lawyers. Sam waited on the porch for me. The truck rattled and spit when I turned it off, but I didn't get out. I sat there, staring into the middle distance, thinking about how everything would be different the moment I opened the door. I'd be living in the after and I wasn't ready for it yet.

Sam rushed over and stood by my open window. She didn't speak or try to get me to talk, unlike Tee, who'd called five times before I left Maiden Lake. I turned my phone off on the sixth call.

Sam should have been running the Calypso Tribune and picking up her twins from school, not holding my hand as my world cracked in two. But here she was anyway. She rested her elbow on the edge of the window and whispered, "Total shitshow, Em."

Sometimes, when you get what you need, you realize you don't need it anymore. A friend validating your feelings, sharing in the misery, is healing. That simple affirmation and empathizing is all it takes to break free from your suffering.

But this wasn't that.

"Did you know?" I asked into the hot silence. I was almost ready to send her away because I didn't know who the hell I could trust anymore. But if I couldn't trust Sam, I would give up on our species.

"Know?" She glanced at me, perplexed. It made little sense that Sam would know more than I did, but I had to get an answer from her.

"Did you know she was here? Also, alive?"

"What do you mean, alive?"

"Don't mess with me, Sam."

"Under these circumstances? Never."

"So you didn't know she was alive?" Good. She knew what I knew.

"Em, I never thought she was dead."

"What are you talking about? I told you the night Dad told me."

"Told me what?"

"That she'd died."

"If she's alive, and it would seem she is, why would he...?"

"Question of the year, right there."

"You never told me that, Em."

"Back when Jake and I broke up. When Dad got sick the first time and I left school to take care of him."

"I remember all of those things and every detail about you coming back home, but you never told me that about your mother."

"I must have..."

"No," she said, shaking her head. Then, "Oh my God, no wonder you're so freaked out."

"How did I not tell you? Dad and I had a huge fight that night, about marriage, of all things, and then he spit that out like it was old news."

"That she was dead?"

"He didn't say when or how or how he knew or anything else about it. We never talked about her again. By then, we hadn't mentioned her in years and he just dropped that bomb out of the blue."

"Well, there's your answer, Em. You and I hadn't talked about her in years, either. Not since we were like eight. You never told me he said that. You haven't talked about her since third or fourth grade."

When I was younger, I'd hoped my mother would walk through our door every day to pick up where she never left off. To take part in my life and be my mother. But as the years went by, hope dwindled, replaced by anger at her continued absence. By the time I went off to college in Maiden Lake, I'd almost given up on the idea of her ever being part of my life.

And then death closed the door on it.

"I, one hundred percent, didn't know she was here," Sam said. She dipped her head to study the side of the truck. Was she hiding something else?

"Tee...knew," I said, trying to breathe.

"Call her. Talk to her. She sounded...wound."

"That mother-person called me Flora. What does that even mean?"

"Flora? Like flora and fauna?"

"I guess." I threw my hands up as if to say, *what the hell with this fuckery,* and sizzled in the heat of my own thoughts.

Eager to check on Bob, I opened the door and got waylaid by the ground. Sam stepped aside, opening the gate to this new existence. The gravel that had been on this driveway my whole life looked different now. It wasn't mine. It was some other person's whose mother was now, and apparently always had been, alive.

Sam checked her watch. She was late for a meeting or a deadline.

"You've gotta get to work. Go on," I said, taking the first step into whoever I was now. The ground felt unsettled under me again. Like I might sink into the quicksand of it and disappear forever.

"I run the place. I get there when I get there. It's almost lunch. I just hope Royce remembers to feed our children." The levity in her voice belied the tension in their marriage. It was on life-support and probably wouldn't survive the year.

"Are they home from school already?"

"Half days this week for parent teacher things."

"Right. You go. I'll be fine. Kisses to the boys."

"You sure?" she asked, following me to the door like a shadow.

"I'm good. It's going to be fine." I'd practiced on Tee and was perfecting with Sam now. How long does it take a person to become a proficient liar?

"Whatever, whenever. You need anything, you call," Sam said, hugging me.

Without another word, I rushed into the house. Didn't want to burden her with my mess. She had enough of her own to contend with.

Bob greeted me at the door with kisses and a few high-pitched whimpers and then wiggled off to his bed to lie down. Maybe it was the medication, but normally he was my Velcro dog, had to be everywhere I was, so that didn't sit right.

"This is a super shitshow, mister. I'm gonna need extra ice cream today."

The snow globe on the top of the bookcase by Dad's recliner caught my eye and a part of me splintered. I raced over and picked it up. Its weight in my hands transported me back to being six years old again, standing in front of my father, staring at the broken glass from this same globe on his office floor.

I'd dropped it and the glass had fractured into a thousand tiny shards. I told him it was an accident, but it wasn't. It had been a gift, the only thing he'd kept from my mother. Inside the globe were two dogs frolicking in a field of blue forget-me-not wildflowers. I thought I was doing us both a favor by destroying it, but he sent it out to have it fixed. It's been in the same spot on that bookshelf ever since.

I shook the globe. The tiny flowers swirled in a frenzy, then floated down, blanketing the dogs in blue florets. *Flora*.

Why would Dad change my name? Why would he and Tee lie about it? I shot straight up the stairs to his office to find answers.

I never would have invaded my father's privacy when he was alive. I'd never had a reason to. But his integrity was a false memory for me now and there was nothing stopping me from rifling through his shit to find the truth.

I stood by his massive mahogany desk, staring at it, willing the right drawer to open. When nothing magical happened, I pulled on all the handles. Each one opened except for the bottom left. Bingo. Locks guard secrets.

I rummaged through the large middle drawer, hoping he'd kept the key in a conspicuous place. Everything in it ended up on the floor. There was no key, so I moved on to the next drawer full of school paperwork and files. They all landed on the floor, too. The next one held all of his piloting paperwork and several instructional books on flying. I threw everything on the growing pile and moved on to the next. Still no key. My agitation grew. I wasn't careful with his things. Why should I be? He wasn't careful with mine.

When I finished with the last unlocked drawer, I sat in the middle of a mountain of paper, like flaming magma in the center of a volcano.

"Can I help?" Sam asked from the doorway.

"Shiiiit! You can't sneak up on people like that," I said, feeling light-headed from the shock of her voice in the middle of my chaos.

"Sorry. Thought you'd hear me coming up those creaky ass stairs."

"I was a little preoccupied."

"I see that." She surveyed my mess in silence.

"What are you still doing here? Your children need you."

"Meh. They eat enough. If Royce doesn't feed them, they won't starve. Need help?" She stepped into the field of disaster.

"I'm not packing."

"Fairly obvious."

"Where the hell would he keep the k—" I erupted through the paper mountain and shot over to the closet in the far corner of the room. Last month, not long before Dad left us, I'd glimpsed the chestnut box hiding on the top shelf in the back, like a secret, nestled under his winter beanies and gloves. I'd fetched a blanket for him in there. He'd been shivering so violently it seemed like he might shimmy out of his skin. It was eighty degrees that day.

Although I wasn't a giant like my father, I possessed some of his height, so I could tippy-toe and grab the Man O'War cigar box without a stepladder. It was clear when I pulled the top up it had been sealed for a while. It still held the nutty scent of the cigars he used to smoke. Cigars that had a hand in killing him.

Inside the box, I found the silver prop plane cufflinks I'd given him for his fiftieth birthday. His initials, JRR, engraved on the bottom of each. There was an old piece of drawing paper folded up on top of a broken Nautilus watch his mother had given him for his high school graduation. She'd thrown it out the window of her boyfriend's VW van as they shed corporate America along with their clothes and went to live in an Arizona nudist colony. She'd never returned. The curse of the women in his life.

I lifted the worn piece of paper out of the box and unfolded it, staring at the hand-drawn picture.

"What is it?" Sam asked.

"My family," I said. I turned the paper over to Sam, standing so close I thought she might be preparing to catch me. "At least how I thought it looked when I was two."

The worn drawing showed a stick figure of a little girl in between two people, holding hands with both of them. A box with a door in it that must have been the house and what looked like a lake in the background. The man was a giant, and the woman was tiny, a fair representation of reality. And a big green blob with black eyes and fangs crept behind them, skulking toward the woman on his long spindly legs.

There was a name on the bottom of the page, written in blue

crayon. The same blue as the lake and the flowers that sprung up all around the stick figures.

"What does that say?" Sam asked, pointing to the name. Someone else had written it, someone older with finer motor skills to print letters. But it was in the middle of a crease so part of it had disintegrated over the years of opening and closing, exposing and hiding. The A was the only similarity that name shared with mine. The rest of it spelled out something else. Underneath the name it said *age 2* in smaller print.

"You said she called you—"

"Flora."

"Whoa. Josiah never told you about—"

"No."

"Damn. He's got a lot of explaining to do."

"Yeah. Little tough now."

The weight of it all kept getting heavier, but the knot in my stomach hardened along with my resolve. I got back to work, rummaging through the rest of the box, but I didn't find a key. What I did find sent chills through me.

It was covered in faded black velvet with a bald patch where someone's large thumb had lifted against the top so many times it had worn the material off.

I put the cigar box on the floor and placed the ring box on the desk.

"You gonna open it?" Sam breathed down my neck.

Dad had told me they hadn't been married. That he didn't believe in the institution. I stared at the ring box, remembering the fight we'd had about marriage and Jake and *the rest of my life* the night he told me my mother had died.

"Add this to the growing list of bullshit."

"So, you're not gonna open it?" Sam stared at me and then the ring box like she couldn't believe I had the restraint to leave it alone. I left it closed.

"Can you unlock that drawer with a paperclip?" I pointed to the only intact drawer in the desk.

"I can try. But, Em, what are you looking for?"

"Please, just open the drawer."

I gave Sam a paperclip and she got to work with no more questions. Hopper, a retired police officer, had taught Sam a few nifty tricks. Certain skills that came in handy for a journalist who might need to research information without others knowing they're after it.

"Got it. Wow. I've gotta tell Hopper. I'm getting better at this."

I almost felt bad for prying into Dad's things. But the bastard lied to me, so I'd rummage all I wanted. Except, then I felt horrible for calling my dead father a bastard.

"Sorry," I said to the room.

"For what?"

"Nothing."

Sam opened the drawer and stepped aside for me to excavate. I squatted down and flipped through the hanging files. They weren't labeled, so I had to search each one to see what it held. About halfway through, I came to a file with the names Cassie and Flora written in pencil on the outside. My fingers became clumsy, like they'd morphed into giant sausages. I couldn't make them work.

"Will you take that file out, please?"

Sam obliged.

"Open it?"

She flipped the folder open, almost in slow motion, and I found it hard to focus. There were health records, vaccination records, old medical bills, but on top of it all, a birth certificate glared back at me as if daring me to look.

Sam lifted it up closer. "Is this..."

I preferred it at a distance, this conveyor of the ugly truth. I'd always dreamed of taking trips out of the country, but didn't have the opportunity. A passport was a luxury I didn't need, so I'd never seen my birth certificate. I'd lived a quiet life in Calypso Springs, taking care of Dad.

Sam glanced over at me and gasped. Maybe because I wasn't breathing, or maybe she noticed my fingers curled one by one into white-knuckled fists. Whatever encouraged her to take my hand before I hurled it through the wall didn't matter. She knew what I needed.

"Yes," I said through gritted teeth. I took the paper from her, trying to breathe. "It's my birth certificate." It said *Flora Marie Rosen*. No running away from that truth.

SEVEN

After Sam left to feed her children, I didn't know what to do with myself. The voices in my head would not stand down. *He lied to you. Tee lied to you. You can't trust anyone.* I didn't turn my phone back on for the rest of the day because I knew Tee would call every five minutes and I couldn't face whatever story she wanted to tell me.

So, I became a day drinker. I wasn't any kind of drinker before, but I'd had a day. This new Flora person, did she like the bottle? We'd explore together and find out.

Dad always stashed a fifth of Jack Daniel's behind his worn copy of *Mythology* on the living room bookshelf. At least that wasn't a well-kept secret. I collapsed on the couch next to Bob and drank it straight from the bottle until I couldn't taste anything anymore. The alcohol, the betrayal.

Maybe this was something I'd do daily now. Get numb-drunk, like Hopper, and drive stolen lawn mowers around town in women's lingerie. I bet my octogenarian neighbor, Connie Speits, had some fancy nightwear hidden in her closet I could steal.

Self-help gurus like to say forgiveness isn't about the other person, it's about healing ourselves. Guess I'd be wounded forever because I'd never forgive my father for this. I'd never be okay with what he'd done. The thought of ever forgiving him made me more angry and more drunk.

So I passed out next to Bob on the living room floor, in the middle of a Monday afternoon, pondering the accessibility of my eighty-year-old neighbor's underwear.

Later, Tee stormed the house and woke me from my drunk nap, pounding on the front door. I commando-crawled across the living room floor and hid with Bob in the downstairs bathroom until she left. I'd locked the doors earlier before the drinking started. Knew I'd have to head her off at the pass.

I'd never hidden from Tee or anyone in my bathroom before, but it felt like something this Flora person might do and not feel guilty about. I was so used to doing what everyone else needed. It was freeing not to be at someone else's beck and call for once.

I woke in the middle of the night with the room still swerving around me and the need to speak my mind. I was curled up on the couch with Bob, which surprised me. I didn't know what time we usually made our nocturnal trek out back to the tree, but apparently it was after two in the morning.

He lifted his head when I struggled up off the couch, groping for purchase on anything that would hold me upright, but he didn't make a move to follow me.

"It's okay, mister. You can stay."

I pet him to sleep, and on my way to the door, I tripped over the pile of willow branches sticking out from underneath the couch. Hopper must have tucked them back under there, instead of throwing them outside when he was 'house keeping' last week. I hadn't noticed them till now.

In a juvenile fit, I kicked at the branches and spread them around the room. Then I felt bad about being ridiculous and waking Bob again, so I gathered the branches and tucked them under my arm to take outside. They were real, soft and bendy, with leaves running the length of them, not figments of my imagination. When I collected them, the leaves moped and then shriveled in my grasp. Weird.

It was a starless, moonless night. A real and metaphorical darkness fitting my mood.

I took the branches down to the tree and laid them on the swing. The leaves were crunchy and dead now, like they'd been sitting in the sun for weeks.

I stood in the middle of the canopy, facing away from the trunk, wondering what the hell had happened to my life in the course of a day. In my still drunken state, I held the rope on the swing for support.

"What the actual hell, Dad?" I said, seething and sweaty. "None of this can be real." I pointed loosely toward to the trunk of the tree, trying not to lose my balance in more ways than one. "But it feels like it is. And then the part that is real, the mother part, you know, why? Why did you do it? Why would you lie to me for twenty years? And Flora? What the double hell, Dad? I feel like everything about our lives was a lie."

The branches rustled and shook like the willow was shivering. Or weeping. There was no discernible breeze, nothing animating it from the outside. Then the canopy converged toward the middle. Walls creeping in.

Like a tree trying to hug me.

"No, Dad," I said, with enough conviction even I believed it. "No one, I mean, no one, has ever betrayed me like this. Not even *her*."

The branches stopped moving in toward me. They slumped down in unison, with one great, heaving sigh, melting into the ground as if they'd given up.

Early the next morning, Bob woke me under the tree with an onslaught of sloppy kisses. My head was a lead anvil. Pretty sure I'd died during the night. "Ugh, mister, please stop punching me with your tongue."

I scratched his ears with the one finger I could move. He wagged his tail and continued assaulting me with love. Seemed like he was feeling a little better. Glad one of us was. I sat up, using the most effort I'd needed for anything ever, and found another orange envelope on the swing next to me. The branches I'd put there the night before were gone.

Sore everywhere and feeling like no person ever should, I didn't move from that spot on the ground. Bob must have already done his business because he was happy to sit with me. He rested his head on my lap as I stared at the familiar orange envelope, willing it to disappear. But I was too exhausted to fight with stationery anymore, so I gave in.

"Screw it." I ripped the envelope open. Inside, I found a folded piece of paper, like the stationery I'd taken out of his desk the day before with his name at the top. Principal Rosen. A chill flew through me and I needed to take a breath before continuing.

When the words stopped moving around on the page, I read the letter out loud to Bob.

"*Kid,*"

That was as far as I got before the waterworks started. I loved that nickname. Even as an adult. The way he said it made me feel like I'd always be his little girl. No matter what, we'd always be there for each other. An unbreakable bond.

And then he went and fucked it all up by lying to me for half of my life.

"No. You don't get to call me Kid anymore," I said, wiping

away my tears. "You've lost that privilege, Father." Bob agreed. He wagged his tail in support.

"I imagine nothing makes sense to you right now.

Ha! You think?

I hope everything will become clear in the end, when it's all done.

When *what's* all done? This is making my stomach hurt." Also, alcohol. "Mister, never drink," I said to Bob, petting his nose with my forefinger.

"It felt like the only way. I regret a lot, Kid...

As well you should.

...and I want you to know I'm sorry, so sorry, but this is going to be good for you both.

Who both?

It's the best parting gift I could give either of you and what I should have done all those years ago. I hope you'll be able to forgive me someday, Emma."

I fended off the sudden rush of emotion as I read the last line. Almost couldn't continue, but Bob pawed at me and rested his head in my lap again.

"Love you more, always. Dad."

The letter struck me hard around the part about forgiveness, because I wasn't used to having anything to forgive him for. Minor annoyances here and there over the years, like if he didn't let me go to a party, or when he showed up at Mort's Mini-Golf on my first date with Jake. Silly, embarrassing things that didn't require forgiveness at all.

But nothing like a life-altering lie. How do you forgive a betrayal that monumental?

Bob wheezed like he had something caught in his throat again.

"Easy, mister, breathe. It's okay. You're going to feel better soon. I promise." I hoped his medication would back me up. He laid down on my lap and fell asleep as I massaged him with my free hand.

The letter burned my other hand so I dropped it. I didn't understand what any of this meant. But I sure as hell wasn't in the mood for any more surprises.

EIGHT

Before I showered, I went to collect the day's daffodil bouquet from the front porch. When I opened the door I almost fell into the two people standing in front of me. Shocked, again, at this person's sudden appearance in my life, I took the only appropriate action. Frankly, when you show up unannounced and alive on someone's porch before seven in the morning, it's well within their right to slam things in your face.

Bob trotted over to stand by me and we both stared at the closed front door waiting for something to happen. Then he looked up, ready for my next instructions. Like maybe go eat the people on the porch.

I took a deep breath, talked myself out of fleeing the country, and opened the door again. "Hello," I said. There was no greeting in my greeting.

Lou Cranston, Dad's irritable lawyer, stood sweating in his standard gray suit and mustache. He held a black briefcase against his side. The mother-person planted herself next to him, barely rising to his shoulder. She'd pulled her dark hair back from her face and the whole ear-filled tableau was distracting. Dressed in all black again, as if in mourning, her two child-sized feet, in matte black sensible flats, crushed my fresh daffodils.

I tried to find humor in the irony of her invading my life, only to mangle my new beginnings. Tried and failed. Also, could a person truly not notice they were standing on top of living things, squashing them? The delicate yellow petals had withered under her weight and turned brown. Did she lack awareness or concern? Both, I imagined.

Bob's tail welcomed the two, but I sent him to bed when he wanted to get more familiar with one of them. I wasn't comfortable with that. She recoiled at his approach, which sealed my opinion of her.

"You need to read a letter," she said, like she was the boss of me.

My skin crawled. Please, for the sake of my sanity, not another letter.

Without warning, she shot forward, attempting to barge into the house like she owned the place. My house. I don't think so. I became a wall. She stopped cold, colliding with my chest. I had a good nine inches on her, so she stepped back and regrouped, staring me up and down in silence.

"Is that what you're wearing?" she asked, like she hadn't ruined anyone's life yet today.

I suddenly identified with those daffodils under her feet. What kind of question was that? Of course it's what I was wearing. I was wearing it. Also, what was I wearing? I checked to make sure I was decent.

"Emma, we need to discuss your father's will. It's imperative we do this today. Now." Cranston peeked inside like he was waiting for something to jump out at him. "May we come in?"

I was sore and achy from sleeping on the ground, still a little drunk, covered in grass stains and actual grass in places. My life had gone off the rails and now these two wanted in for more. Maybe they'd light the house on fire.

"Sure, why not? How much worse could this get?" I said to myself out loud.

Never ask that question of the universe.

Cassie had concerns about being on the property that morning. Would she feel what she'd felt the day before? Would she be able to get in the house? The sweaty lawyer had told her she needed to accompany him for legal reasons. Josiah's will and all that. But she wouldn't agree to it until he told her precisely what those reasons were.

She approached the front of the house with trepidation. He waited for her on the gravel driveway, urging her on with wide-eyed irritation, like he had somewhere else to be. But she stood her ground, taking slow, measured steps forward. She would not be rushed.

After each step, she probed her body to see how it felt. She reached the door without seeing Josiah and with no discomfort. Perhaps the intense attack she'd had the day before would only occur when she saw him in the flesh, so to speak. She'd keep her distance from the backyard.

The moment Cassie crossed the threshold into the house, something twisted inside her. Like a long dormant voice awakening deep within, needing to speak and be heard. To say things unsaid for so many years.

She ignored it. None of that mattered. Everything depended on what came next. Convincing the daughter to comply with Josiah's wishes and finding that box.

"Watch your step, it's a little...wild in here," the lawyer said, holding his briefcase up to his chest with both hands.

Everything was unacceptable. Did the daughter not know the simple mechanics of housekeeping? Had Josiah never introduced her to a broom? A dishwasher? A maid? What was that thing growing in the corner? The inside of the house matched the outside. Cassie heroically resisted the urge to set it all on fire and declare it a complete loss.

"Good lord, what was that?" Something warm and wet slid across the back of Cassie's hand. That rabid mutt licked her.

"Germs and disease. Go away, you. Shoo, you dirty beast." He sat at her feet, staring up and panting, sticking that terrible giant tongue out at her. Why would any civilized person have this creature in their home?

"First, he is not a dirty beast," the daughter said, leaning over the staircase to talk at Cassie. She best be on her way to change into something more respectable than that hussy outfit she wore to answer the door. From the look of her and this house, Cassie questioned whether they were related at all. She did not recognize one cell of herself in that disheveled woman on the stairs.

"Bob is a beautiful good boy, a superhero, and in my house, he rules. Yes, you do, mister."

"Shoo, you," Cassie said again, ignoring the daughter. The dog wouldn't leave her alone. Licking at her hands like she'd dipped them in peanut butter. She grew so desperate to escape the dirty thing, she locked herself in the bathroom down the hall.

No, this would not be as easy as Cassie had hoped.

Gauntlet thrown, lady. You don't like my dog? We're going to have a problem.

I returned downstairs more presentable in a sundress. The mother-person sneaked from the bathroom trying to avoid Bob's superior ninja skills, but she didn't stand a chance. He was there before she took two steps into the hallway.

But unrequited love is devastating, so I sent him to bed for his own good. And mine. I couldn't stand to watch him give this person all the love he should have been giving other, more worthy, people. Like the one who fed him and picked up his poop.

"Though you ambushed me without warning or common decency, can I offer you a cup of coffee before we start?" I said to Cranston. Or some part of that sentiment. He still stood awkwardly by the front door, like he needed a quick exit strategy in case things went sideways.

"I'm fine, thanks. Had my five espresso shots this morning."

Five shots? How was he not vibrating? No wonder he was sweating.

"Excuse me," I said, moving Cranston out of my way to retrieve the daffodils from the porch. They were in bad shape. Worse when I picked them up. Like the willow leaves I'd taken out back last night, every flower, from stem to stigma, shriveled up and turned black when I touched them.

I rarely express myself in hyperbole, but it was like holding death in my hands. My touch had killed them all. What the fresh hell was that nonsense?

I checked to make sure they hadn't seen what just happened and hid the dead flowers as I swept past them into the kitchen. They both stood by the door now.

"Have a seat, please. The couch is there for a reason," I said, because it seemed like they needed instructions about where to sit. "I'll be there in a minute."

One might put dead flowers lower on a list of things to handle than a father's will, but I'd just murdered living things with my touch, so I needed to sit with that for a minute.

I threw the flowers away, making sure no one watched me. When I turned to check the vases around the kitchen with all the other— "What the hell?!" I said, before I even realized the words had escaped me. All the other daffodils blooming yesterday were now crispy and falling off their stems, too.

Did it happen when she came into the house? They were perfectly fine before. Then I remembered what Tee had said about rotting flowers in my kitchen last week. I thought she was delusional. Was I the delusional one? How long had they been like that? I needed to check my garden out back.

"I'll take a glass of water while you're in there," the mother-person said, more of an order than a request. She sat on the couch next to Cranston.

"We ran out."

"Of water?"

"Of glass." I sauntered past her, holding an enormous glass of cold water. The flowers could wait. She was plucking my last nerve, and I needed to handle her.

I reclined in Dad's old chair in the corner and took a nice, long swig of water. Drank half the glass in one gulp as they watched. I was irrevocably connected to my inner jerk around her now. All Flora's fault. Buried for thirty-eight years, maybe I should have thanked the mother-person for digging her up for me.

She battened down her hatches and sat up on the edge of the couch, hands clenched, eyes focused. On me.

This was going to be fun.

"Okay, then. Let's talk about your father's will." Cranston opened the briefcase on his lap and pulled out a stack of papers. Bob had settled in near the tiny woman's feet. His bed was nearby. That was why he lay next to her instead of me in the chair. Except he'd missed his bed by about four feet at the other end of the couch.

As Cranston pored over his paperwork and yammered on about this legal thing and that, I watched the mother-person's hand drift to her chest. She grasped the cross dangling on the gold chain around her neck and twisted the end between her thumb and forefinger, back and forth, like she was nervous. What did she have to be nervous about?

She whipped her focus over to me; her gaze white-hot and intimidating, like nothing I'd experienced with anyone before. She was a force of nature.

"Does that sound fair, Emma?" Cranston asked.

I'd heard nothing he'd said and had no idea what he was talking about. "Great."

"Very good. I'll read his letter of intention then."

"His letter of what now?"

"His letter of—you said great. Is there a problem?"

"No no. Didn't know...so, what's this?"

"Josiah's letter of intention. It's what needs to happen before I can release the contents of the will. He left specific instructions I'm going to read to you now, if you'll allow it." They both looked at me like I needed quality time in therapy. They weren't wrong.

"Fine. Good. Yes, bring it on."

When would I learn to stop antagonizing fate?

Cranston nodded curtly and read the letter. I could see through the paper as he held it into the light. It was Dad's fancy letterhead.

My last request is for my daughter, Emma Rosen, and her mother, Cassandra McCormack, to prepare our family home for sale together. The new buyer will take ownership forty-five days after my passing, per the purchase agreement. This includes donating my belongings to Rainbow House or Nifty Thrifty in Maiden Lake. When Cranston & Associates receives proof of delivery, they will dispense my assets to all parties involved.

Why had I let them in? How does breathing work again?

"You see why this was so time sensitive. It would have been better handled immediately after the funeral," Cranston said, like he hadn't ripped the proverbial rug out from under my life. "Today is Tuesday, June 18th. You're already in the middle of the sixth week. Not counting today, you have twelve days to prepare everything by the deadline of June 30th. The new owners graciously offered you four extra days, given your circumstances. They'll take possession of the house July first."

I had to give it to my father. He'd never half-assed anything in his life and maintained that discipline in death, too. This was the Mount Everest of betrayal.

"No," I said, flipping the recliner up. It sprang forward with more velocity than I expected, launching me like a trebuchet toward them on the couch. Bob was startled, but didn't stand. I steadied myself and tried my very best to stop feeling murdery.

"No?" Cranston asked, perplexed. "I'm afraid you don't have a choice, Emma. These are legally binding documents." He held up the stack of papers like they should mean something to me. "You have to—"

"I have to eat breakfast and wear deodorant. I have to take care of my dog and go to work. I have to brush my teeth and—"

"Would you like to read the letter? He was quite clear. It says here—"

"I don't care what it says. I'm not doing this. Especially not with her."

The mother-person wasn't innocent. She sat there basking in deep smugness. Had she put Dad up to this? What could she get from him that would make it worth her while to come back now? The worn ring box on his desk upstairs popped into my head and I wondered if that had anything to do with why she was here.

Bob's nervous panting filled the silent room.

"Why are you here? Who called you?" I asked her.

"Emma, she's here because—"

"Eh!" I threw my palm up to shush Cranston. "She's a grown woman. She can speak for herself." This Flora person was growing on me. She was assertive and not here for your shit.

The mother-person didn't speak.

"Did you know about him selling the house? Did you talk to him before he died?"

"I called her, Emma," Cranston said.

"Why are you here *now*? Why didn't you come, you know, like forty years—"

"It's time to move forward and stop dwelling on the past. I'm here to help you fulfill your father's last wishes."

"Help me? Ha! I've lived forty glorious years without you," I said. The Flora side of me wanted to say, "Bitch, please! I didn't ask for your help and I don't need it."

They both stared at me again, like I'd said that out loud.

Oh.

Well.

I couldn't sugarcoat anything anymore. Flora had taken over. "Both of you, out. Now."

NINE

Later that morning, Lenny from Meals on Wheels called me at the flower shop. One of the usual drivers was sick, and they needed me to deliver food that evening. Happy for a reason not to go back home, I accepted the request.

I took Bob instead of dropping him at the house, because it didn't feel right not having him with me. He was always there, my little helper. But I heeded Dr. Dixon's orders and left him in the truck for the deliveries. No excitement allowed.

I'd never delivered to the last house on our list. It was on old Kramer Road, about two miles outside Calypso Springs.

We pulled into the dirt driveway just after sunset and I felt a strange foreboding. Like something wasn't right with this place. The gloomy, fading light made the mess of vines growing over the front of the house seem even more spooky. Growing was a misnomer. They were overtaking it. Taking over. Grisly and warped, a giant hand strangling the house.

They looked like the vines at the nest, the natural spring the founders named our town for. Calypso's spring was deep in the creepy end of Calypso Woods. A tangled heap of dead, tentacle-like morning glory vines grew across the entire surface of the pool.

Hence, the nickname *the nest.* No one ever swam there. It was not inviting.

The whole haunted murder-house tableau made me rethink the do-not-bring-Bob order from Dr. Dixon. I might need him for protection. Though his capacity for security would be sketchy at best. My boy was many things, but a fighter was not one of them. I left him in the truck because he was already anxious, glancing around like a wild animal was going to charge at us from the house.

"Be back in two minutes. You rest, mister." I kissed the top of his head and tried to calm him with a few scratches behind the ears. Didn't work. He still panted like he'd just run a mile top speed.

The lawn at this place was unkempt and unwell. Long, brown, and crunchy underfoot. An old garage squatted at the end of the driveway, as dilapidated as ours, minus the severe lean angle. Behind it, deeper in the yard near the edge of the woods, lay a fallow garden. A sad plot of scorched, brittle soil. It reminded me of a scar that had never healed.

I reached the door, panting from speed walking, also fear, and dropped the food bag on the creaky porch. There was no bell or knocker, so I announced myself the old-fashioned way. Waited. And waited. Before I knocked a second time, the door opened a sliver and a tall, white-haired old woman peeked through the small opening, smoking a cigarette. She peered at me for a second, glanced down at the bag, then back at me.

She seemed to recognize me. It wasn't surprising, given how popular my father was in town and how often we'd volunteered together. I didn't know who this woman was, but we may have run across her in the past.

"We don't need any." She took a long drag on her cigarette, blew the smoke in my face and slammed the door. My life had fallen apart in the course of a day and a door slammed in my face didn't help my mood.

I knocked again, hard and long. No answer. "Hello. Hello!

I'm Emma from Meals on Wheels. I just want to deliver your food and then I'll be out of your hair." Hushed muttering from behind the door. Two people whisper-shouting at one another.

I eavesdropped on the two women from the open window across the porch. The one who didn't answer the door was tiny and frail, slumped over in a wheelchair. Boy, was she giving it to the tall one.

"Me again," I said, waving at them from the open window. Refusing food made no sense. If they were on this list, they needed help. By the look of their house, they needed more than food. The floor hadn't seen a broom in fifty years.

The tiny one in the wheelchair appeared feeble, but her unruly red hair painted a chaotic scene all around her face, like her head was on fire. She pointed her finger at the tall one, almost using it as a weapon. It was long and gnarled, but she could have done damage to an eyeball if she'd had the opportunity. Seemed like she wanted to make the opportunity.

"Tell them Meals people we don't want no more food. They were supposed to stop delivering last month." Smoky yelled at me from the kitchen like I handled the schedule and how dare I help them.

"Okay, I'll let them know. But why not take what I've got with me now? Since I've got it and it's yours."

Little Red yanked Smoky's shirtsleeve and pulled her down to whisper in her ear. Whatever she said convinced Smoky to stroll over and let me in. The door creaked open.

I took a deep breath, questioning my haste to deliver their food, but there was no backing out now.

Inside, Little Red sat watching me with great interest next to the biohazard that was their kitchen table. Smoky leaned back against the counter, eyeing me with great suspicion. The lines on her face told a story and it wasn't a comedy. She held her cigarette about an inch away from her lips and kept it there. Didn't move. It was unsettling.

"Where would you like your food? Can I put it in the fridge for you?" I searched for the fridge but only found an old icebox.

"Put it on the table. No. Nevermind. Here, gimme it," Smoky said. She grabbed the bag from me and raced over to the kitchen sink with it like a sloth.

I stood there, uneasy, with nothing to do. Glancing at the cluttered shelves and wall of photos, the largest picture caught my eye. It was a vintage black and white of two young girls, one about three inches taller than the other, standing awkwardly in front of a lush flower garden. A large shaggy poodle snuggled in between them stared up at the shorter one with adoration. I'd guess that was Little Red. Neither of them smiled. In fact, they weren't smiling in any of the photos. Especially the one where they held hands.

How things stay the same.

Little Red glanced up at me with a gleam in her eyes, like she knew something about me. Everything in this place was unsettling, especially the people.

"She's got his eyes," Little Red said. She stared at me, but hers was a different sort of gaze than her sister's. It held awe. Not of me, surely, but maybe I reminded her of someone she'd loved long ago.

"Whose eyes?" I asked.

"Nobody. You don't know him," Smoky said from the counter, looking like she might bite. She glared at Little Red.

Red ignored her and kept staring at me. Then she did something that ran counter to everything I knew of her from those photos on the wall. She smiled. It was a revelation, like a flower blossoming in front of me. I returned her gesture, though not so exuberantly.

Something in that crooked smile seemed familiar. "Did you ever spend time at Connie's Convalescents? Or Rainbow House, the shelter in Maiden Lake? You seem familiar..."

"Come here, dear," Little Red said, ignoring my questions.

"Sure." I took a few steps toward her.

"No!" Smoky erupted. I couldn't tell if she was yelling at me to stop moving or answering my previous questions, but I stopped. "We ain't from here," she said. Every word felt like a stop light flashing in my face. Go no farther, peasant!

Flora was strong in me, though, so I kept inching toward Little Red. Smoky dropped the bag of food on the filthy floor in front of the sink. She rolled upright, her spine creaking at every inch, and stood like a bodyguard, arms crossed over her chest, watching me.

"Closer, dear," Red said.

I moved toward her and that moldy old table piled high with bills and garbage. A sharp twinge struck the middle of my chest and radiated out to my whole midsection the closer I got to that table. Like someone was squeezing me and wouldn't let go. It became difficult to breathe.

I didn't do well with mold. Must have been a lot of it there.

I was about two feet away and Little Red clutched her own chest like someone had hit her there. "Pearl, it's starting."

"Course it is, Fern. I told you it would. But you ain't gonna listen to me. Gotta see for yourself. Well, see?" Pearl took two long strides and grabbed the wheelchair, spinning Fern away from me. Fern whimpered, still holding her chest, and Pearl wheeled her into the dark abyss of their living room.

"Leave the food on the counter. We'll handle it later," Pearl barked at me. My cue to leave. I couldn't get out of there fast enough.

I left the food and raced back to the truck in the dark to find Bob in the middle of his worst coughing fit yet. He couldn't stop and I couldn't calm him. There was something different about this attack. More aggressive. It terrified me. Eighteen minutes later, I screeched to a halt in our vet's parking lot.

TEN

Cassie waited on the daughter's porch into the early evening, but she never came home from work. There was no spare key, at least none Cassie could find. She'd considered breaking and entering through the back door, but wasn't quite to that level of desperation yet. If she got anywhere near Josiah, it would cause sorrow and suffering, even more than she'd experienced when they were together if the other day was a gauge. But if she couldn't get in soon, nothing was off the table. If she couldn't get in soon, she wouldn't need to get in at all.

To move things in the right direction, she went to the only person she could persuade to help her. The last person she'd ever want to talk to, but life is full of things we don't want to do and things we need to get done.

Cassie knocked twice and waited. The door swung open and Tee stood with her arms crossed, glaring, a redwood to Cassie's bonsai. It was a standoff, neither of them spoke. Besides, Cassie felt it was only fair to give Tee the opportunity to go first and apologize.

"I can't decide if you're brave or stupid coming here," Tee said.

Apparently, she was going to choose an option other than apologizing.

"And by here, I mean home. After all this time? What are you doing, Cassie? You didn't even come back to say goodbye to him."

Him. Josiah. It took all the restraint Cassie had, which wasn't much, not to strangle Tee where she stood for speaking about Josiah to her.

"I'm not here to talk about him."

"What then?"

All Cassie could think about was how much Tee had weathered from the gawky girl she'd grown up with. The top of her head had bled out all the mousy brown and left her hair thin, wilted, and monochromatic gray. That would not stand. Show a little pride in your appearance, for Pete's sake.

"Are you in between dyes?" Cassie asked.

"What?"

"Your..." Cassie pointed at Tee's head. That gray disturbed her. It was aggressive. Maybe even contagious. She backed up a step.

"For God's sake. Are you actually criticizing my hair right now?"

"Have a modicum of pride, Teresa. It's a disgrace." Maybe she would be the catalyst for change. One could only hope.

"You narcissistic, ego-maniacal bi—no. You will not pull that out of me." Tee took a deep breath and let it out all over Cassie's face.

"When did you start wearing glasses? Red frames don't do your olive complexion any favors. But I suppose you already knew that."

"Do you have a purpose in being here?" Tee asked.

A stray, curly gray eyebrow hair sprang up under the top part of Tee's ugly glasses and Cassie fixated on it. *Oh, that won't do.* She wondered, but only for a moment, if Tee would allow her to pluck it.

"What are you—get your hand off—don't touch me, Cassandra." Tee swatted Cassie's hand away from her face. "What's wrong with you?"

Tee stared at her for a few seconds and then seemed to give up on the conversation. But before she could slam the door in Cassie's face, something that happened far too often lately, Cassie held her hand out and stopped it from closing. She may have been sick and tiny, but she was still a force to be reckoned with.

"You didn't fly three thousand miles just to pick me apart. So what the hell do you want, Cassie?"

Cassie hadn't created a concrete plan on her walk over to Tee's house, so she pondered how to go about the business of blackmailing. It was so gauche and tacky, but she didn't have a choice. It was this or breaking and entering, and this was much easier on the back. Plus, it would be fun to make Tee sweat. Cassie had never sought revenge for her ex-friend's betrayal. Maybe now was the time. Carpe diem and all that.

"It's not what I want. It's what you want. Rather, what you don't want. It would be a shame for Flor—Em-ma to find out the terrible truth. Don't you think?"

Tee edged forward, a lioness stalking her prey.

"Tread lightly, old friend," Cassie said, with more confidence than she felt. "I know the truth, and I'm not afraid to use it."

Tee's face turned from olive to magenta in a breath. "What do you want, Cassie?" If words were daggers, Tee would have impaled Cassie against her porch swing.

"Get me inside."

"Inside where?"

"That house."

"What house?"

"You know what house."

"It's not your house anymore. It's Emma's."

"In twelve days, it won't be."

"What are you talking about?"

"Oh, didn't she tell you? I thought you were close. Josiah sold the house. His last wish was for us to get it ready for the new owner. And by us, he meant not you."

She smiled at Tee, letting that information soak in. Tee hung her head, staring at the ugly burgundy shag carpet on the floor. Did no one have good taste anymore? Cassie couldn't tell if Tee was thinking or crying. She *should* have been crying over that terrible shag. It didn't look like she was breathing. Cassie tried to care either way, but couldn't muster it. Then Tee's head popped up like it was on springs and she glared at Cassie.

"What do you need me for, then?" Tee asked.

"Have you gone dull with age?"

"Why do you need me to get you in the house if you're mentioned in Josiah's last wish?" Tee towered over Cassie, crossed her arms, and smiled. It was a nasty, knowing, Cheshire Cat grin. Cassie refused to answer her because Tee had figured out the truth. The daughter wasn't a cooperating partner in that wish.

"I want you to do something else too," Cassie said, without acknowledging the purple elephant on the porch. She pulled a small, folded scrap of paper from her pocket and held it out to Tee. Tee glanced at it, then back at Cassie. She didn't take the paper.

Cassie unfolded it and stood her ground, holding the paper up to Tee with an outstretched arm.

"Ugh. Tattletale," Cassie said, moving things along. She did not have all the time in the world.

Tee growled and snatched the note from her. Cassie checked her hand to make sure it was still attached to her arm.

"Esther Blum. Who's this?" Tee asked, reading the name on the paper.

"That's what I need you to find out. Who. Where. How to contact her."

"Why?"

"Get me in the house and find Esther Blum." Cassie spun around and marched off Tee's porch with her head held high. That went well.

"Jocelyn Prescott," Tee said out of the blue, as if that name should mean something.

Cassie stopped at the bottom of the stairs and indulged her. "Is she of any significance, or are we shouting out random names now?"

"She was one of Emma's best friends in grade school."

"Thrilled for her."

"She accused Emma of stealing their teacher's purse in fifth grade."

"Gripping tale, Tee, but I have neither the time nor the patience for an adolescent soap opera," Cassie said, turning to leave again.

"They caught Jocelyn with the purse a few days later. A simple case of school girl jealousy. The boy she liked had a crush on Emma."

"You might need to get your ears checked, Tee," Cassie said, still walking away.

"Over the years, Jocelyn tried to mend things with Emma. But Emma never talked to her again." Cassie stopped, but didn't face Tee. "Walks the other way when she sees her in town. Even now."

"This darling anecdote pertains to me how?" Cassie said, turning back toward Tee.

"She'll never forgive you."

"Why on earth would I need her to?"

"Jesus. You really don't give a damn." Tee stood tall in the doorway now, taking up the entire space from floor to ceiling.

"I'm not here for that, Tee."

"Obviously."

And obviously that disgusted Tee by the sour look spreading across her face. But Cassie didn't need to explain herself to anyone. Certainly not to Tee or the daughter.

"Well, if it ever crosses your tiny mind, I'm telling you now, it won't happen. Emma doesn't forgive. She's not built for it."

"I'm sure you'll keep that in mind while you're doing your

homework for me. Chop chop," Cassie said, snapping her fingers at Tee. "Times a wastin'."

ELEVEN

Thankfully, my vet's office was a 24-hour emergency clinic. "Okay, mister. We're gonna figure this out now," I said, petting Bob's head as I took him out of the truck. "We're gonna make you better, okay?" A stone settled in my gut. I didn't believe my own words anymore.

He had stopped coughing and wheezing by the time we arrived at the clinic in Maiden Lake, but I knew he wasn't out of the woods. As he lay against my chest, my shirt clung to my body. It wasn't soaked from running around in the middle of the warm night, or the weight of him in my arms. I was sweating from the weight of what I could be facing. It almost brought me to my knees right there in the parking lot.

Tee pulled in and parked in the spot next to me as I fumbled with the truck door, trying to close it. She was stalking me now. I had armfuls of Bob and couldn't navigate well, so I was grateful for the help, but I would never admit that in court.

She raced from her car and opened the door to the clinic for me. I didn't look at her as we rushed Bob in to the front desk together. She stood by my side while I checked him in and rubbed his feverish head.

We didn't have to wait for the vet to show up. He charged out of the exam room and around the corner to greet us. I was expecting Dr. Sax or Dr. Crow, the usual after-hours vets.

Instead, I got Jake.

Time moved backward in the second it took him to recognize me. I relived our entire relationship with his approach. The proverbial life flashing before your eyes moment. Meeting for the first time in the observatory at school. Late night ice cream secrets in the snack hall. Long walk-and-talks by, under, through the waterfalls. And sex. Everywhere sex. Oh my god, the sex.

Things happened in my body that hadn't happened for twenty years.

"Emma," Jake said, clearly shocked to see me late on a school night. Or any night. Or ever again. As shocked as I was to see him the day before. It couldn't be him, but it was. "And Tee, wow. It's been..." He stood in the middle of the hallway several feet from us. I wondered if his legs and heart had stopped working like mine had. "Sorry, I'm just surprised to...Did you know I transferred...I mean..."

Questions cluttered my mind. When had he come back to Maiden Lake from Indiana? How long had he been here? Why was he here, in my vet's office, standing in front of me more sexy than ever? But there was no time for *so, you still exist and haunt my dreams,* because Bob.

He took another moment of silence and then remembered where we were. "I'm so sorry, what's going on with this big guy?" he asked, back to being our emergency vet instead of *the one who got away.*

"Little help," I cried. My arms were giving out from carrying eighty-plus pounds of golden retriever. He almost slipped from my grip, but Tee swooped in and supported him under me until Jake reached us and took him.

Jake smelled amazing, like clean laundry, crisp winter air, and cigarettes. An odd combination on anyone else, but somehow he pulled it off. And he didn't smoke, so that was strange. Or maybe he did now. I didn't know. I knew nothing about him anymore. This man I'd given everything to once upon a time.

"Hey buddy. How you doin'," he said tenderly as he took Bob in his arms. "He can't walk?"

"He's so tired I didn't want to stress him more."

"All right, let's have a look. What's your name, mister?"

"Bob. This is Bob. Redford, actually. Bob for short."

"You always had a thing for The Sundance Kid." Jake smiled and turned away with Bob, carrying him into an exam room. His smile did things to me. The sheer wattage of it could light up a stage. It had electrified so many of my days and nights when I was struggling in college, and I couldn't believe it was in my life again.

I followed Jake with Tee on my heels. She was right behind me, close enough to reach out, but far enough not to impose. She always seemed to know where to be for me. That's why her betrayal hit me so hard. I didn't tell her to stay or leave. I didn't acknowledge her at all yet.

Bob flopped his head over the side of Jake's arm, looking for me. His tongue hung out of his mouth as he panted. He always had to know where I was.

"I'm right here, mister. I'm not going anywhere."

He panted and wheezed and I stroked the little notch on his head with my forefinger as we approached the exam table, hoping to soothe him. The perk was a certain closeness to Jake. My Jake. I was standing next to Jake. *Not the time, Emma.* Why was sex all I could think about?

"Tell me what's going on," Jake said, easing Bob down on the exam table. Bob, abnormally stoic in general, whimpered when he touched down. I reached out to soothe him, but he flinched, like my touch hurt him. It broke me.

"How's his appetite?"

"Slow for the last couple of days. I thought it was because of the infection."

Bob didn't try to stand. "Infection?" Jake examined him,

feeling all over his body for sensitive spots. I'd never wished to be a dog more in my life. *Handle yourself, Emma!*

"Dr. Dixon diagnosed him with a lung infection yesterday. He's on antibiotics and they're obviously not working yet."

Jake massaged Bob's chest and continued performing the regular exam of his heart and lungs. Bob seemed fine with Jake touching him, but every time I tried to get near him, he whimpered. *What was going on?*

Bob coughed and it wrenched his whole body. He went stiff with the effort. I didn't know what to do if I couldn't pet him, so I whispered into his face over and over. "You're gonna be okay, mister. You're gonna be okay."

"How long has he had the cough?" Jake asked, listening more intently to Bob's lungs.

"It wasn't like that when I brought him in yesterday morning. This is as bad as he's been. He's had a simple cough for a little while. A few weeks maybe, since...but never this bad."

Jake listened to Bob's lungs again with his stethoscope and made an odd noise. "Has he been in the woods recently?"

"No."

"Near water? You still live on the lake?"

I nodded. *He remembered.*

"Has he been digging?"

"There's an old tree stump out on our shoreline. He never paid attention to it before, but in the last month, since Dad..."

"I heard about your father. I'm really sorry."

I thought he might reach for my hand or touch my arm, a warm gesture from an old...friend, but he didn't. He kept things professional. Probably better. That old familiar twinge flared up in my belly whenever he glanced my way and reminded me not to get too close. I hadn't experienced it in twenty years. Not since we were together in college. So I nodded, unable to respond with much else.

Wait. He'd heard? And he didn't...never mind. Didn't matter. Stay focused.

"So he's been digging at a tree?" Jake asked.

"Like he was trying to dig it up or something. It's hollowed out and has holes all around the trunk. More now that he's been digging at it. He's obsessed." That was not good news, given the way Jake's face fell.

"We'll need to do blood tests and a chest x-ray to confirm, but I think he might have blastomycosis. It's rare in this region of the country. Over the years, I've only seen a handful of cases in Maiden Lake, but I saw one a few months ago at our other clinic before I transferred over here with Dr. Dixon. They all presented similarly to Bob."

Earth shifted on its axis and came to a screeching halt, full-stop mid-rotation, sending me hurtling into space. "I'm sorry... you were here? In Maiden Lake?" Jake had been thirty minutes down the road, not in Indiana, for the last however many years?

"You didn't...I thought..." He seemed derailed by my question, as if he assumed I knew he'd been here all along.

"Sorry, not important right now," I said, trying to get us on track with Bob and bring me back to solid ground. "What does it mean, blast...?"

"Blastomycosis," Jake said, distractedly, like he was trying to remember something.

"Right. What do I need to do?" I asked, ever the soldier of doing.

"Emma, I..." He looked directly at me for the first time. It wasn't the look a vet gives a client. It was the look a man gives a woman he has a certain history with. He was about to say something profound, something that would change my life forever. I could feel it. The air between us had become electric.

"I...have to warn you..." A switch had flipped and he was back to being my emergency vet. "Don't go online to look this up, okay? I know you'll want to arm yourself with a lot of information and that's good to have, but blasto's a beast. And there are a lot of stories online. Considering everything you've been through with your father, I think..."

There it was again. He was here, he knew, and he didn't even try to get in touch. *Is everyone in my life an asshole?*

"I'm sure that was hard on you. I really am sorry."

Right. Well, joke's on him because he said 'hard on' and my father's a tree now, so it's all good. And I should never ever think about those two things together again.

We both rested our hands on Bob's back, almost touching. "I don't want to jump to conclusions yet, but if this is what I think it is, it's going to be a long and expensive road to recovery for him."

"We'll figure it out. Whatever it takes," I said, not knowing where the hell I would get the money I needed for this, too.

"He may get worse before he gets better. If he gets better. Emma, I have to tell you this because—"

"No, you don't." I couldn't stomach the idea of losing Bob, so it wasn't worth setting the table with that information.

"If it is blasto, there's a high probability he'll—"

"Nope." I waved him off. What was I thinking? Jake wasn't sexy at all.

Tee's hand materialized on my back. It burned where it lay, an open wound. I shrugged her off without a word. She pulled away, but my body didn't release the pain. It stayed with me, the cut that wouldn't heal.

"As long as you understand," Jake said.

My father had faced two successive death sentences with different cancer diagnoses. He succumbed to one. So I understood more than I wanted to about high probabilities and the cruel certainty of uncertainties.

TWELVE

The vet tech took Bob's blood and x-rays, but the clinic's computer system was down, so I wouldn't be able to see his results until it was back up in the morning. We threw away the antibiotics and Jake gave him his first dose of Itraconazole, which, thankfully, knocked him out on the ride home.

Tee escorted us back to the house. Her steady headlights in my rear-view mirror were a comfort, but I still didn't want to talk to her. When we arrived home, she made herself useful. Closed the truck door behind me after I coaxed a groggy Bob from the seat into my arms, then ran ahead of us to light the porch and open the front door. I'd never seen her move so swiftly. She was generally more tortoise than hare.

Inside, I settled Bob on his bed and laid next to him on the floor, petting him back to sleep. Tee crouched to sit with us. Her entire body creaked with the strain of bending. I held up a hand as a stop sign, trying to keep her from getting comfortable.

"Thanks for your help tonight, but it's late. You should go—"

"Honey, we have to talk."

She sat with a thump on the unforgiving hardwood floor. Half of me enjoyed seeing her wince, and the other half slapped myself upside the head for feeling that way. She massaged Bob's hind legs while I snuggled his head. His breathing settled into the consistent rhythm of deep sleep, and we settled into another stretch of agonizing silence.

"Quite the surprise with Jake." Tee's sudden voice was a thunderclap in the quiet room. "He looked good." She wasn't wrong. "So, he didn't move back to Indiana after college?"

"Guess not." Knowing he lived this close now stirred a certain hope I didn't welcome because it wasn't possible. Love was not in my future.

"You didn't know he was here, working at the—"

"Let's not worry about what *I* knew. Yeah?" I didn't want to talk about Jake with her. Not now. I could only concentrate on one fire in my life at a time. I leaped up and charged into the kitchen to get a snack. She wasn't invited but followed me, anyway. Leaning against the doorway, she watched my every move. I put pomegranate seeds, almonds, and grape jelly in my cottage cheese to see what she had to say about it, but she remained mute. Normally, she would have had a lot of opinions about the weird foods I mixed together.

I didn't offer her anything to eat or drink. My rudeness felt so wrong, but so right. Thank you, Flora.

A strangling silence overtook the room as we faced off. I thought I might need to break a window or door to let in some air, but then Tee spoke, breaking everything apart.

"I didn't know, honey. I had no idea she was going to be there." Her words and expression were sincere, like they always had been.

"Okay. But you didn't seem to think you were talking to a ghost yesterday, so how do you explain that?" I shoved a big scoop of cottage cheese with grape jelly in my mouth.

"A ghost?" She took a step toward me with confusion etched on her face. "Honey. I don't know what..."

"You didn't lie to me about that for the last two decades?"

"Apply the brakes and reverse because I don't know what the hell you're talking about."

Was I the only one Dad had lied to about the mother-invader?

"She's alive, Tee. Maybe you didn't know she was going to be there, but did you know she was alive enough to be anywhere?"

"Why would I think she wouldn't be?"

"Because Dad told me she wasn't."

"Cripes, no wonder you were so shocked. Why the hell would he..." She seemed dumbfounded by this information.

"When he came back from his trip to California, remember? He went to visit some old friend from high school. I didn't know the guy's name. Dad had a terrible time. And when he got back, he was different. Angrier."

"Oh...oh no." She dropped her head and hid her face from me like she was remembering something very different about that trip.

"He didn't tell me what happened. But he talked to you about everything back then," I said.

"Josiah, you damn idiot." Tee shook her head and scolded him like he was in the room with us. She sat on the stool across the island, but wouldn't look at me. It took her a few months to speak again and as she did, her breathing became shallow, thin.

"A couple nights after he came home from that trip, we all had dinner, your dad, my dad, and me. Josiah said..." Tee glanced at the ceiling, at the rotting flowers on the counter, everything but me.

"Just say it. You're not betraying him now."

"'She's dead to me.' He said 'She's dead to me.'"

"Dead to him. Not actually dead."

"Right. The figure of speech."

"Yeah, well, he figured his speech a little differently to me."

"So I'm gathering."

"Right after the trip, when he got sick the first time, he told me she was dead. As a doornail. Six feet under. Pushing up daisies."

Tee winced, waving her hand in front of her face for me to stop. "Okay, honey, I get the picture. Josiah. Ugh." She shook her fist at the ceiling. "I'm so sorry. I swear I didn't know he told you that."

Given her reaction, I believed her. It helped calm the brewing storm inside.

"But he must have had a good reason. Your father was not—"

"A lying liar? Because that's exactly what he was. How can you defend him?"

"I'm not defending—it was inexcusable. But it was also not like him. Something must have made him believe it was the right thing to tell you." She didn't meet my gaze when she spoke, studied the floor instead. That wasn't like Tee. When she had something to say, she looked you in the eye.

I felt like she was still keeping something from me, but I couldn't ask, didn't have the stomach for any more truth or lies, so I melted to the floor where I stood. My legs weren't strong enough to hold me after the emotional shit storm of the last two days. Tee sat, struggling to get down on the floor next to me.

"Don't," I said. But she did anyway.

"Your father was many things, Em—"

"Lousy rotten lying liar tops the list."

"He was protecting you from something. Some deep suffering. I'm sure of it."

"The deep suffering of getting to know her?"

Tee smirked. "Too right. Welcome to the joy that is Cassie McCormack. Please know this, honey: He loved you more than anything in this life, more than he loved her. And that's saying a lot."

I couldn't imagine how my father had ever fallen in love with that tiny woman-tornado. In my limited experience, her first and second impressions left everything to be desired.

"Right now, all I know is he lied to me, betrayed me, and lied to me some more. He sold the house, left me with no money and piles of bills. On top of that, my beautiful boy is sick, and I have to move because, if I didn't mention before, he sold the house.

I'm like a goddamn country song on steroids. Those are the things I know."

"At least you're not in denial. He really, he sold the house?" Her voice was strained, like this wasn't as much of a surprise as it should have been.

"They came earlier. And I mean earlier. Question: Who shows up unannounced at someone's house to deliver The Worst News Ever before seven o'clock in the morning? Answer: The mother-invader."

"Mother-invader?" Tee scoffed. Then nodded. "Fits."

"Dad sold the house, Tee." I deflated with the statement. She sighed and took my hand in hers. I didn't pull away. The part of me that needed support argued louder than the part that was still suspicious about her keeping secrets. "And he wants her to help me pack everything up. They won't release the will until we've donated all of his things to charity."

"That brilliant bastard," Tee said, like she'd had a grand epiphany.

"He's one of those things."

"Who bought the house?"

"Don't know. We have twelve days. I'm not doing it."

"Of course you're doing it."

"Uh, no."

"You're never going to understand anything about what happened, why she left and stayed away, until you talk to her. She's the only one who can answer those questions."

"Now you want us to be besties?"

"Want is a strong word. It connotes a certain level of desire. And never besties. She's not the softest plushy in the toy bin."

"Loud and clear."

Tee chuckled for the first time in months. I'd been keeping score for both of us.

"You were friends with her once upon a time. You should do it instead," I said. "Wouldn't it be nice to reconnect? Reminisce

about the old days and, you know, find out why she abandoned
her family."

"You are your father's daughter."

"How dare you."

We settled into a contemplative silence, this one less fraught
with tension. On my part, at least.

"Honey, I'm so sorry this is all happening. Your idiot father
notwithstanding, it's a lot to deal with. But Bob is going to be
fine. Know that. We'll do whatever it takes. And no matter what
happens with the house, you always have a room with us for as
long as you need."

Damn. She'd popped our bubble and brought us back to reality. All I wanted was her unwavering support for my fantasy that
doing nothing would make everything okay.

"I want to know what happened and why," I said. I'd spent
my life chasing those questions with no answers. "It's just, after
meeting, I don't know if I want to hear any of it from her."

"Understood, believe me, but it sounds like you don't have a
choice. At least about the house."

There I was again, backed into a corner with no control over
my life because of that mother-person. I wanted answers from her,
but I needed answers from the mother sitting next to me. The
thought of grilling Tee made my breath quicken. Sweat trickled
down the nape of my neck and my body was jittery, unsteady. I
was teetering on the edge of a precipice in my relationship with
her, terrified to jump and know the truth, but also unable to walk
away from the danger of it.

"Why didn't you ever tell me about Flora?" I asked.

The question caught her off guard.

"It was so long ago. I didn't..."

"You didn't think I had a right to know?"

"It's not that...I was—"

"Keeping his secrets."

"I made promises." She let out a heavy sigh but said nothing
else.

"What kind of person asks you to make that kind of promise? I feel like I didn't know him at all."

"He didn't ask me. I offered. Back then, I did anything I could to help ease his heartache."

And she had never stopped.

"Why did he change it?"

"Your father believed in the power of a name. He needed a fresh start, a clean slate. Cassie wanted to name you Flora from the moment she found out she was pregnant. And so it was when you were born. But when she left that night and never returned, you became his whole world. You were so joyful and brilliant, and had this magical way of putting everyone at ease around you. After two years of agonizing over Cassie, he changed your name because he wanted it to reflect who you were and what you'd become to him. You were Emma, not Flora."

"Did you want him to change it too?"

"You lived up to the meaning of your new name. Universal. For everyone. You were his little helper at school from the beginning. Everyone adored you."

Everyone's savior but my own.

"Did you help him decide to rename me?"

"Whatever you're asking, just ask it, honey."

"Did you help him in other ways with the fresh start?"

"No. We never..." she trailed off, lost in thought.

What was she hiding? I couldn't get the image of her shielding me from the mother-invader out of my head. She'd tried to drag me out of the conference room, away from the truth. What was she afraid I'd find out? A storm swirled in my stomach, gathering strength by the minute, but I plucked up the courage to ask the question.

"What aren't you telling me, Tee?"

She exhaled like she'd been holding her breath for forty years. "He never stopped searching for Cassie."

"I know. It was unhealthy. He thought he was hiding it from

me, but I knew. I saw the checklists with addresses crossed out on his desk."

"After that trip, he told us she was never coming back. I figured he'd finally found her, but things didn't go the way he'd hoped, because he asked us not to mention her again. To you or anyone."

"Are you kidding me?" Lightning in the middle of my kitchen. A category five brewing inside me.

"He didn't talk to me about everything. Especially not that trip. When he returned, he didn't tell me what happened or if he'd even seen her. I never asked. I didn't want to open his wounds any more. I assumed he had because of what he'd said."

"You knew he found her? Went to see her. And you never told me?" My body raged like I was made of a hurricane. I wanted to kick her out before she spoke another word.

She was sweaty now, too. Pasty-faced. She fiddled with her hands and stretched her neck, clearly uncomfortable. "I didn't know for sure, but yes, I thought he had. I never imagined he told you what he did. I wouldn't have let that stand. It wasn't right."

"But you keeping that secret about her was? You could have asked him where she lived. You could have pressed him for my sake so I could at least talk to her. He found her and you both kept it from me."

"I'm so sorry, honey." Neither of us spoke, dealing with the weight of her admission.

"That night, his words sounded so final, like he'd simply repeated what she'd said to him. I guess I thought it would be better if you didn't know where she was, so you wouldn't..."

"Wouldn't what?"

"I don't know. Hope for some kind of relationship with her in the future."

"But it wasn't your decision to make for me. And it wasn't his either."

"You're right. I know you're right. Please understand, we only ever had your best interests at heart."

Did she though? Do you ever have someone else's best interests at heart when they directly conflict with your own? I had a feeling there was something else behind her promise and secret-keeping for my father. Especially after her efforts to steal me away from the mother-invader the day before.

Had she been worried, all those years ago, about the mother-invader replacing her in my life? Or did it run deeper than that? She'd been trying to win my father over since I'd known her and had never abandoned that pursuit, even after she was married. If I'd developed a relationship with my mother, it could have opened the door for her to come back into his life again. The last thing Tee wanted. Even though he'd kept her at arm's length romantically, I know Tee still hoped for someday with him.

Like I'd always hoped I'd meet my mother someday.

Careful what you wish for.

"I'm sorry, honey. I thought I was doing the right thing for you. You were already grown and so independent at school. I...I should have told you."

I stood on wobbly legs and drank straight from the tap to ease my burning body. Tee hauled herself up next to me, using the counter for balance.

Other than her staggering personality deficits, why wouldn't Tee want me to know who the mother-invader was yesterday? And why was she pushing me toward her now? It was fickle and unlike Tee. The more I thought about it, the more it felt like she didn't have my best interests at heart. Then or now.

"I'm not doing it," I said. "I'll squat here. They'll have to remove me by court order. It'll be ugly. Don't care."

"That's one way to handle it. Or you could—"

"If you didn't want me to know who she was yesterday, why are you pushing me to do this with her now?"

"Because you're right. I shouldn't have kept that from you. It was wrong. And because sometimes what we want and what we need may be two very different things."

Before this, there had never been a time I questioned whether

I could believe Tee, trust her. It had always been a given. She was my rock. It felt ugly and wrong to suspect everything she said, but how do you trust someone again after they've lied to you for so long? How many other secrets had she kept from me? How many was she still keeping?

"Well, right now they're the same for me," I said.

"Oh?"

"I want and need you to go. Don't check in on us. We'll be fine."

I left her alone in the kitchen, leaning against the cold counter for support. It's true what they say, the first cut really is the deepest.

THIRTEEN

Early the next morning, I woke under the dad-tree with Atlas's world and Bob's soft head on my shoulder. Thoughts of Tee's betrayal made my body heavy. If I'd had my way, I would have crawled into one of Bob's holes by the lake and taken a fifty-year nap until everything worked itself out.

Instead, I dragged myself off the cool, wet ground and trudged inside.

On my way upstairs, a strange noise blew in from the porch. I opened the front door and noticed two things at once. Thing One: a gorgeous man who used to be *my* gorgeous man, stood in front of me holding a bouquet up to his face with his forefinger pressed against his lips, shushing me. His sudden presence again, on my porch no less, incited more storms inside me.

Before I could say anything, Jake used the flowers to point to Thing Two: the mother-invader on the side of my porch. Cocooned up, chopping logs inside an old sleeping bag atop a stack of flattened moving boxes.

That woman would be the death of me.

Embarrassed by everything, I had the same clothes and head from the night before, I almost jumped inside and slammed the door on both of them. Seriously, though, did no one call anymore? A little notice and I could have wiped any crusty things off my face and porch before he arrived. The curse of small towns. Everyone lived close enough to drop by. Except, as far as I'd Googled last night, Jake lived on the far side of Maiden Lake, so a stop in Calypso Springs was definitely out of his way to work. I tried not to read too much into it. Like I said, one fire at a time.

The nervous concern etched on Jake's face worried me. It likely wasn't about the random homeless person sleeping on my porch, so it must have been about Bob.

"What's that?" I whispered, pointing to the manila envelope in his other hand. Unable to ignore the tiny snoring elephant on the porch, I stepped aside and waved Jake into the house. "Maybe you should...yeah." He nodded and crossed the threshold into my living room. Why did he have to smell so good? Pretty sure I smelled like dirty clothes and regret.

"This is why I'm here," he said, lifting the envelope up to show me after I eased the front door closed. "Also, these are for you." He held the daffodils out to me, a sweet offering. My heart went all aflutter until I realized it was just the usual morning bouquet from my anonymous porch donor. I wanted to be those flowers, held tight in the palm of his hand.

"I mean, I found them...out there." He pointed toward the porch, the land of lost things, and glanced around like he didn't know what to do with himself. It had been twenty years since he'd been in this room. "I can put them in a vase for you."

Strange thing to say in someone else's house.

"I don't know why I said that. Here you go." He held the bouquet out to me, but didn't meet my gaze. He was nervous. That made two of us, which helped me feel less buzzy and awkward.

When I took the flowers from him, my fingers brushed against his. The contact sent shock waves through me. I tried not to think about how many mornings I'd woken in the last twenty years in a cold sweat after dreaming about the simple act of touching his hand again. And now, the inevitable ache followed, starting in my middle and spreading to the rest of my body. Like it had back in school when I fell in love with him.

"You okay?" he asked, putting his hand on my arm to steady me. It made things worse, so I pulled away, like I didn't want him to touch me. I'd never told him how much it hurt me in school, and I wasn't about to start now.

"Yep. Great. I'll..." I scrambled with the flowers into the kitchen, trying not to think about what a mess I was making of everything. Creating distance between us held off the impending storm.

Like opposite ends of a magnet, Jake was drawn to Bob. He shot straight for him and laid down on the floor next to his bed. Bob hadn't jumped up to greet Jake when I'd opened the door, and that worried me. He was my wiggly greeting machine. Always needed to know who was visiting and find out how many kisses he could fit in before they'd reach their slobber threshold.

Jake was so gentle it made me jealous of Bob too. You had me at lying on my dirty floor in your work clothes to comfort my sick boy. *Damn it, Emma. Focus.*

I'd gone to the kitchen to put the daffodils in a vase, but why? They were dead already. Shriveled and crispy in my hand, like the others the day before. This was a thing I did now. I threw them in the sink and tried to ignore the haunting feeling that I was broken. So much for new beginnings.

"How was he when you got home last night?" Jake asked.

"He slept at first, but then he was restless. Like he couldn't get comfortable," I said, sitting on the floor with both of them. I made sure not to let my hand wander into Jake's territory again.

"It'll take a few days for the meds to kick in and start working if they're going to."

"If they're going to?"

"That's why I'm here."

"Right. The envelope."

A loud burst from the chainsaw erupted from the front

porch. Hard to ignore that kind of elephant when there's a wide-open window in the room.

"Can we...um, who is that?" Jake gestured toward the area where Thing Two slept on the porch. How to explain? Best not to until necessary.

"Long story. So, the envelope?"

"Right. Sorry. Listen, Em, I don't do house calls, especially this early, but..." It had been so long since he'd been familiar with me, calling me Em.

"But..." I said, racking focus back to Bob.

"I saw something strange on Bob's x-rays and I wanted to show you as soon as possible. Dr. Dixon's out sick and we're booked solid at the clinic today, so this was the only time I had. Sorry if it was inconvenient." He glanced in the chainsaw's direction on the porch.

"Not a problem. I appreciate you taking the time. House calls, cell calls, landline, all the calls. Make them any time, day and night." Some idiot had kidnapped my mouth. But I didn't let that deter me. "Anything to do with this guy is top priority. Knowledge is power and...we must speak truth to the...whatever. Lost the thread."

Jake lowered his head and smiled, like he'd heard a joke only he understood. He glanced up at me, and inside his hazel eyes, time slowed and stretched, suspending us in the middle of the vast universe, alone. We stayed there in each other's gaze for centuries, eons, millennia. Then Bob coughed and I looked away. We snapped back into place in my living room on a hot Wednesday morning like nothing extraordinary had happened at all.

Also, it's possible nothing had.

Jake rubbed Bob's head near my shaky hand, getting close enough for me to feel the heat coming off his fingers. I pulled away. He didn't seem to notice.

"I'm glad you haven't changed," he said. The smile that followed was genuine and bright and made of gold dust. I wanted to dive into his mouth. "I haven't either."

Did that mean what I thought it meant? He didn't look at me when he said it, he focused on Bob. Was I reading too much into it? Possibly. Probably. Definitely. But it had been twenty years, and he was here, here! In my living room, in front of me, and I had so many questions. It was almost like he wanted the idea of our potential to float there between us, marinating in the tension of unspoken things.

But I'd had enough of that. I wanted answers.

"When did you come back?" I asked with barely enough breath in my chest to get it out.

He looked at me like I'd asked him to explain quantum physics. "What do you mean, back?"

"Well, you went home to Indiana to take care of your mother, so I was wondering when you came back to Maiden Lake."

"I can't tell if you're messing with me."

Uh oh. His smile faded and the air cooled about ten degrees between us.

"I'm not messing with you."

"Emma, I left to go home for a long weekend at the beginning of our junior year. My mom had pneumonia, and I took care of her for a few days."

"Okay."

"When I got back, you..." He paused so long I thought he might have forgotten what he was going to say.

"I what...?"

"You really don't remember?" His gaze pierced me, like he was trying to figure out if I was lying or not.

"I'm sorry, I...I thought you were..."

"You know what? Doesn't matter. It was twenty years ago. We've both lived life and moved on, right? Water under the bridge." He pulled away. I could almost see him closing the door on me in his mind. That chapter of his life over and done.

"You stayed?" I whispered, more to myself than anyone else in the room. Still trying to make sense of it.

"I stayed."

"All these years." A profound sense of loss, lost time, lost opportunities, washed over me as we marinated in that truth. But he released the tension between us and got us back on track. Bob, the reason for his visit. Or, maybe, the other reason for it.

"We should, uh, let me show you these and I'll get out of your hair." Jake pulled Bob's x-rays from the envelope, back to business being my vet.

He held the film up to the light of the windows facing the front yard. When I glanced through them, I noticed something moving. A willow tree, with long branches dancing in the breeze, near the front porch.

"We should use the window in the kitchen," I said, standing. I had to get Jake out of there before he saw my dad-tree. Also, what if he didn't see him? That could only mean one thing, and I still wasn't ready to face that kind of reality about myself.

"What am I looking at?" I asked, trying to erase any trace of emotion from the conversation we'd just had. I stood in front of the kitchen window, holding up the other side of the x-ray film. Jake wouldn't be able to see past me to the front yard, in case the dad-tree made another appearance.

"This is Bob's left lung. And here's his right."

"What...are those? They look like..." I didn't want to say it out loud. I'd made enough of a fool of myself already.

"The results aren't back from the lab to confirm blasto, but this is not a normal scan for that diagnosis."

"I wouldn't think this is a normal scan for any diagnosis."

"It's a mystery," he said. A mystery. Much like most of my life at the moment. "Blasto presents like a snowstorm in the lungs. A lot of static everywhere in this area here." He pointed to the middle section where Bob's lung was. "Normally, it would look a lot like this one." He pulled another x-ray film out to compare with Bob's. It was nothing like it.

"So, what do you think this is?"

"Honestly, I have no idea. I've never seen anything like this before."

It wasn't a snowstorm we saw in those films. It looked like a handful of seeds had taken root in Bob's chest and blossomed into a field of wild forget-me-not flowers.

Cassie snorted awake. Damn it. She hadn't meant to fall asleep and stay that way. She had prepared to greet the daughter with the dawn, bright and fresh and ready for battle, but she was more exhausted than she'd thought. Her conversation with Tee had drained her. For a woman of such stature and strength, Tee was useless. As persuasive as a potato with that daughter-person. Cassie would have to do everything herself.

Two voices drifted out of the living room window over Cassie's head, so at least she hadn't missed her. But who was in there with the daughter? Had they seen Cassie on the porch? Mortifying. Speaking of, the zipper on the sleeping bag had caught on her sleeve and she struggled to get out of it. This was not her best look. On all fours, twisting like a trapped animal to free herself from the jaws of a demonic blanket.

The front door swung open the moment she burst free from the zipper. She stretched up, still on her knees, and almost shouted hallelujah, but a stunning man stepped out of the house and onto the porch. She'd never sprung to her feet faster.

"Bring Bob in as soon as you can today to get another x-ray. And don't forget to have the stump taken out in case it's the culprit. This could have been a glitch in the Matrix last night, but if it shows up again, I think we should do a CT scan to get a better idea of what we're looking at. It'll be costly, but I'll see if we can put you on a payment plan," the man said, directing all of his attention inside the house, unaware of his audience on the porch.

"Whatever it takes," the daughter said, still inside. Cassie wondered why that mangy creature would require a CT scan, but it didn't involve her, so she lost interest halfway through the thought. Why was this person here at whatever ungodly hour it was in the morning?

"You are?" Cassie said, charging him as he leaned on the door frame facing the daughter. Did that woman ever put a comb through her hair? Good grief.

"Oh god," the daughter said, loud enough for everyone present to hear. Cassie wasn't the only mortified member of the party. She didn't take it personally.

"I'm Jake. Bob's emergency vet."

"Uh huh," Cassie said, sizing him up.

He smiled, gazing at her like he was waiting for her to do something for him. "And you are?"

"My realtor! She's my realtor." The daughter spit it out before Cassie could say a word. Cunning girl. Cassie would go along with her lie because she didn't see a reason not to. Yet.

"My father sold the house and she's taking care of...everything."

"He sold the house?" Jake repeated. The daughter nodded but didn't say a word, which spoke volumes. Cassie had a feeling she should care about that, but as quickly as it had come, it passed.

"Your plate really is overfull. I'm sorry," Jake said. Cassie wondered what he had to be sorry about. "We'll figure out what's going on with Bob, get him fixed up soon."

The daughter nodded and smiled. A limp gesture filled with no joy. It may have fooled Jake, he looked easily fooled, but Cassie recognized that smile for what it was. A fragile forgery of happiness, putting others at ease, while she's shattering inside. Cassie had perfected it with her parents in the early days after they'd left Calypso Springs.

So, apparently, she and the daughter did have something in common.

"That's some kind of dedication," Jake said to Cassie, turning to leave. He glanced over at the temporary bedroom she'd set up on the flattened boxes. "Wish my realtor had that kind of work ethic." He glanced back, smiled, and winked at the daughter. It was subtle, but Cassie recognized it, that spark. She'd felt it herself a lifetime ago with Josiah. As he moved off the porch and down the driveway, she understood exactly why he was there and what she needed to do now.

"I think it's time we came to an agreement, don't you?" Cassie said, peeking around the edge of the front door she'd stopped from slamming in her face again.

FOURTEEN

It was getting harder to ignore the person barging into my life as she used her tiny, yet formidable body to stop the front door. Her sleepover stunt reminded me of the time I'd spent two weeks camped out in front of Fussy's flower shop, waiting for her to open every morning at five. It took thirteen days before she broke down and hired me for a job that didn't exist.

If this tenacity was in any way hereditary, I was in trouble. I didn't have it in me to resist anymore. There was too much to get done. The last thing I wanted to do was admit Tee was right about letting the mother-invader in. Didn't want to give Tee credit for anything, but maybe it was time. If only to find out the truth and move on. I hoped it wouldn't be the biggest mistake of my life.

"Ground rule number one," I said, walking away from the door. "This is still my house for the next twelve days. You're not allowed in it without me here."

"Nonsense. I'll pack while you're at work. We'll be done in no time."

"Not going to happen. My house, my rules. If you don't like that, you're free to leave by the door you're hanging from."

"We'll continue to negotiate. Right now, I have to use the facilities."

The minute she marched into the house (like she owned it) Bob perked up. She shuffled straight to the bathroom with him hot on her heels. He almost wiggled his way in behind her before she slammed the door in his furry little face. I didn't enjoy how he reacted to her.

I put the envelope with Bob's weird x-rays on the bookshelf by Dad's recliner in the corner. Jake let me keep them since we were redoing them later. The snow globe she'd given Dad sat on the top shelf, daring me to shake it. Challenge accepted. The inside swirled around in a chaotic flower storm, eerily similar to those x-rays.

"I need to take Bob back to the vet," I said to the bathroom door. "We can talk about the rest of my rules in the truck."

The door cracked open enough for her to peek out at me. She held it tight while trying to shoo Bob away with her kneecap. "Why don't I stay and assemble the boxes for you? They'll be ready to pack when you return."

"You're welcome to use either exit to leave when you're done in there." I started up the stairs toward my room, calling Bob. She flung the door closed again.

After I'd changed and run a comb through my hair, I made a quick call to Fussy at the shop to let her know I'd be late. Her voice sounded odd, wound tight, like she'd heard bad news.

"Emma, dear, oh jeez. I'm happy you called. I mean, I'm not happy. Nobody's happy in this situation, you know." Dread sparked in me with every heavy sigh she breathed. "I hate to do this after everything you've been through." She exhaled like she was putting her favorite cat to sleep.

"What is it, Fussy?"

"Well, dear, I'm going to need you to take time off for a while."

"A while?"

"A while."

"Like a couple weeks?"

"Little longer."

"A month?"

"A month plus…"

"Plus?"

"Plus forever."

My cell phone felt like a fifty-pound weight against my head. "Fussy, I know I've been a little scattered lately, but I'll do better, I promise. I have a lot going on right now. I need this job—"

"Oh, Emma, it's not you. You're the best. Business isn't picking up the way I'd hoped. I can't afford you anymore."

This was the last thing I needed, but I couldn't make Fussy feel worse about her circumstances. Now I was the one sighing. "Okay, I get it. It's fine. I mean, it's not fine, but I understand. Call me as soon as you need me back, okay?"

"I won't, dear. I'm so sorry, Emma."

"I know."

And like that, I was unemployed with a tsunami of bills rushing in, ready to sink me where I stood. But I didn't have the luxury of dwelling on it because there was too much to get done. Now I'd have to add finding a job to that burgeoning list.

After I screwed my head back on straight, I called the tree guys to uproot the rotting trunk out by the lake so Bob wouldn't dig in it when he got better. His health was a *when* situation. *If* was not an option for us.

The truck wouldn't start. I had Bob all loaded up and ready to go, waiting for the mother-invader to appear, and the truck decided on unreliable. Wouldn't even turn over.

Luckily, there was another car parked in the driveway. But when I searched inside the house, the driver was nowhere to be found. The bathroom was empty, and somehow, her suitcases now blocked the bottom of the staircase. How did she bring them in without me noticing? The woman was crafty. I'd need to keep both eyes open around her.

"We're leaving now. My truck won't start. We need to use your car."

"Be right there," she called from upstairs. Upstairs.

"What the hell?" I said, clearing a path between her rolling cases. I shot up the stairs two at a time, regret racing through me like ice in my veins. I knew I shouldn't have let her in. The last thing I needed was to babysit a sixty-year-old with shady intentions.

"What about 'not without me' did you not understand?" I asked, huffing and puffing into the office.

"Confusing syntax. I'd rephrase," she said.

I was wrong. The last thing I needed was an English lesson from a sixty-year-old pedant. She stood by the desk holding the ring box, and didn't look at me when she spoke. Was that what she was after?

"Did you open it?" I asked.

"No," she said, gazing at the box like it might do something.

I hadn't opened it either. Didn't know if there was a ring in it or not.

"I'll take it." I held my hand out to her, palm up.

"What we could have had," she whispered to herself, like I wasn't there. Like she was somewhere else with someone else. And then, snap, she was back. "What's done is done." She slid the box into her jacket.

"We're going to have a tough go if you start like this," I said, taking the box back like I was pulling contraband tater tots from a first grader's pocket.

"Where are your keys? My truck won't start. You need to drive."

"I'd like a nap."

"I'd like a different life, but we work with what we've got."

"Take my car. I trust you know how to drive without incident?"

"You're not staying here. If you need to sleep, you can do it when we get back. I'll drive if you're too tired."

"I'm thoroughly capable," she said, and stomped from the room like a toddler in need of a nap.

"By the way, I have a perfect driving record," I said to the empty room. The velvet box felt heavy in my hand. I opened it to find out why.

"Navigate, please. I don't know our destination," the mother-invader said, perched in the driver's seat. Her head barely reached the head rest. Bob's head rest was my lap in the back seat.

"Turn left at the stop sign and go straight to hell," I said. Or maybe that's just how it sounded in my mind. When you're sitting in the back of your estranged (strange) mother-person's car, thoughts ricochet through your mind like a horde of hangry bats at dusk. Things you want to ask her, but don't have the nerve to, because what if she answers you? Better not poke that sleeping bear.

"How long have you worked at the flower shop?" she asked out of the blue. And then said, "Rutgers Hardware," as we passed Rutgers Hardware on the way out of town. Odd bird, that one.

I had mixed feelings about her question. Why should I tell her anything about me or my life? I wouldn't tell her the truth about being let go. Didn't want to fuel her obvious disdain for me with evidence I wasn't worthy of her time. She didn't deserve an answer.

"Almost twenty years." Note to self: Connect mind to mouth for better resolve.

"You're an accountant?"

"I handle the books. And manage the store. Everything behind the scenes." Saying that out loud, I realized Fussy was right to let me go. We'd been in the red for a while. Was it my fault? Could I have done more to bring customers in? I was so preoccupied with taking care of Dad, the last six months at the shop were a blur.

"Why not in front of the scenes? Creating the bouquets."

Getting a little too nosy. I wasn't about to tell her that Fussy never let me anywhere near the showroom. Not since the first week when an entire shipment of mums shriveled up and... "Oh my god."

"Did I miss the stop?" she asked, slamming the brakes in the middle of the road.

"No. Keep going," I said, checking behind us to make sure no one was about to rear-end the car. I'd rethink letting her drive next time. If there ever was a next time. Which there wouldn't be.

Last week Tee had said my garden was rotting, that I had vases filled with dead flowers, and I thought she'd lost her mind. They were all in full bloom, stunning to me. I couldn't see what was actually there. How long had this been going on?

I understood now why Fussy never let me in the shop showroom. Why she asked me to use the back door to enter and leave. Why Cara and Bobbie always took delivery of the shipments, not me. I was the accountant and *only* the accountant. I thought I was running the shop, but all I did was crunch numbers and answer the phones.

Poor Fussy, all the time I'd spent at the shop. How it must have plagued her every time I approached the flowers. I wondered how much inventory I'd ruined over the years. No wonder she let me go. Why would she keep me on for so long in the first place?

I murdered flowers and hadn't seen the truth of it till the mother-invader came to the house. How was that possible? This was gettin' real weird.

"You like numbers, do you?" the nosy one asked.

"I prefer being behind the camera." I didn't owe her the truth. Didn't owe her anything.

"Do you?" She peered at me in the rear-view mirror like she knew I was lying. It set me on edge. I wasn't in the mood to be analyzed, especially by her. Bob coughed, almost on cue, getting me out of the conversation.

"Please watch the road. Speed limit's fifty-five here. You can put your foot down," I said, putting mine down. She was quiet for the rest of the trip.

Before I could stop her, the mother-invader shot straight to the front desk at the vet's office while I guided Bob through the heavy door.

"Hi there," Jake said, greeting Bob as she signed us in. I'd never admit I appreciated her help.

Jake glanced at me and offered a subdued smile as he pet Bob. Remnants of our earlier conversation charged the air between us and made it a little harder for me to function properly. Not Bob, though. He perked up as soon as he saw Jake. Wiggled his butt and whimpered as he spun around Jake's legs. Brushing against your legs was how Bob showed love if you were new in his world. Also, if you were old in his world. Any time you were in his world.

"You pass the dog test, I see," the mother-person said to Jake, shaking his hand.

"Pretty good with the canines. Hence, the white coat," Jake said, smiling at both of us. He seemed perplexed by her presence, and then I realized why.

"My truck wouldn't start, so she was kind enough to give me a ride."

"You really do show up for your clients," Jake said. His snarky but lighthearted remark made me think he didn't buy any of it. It also gave me hope we could get past our past sooner than later.

"Like you show up for your patients," she said. "Do you make early-morning house calls to everyone, or just the pretty ones?" My face turned to lava. I stared daggers at her, but she didn't seem to notice. She was too focused on getting an answer out of him.

"Only on specific occasions for old friends." Jake smiled at me and ignored her altogether. Something petty deep inside appreciated that slight.

"Old friends? Wonderful," she said, interested. "How do you know each other?"

"Once upon a time, we—"

"Dated. We, in college. For a bit. A lifetime ago," I said, downplaying my relationship with the love of my life to the love of my life. *Way to chase your dreams, Emma.*

"Yeah," Jake said, taking a small, but noticeable step back from me.

"Hardly a lifetime ago. I'd say long enough to become curious again," the mother-person said, making our awkward conversation even more so. "Wouldn't you?" She directed her question straight at Jake, and I saw a flash of the cornered animal he'd become. That woman was a menace.

"Please, I imagine you're married with three beautiful kids now, right?" I said, trying to take the pressure off Jake and lighten the weirdness.

Thankfully, someone saved him with a page over the loud-speaker. "Duty calls." He pointed to the ceiling, like we hadn't heard them call his name. When he reached the hallway leading to the back of the clinic, he turned and said, "Not married. No kids I know of." And then he was gone.

"He likes you," she said simply. But I couldn't let that notion, the hope that it might be true, in. The more I saw him, the more everything in me hurt. Standing close to him made my chest burn like it had back in school. It was nervous energy gone nuclear in my body and I didn't know how to get rid of it. So I let it out on the closest person to me.

"Don't be ridiculous. He's doing his job."

"Oh, crystal clear."

"What?"

"You want to get naked with him, too. It's so obvious it's boring." Though they didn't look over at us, the front desk staff and at least three other clients heard her.

"Keep your voice down."

"Truth cannot be silenced."

"Speak it softer."

Without Jake to pay attention to, Bob focused back on the mother-invader. She shooed him away as he sniffed at her hand. "Know when you're wanted, Robert," she said, using Bob's full first name. No-one ever called him that. Redford, sure. Robert, never. It suited her. Made perfect sense.

I sat on the bench with Bob lying on the floor in front of me and she slid all the way to the other end by herself.

"Question is," she said, gazing out the glass door like she wasn't talking to anyone in particular, "what are you two fools going to do about it?"

FIFTEEN

Bob's second x-rays came out the same, a wild storm of forget-me-nots growing in his lungs, so we scheduled a CT scan. The mother-invader lived up to her name on the way home from the clinic, asking non-stop questions about Jake, like she had a stake in my future with him. But we had no future, no matter how magnetically attracted I still was to him. We'd had a youthful, passionate, and painful love affair twenty years ago. End of story.

Early the next morning, on my way inside from the tree, I found a single lavender rose on the back stoop. Forgetting myself, I picked it up and the moment I touched the stem, it shriveled and died. The dad-tree rustled behind me, but I didn't acknowledge him.

I walked into the house holding the rose like a pulled weed. The mother-person surprised me, marching in from the front porch holding what looked like a shriveled pink and black carnation. I hated carnations, but especially pink ones. *A mother's love.* I'd had zero experience with that phenomenon.

"Where did you find that?" I asked, wondering who'd sent that message.

"Front porch. You?" She nodded at the dead thing in my hand.

"Back stoop. Were there daffodils out there too?"

"Only this." She held up the sad carnation. The pink tinged black head flopped over and kissed the dead stem.

No daffodils. First time in over a month I didn't get a fresh bouquet. Was my new beginning over? They stopped the day after the mother-invader breached the house. Coincidence?

"You know what lavender roses mean," she said, taking a step toward me. It wasn't a question.

I did, though I never understood how or why I knew. It had always been an instinctive thing for me. When I was young, I had the ability, holding a flower, to know what its message and purpose was and, sometimes, who it was meant for. I couldn't explain how I knew that without sounding loopy, but it was like the flowers spoke to me, whispering their secrets. Telling me how they could make the biggest difference in someone's life.

I'd never told anyone what I could do. Not Tee or even Sam. How do you explain that to someone without sounding batshit?

This magical connection with flowers was why I wanted to have my own shop growing up, why I'd settle for only working in one when I realized having my own wasn't in the cards. We'd never had a florist in town until Fussy's Tussy Mussies moved in the year I came home to take care of Dad. I saw it as a sign. Kismet.

But after my relationship with Jake, the ability I'd cherished disappeared and I couldn't hear the flowers anymore. I'd fallen in love and lost my magic, which didn't seem right at all. I thought working at Fussy's might bring it back.

And now I realized, not only had I lost the gift, it had become a curse, destroying the beautiful things I'd once used to help people. I'd never understood why falling in love with Jake had hurt me so much physically and taken the one thing I felt destined for. Love had destroyed me, which was why I never pursued it again.

"We're well past love at first sight. Jake didn't leave this," I said, though every fiber of me wished he had. I knew better than to hope for that, but the pull was still so strong with him.

"He's smitten with you. Enchanted, one might even say. Who else if not him?"

Chills flew up my spine at the mere possibility it might be true. Was he sending me a message? We used to communicate in flowers when we met.

"What about yours? I can't imagine who left it," I said, pointing to the dead thing in her hand. "You didn't leave it for me. That's a given." She scoffed in my general direction.

I wondered if Tee had left the carnation, but she wouldn't be so brazen with the actual mother alive and sleeping here now.

"Was it dead when you found it?" I asked. She didn't answer me, so I figured it wasn't. I could already read her tells and when she wouldn't look me in the eye, I knew I'd hit on the truth or something close to it. How long were we going to communicate like that?

"Mine wasn't either," I said. "Why is this happening?"

"Why is what happening?" Her voice raised an octave.

"Why do we murder flowers when we touch them?" It was true. I saw all of that now, thanks, apparently, to the mother-invader's presence in my life. But this had been happening before she came to town, so I couldn't blame it all on her. "Are we... cursed or something?"

"Don't be ridiculous," she said and threw the carnation in the kitchen trash.

Don't be ridiculous. This situation was ridiculous. "I won't stop asking questions, even if you don't answer them. Especially if you don't."

"We've got work to do. Bring the boxes when you come." She trotted up the stairs, without a single box, and headed toward the office with Bob following on her heels. Damn it. His fascination with her was exasperating. Also, I didn't appreciate being told what to do in my own house. Especially by her.

When Cassie ordered the lavender rose from Fussy's flower shop, she thought it would at least arrive in a small vase so Emma wouldn't ruin it. She'd need to be more specific next time.

But where had the pink carnation come from? And who was it meant for? The daughter was right; it wasn't from Cassie. She stood in the doorway of Josiah's office trying to make sense of it, and a flood of memories swept through her. Beginning with the first flower she'd discovered on the same porch when she was five.

She'd found a pink carnation on the porch every day after that until her parents kicked her out of the house at eighteen. On special occasions, birthdays and significant events at school, she would find a bouquet, like the day she'd won a coveted place on the debate team. The first girl in her school to accomplish that feat.

What struck Cassie most when she'd touched those carnations was the rush of warmth she'd felt. Like love itself was flowing into her through them. She'd never experienced that, even with her own mother, Mary. Her father, Jack, never touched her or offered any sign of affection, so it thrilled her to receive the gift of those flowers.

But she never discovered who sent them or why. It wasn't her mother. Mary threw them away any time she found them on the porch. On her seventh birthday, Cassie had hidden behind the curtains in the living room by the front door to catch the person leaving the flowers.

Instead, she caught her mother burying them in the mulch pile out back.

From the beginning, Mary had made a practice of taking everything Cassie loved away from her. And when Cassie cried on her birthday after watching her mother bury the only gift she'd been given, Mary said, "Get used to disappointment," and stalked away.

It all came back to her now. This office used to be her

bedroom. She knew where she needed to look for the box. If only that mutt would leave her alone. He kept trying to lick her hand. She shooed him away and closed the door in his face. Not much time now. The daughter would be up there soon to spy on her and make sure she wasn't stealing everything. She didn't want everything. Didn't want anything. Only that box.

As I headed upstairs, someone pounded on the front door, startling me. Were they trying to break it down? Then I remembered I'd called the tree guys the day before to pull up Bob's stump. I was still shocked to be greeted by a Mack truck of a man on the other side. He had the largest arms I'd ever seen on a human.

"Emma Rosen?"

"Hi, yes. You're here from—"

"Tree removal." I wondered if he was going to pull up the stump by himself. No need for equipment with equipment like that.

"Great, I'll show you where it is."

He followed me out back with his crew of other large men, and I set them to work.

It had been almost fifteen minutes since the mother-invader went upstairs without me. Plenty of time to pillage, so I raced back to the house and took the stairs two at a time. Bob sat outside the office, pawing at the door, whining to be let in.

"Wow, mister," I whispered, scooping his face into my hands and massaging his head. "I won't lie. This hurts." Why was he so into her? I kissed him and swung the door open wide.

How to describe the scene that greeted me? If it were a painting it would have been titled, *Pantsuit, Bottom's Up.* The mother-invader, crouched on all fours under Josiah's immense mahogany desk, prying at the floorboards.

"Looking for something?" I asked.

She sprang up into the desk like she was trying to run away, but forgot where she was and which way was forward.

"What are you doing?" I tried not to lace my voice with her brand of smug superiority.

"Oh, I...I lost my contact." She scooted out from under the desk.

"I see. The contacts you wear with your glasses?"

"Yes." She stood her full five feet, level with my collarbone, staring up at me through said black-rimmed glasses.

"Okay then." I crossed my arms. It was going to be that kind of conversation. *Bring it, you tiny tornado.*

"Okay then," she repeated, like a dare. She smoothed her blouse down over her pants, took a deep breath and a step toward the door.

"Where are you going? We've got work to do," I said, using her own words against her.

"And very little time. We can get more done if we do it separately. I'll take his bedroom." She grabbed a flattened cardboard box leaning against the wall by the door. Bob perked up when she approached him.

"I don't think so. For some sadistic reason, my father wanted us to work in this hellscape together and we're going to honor his wishes to the letter."

"What does that mean?" The horror was clear in her hazel eyes.

"It means we're stuck with each other. We'll do this side by side or not at all. My house—for the next two weeks anyway—my rules." She mulled it over like she had a choice. "You can leave now if you want. Never come back. You've got a lot of practice with that."

"Is there something you'd like to say to me?"

"Think I just did."

"You're a smart girl, Emma. Careful what you wish for."

"Don't worry. I stopped wishing for things a long time ago.

I'm going to get to work. Join me if you'd like or use the front door when you leave. I left it open for you."

Without another word, she grabbed the packing tape off the floor and aggressively assembled the boxes. The room filled with her irritation and heavy breathing, but I didn't let it distract me.

I cleared the closet and stacked everything up in the middle of the office. "We'll do three piles," I said. She kept taping while I spoke. Didn't look at me or pay any attention like she was participating in the conversation. Such a child. "One for charity with his things, one for me moving, and one for trash."

She kept taping her boxes. I took one and folded a couple of Dad's winter jackets into it. She still didn't speak. One after another, I filled the boxes with the rest of Dad's clothes and shoes. After an hour, a pyramid of packed boxes sat in the far corner of the room. I'd accomplished a great deal already, and it wasn't even lunchtime. I thought it would be harder to pack everything up, but this wasn't so bad after all. We'd be done in no time, and she could leave again.

"Which ones are those?" she asked, pointing to the boxes in the corner.

"Those are moving with me."

She glanced around the room. "Where are the others?"

"What others?"

"The other boxes."

"We still have to put them together."

"No, the other boxes for your father's things to take to the charities. And the trash. Where's the trash?"

I'd packed nothing in those boxes because I'd put everything, everything, in the boxes to go with me.

"Damn it," I said.

"Well, that won't do at all."

She was right. It irked me to no end.

The box wasn't under the floorboards. Jack had told Cassie he'd hidden it there before they'd left town all those years ago. So where was it? And how was she going to find it with Little Miss Rules handcuffing Cassie to her side?

She'd have to be clever. Get the daughter out of the house for a while. Or gain her trust.

It was clear the daughter wasn't up to packing by herself. She'd put everything in the moving boxes and nothing in the trash or charity boxes. The point was to give his things away, and the daughter was bungling it already.

But Cassie understood the need to hold on to Josiah's things. The night she and her parents left Calypso Springs, she'd taken Josiah's gloves with her. He'd forgotten them on the stand in her hospital room. They were the only things she had left of him, or so she'd thought for twenty years. She'd kept them through every move, never willing to part with them. For the longest time, she would have given everything to touch the hands that fit in those gloves again.

And now the daughter stood in the middle of the room, a bereft, lost little girl. She stared at the boxes of Josiah's things like she didn't know what to do with them or herself. It stirred something in Cassie she hadn't felt in a very long time. The need to protect her child. Compelled to comfort the daughter in some small way, Cassie stepped toward her, but as soon as she did, she felt woozy and weak.

"I know how hard this is. I want to help. Please let me." They flew from her mouth without warning. The words felt strange and misshapen, foreign coming from her because, in that terrifying moment, she meant them.

The mother-person came at me with a strange look in her eyes. Strange because, contrary to all prior impressions, she now seemed sincere. She also seemed a little drunk. I wasn't sure how to respond, so I averted my eyes and put distance between us so I could work out what was happening. Did she genuinely want to help me through this emotional minefield of packing and letting him go? Against my better judgment, I believed her. Didn't mean I was ready to divulge my darkest secrets, but maybe I could accept her being there.

Bob perked up. I imagine the scent of my confusion filled the room because he came to settle my nerves like he always did when life frazzled me. I took his face in my hands and massaged his ears. Gave him kisses on his hot black nose. He coughed again and didn't stop.

"Good grief. Get that dog a drink," the mother-person said. Looked like she might crawl out of her skin listening to Bob wheeze and hack. "Does he need medication?" Her face was sheet white when she spoke from the farthest corner of the room.

"Are you okay?" I asked, shocked by her sudden ghostlike appearance. I thought of the stump and wondered if Bob was contagious. Had he passed something on to her?

The mother-person stumbled from the room, coughing. We followed her downstairs. She raced to the back door like she was going outside, but something stopped her cold when she opened it. With a look of sheer panic, she swung around and darted out the front instead. Had she seen Dad?

"Bed, mister. You stay here." If he was contagious, I needed to keep him away from her. Bob snuggled up on his bed in the living room. Thankfully, he'd stopped hacking. Before I joined her, I rubbed the top of his head so he didn't feel neglected.

The mother perched on the top step of the porch, still struggling to breathe a little, but at least she had some color back in her face. I sat next to her, not knowing what to say or do. If she were Tee, I would have massaged her back, but we weren't anywhere near that kind of intimacy in our relationship. Doubtful we ever would be, but I hoped my presence would be some kind of comfort.

"Can I help?" I asked, feeling helpless. She shook her head

without looking at me. Her breathing became less labored as we sat in awkward silence together. A warm breeze blew across the porch, ruffling our clothes. It cooled my sweaty face.

"Was that an asthma attack?" I asked, hoping the answer was yes so I could let Bob off the hook.

"I don't have asthma," she said, holding her hand to her chest.

I remembered the first time I saw her crossing the street toward us. She'd had some sort of attack then, too. Maybe this wasn't Bob's fault after all. "Has it ever happened before?"

"I'm fine. Remnants of a cold."

Her clipped answer and tone of voice closed the door on the conversation. She was lying about something, but I didn't press her.

"Okay, well, it's already a scorcher out here today. Can I get you a glass of water?" I stood up on the step next to her, ready to go inside.

"Are you back in glass now?" she asked, glancing up at me.

"Excuse me?"

"Yesterday," she said, taking a deep breath, "you were out of glass. Her eyes held mischief in them, something I hadn't seen before. It cracked my walls and let a little light through.

For a moment, she reminded me of Dad when he used to play his practical jokes on me. He always laughed the loudest, but I found joy in the way he entertained himself at my expense. With love, of course. This was a revelation. I wouldn't have guessed she had any humor in her.

"We got a big delivery after you left."

"After you kicked us out?"

"Ice?"

She nodded and held her hand to her mouth as she coughed again. It racked her tiny body. The urge to help steady her struck me, but I fought it and stepped inside.

I brought Bob's bowl of water into the living room and put it next to his bed so he didn't have to move to get a drink. The mother-person had come in from the porch and deposited herself on the couch. Her body fit without extending over the armrests. I put her glass of ice water on the stand closest to her head. She didn't take a drink, didn't move at all. A week ago, I never would have imagined I'd be taking care of either of them like this.

"I'm going to rest," she said without opening her eyes. She seemed exhausted. Bob was too. It took him four seconds to start snoring as I snuggled with him.

What happened to them? And why?

The heavy knock on the back door came a few minutes after they'd both fallen asleep. Luckily, neither woke as I jumped up to take care of it. I opened the door to the same truck of a man and stepped out onto the back stoop, closing the door so they couldn't hear us talking. The dad-tree rustled when I appeared.

"We're done. Stump's gone, but we found this in it," the truck said, holding a soil-covered box out to me. From what I could see, it looked like one of those old bank safe deposit boxes people store gems and cash in. "You'll want to clean it off before you open it. Don't want to contaminate what's in there with whatever's in the soil, if there is something."

"Right. Thank you," I said, taking the box from him.

He stared at me, waiting for something. "So that's it then? It's all gone?" I asked.

"All gone."

"Where did you say you found this?" I lifted the box.

"Inside the stump."

"It was that hollow?"

"Hollow and rotting."

I could relate. "Okay, well, thanks again."

"Should we bill you or what?"

"Oh right. That would, yes, that would be best. Thanks. Thank you." My head spun at the thought of another bill.

"Right," he said, and trudged off without another word.

The tree rustled again, lifting and lowering on the breeze that had picked up, like he was beckoning me to him. I still didn't want to talk.

The box was heavy, made of steel or some other sturdy metal. But I got a strange feeling that wasn't why it was heavy. The minute he put it in my hands, I felt a jolt of energy coming from it. Like it was vibrating, alive.

I tipped it upside down and brushed the dirt off to see if I could find any information about where it had come from or who it belonged to before. It had *Calypso One Savings and Loan* engraved on the bottom. And three initials inscribed on the side, in large, heavy script: *JRM.*

No one I knew had those initials. My father was JRR, Josiah Ravi Rosen, so the box wasn't his. He wouldn't have a safe deposit box from that bank, anyway. Like most of the older institutions in Calypso Springs, it didn't exist anymore. Our bank was in Maiden Lake. It must have belonged to the person who lived in our house before us. I could find out who that was at some point, but at the moment, I had a million more important things on my mind.

I didn't want to open the box or bring it inside before I cleaned it in case it was contaminated with something deadly. I also didn't want to advertise it to my new guest. My gut told me not to let her see it. Maybe it had been Dad's, from before I was born, and that's what she'd been looking for earlier. I couldn't let her have it. If she got what she wanted, I had a sneaking suspicion she'd leave again.

I wasn't sure I was ready for the truth, but now that she was here, I wasn't ready to let her go again. Not yet. I'd seen a glimpse earlier, something else under that dumpster fire of a personality, and I wanted to find out what it looked like.

So I hid the box under the dense weeds of my dead flower garden at the back of the house. One more puzzle piece in the mystery of my strange new life.

SIXTEEN

S ince I'd let the mother-person in, the dad-tree had grown more full. Its canopy was so thick and long most of the branches touched the ground, obscuring everything underneath. So, at midnight that night, I hid under it, wide awake and ready for battle.

My neighbor's backyard floodlight filtered in through the thick branches so I could see the outline of the tree trunk. I paced back and forth in front of it, riling myself up as I interrogated my father.

"Why now, Dad? Does she need money? Are you giving her something from the sale of the house? In the will?" He'd sold everything we owned to help pay for his medical bills when he got sick again. But it wasn't enough. I thought about the empty ring box I'd taken from her in the office. "What the hell is she looking for in there? Did you leave something for her? There's no ring. Where is it? Did you sell that too?"

No one answered my questions. The branches rustled a bit, but they didn't dance in toward me like leafy stalkers. "Bob's sick. Really sick. I don't know what's wrong with him." Saying it out loud, even to the dad-tree, deflated most of my anger and weighed me down with worry. I'd called Jake earlier to check on Bob's blood test results, but they didn't reveal anything unusual. "Everything feels so out-of-control right now. Thanks to you."

Sam and Tee had both called several times in the last day. It felt wrong not talking to them about everything. But I couldn't trust Tee anymore and Sam had the paper, the twins, her parent's divorce, and her own failing marriage. I didn't want to add to her trouble, so I sent them both to voicemail.

I loathed feeling that kind of tension. Unresolved anger and doubt about the two people I'd trusted most in my life. The anger was justified, but it still made my stomach ache.

"I'm not running away tonight." Tee's sudden voice crashed under the canopy like a breaking wave. I spun around and saw her silhouette swaying on my wooden swing.

"Tee, God! You've got to stop doing that!" I yelled, jumping out of my skin.

"Sorry, honey."

She'd heard everything I'd said. "I wasn't talking to...sometimes I need, you know, and since the house is occupied now, I come out here to..."

"No explanation necessary, Em. I'm mad at him, too. For you."

The Flora part of me wanted to say, *Like hell you are. You understand nothing!* Then spin around and huff away like a petulant child. The Emma part wanted to kick her off my swing. Surprising how similar my two parts were when it came to Dad. This tree, this was our place.

But Tee missed him as much as I did. Why else would we both be out there at midnight? Like she could read my mind, she rose from the swing and offered it to me.

"It's fine. You can—"

"—sit." It was not a request, and I didn't feel like I had a choice in the matter, so I sat. Shocking how she could still reduce me to a five-year-old sometimes with one stern word. But I didn't swing. She couldn't make me swing.

A cool breeze whispered in under the thick layers of

branches and they swayed in a soothing rhythm. Like the tree was breathing or dancing. Then I realized it could breathe and dance and I wanted to go back inside before anything weird happened. I tried to slip from the swing, but Tee rounded on me as my toe hit the ground and I popped back up onto the flat wood.

"Sometimes I still see you as that bouncy little rugrat with eyes too big for your head," she said. "I know you were never my rugrat, but sometimes it felt like…"

"Tee, what are you—"

"—always dirty, never satisfied. Eternally curious about things in the soil. Those deep summer days after we'd barbecued, you'd bring me the book and crawl onto my lap, grubby as all get out from exploring again. Do you remember?"

"How is this—?"

"—that book. You loved that book. Of course, I would have read it to you at least twice already. Once to start the day and once at lunch. Then, right before sunset, you'd crawl up onto my lap for one more reading before you conked out on my shoulder. Always one more time."

"The Giving Tree's a classic. Once is never enough."

She nodded and turned away as if my answer was a disappointment. "You always wanted to be the tree," she whispered. "I thought it was so noble."

The tree surrounding us shook its branches, like someone had tickled it or given it chills. I hoped Tee wouldn't notice.

"Between the tree and the boy, the tree was the better choice. The only choice," I said.

"Even when you were five. The boy was…"

"A selfish asshole."

A shockwave of Tee's laughter careened around the inside of the canopy. "Good to see your understanding of the story is more nuanced and mature."

I didn't know why she was taking me down memory lane and I also didn't want her thinking she was off the hook.

"What are you doing out here, Tee? If you've got something to say, say it."

"Are you going to have me arrested for trespassing?"

"Don't be daft."

"You could. Then I could share a cell with my father."

"He's back in jail?"

"Dick found him slumped over Sandra Jenkins' Segway in the deep end of Jackson's meadow."

"That far out on a Segway? His persistence is impressive."

"I don't know how he did it."

"Drunk?"

"Wearing Sandra's nightgown."

"Anything I can do to—"

"No. See, *this* is your problem, honey."

"My problem?" That sent my hackles skyward.

"You're not responsible for everyone's happiness."

"I know I'm not responsible for *everyone*."

She took my hand in hers, squeezed it, and didn't let go. It was warm and soft and strong. "Listen to me very carefully when I say this, all right?" she said. "I can't see you very well, so I'm going to wait until I get verbal confirmation I've got your full attention." Tee, ever the teacher.

"I'm listening."

"We love you. We all love you. But you are not The Giving Tree, Emma. And if I'm at all responsible for planting the seed that you should have been back then because we shared that book, I'm sorry. It's just not true."

"I appreciate that, but it wasn't the book."

"Well, somewhere along the line, you got this wrong-headed notion you were supposed to take care of everyone else. You've been twisting yourself into knots doing that your entire life. The only person you're responsible for is you. And she's the only one you seem to ignore time and again. Why is that?"

I didn't have an answer for her, but she was wrong. I *was* responsible for my father's happiness. Someone had to fill the void that mother-person had left. And who else was going to take care of him when he got sick?

Why were Tee and Sam so gung-ho about this now? They'd said nothing to me before their intervention a week ago. Not when I was helping Tee pick out vacation destinations for her 25th anniversary. Or painting her house. Or restructuring Sam's garage for storage. Or designing Sam's garden or...oh shit. Snippets of conversations I'd had with both of them in the last year hit me. They had said something before. I just wasn't listening.

But I didn't want to argue with Tee at midnight about it when my entire life was blowing up.

"Do you know anyone with the initials JRM?" I asked.

"That was a detour. Think I've got whiplash."

"I found an old bank safe deposit box in the stump Bob's been digging into. Well, the tree guys found it. It's ancient. Has the initials JRM engraved on the side."

"Can't help you there. But since we're changing the subject willy nilly, how is Bob? Any better?"

"Jake still doesn't know what he's got. The x-rays were...interesting. He's going to do a CT scan of Bob's chest next." I didn't need to fill her in on the flowery details of what was growing in Bob's lungs.

"Honey, Bob's young and strong and loves you more than a steak bone. He's not going anywhere. Count on it."

"These days, I can't count on anything."

She sighed, like I'd closed a door in her face, but didn't defend herself.

"Jake definitely got better with age," I said, cracking the door open.

"Yes, he did. Careful there, Em. I saw the way he looked at you when you weren't ogling him the other night." A twinge of excitement sparked in my belly.

"I wasn't—doesn't matter. I've got enough craziness in my life at the moment for ten clowns at a circus. No need to bring anyone else into this nightmare with me."

"Good."

The way she said it, so final, made me want to rethink my decision. *You're not the boss of me, Tee. Not anymore.*

"You were suffering with him, honey. It made no sense. As soon as you broke up, poof, your pain disappeared. That said something to me."

"What did it say?"

"He wasn't right for you. Love shouldn't make you suffer, Em."

"Do you remember what happened when we broke up?"

"You quit school and moved home the week they diagnosed your father. You said Jake had moved back to Indiana to take care of his mother and you never spoke his name again."

"Why didn't I?"

"I don't know. You brushed us off any time we brought him up. You weren't hurting anymore. But you weren't happy either."

"I don't remember any of it," I said, frustrated.

"It's a mystery."

"Well, we're not going to be a thing now."

"You want to write that down and get it notarized?"

"Very funny. Seriously, it's not...going to happen."

"Was he in Maiden Lake this whole time, then?"

"Yes."

"Puzzling."

"Yeah."

Silence fell between us, heavy with regret.

"So...Cassie. How's that?" Tee asked.

Speaking of regret.

What to say? "Surreal. As I might have expected had I expected her to show up on my doorstep one day. Alive."

"Nonstop party then, yeah?"

"Was she ever happy, Tee?"

She'd been pacing back and forth in front of me, but stopped moving. The question seemed to catch her off guard. "Yes."

"When?"

"I'd never seen her happier than the night you were born." Not the answer I was expecting. I wasn't sure what to do with it.

"You were there?"

"I was."

"Why don't you know what happened to her? Why doesn't anyone?"

"We left when visiting hours were over for the night."

"Dad too?"

"He drove home to shower and get a little sleep. When he went back in the morning, she was gone." Melancholy lived in Tee's voice. It resurfaced whenever she spoke about Dad back then, which wasn't often.

"It's hard to imagine her ever being happy. Or him being happy with her. Or them being together at all."

"They were mad about each other. No denying that."

"I always thought..."

"What?"

"I never thought they were in love. Dad was always so angry about her when I was little."

"With good cause, don't you think?"

"But I never thought they started out happy."

"I see. Well, they did. But, as so many love stories go, life derailed them."

"'Derailed by life?' You make it sound like abandoning her family wasn't her fault."

"I think there were a lot of factors involved. Only she knows the truth."

"Yeah, well, she's not exactly forthcoming about the past."

"Shocking. Try harder."

"Why aren't there any photos of us? Or of them before I came along?"

"He took rolls of photos of both of you the night you were born."

"News to me. I've never seen them."

"After a few years of waiting for her to come home, he...let them go."

"None of it makes any sense."

"Got that right. The Great McCormack Mystery."

"Love makes you foolish."

"It can. Especially first love—" Tee stopped like someone had flipped off her switch.

"Tee?"

"Where did you say you found that old box?"

"In the rotting tree stump by the lake. Why?"

"It was their first kiss. Behind that tree."

"Who's first kiss? What are you—"

"Your mother and Josiah. That was the tree. They were hiding from her father. She told me about it the next day."

"I don't understand. Why were they hiding from her father?"

"Your grandfather, honey. Jack McCormack was...well..." Tee stopped and looked up toward the house. "It's not my place. I think you ought to hear it from her," she said, pointing to the window in the attic where a light had come on. It winked down through the branches at us.

"John Robert McCormack. *Jack*, to the few people he allowed familiarity. JRM were your grandfather's initials, honey. Might want to ask her about that box."

SEVENTEEN

The first thing I heard when I ran back into the house was the distant coughing two floors up. This time, it wasn't Bob. Where was he? His bed was empty when I rushed through the living room on my way upstairs.

I stood, breathless, at the base of the attic staircase. How did she know where this door was? The entrance to the attic was in a hidden alcove in the back corner on the second floor. You'd have to know the funky layout of this house in order to find it.

Bob and the musty smell of things unseen for decades greeted me when I reached the top floor. Why was Bob up there with her? Would he follow her anywhere?

In the stark white light of the one bare hanging bulb, the mother-invader seemed surprised to see me. She popped up from behind a mound of boxes she'd been rifling through, all innocent and doe-eyed. And trying her best to stifle the cough that was overtaking her.

"Trouble sleeping?" I asked. She didn't respond, still trying to hold a cough in, but it got the better of her. "After what happened earlier, you think maybe you should go to a doctor? That sounds pretty serious."

"I'm fine," she said, between hacking coughs. "I told you, remnants of a cold."

"So, what's happening here?" I pointed to the shoebox in her hand and she glanced down at it like it was the first time she'd seen it.

"I couldn't sleep. I thought I'd prepare some things to pack." It was almost as if she believed what she was saying.

"Guess you forgot about my rule."

"It's a stupid rule."

"You're entitled to an opinion."

"We have ten days to pack an entire house."

"Still my house."

Bob lay between us, glancing back and forth like he was watching a tennis match.

"I'll take that." I held my hand out to her for the shoebox.

"I don't know what it is you think I want from you, but—"

"I don't think you want anything from *me*."

She held my gaze until I had to look away.

"I'm trying to help," she said, like I was in the wrong for thinking otherwise.

"Why?"

"I don't understand the question."

"Why do you want to help?"

"It's what your father wanted."

"Right. Not what you wanted. You never would have come back if Cranston hadn't called about the will." It surprised me to realize I cared whether that was true.

"That's not—it's not that I didn't want—" She couldn't finish because another bout of coughing racked her body. Bob sighed, watching her. He could relate. She gathered herself together, but it took so long I felt terrible watching her without helping.

She stared at the floor in front of us and then glanced up at me. Her face changed, like time had spun her backwards and she'd become someone else. Those jagged edges of imperiousness had softened and left a woman who seemed contrite. The look in her eyes terrified me because it was so vulnerable. So open. Without a word, it seemed like she was begging for understanding. Like she wanted to tell me something, but had lost the words.

I became the little girl who never stopped needing her mother. It was frustrating to still feel that way because it gave her power over me.

Neither of us spoke.

And then it was over. The transformation hadn't stuck. She became angular and overbearing again. "Well. We're not going to get any work done up here tonight," she said, smoothing her hair back, exposing those ears once again. It wasn't such a shock to my system anymore. She headed for the door, trying to sneak the shoebox out without me noticing.

"I'll take that." I held my hand out to her again. This time she put the box in it, scowling. Again, the weight of it surprised me. Like there was lead in there. *What was going on with these boxes?*

"Night," I said, smiling, as she crept out the little door and down the steep steps. She didn't respond. "No, Bob, you stay with me. Come here, mister." He was halfway down the stairs, following her, when he switched gears and came back. Was it my imagination or did he return to me grudgingly?

When I turned to put the shoebox back, Bob was there under my feet. I sidestepped around his wiggly butt and ran into the ancient steamer trunk filled with the shoeboxes, flipping it. Everything splayed on the dusty attic floor.

"Damn it!"

Letters everywhere. Hundreds of them spread out across the dirty, dark wood. Rubbing the growing goose egg on my knee, I examined the envelopes closer. The writing was familiar. Beautiful block letters that had become my father's signature style before cancer stole the steadiness from his hands.

I squatted in the middle of the sea of white envelopes. They were all for Cassie McCormack, but didn't have a mailing address underneath her name. Most of them had our return address in

Calypso Springs, but a few of the more yellowed ones had a return address I didn't recognize. From Maiden Lake.

Each envelope had a stamp on the upper right corner. A sign of profound optimism.

I picked up a few letters and dusted them off. All of them sealed, ready to be mailed, but for that last essential detail. I began to understand what it must have felt like for my father to have lost her overnight. Not knowing anything about where she went or why or whether she was ever coming back. That blank space underneath her name was the mystery of my lifetime and the bane of my father's existence. The weight of it was heavy in my hand.

I drew a shaky forefinger under the flap of one envelope. But the moment the paper started to give way and tear, Bob had another coughing fit.

The letters would have to wait.

The weight in her chest had grown heavier. Cassie was running out of time. Being back in the house must have accelerated the disease. Lying to the daughter about it would only work for so long. She was a smart girl. She would figure it out soon enough.

At least Cassie knew where she needed to keep looking. If the box was anywhere, it was most likely up in the attic. Finding those letters was a shock. Boxes and boxes of them. He must have written to her every day for years.

Cassie sat on the edge of the tub in the downstairs bathroom with it resting on her lap. The one letter she'd been able to smuggle into her waistband before the daughter caught her snooping. The return address on the yellowed envelope was their old Lilac Cove apartment in Maiden Lake. She remembered it now. Every minute she stayed in this house, more and more of her past came alive for her.

She closed her eyes and saw the shabby yellow exterior of the Lilac Cove apartment building the day she and Josiah moved in.

Her mother had kicked her out because she fell in love with him and brought shame on their family. They thought Mary might retaliate or stalk them, so they kept their new address a secret from her parents. By then, Mary had grown into an angry woman, capable of terrible things. Everyone in town knew it, especially Cassie.

She opened her eyes and focused on the space below her name on the envelope, where an address should have been. In all these years, it hadn't crossed her mind to consider what Josiah had gone through when they left. Not knowing anything about why she'd disappeared or where she'd gone. The burden of his heartache, the weight of his anger, lived in that letter. She felt it.

Cassie flipped it over in her hands, mustering the courage to open it and find out what he was thinking then. This wasn't hard, why was she hesitating? Cripes' sake, she'd had a child. That was hard.

The sudden queasiness in her stomach told her otherwise. She'd felt nothing close to this kind of sick overwhelm for the last twenty years. Being back in the house, so close to the tree-love. Hearing the ghost of her mother on those stairs. And those moments in the office and the attic with the daughter. Connections she did not plan for and vulnerability that would no doubt turn into a liability. Where had it come from, the desire to talk and tell the daughter things?

Too much input there. It had been so long since she'd felt anything at all. She was ready to pack up and get the hell out. With or without the box.

Then she opened the letter.

EIGHTEEN

I woke with a start the next morning. Bob wasn't with me. For a split second, I wondered if all of this had been a terrible dream. Then I thought about last night with Tee, the attic, those letters, and worried the mother-person was upstairs rifling through all of them as I slept.

I scrambled to my feet, ready to go on the attack, when my mind caught up to my body. I'd locked the attic door last night so she couldn't get in. But where was Bob?

On my way to the back door, I scanned the yard out to the lake and there was no sign of him. He'd never not slept by my side until the last couple days. Since I let her in.

They were both asleep on the couch. She lay balled up at one end, her legs tucked into her torso like she was going to pack herself into a suitcase. And he lay next to her. He'd probably tried to rest his head on her legs, like he always did with me, but I imagine she wouldn't allow him to touch her.

Her disdain for Bob didn't bother me. It wasn't surprising given her particular personality. What drove me to madness was that he couldn't get enough of her. He was too sick to come sleep with me last night, or he wanted to stay with her. Both options made my heart hurt.

I tiptoed back toward the stairs, taking this opportunity to have another look at those letters in the attic since I didn't get to read any of them last night. Prepared for the inevitable, I'd put all the keys I'd need in my pocket before I went to bed. I'd become efficient at this sleepwalking routine.

Heading up the attic stairs, my stomach would not settle. Leaping and somersaulting with every step. I was about to learn things about my father and mother-person I wasn't ready to know. But when would I be ready? How do you prepare yourself for the truth when lies have been your truth for so long? Midway up, my phone rang into the stillness. The sudden noise almost sent me sailing backward down the stairs.

I fumbled for it in my pocket and answered before I looked at it, hoping it hadn't been loud enough to wake anyone.

"Hello?" I whispered.

"Em, it's Jake." His voice didn't sound hopeful.

"Any news?"

"The results for the blasto test came back negative. You should stop giving him the meds. They're powerful."

"What about the other tests?"

"They all came back negative."

"So we're at square one still."

"We'll do the CT scan and hopefully have a better idea of what's going on with him. If we still don't find anything, exploratory surgery isn't out of the question. If you can swing it."

Exploratory surgery? Sure. Maybe we should replace all of his joints with titanium while we're at it.

"Of course. Whatever it takes."

"When can you bring him in?"

"Now?"

"Great. I'll have them prep and be ready for you when you get here."

"Okay." I sighed.

"Em?" My nickname in his mouth felt intimate.

"Yeah?"

"We'll figure it out. Okay?" I wanted to believe that. Needed to. Jake had always made me feel like anything was possible. His unwavering optimism was the thing I loved most about him.

"See you in a few," I said, hitting the end button. I needed to nip this emerging connection in the bud.

Dad's letters and their stories would have to wait a little longer.

While we were at the vet waiting for Bob, my phone rang again. This time it was Sharon from Meals on Wheels.

"I hate to ask you, Emma, but half of our staff is out sick with the flu and the other half are taking care of the first half. And Jimmy, our emergency driver, called in sick again."

"It's a difficult time right—"

"Trust me, if we had anyone else, I would use them. I almost considered having my twelve-year-old do it, but, you know...illegal."

"A full route?"

"I'll make some calls. Pare it down to the bare minimum."

I didn't want to leave Bob in his state, but it was clear by the frantic tone of Sharon's voice she was desperate.

"When do you need me?"

"About an hour ago."

As soon as they brought Bob back out, the mother-person and I kicked it into high gear. Jake had to walk and talk with me out to the car.

"We should have the results back in a day," Jake said, after lifting Bob into the back seat of the car. He turned to me like he wanted to ask something, but wasn't sure if he should. The mother-person stood on the passenger side of the car with the door open, watching us. Nothing awkward there.

"Em, when I, uh...when we talked," Jake whispered, "I didn't mean to—"

"Oh, we don't need to right now—"

"You like flowers, Jake?" the mother-person asked, barging into our private conversation.

"Flowers?" he said, like he'd forgotten she was there.

"Roses are a lovely gesture," she said.

"Okay." It was clear Jake didn't know what the hell she was talking about. I knew he hadn't left the rose. It wasn't even our flower.

"Please, disregard," I said to Jake, glaring at the mother-person to get in the car. "Let me know as soon as you hear anything, okay?"

"As soon as I know, you'll know." Jake smiled and closed my door for me. He waved as he walked back into the clinic.

"Certainly is attentive to his patients," she said.

"Told you." I started the car with more vigor than was necessary. The product of excess tension.

"Told me what?"

"He didn't give me the rose." I put the car in drive and sped out of the parking lot.

If we were going to deliver meals, I'd have to leave Bob home and I needed someone to be there with him. But I wasn't about to leave the mother-person home alone, so I made the call.

"Tee?"

"What is it, honey?"

"I have to work Meals today and she's coming with me." I didn't explain who she was or why, but Tee could figure it out. "I need to leave Bob home so he can rest. Can you watch him?" I hated to ask her.

"Damn it. Parent-teacher conferences this morning. If I'd known, I would have switched days."

"I'll see if Sam—"

"No, I'll send Dad. He loves Bob."

"He's out of jail?" The mother-person gave me a strange look at the mention of jail.

"This morning. Miracles never cease, right?"

"Okay, well, we'll be home in twenty. We've got to get going as soon as possible."

"I'll send him right over. Bye hon—"

I hung up before she could finish. My anger came in waves, like grief, and hit me at the oddest times.

How Cassie had been wrangled into going on a Meals On Wheels delivery she would never know. It all happened so fast that morning. From the minute the daughter woke her, they were go go go. No time to think. Taking the beast to the vet and then committing, without her consent, thank you, to work for other people instead of packing like they should be.

After they returned from the vet, Cassie took a moment for herself on the couch. Unfortunately, thoughts of Josiah's letter consumed her. Before she read it, she hadn't considered why Josiah and the daughter lived here in her childhood home. But now, knowing how much he'd done for her after they left. Well. So much love and grief in his words.

Thunderous pounding on the front door shocked Cassie and sent her heartbeat through the roof.

"Can you get that?" the daughter called from the kitchen. She was busy feeding and watering the mutt. Cassie didn't appreciate being babysat or babysitting. And she wasn't anyone's employee. But the knocking was obnoxious, and she wanted it to stop, so she obliged.

When she opened the door to that redwood of a man she knew as Raymond Potrero, she almost slammed it in his face. It had been forty years since she'd seen him and it was quite a shock. She hadn't thought about him once in the last three decades. Not since the argument with her father before he died. Ray had wreaked his havoc on her family back then, nothing to be done about it now.

He stood there, speechless, staring at her like he wasn't sure if she was real or not. He damn sure was. The flesh and blood reason her life had unraveled all those years ago. It seemed like life had taken its own revenge on him for that. Chewed him up and spit him out much the worse for wear. He did not look well.

And she did not want to be near him any longer. The daughter would most likely rectify the situation, but not before he got the hint loud and clear from Cassie about how she felt seeing him again.

It was like a shotgun, the sound of the door slamming in his face. She sauntered into the kitchen and grabbed a drink. A stiff one.

"Where's Hopper?" the daughter asked, confused.

"Who?" Cassie hated that nickname. *Hopper*. It was juvenile, so it fit him, but it would never escape her lips. She took a long swig of whisky straight from the bottle.

"Breakfast of champions right there," the daughter said with surprise. Cassie wondered if Josiah or Teresa had taught her that sass. Probably both.

"Hopper. Big guy. Old as dirt. Hard to miss." The daughter was still flummoxed. It took so little to confuse her, poor thing. She didn't understand Raymond was where he belonged—outside of this house.

"He decided not to stay. I'll watch the beast. You go."

"Uh, first, Bob is not a beast. He's the best boy in the world." The daughter gazed at the mutt with a daft mix of admiration and love. It went on so long Cassie thought she might need to snap her out of it. "And second, Hopper wouldn't—"

Knock. Knock. *Damn it.* He was persistent, like everyone else in that stinking town. The daughter gave her a quick, quizzical glance, and before Cassie could stop her, she raced to the door to greet the menace.

She tried to lead him in to talk to Cassie, but he stopped at the threshold of the kitchen. Wouldn't go any farther in, like there was some force blocking his way. He'd done that before, too. A lifetime ago, when he shouldn't have been there at all. He leaned against the doorjamb, like he needed it to hold him up, and stared at Cassie. She didn't look away. She would be damned if he was going to cower her in her own house.

"Hopper, you remember my...uh, Cassandra?" the daughter said.

"Boy, I tell ya. It's been a minute since we seen you 'round here. Where ya been all this time?"

She didn't answer him, but didn't look away either. He fidgeted with his hat and belt.

"How's your mother? How's Mary? Is she..." His voice faded away. Cassie didn't answer his question. It was none of his business what state her mother was in. It never was and never would be.

"All right, well...this has been..." the daughter said, glancing back and forth at each of them, understanding nothing. "We need to get going, so...you good, Hopper?"

"What's he need?" he asked, referring to the beast.

"Nothing. All you have to do is be here with him. I fed him and he's been out to potty, so hopefully he'll sleep the whole time."

"I could use some of that," he said.

Cassie wished him the eternal kind.

"Feel free to join him on the couch," the daughter said.

"Boy, I tell ya. Been a rough week. Think I might."

"If he coughs, try to calm him by rubbing his chest, okay?"

"Roger that."

"If you can't get him to stop, call me. We'll come back."

The daughter took the car keys from the kitchen counter like they belonged to her and headed for the front door while she spoke to Raymond. Cassie followed, not acknowledging him as she passed through the kitchen doorway.

"Good to see you," he said.

She'd never been a violent person, but Cassie had an urge to strike him in an inappropriate place. Instead, she followed the daughter out and slammed the door. The house shook. Much like the last time he was there with her mother.

The more time she spent in that house, the more memories flooded back. They made it challenging to maintain a positive mood. She began coughing as she approached her rental car in the driveway and felt like it might never stop.

We were on our way out to the Blackwell's again. After my first visit, which I thought would be my last, I'd made sure Meals had canceled their account, so I didn't understand why their address was on my list. I called into the office to double check and Sharon confirmed.

The mother-person was in the middle of her fourth coughing fit since we'd left the house. It sounded tender and raw. I didn't understand why she wouldn't let me help her.

"I think you need to go to the hospital."

"I'm fine," she said, through labored gasps.

"You don't sound fine. You might have an infection. Maybe walking pneumonia. That's nothing to mess around with."

"No," she said with such finality I left it alone. She calmed herself enough to sound almost normal again. If normal was shallow wheezing.

"So, what was that business with Hopper about?" I waited for a response I knew would never come. She hadn't answered any real questions yet, but I was undeterred. I'd get to the bottom of something if it killed me.

"The past is the past. Best to leave it there," she said, glancing out her passenger side window at the wildflower meadow on Kramer Road.

"Didn't seem like it was in the past. Did Hopper steal your mother's lingerie too?"

"Excuse me?"

"It's his thing. He wears stolen lingerie and drives around

town at all hours of the night on lawn mowers that don't belong to him."

"Raymond did not steal my mother's—" She waved off the rest of her sentence like saying it was beneath her dignity.

I'd almost forgotten Hopper's real name was Raymond. Nobody in town ever called him that. He'd been Hopper my whole life.

"So why the animosity toward him? You and Tee were close, weren't you?"

"We used to be."

"What did he—oh my god. Did he do something inappropriate?" I couldn't imagine Hopper ever being that guy, but who really knew anyone? I never imagined my father would do what he did to me. I'd learned a hard lesson from all of it. There was no guarantee about anyone's character in this world.

"I am not stepping foot in that house," she said. Not the response I was expecting, but then I realized I'd pulled into the Blackwell's driveway. We both stared at the decaying property and I wondered, not for the first time since my father had died, who the hell my friends were.

"Do what you want, but I'd appreciate the backup. It's scary as hell in there," I said.

"You should be in sales."

Another glimpse of that buried humor flickered in her eyes.

"Going in," I said, taking the last cooler bag from the back seat of the car. She would come or she wouldn't. But I wished she would. I didn't want to head into the murder house alone again.

The sound of swift footfalls catching up on the crunchy grass beside me as I crept past the leaning garage toward the house. I didn't know what had compelled her to join me, but I let myself believe it could have been a sense of motherly...something. Duty? Love? Nope. But maybe something like that.

The property was a disgrace. Everything in decay. Cassie would never have put a toe in a place like that, but the gesture might endear her to the daughter, who might loosen her leash at home.

She stood on the rickety porch behind the daughter while she knocked. They both stepped back when the door swung open. A tiny redhead sat alone, hunched over in her wheelchair. Life had had its way with this woman, that was apparent, but when she glanced up and connected with Cassie, her demeanor changed. Her shoulders lifted and her body seemed to inflate in front of them. Then she smiled.

"Oh! I didn't know we were having company." The old woman glanced behind her into the dark cavern of the back room like she was looking for someone. "Please come in," she whispered to Cassie. She gestured with her gnarled hands for both Cassie and the daughter to enter, so Cassie let the daughter go first. Given the state of the place, she was not interested in becoming its first victim. Or its second. She remained close to the door.

"Hello, Fern. How are you today?" the daughter said. Kindness lived in her voice, something Cassie had never possessed. This daughter person was good. Generous.

"Delighted to have company," Fern said.

"Well, that's...refreshing," the daughter said. "Where's Pearl today?" She glanced around the empty rooms, looking for someone Cassie assumed was Pearl. She acted strangely. Sharp, quick movements, like she was nervous. Understandable, given the state of the place.

"Napping," Fern whispered, and then she raised a crooked forefinger to her lips. "Shhhhhhh."

Cassie felt exposed standing in that filthy kitchen. The tiny redhead stared at her with great interest, but didn't say a word, so she approached the daughter at the kitchen counter and helped her with the food.

"Thank you." She seemed surprised again by Cassie's gesture.

The faster they could offload the food, the faster they would be out of that wretched kitchen. Away from the strange little woman who had followed her to the sink.

Cassie finished putting the last of the meals in the icebox and turned to leave. The woman was right behind her, so close she nearly fell into her frail, skinny lap. This nymph was even more aggressive than the beast stalking her every move at the house. Cassie took a step sideways to avoid falling into her and slipped on a horrifying wet spot on the linoleum.

"Oh dear!" Fern said, reaching for Cassie. She failed to make contact.

"Careful," the daughter said, as she reached for her too.

Cassie groped at the foul countertop and held herself up.

"I'm fine," she said, waving away the help the two women were trying to force on her.

After she struggled to stand, a coughing fit took her and didn't let go. The daughter filled a glass with water and offered it to her, but she couldn't take it.

"Why don't you sit for a minute? Is it okay if she sits, Fern?"

"Of course. Please." Fern reached up from the side of her chair like she was going to take Cassie's hand and lead her to the table.

"Stop!"

An aggressive, white-haired beanpole of a woman charged into the kitchen. She pointed at Cassie and Fern like they'd stolen something precious from her.

"Fern! No! Don't touch—"

Fern yanked her hand away. Cassie continued to cough, harder now, struggling to get to the chair at the cluttered kitchen table.

"What're you doing here again?"

"I'm sorry, Pearl. We had these meals for you, and I didn't want them to go to waste. I even confirmed with the office and Sharon said you were still on their list."

As Cassie struggled toward the table, the daughter put a hand on her back, to help her sit down. A simple, kind gesture, but her touch burned Cassie's back.

"Don't," Cassie said, swatting at her hand. Her tone was much more stern than she'd meant it to be, but she didn't have the energy to be nice. She was trying to survive whatever was happening to her. She could tell the daughter had felt something too because she yanked her hand away the minute it made contact.

Before Cassie could get up and out of that terrible place, Pearl swept Fern away into the darkness of the living room. Grumbling about unwanted visitors and how she knew this would happen.

What the hell happened there? It was like I'd held my hand over an open flame when I touched the mother-person's back. And the darkest thoughts flashed through my mind. I felt empty, hollow, like I would never be happy again. That one brief touch had sucked away all of my energy. It came back, but the desperate sadness lingered. None of it made sense.

"Can I please take you to the hospital now?" I asked, driving like a maniac away from the second and, hopefully, last delivery disaster for the Blackwells. I'd make damn sure we never had to go back there again. The mother was affected by something in the house, too. I'd bet there were twenty kinds of toxic mold growing in the kitchen alone. Who knew what was festering in that cave of a living room?

"Take me home," she ordered, in between bursts of coughing.

The way she said home like it was hers, where she belonged, didn't surprise me. It was presumptuous, as usual, when she'd been there all of three days. But it made perfect sense.

She fell asleep on the way. I welcomed the quiet. Even if it was short-lived.

NINETEEN

It was almost dark when they arrived at the house. Cassie lumbered along behind the daughter. She wanted to collapse on the porch, but the minute Tee opened the door instead of Raymond, fight or flight kicked in and she was in the mood for fight.

"Tee," the daughter said, sounding as surprised to see her as Cassie was.

"Dad had to go, so I took over. Hope you don't mind," Tee said, ignoring Cassie.

"How's my boy?"

"Slept the whole time."

"Coughing?"

"Not with me."

The daughter rushed in to greet the beast lounging on the couch and Cassie confronted Tee at the door. "Care for a drink in the kitchen?" she whispered up at her. Tee didn't seem interested in joining her for that drink, but Cassie waited, arms crossed, for her to remember what was at stake.

"Sure," Tee said through gritted teeth. She let Cassie lead them into the kitchen, hovering close behind her.

"What?" Tee hissed when they were out of the daughter's earshot.

"What what? You know what."

"We're going to play a game now?"

"Did you send him over here on purpose?"

"No idea what you're talking about."

"Liar."

"You'll be shocked to learn this, Cassandra, but the world does not revolve around you. Emma needed help. I sent help."

"Help you knew I would never want to see again."

"Unintentional benefit."

"I didn't appreciate it."

"Noted."

Cassie narrowed her eyes at Tee. She checked the living room to make sure the daughter was still preoccupied with the sick mutt.

"What did you find out about Esther Blum?"

"Why don't you want her to know about Esther?" Tee asked, glancing into the living room too.

"It's got nothing to do with her."

"What are you after?"

"Right now, a bit of whisky," Cassie said. She searched for the bottle she'd been drinking from earlier.

"Are you looking for your diaries here?" That stopped Cassie cold. She'd forgotten about them. Musings of a foolish young girl a lifetime ago.

"Don't be ridiculous. They're long gone," she said, lying.

"If you say so."

"Did you find Esther or not?"

"Why do you need her?"

"Enough with the twenty questions. How about I give that one out there a history lesson instead?" Cassie said. She took the bottle and approached the doorway into the living room. Tee stepped in front of her, blocking her path.

"If I find Esther, are you going to leave again?"

"Depends," Cassie said. She knew nothing about Esther Blum. Whether or not she could help her, but she had to try. "I'm sure *you* want me to."

"Astute of you."

"I get the feeling that one may want me to stay a while longer." Cassie nodded toward the daughter.

"Well, you never know what anyone's thinking, do you?"

"Not even when they say it to your face," Cassie said, smirking. She sauntered back to the island and rested her torso against it as she took another swig of whisky. Then she offered the bottle to Tee. Tee refused, like the prude she always was.

"I didn't find anything concrete about Esther," Tee said. "At least nothing recent. I don't even know if she's alive. She was from a Jewish family here in town. They left about sixty years ago, much like your family did, suddenly, overnight, without explanation."

"Sixty years ago. You don't know where she is now?"

"Like I said, there's nothing recent on her at all. She disappeared and stayed that way. But if she's still alive, she would be your father's age."

There was only one person Cassie knew who might have information about her father's old friends. She'd slammed the door in his face that morning.

"Ask Raymond about her," Cassie said.

"Excuse me?"

"Ask him. Maybe he'll know where to find her."

"I don't know if you should find her. The things I read about the Blum family were not rated G. Of course, who knows if any of it's true? Could be all small town gossip and internet rumors."

"Indulge me."

"Don't say I didn't warn you."

"I'm a big girl. Think I can handle it." Cassie took another swig of whisky, just in case.

"The Blum father, Ira, supposedly embezzled a lot of money from Calypso One while he was branch manager there."

"Big whoop. Esther's father was a thief. Is that it? Thanks for nothing."

"There's a lot more."

"I'm all ears."

"Yes, you are."

Cassie let Tee have that one for free.

"Allegedly," Tee said, probably feeling very good about herself now, "Blum was running an underage prostitution ring in Maiden Lake. The story goes the FBI was closing in on them, so they left town without a word."

"Prostitution ring? Seems far-fetched."

"Rumors about sexual deviancy in his own house, too. Keeping their kids handcuffed to the beds. Forming a sex cult. Everything was unsubstantiated. Could have come from some sicko's imagination. I don't know where the stories originated, but the Blums never returned to clear their name, so who knows? I'd heard nothing about a Blum family until you stormed my door the other day."

"None of this is helpful."

Tee shrugged, unapologetic.

Cassie switched gears. "Why didn't you ever leave this place?" she asked. "You had grand dreams to conquer the world when we were young."

The question seemed to throw Tee off guard. She fidgeted with her blouse like it was too tight.

"Dreams change."

"You were going to be the next supreme court judge. Or president. I forget. One or the other. What happened?" Cassie didn't tone down the judgment in her voice.

"People needed me. So I stayed."

"Loud and clear, old friend. Holding on, hoping someday someone in this house might need you enough."

"You gave up the right a long time ago to make assumptions about anyone in this house," Tee said, spitting nails at Cassie.

"I'm making an observation. You were smart. You could have made something of yourself."

Tee straightened and took a deep breath. She appeared twice as tall. "I know this concept is foreign to someone like you, Cassandra, but I believe being present for the people you love is the most important thing anyone can do in this life."

"Someone like me?"

"Being a grade school teacher may not seem like much to you, given the great heights of achievement you've accomplished in your own life. But I'd like to think I've made a difference in a few children's lives. One in particular. A helluva lot more than you did."

"Careful where you throw your stones, Teresa. They might just ricochet back at you."

Tee glared at Cassie. Without warning, she marched straight at her, grabbed the bottle of whisky out of her hand, and took a long, hard swig. Cassie watched Tee's throat swallow and swallow, and stood her ground without a word. Time and gravity had been unkind to Tee. When they were young, Cassie stood eye level with Tee's ribcage, but now she was eye to eye with her sagging chest.

"Regardless of what you think I felt for him, I did nothing out of malice to hurt you," Tee said, blowing hot, sour whisky breath into Cassie's face.

"I imagine that's the story you've told yourself for the last forty years to sleep at night." Cassie knew she shouldn't prod Tee, but it felt good to release some of her pent up anger after all this time. Tee's face turned an unnatural shade of rage.

"What story?" the daughter asked. She watched them from the doorway. They'd been so preoccupied with their old fight, neither had noticed her sneaking up on them.

"Oh, nothing, honey. Just recounting things of the past," Tee said. Cassie and Tee both stood a little straighter and separated. "Best they stay there, don't you think, Cassandra?" Tee took another long swig of whisky and then shoved the bottle into Cassie's hand.

"Since when do you drink, Tee?" The daughter was as surprised by this whisky-guzzling Tee as Cassie was.

"When the need arises, honey." Tee gave her a kiss on the forehead, then disappeared into the living room to pet the beast without another word to Cassie.

"Say hello to your father for me," Cassie said, moments later as Tee walked out the front door. The daughter stared at Cassie with too many questions in her tired eyes.

Those two were up to no good and it was time they started talking to me.

"What happened between you two?" I asked the mother after Tee left.

A brief smile pulled at the corners of her mouth. Not a sign of happiness, rather a nervous tic. She was uncomfortable with the question. Good.

"The past is a dead thing, and dead things should stay buried. No point in opening old wounds that will never heal."

"Poetic, but not an answer. What about Hopper? You slammed the door in his face earlier and now you want Tee to pass on your regards? That makes total sense. In no way at all."

She took another swig of whisky and ignored me. Verdict in. She was the most frustrating human I'd ever encountered. I'm not a fan of being ignored. It brings out my inner Flora.

A storm brewed inside me when I'd touched the mother's back at the Blackwell house. I hadn't mentioned it to her because I didn't understand what *it* was, and, frankly, it scared the hell out of me. Made me feel like I was losing more of my mind and I didn't want to add fuel to that fire. But there was only one way to find out if it ran in the family.

"I tried to help you earlier when you were struggling in that terrible kitchen. I touched your back and felt..." What? How to describe what that hellishness was? "Okay, let me preface this by saying I know it's going to sound absurd. It is absurd, but it was like I could feel your soul's sorrow. A deep, unending grief. Like it flowed into me from you. What *was* that?"

She wouldn't meet my gaze, but didn't hesitate to answer in her sharp, accusatory tone as she raced from the kitchen. "You sound mad. Have you tried therapy? I've no idea what you're talking about."

Something in me snapped, letting loose The Flora.

"Okay. Yeah. I'm *mad* and you're what? Sane?" She stopped at the threshold of the living room but didn't turn around to face me. "I've lived here all my life. You think I wouldn't hear about your meltdown the night I was born? It was all anyone talked about for years after you left. I knew what they were whispering about, even when I was too young to understand. You lost the plot when you gave birth to me. So, what's wrong with us?"

The whisky bottle fell to her side. I thought she might let it drop to the floor. "You ask so many questions," she said, still turned away from me. "Did you ever stop to consider the things you heard might not be true? People dream up wild stories to explain things they don't understand." She peered out the door toward the backyard. She seemed wistful, full of melancholy. Like she was connecting with someone she once loved.

"You see him," I said, recognizing the look. "Don't you?"

"I don't know what you're—"

"You do." She didn't turn away from him as I spoke. My apple had not fallen far from her tree. "Have you talked to him?"

She took a deep breath and spun around to face me. "Why the third degree? Can't you be happy I'm here now?"

It took me a few seconds to glue my mind back together after she blew it up. "In what fantasy would you think I'd be happy you're here now? Forty years late. Without one call or letter or birthday card. You barge in here, unannounced, uninvited, without ever having reached out to me or shown me you give a damn I exist before. Happy? You've written me off my entire life. Do tell, what the hell should I be happy about?"

She'd turned away from me mid-rant and didn't move or say anything for a while.

"Your father seemed to think we might need this time together."

"Well, he turned out to be a rotten lying liar, so I think his judgment was fatally skewed."

"Don't disrespect your father."

"Oh, now you care about him?"

"I never stopped caring about him."

"Right. You just didn't give a damn about me." I sounded needy and desperate, but I didn't care. I wanted her to want to know me, to know the woman I'd become with no guidance from her. I wanted her to apologize for all the suffering she'd caused us.

Still holding the bottle, she opened the front door without looking at me and left.

There it was. She didn't even try to deny it. I'd spoken the truth she didn't have the courage to say out loud, and now it hung in the air like a toxic fog. I wasn't any part of the reason she'd come back. I hated myself for letting that matter, for letting it take up any space in my heart at all.

TWENTY

After the mother left, I raced to the attic. Bob stayed close and followed me upstairs.

I sat on the dirty floor encircled by a wall of shoe boxes. Each filled to the brim with letters. He'd labeled each box with a month and year date, so I went back to the one closest to my birthday in April 1979. It looked like he'd written her a letter every day for twenty years.

Growing up, I'd spent no time in the attic because Dad wouldn't allow it. It had always been off limits for me. I'd done everything he'd asked like a good little daughter. I felt like a fool. An obedient fool who knew nothing about her own father. The man I gave up everything for.

Bob lay next to me, sleep wheezing. I pet his head as I lifted the first letter on the bottom of the pile in the box and pulled it from the yellowed envelope. It was folded up inside like a secret note, dated April 17, 1979. Three days after I was born. There were a million creases in it, like it had been crumpled up and thrown away, then smoothed out and read, over and over again. Much like my crayon family portrait. This paper had a fragile quality too. Like it might not bear one more reading before it gave up the ghost and turned to ash in my hands.

I took a deep breath and snuggled with Bob, not sure I was equipped to read something like this. And then I dug in.

April 17, 1979

Cass, my love,

I don't know where you are or why you left, but Flora and I need you here. All she does is cry. She needs her mother, Cass. We need you back here with us. It's been three days and it feels like a lifetime without you. I filed a missing person report, but they've done nothing about it. How the hell did Jack know where we were? I'm going to find you. Bring you home. You belong with us, Cass. We're your family. They never were. We love you. Always. Come back. Please. Come back to us.

How did Jack know where they were? Such an ominous question. Did my grandfather actually steal my mother away like people had said? If that was the truth, why wouldn't she come back? Did she go willingly?

Tee said Jack and his father, my great grandfather, worked for Calypso One bank. The safe deposit box was Jack's. It had his initials on it. I had a feeling something in that box would answer my questions. Time to find out if my hunch was right.

TWENTY-ONE

Bob was worn out again, so I put him to bed. The mother had come back while I was in the attic and lay snoring on one end of the couch. I covered her with the blanket hanging over the back of it and sneaked outside. Bob didn't follow me. He was asleep before I reached the back door.

A cool breeze swept under my shirt and sent chills through me as I dug the box out from under the dead leaves of my garden. Its heaviness caught me off guard again.

I sprayed it off with cold water from the hose. Since the blasto test was negative, there was no need to worry about being infected with that horrible disease, but it still needed to be cleaned.

Holding the wide part of the cold, wet box against my stomach, I tried to pull it open, but it wouldn't budge. A small latch on the front lay over a metal half loop where a lock would go, but there was no lock on it. I yanked on the latch, thinking there might be dirt or rust lodged in the crevice between the top and bottom, fusing it together. Nothing moved except for the latch. I used a spade to clear out any debris and tried to pry the box open with it. Nothing worked.

"Why the hell won't you open?" I snapped. Frustration burned in me and the flame grew stronger with every fail. I needed to open this damn box now. To be in control of one thing in my life. What did it say about me that I couldn't even open a simple lockbox?

I marched into our garage with it and sprayed WD-40 on the hinges and anywhere else it might loosen up. Still wouldn't budge. It was personal now. Felt very much like my patience and resolve were being tested. *Challenge accepted, Universe!*

Maybe brute force would do the trick. I hurled it onto the cement floor as hard as I could. It bounced and landed upright, taunting me. I did that three more times. It became exponentially heavier each time I raised it above my head. Who needs a gym when you've got old boxes full of secrets that won't open?

Frustration got the best of me after the last try, whipping me into more of a frenzy. I used an old tee-shirt from Dad's workbench as a sweat rag for my face, then grabbed a rubber mallet from the same bench and beat the box to within an inch of my life. I hadn't exercised that much in years. It felt good to release so much pent up anger, but that anger doubled down when I realized I didn't even dent the box. And it still wouldn't budge.

So much for answers.

I cleaned myself up the best I could with the old shirt and crept back over to the house with the box. The breeze was crisp on my clammy, hot skin, cooling me from my nuclear meltdown. I buried the box in the same spot under the house and went to bed frustrated and sweaty.

Cassie snorted awake, disoriented. She'd been snoring again. This was not normal. It must have had something to do with the house. She scanned the dark room to make sure she was alone. Finding an audience would have been mortifying.

It took her a moment to gain her bearings. When the living room straightened and stopped spinning, she thought of things said earlier that night. There was nothing pleasant about the way they'd ended their conversation. The way she'd ended it. Cassie had planned to talk to the daughter when she returned from her angry walk. To at least apologize for her rudeness, but the deep exhaustion and alcohol put her to sleep almost before she'd reached the couch.

The beast lay sprawled on his back next to her feet again, snoring. Lord. Now she even had something in common with the mutt. What a world. He wasn't close enough to touch her, because she wouldn't let him, but he was close enough to be a nuisance, pushing her to the absolute edge. Why wouldn't he leave her alone? Weren't these creatures supposed to be intuitive? *Read the room, Robert. Know when you're not wanted.*

The living room was lit by the street lamps in the front yard. Cassie noticed the outline of Josiah's ratty old recliner in the corner. It was his favorite chair when they'd moved in together. She wasn't at all surprised he still had it forty years later. When he loved something, he held onto it no matter how much it fell apart on him.

Something stirred in her, wishing she'd been here to snuggle with him in it the way they used to in their old apartment in Maiden Lake.

All the things she'd missed with him here in this house, all the lost moments with the daughter too, they began weighing her down. It was frustrating how angry Josiah still was with her. But she couldn't dwell on it. She couldn't do anything to make it right with him, as much as she wanted to. There was no fixing it.

A noise from the backyard startled her. Cassie crept over to the door to investigate, peering through the small window into the dark, very much like a spy. The daughter was struggling with something.

A box. *The* box.

A twinge of excitement prickled her belly. Cassie watched and waited until the daughter marched back out of the garage with it under her arm, looking worse for wear and quite disgruntled. She hid it under the house. When she charged toward the back door,

Cassie raced to the couch, nestling herself under the blanket opposite the snoring beast again.

How had the blanket gotten there? Cassie didn't remember putting it over herself when she fell asleep. The daughter must have done it. Lovely gesture, given Cassie's exit earlier.

A few minutes after the daughter sneaked past her and up the stairs, Cassie crept to the back door again to fetch the box. The minute she stepped outside, the ache seized her and she couldn't move. The tree shook in the breeze, thousands of frantic branches. Except there was no breeze and it was shaking directly at her. It took all her strength to close the door. She trudged back to the couch, holding her chest with both hands.

Well, that wouldn't do.

Too miserable to fall asleep, she lay against the armrest of the couch, trying to figure out what her next move would be. If she couldn't go to the box, the box would need to come to her.

Something caught her eye on the bookshelf next to Josiah's recliner in the corner. The silvery outline of a glass dome. She knew what it was before she was close enough to touch it. The custom-made snow globe she'd given him for their two-year anniversary. She'd been an elephant, eight months pregnant, but he still carried her over the threshold like he had when they'd moved in together the year before. Of course he did. He was a giant of a man in every way for her.

Cassie caressed the cool glass of the globe. When she shook it, the storm of tiny flowers swirled in the chaos of water, then settled onto the backs of the dogs playing in the field. Touching it opened up too many memories in her. Her stomach ached, and it was getting harder to breathe the longer she held the globe. She dropped it on the top shelf. Thankfully, her reflexes were sharp enough to catch it before it toppled off onto the floor and shattered.

A large manilla envelope lay on the bookshelf next to the globe. In the darkness, she could barely read the writing on the front.

Bob Rosen X-Rays 6/18/19

She pulled the films out. It was impossible to see anything in the corner, so she took them over to the windows facing the street lights and held them up. Everything was suddenly illuminated.

"Son of a..."

She still didn't understand the daughter's role in all of this, but Cassie needed her on her side. Now she knew exactly how to get her there.

TWENTY-TWO

I woke later than usual under the tree the next morning. Bob was nowhere to be found and everything got weird the minute I entered the house. The scent assaulted me before I reached the back door. Sulfur and burned toast. Who had broken in to murder breakfast? And how could I flee that horrifying smellscape?

Bob greeted me with more energy than he'd had in days. I think he was trying to get away from the stench in the kitchen. He almost seemed normal, except for the occasional coughing spell.

"Hi mister," I said, massaging his front legs. "Are you cooking?" He slathered my face with kisses and wiggled to the ground, flipping over so I'd rub his tum. I glanced into the kitchen and there she was. If I hadn't seen it, I wouldn't have believed it.

The mother stood with her back to me at the stove, scraping the charred remnants of things that used to be eggs from the frying pan. She mumbled something under her breath. Not a positive affirmation. Two pieces of blackened toast stood in the toaster like torched soldiers awaiting her commands.

"Bribery or atonement?" I asked, thinking of last night as I approached her in the kitchen. More like punishment, I thought, but didn't say. That would be mean.

She jumped back, startled, and let loose a high-pitched screech. "A little warning next time!"

"Sorry, I thought you heard me talking to Bob."

"I'm too busy burning the house down."

"I smell that."

She glared at me. First mother-daughter breakfast off to a great start. I glanced into the frying pan and couldn't understand how she'd done what she'd done. I'd never seen eggs that looked less like eggs in my life.

"That looks...salvageable," I said, trying to support her efforts.

"It's not my fault. Your stove has two settings: Off and flamethrower. You don't have to eat them."

"But then I would miss..." I caught myself before I said, out loud, what I couldn't believe I was thinking. *I would miss my first breakfast with my mother.* "I would miss the unique culinary experience you've created. Mmm. Dee-lish."

The corners of her mouth rose, but I couldn't tell if it was the beginning of a smile or a smirk. I grabbed the toast and scraped the crusty top layers off into the trash and put them on plates. Our domestic activity was remarkably unremarkable. Standing in my kitchen on a Saturday morning salvaging a ruined breakfast like we did this every day.

"It's garbage," she said. "I saw yogurt in the fridge. We're having that."

Thank god because I could not bring myself to go near those stinky charcoal nuggets.

"A plus for effort. I appreciate it." That time, there was a smile, albeit a small one.

We each fixed a bowl of yogurt with pomegranate seeds and sat at the island in the middle of the kitchen. At opposite ends, we dug into our breakfast in silence. The morning sun streamed through the kitchen window, melting some of the frost that had set up between us over the past couple of days. The air was still heavy with things unsaid, but when we sat down, there was a shift in the energy. It was palpable. I thought, finally, some of those things might find the light.

"Have you always been a sleepwalker?" she asked, pointing outside.

I hadn't given my nocturnal wandering much thought since she'd come to town. It was my new normal. Like everything else in my life at that point, all askew.

"No. I—"

"Unresolved issues," she interrupted with unearned authority.

"Dad didn't tell me you were a shrink. Will you take a check?"

"Oh. A comedienne. Don't leave your day job."

Damn, even said wrong, her burn wounded. Mostly because I didn't have a day job to quit anymore.

"Your father..." She spoke into the stillness of the kitchen, but then stopped. Something different lived in her voice, a gentler, less brash tone. She'd whispered the two words that carried more weight than anything in my world and closed an inch of the enormous gap that spanned between us. I could see it in her eyes, the love she had for him. It hadn't disappeared like I'd thought. I only saw an ephemeral glimpse, but it was there. She'd let her guard down, become vulnerable again. It cracked open a doorway and I tiptoed through.

"My father?" I said, encouraging her to finish. To keep closing the gap. She glanced around the kitchen, but her gaze returned to the shriveled daffodils in the vases on the island in front of us.

"Your father was a complicated man. Loving and loyal, but not one to forgive easily."

"True. He waited for you, you know. All these years. I shouldn't tell you that, but he did." I didn't want to give Dad's secrets away to the one who had destroyed him, but maybe it would get through to her a little.

"Surely, he dated?"

"He waited for you. To come back to us." As she absorbed what I'd said, it seemed to weigh her down. Shrink her.

I wasn't sure how any of this was going to end, but at least we were talking. A miracle. Whatever had changed between last night and this morning, I'd be lying if I said part of me wasn't grateful. And part of me was angry at that part for feeling grateful. It was a complicated relationship.

"Your father..." Her focus wandered off again. She had a dreamy look in her eyes, like a teenager in love. "Did you know he used to bring me one sunflower every day when we first met?"

"I didn't. Guess that explains why he kept our house in fresh sunflowers for years. Did they die like these? I mean, when you touched them?"

She shifted her gaze away from the flowers and smoothed her top over her belly, a nervous habit. It seemed like she might change the subject again, but then she looked right at me and said, "No, they didn't. Not at first, anyway. He left them every morning on our back stoop, very much like your porch daffodils."

"What do you mean 'not at first'?"

"Why do you wake under the tree every morning?"

I hate it when someone answers a question with a question. "What does that have to do with flowers?"

"Don't answer a question with a question."

"But you just—"

She wore that *don't sass me* look all mothers master. I couldn't believe it worked.

"I haven't given it much thought."

"Lying is a bad color on you. "

"Do you have a point?"

"Your father."

"What about him?"

"Maybe your sleepwalking has something to do with him being a tree now?" She held my gaze and didn't look away, wouldn't let me either. My spoon, loaded with a heaping mound of yogurt, froze halfway up to my mouth.

"I knew it!" I dropped my spoon into the bowl. Yogurt splashed out of it onto the countertop. "I knew you saw him too!" I pointed my forefinger at her like I was trying to impale her with it. If I was losing my marbles, she was on that journey with me. Still, not much comfort.

"But why...do you...what's wrong with us..."

"You haven't lost your mind, if that's what you're wondering," she said.

Was it legitimate for her to say that to me if she had? And if she had, wouldn't it follow that I had too, since we were having the same symptoms?

"It's the family curse," she said, like she was telling me the forecast. *Partly cloudy with a chance of a family curse today.*

"The what now?"

She put her dish in the sink without a word and stood with her back to me, her hands gripping the edge of the counter. Either she didn't want to face me or she needed something to hold her up.

"Family curse?" I repeated. "Like, from a witch?"

"Don't be daft," she said, dropping her head.

"You're telling me we're cursed? Like actually cursed. Who's the daft one here?"

"Should I repeat myself?"

"Who cursed us then? How?" I hopped off the stool and stood next to her at the counter, glaring at her profile as she inspected the corners of the sink. "Yesterday, you said I was an idiot for thinking such nonsense. Though, to be honest, I wasn't thinking it could possibly be true."

"What would you like from me?" She spun around from the sink, coughing, and charged into the living room looking for something.

"How about explaining what the hell you're talking about and why my father's a tree now. None of this makes any sense. And yet, now all of it does." I leaned up against the doorjamb in the kitchen, watching her tear the couch apart in the living room. I was that couch.

"I don't know why, in particular, your father is a tree. It's not like there's a manual for this. Ah." She found what she'd been searching for. The whisky bottle wedged in between the end cushions. She sat and drank deeply from it between coughing spasms. "But I can only assume it has something to do with our curse. Nothing else would make sense."

"Sure. That's reasonable." Or, maybe we've both come unglued. "I'm sorry, I didn't know it was happy hour. Let me pull up a stool," I said, carrying a stool from the kitchen into the living room to sit next to her.

"The alcohol helps relax my situation. It helps me breathe."

"Situation?"

"The curse."

"Right. Family curse."

She sat all the way back on the couch like a child, holding the bottle close to her chest, staring straight ahead out the windows.

"We need to open the box," she said out of the blue.

"What box?"

"The one you're hiding under the house."

"How do you...?" Had she been spying on me? Of course she had.

"You've noticed we have...certain skills."

"I wouldn't call what we have skills, but yes, I'm aware."

"It wasn't always like that for me and I imagine it wasn't for you either."

"I didn't realize the murdery part until you got here."

"Well. I don't know how it started. My father didn't tell me before he died. But he told me to get the box. Whatever I have is the manifestation of the curse, and that box is the key to breaking it. So you can help me or you can stand by while it takes me too. Your choice."

"Takes you *too*?"

"*He* needs you to do this," she said, pointing to Bob with her outstretched arm, her hand still holding the whisky bottle.

"What does Bob have to do with a curse?"

"Your vet boyfriend won't be able to help him."

"How do you know that?"

The mother person pulled a large envelope from her suitcase next to the couch and handed it to me. "Open it."

I glanced at Bob, lying by her feet, racking my brain to figure out what his illness had to do with her. "What is this? I don't understand."

"Open it and you will."

"I don't like you telling me what to do all the time. You've done nothing to earn that right."

"Fair point. Open it."

I opened the envelope grudgingly and pulled out an x-ray film. It had Cassie's name at the top and was dated Monday, May 13th, 2019. The day after Dad died.

"Look at it in the light."

Something told me this was going to be another before and after scenario. I held the x-ray film up into the light. If I hadn't seen Cassie's name on the top, I would have thought I was looking at the x-ray of Bob's lungs. The same field of wild forget-me-not flowers grew in hers.

"If you want to save your dog, you need to help me break this curse."

TWENTY-THREE

"Please retrieve the box," Cassie said, hoping to move things along.

"I have to warn you, I couldn't open it last night. And really I tried."

"Perhaps it requires the proper technique, the right touch."

"I suppose *you* have that touch?"

Cassie smiled at the daughter, not questioning for a moment whether she would be able to open the box. Of course she would.

"That's what you've been snooping around for, isn't it?"

Cassie shrugged. "Guilty."

"If you knew the box was out there, why didn't you get it yourself?" the daughter asked, putting Cassie's x-rays away.

"I can't...go out there." She glanced toward the backyard.

"Near Dad? You can't or you won't?"

"The pain is..."

A realization flashed across the daughter's face and softened it. "You have that too?"

"I do."

"You?" Cassie asked. But she already knew the answer. The daughter nodded her head without making eye contact. "I'm sorry to hear that." Cassie knew her words were inadequate for that kind of loss, sacrificing love because the pain was too much to bear. "It's all part of the curse. Another reason we need to figure it out. You deserve...more. We both do."

The daughter twitched like she didn't know how to react to Cassie being nice to her. Cassie was uneasy with this level of intimacy, too.

"If the box was your father's, why was it in the old stump out back?"

"I don't understand your question," Cassie said.

"The tree guys found the box inside a rotting stump by the lake. Bob had been digging in it for weeks. That's why Jake thought he might have blasto."

"I still don't know how this pertains to me."

"Right. Because everything is about you," the daughter said, shaking her head.

"Right now, everything is about that box." Cassie didn't give a damn about an old stump or where the box was found or who was digging where. She needed to find out what was in it. "Time's a wasting."

The daughter moved toward the back door, ready to open it, but she paused there a moment, glancing toward the lake.

"Tee said that was where you and Dad had your first kiss."

Their first kiss. It came back to Cassie fully formed, like a living, breathing thing. She could feel Josiah's hand, the warmth and strength of it, on her cheek, caressing her. No boy had ever touched her like that. His skin against hers was fire. Her body vibrated with energy.

"Cassie. Cassie? Hello?!"

"I was..."

"I see that."

"The stump. Where was it? Will you show me?"

Standing in front of the window at the back of the house, the daughter pointed out to the spot by the lake where their tree had been forty years ago. The spot that changed her life. Cassie's father would never have put the box there. The tree was still alive when they left this house. Josiah must have found it where her father had hidden it upstairs and put it out there. But why?

"What happened to the tree? Did it die?" Cassie asked.

"I woke up one morning and Dad had cut it down. I didn't understand why. It was perfectly healthy."

"When did he do that?"

"Long time ago. Must have been...huh." The daughter didn't finish her thought. She seemed caught up in a memory.

"What is it?"

"Nothing." She wouldn't make eye contact. Definitely hiding something.

Without another word, the daughter raced out the back door, and the beast followed behind her. Cassie could breathe again. Being sick was hard enough, but engaging in this manner with the daughter, answering all the questions, it was exhausting. Hopefully, she wouldn't have to keep this up much longer. With the box in hand, they would be one step closer to resolving this familial scourge.

Before he died, Cassie's father had said a great sacrifice of love would break the curse. She'd already made hers long ago with Josiah and nothing changed, so it must be up to the daughter now. But it wasn't Jake she would have to give up, like Cassie initially thought. After seeing those x-rays, she knew it was the mutt. There was nothing the daughter loved more than that beast.

But Cassie wouldn't share this detail with the daughter until it was imperative. How could she?

The daughter charged back into the living room, followed by the mutt. She held the safe deposit box out to Cassie. "I hope you have better luck."

The weight of it surprised her. She almost dropped it.

"Yeah, it's heavy. Like our family," the daughter said.

Cassie smirked and carried the box over to the coffee table in front of the couch. It seemed to vibrate in her hands, like trillions of high-speed atoms careening off one another with no place to go. It contained an energy she'd never felt before.

She drew a tight, shallow breath and pulled on the silver latch that should have opened the top. Nothing happened. It wouldn't budge. She tried again and again.

"Trouble?" the daughter said, chewing on a piece of smug sandwich.

"Get me a screwdriver. I'll pry it."

"I've already tried."

"What about that DW stuff?"

"You mean WD-40?"

"That's it."

"I sprayed half a bottle on it last night. That's why it's all greasy and smells like oily vanilla."

"What about dropping it?" Cassie said. "Did you try that?"

"Only on the garage floor."

"How are you with heights?"

As a last ditch effort, they ventured out to the tallest building in town, the brick stalwart that used to be Calypso One Bank, six stories high. They threw it with gusto from the roof to the blacktop alley below. It bounced and tumbled, but stayed locked tight.

"God...damn it!" the daughter screeched. She became increasingly frustrated with the futility of their efforts. Her quick temper surprised Cassie. In a moment of reflection, she allowed herself regret for not being there to help raise the daughter with Josiah. But when she let that through, all the other garbage came too and she succumbed to a severe coughing fit. The daughter insisted they go home to take a break.

"Deep breaths if you can. Slow and steady. In...out," the daughter said back at the house, handing Cassie a glass of water. She sat down on the couch next to Cassie, trying to coach her how to breathe. A gracious gesture, but Cassie moved away, concerned with keeping a few feet of distance between them at all times. She didn't need a repeat of the other day at the hoarder house. It was hard enough to breathe on her own without the weight of her daughter's grief living in her cells, too.

"I'm fine. You can go do something else."

"Fine," the daughter said, offended. "I need a break. I'm going to go..."

"Where?"

"I don't know. I'll figure it out when I get there. Go or stay. I don't care anymore. If you leave, lock the doors. Or don't. Whatever."

"You won't be gone long, will you?"

"I don't know. Maybe. You can keep working on the box. Or go drop it off another building." Cassie got the distinct feeling the daughter wanted to drop her off a building instead.

"We're getting worse," Cassie said, anxious about not being able to open the box. About Tee not finding Esther Blum. If they couldn't get any answers, soon enough, she would come to her own dark resolution.

"Bob seems better, so maybe it's only you getting worse."

"And that would be okay with you?"

The daughter stopped and stared at the floor before she glanced up at Cassie. "I'll be back in a while. Come on, mister."

She left without another word.

TWENTY-FOUR

I couldn't believe that damn box didn't open after we dropped it off the top of a building. What if we couldn't open it? I wouldn't be able to save Bob. Or her. Knowing its importance left me spinning. I needed time to process everything without the mother in my personal space being...herself again.

It's not every day you find out you're the unlucky heir of a family curse. A person might need a moment. The silver lining in my case/curse was that it would end with me. There was no next generation to pass it on to. And if my life kept going like it had been for the last twenty years, a black hole of love, there never would be.

Miraculously, my truck started on the first try, so I took Bob and headed to the nest, the natural spring in the middle of the woods. Locals had called it the nest for as long as I could remember. Fitting, as it was overgrown with dead vines and resembled a giant bird nest.

No one else I knew ever explored that end of Calypso Woods. Probably because of the rumors about it being haunted. Nonsense if you ask me. Not to say it wasn't spooky, but there were no demonic spirits or haunted beings there. Unless you included the frustrated forty-year-old woman trying to make sense of her bewildering life.

I'd accidentally discovered the nest when I was ten. Took a wrong turn on a bike ride with friends and fumbled alone through the empty woods toward...how to describe it? A voice? A feeling? Something or someone beckoned me to that place and kept me coming back year after year.

I used to sit on the top edge with my bare calves pressed against the steep, cold granite wall, searching the water below for any sign of life. Being there always settled my frantic mind from the rumors flying around town about my family. Whenever I was close to the water, some benign presence down there made me feel protected and supported. Like everything in my life would be okay in the end. I suppose that's what I'd been searching for without knowing it. What I imagined my mother's love must have felt like.

At twenty, when I quit college and moved back to Calypso Springs to take care of Dad, I stopped going out there. This was my first time back.

Bob and I climbed the craggy hill up to the railroad tie staircase that led down to the spring. Everything was the same. Dark, quiet, overgrown with dead things of the forest. I imagined it had been beautiful once, but something had destroyed it long before my time.

About fifty feet in diameter, the actual spring was a substantial pool. Twenty feet below the top, the water hid under thousands of twisted dead vines. A chaotic crosshatched quilt, they stretched from one side to the other, covering the entire thing. Those vines were nature's *Keep Out* sign.

Similar to the Blackwell house.

I dangled my feet over the top edge, a familiar feeling even after so many years, and Bob laid on the crunchy leaves next to me, resting his head on his front paws. He'd never been there before, but he was handling it like a champ. Gloomy as it might have been for most people, I always felt safe there. If anyone had asked, I wouldn't be able to explain why without sounding like I'd gone round the bend, so I was grateful no one ever did. Probably because no one ever knew this was my place. It was my little secret.

Looking out over the chasm, I realized with a sudden deep sadness Tee and Sam were right. My life had stopped moving forward the day I returned home two decades ago. I wanted to change that now. Calypso's spring was already working its magic on me.

The letter Cassie had taken from the attic burned a hole in her pocket. She'd read it several times and decided one more couldn't hurt.

April 14, 1981

Cass,

Where are you? I know I ask this in every letter, but I can't wrap my head around it, even now. Why you would do this to us? Some days I'm so filled with rage I don't know what to do with myself. No part of me believes you would want to leave us, but the evidence is pretty damning at this point. It's your daughter's birthday today, Cass. Flora's two. She's so much like you. Stubborn, feisty, beautiful. She takes shit from no one, even her daddy. She's turning into a miniature you more every day. Makes me miss you so much. I haven't found one clue about where you are or if you're okay. But I will not stop looking. I'll never stop, Cassie. We belong together. I bought your old house from the bank. Thank Jack for me. Because he defaulted on his loan, it was a steal. Didn't want to say anything until the deal was done. We'll be closing Escrow in a week and move in after that. I wanted to be here when you come back, when you come home. I wanted you to feel like you're home. Tee's been great. She comes over every day after her classes to help with Flora. No one will ever take your place, Cass, but I have to admit, it's been nice to have the help. And the company. I miss you. So much. Love you more, always.

The warmth of that love pulsed through Cassie's fingers as she held the letter. She was seventeen and falling for him all over again. It had been so long since she'd allowed herself to feel like this. Her body vibrated with the energy of it, the heat. She let it wash over her, remembering what it was like to love someone with a full heart.

Then, a building fell on her chest. She couldn't breathe. As long as she held the letter, it felt like she was sucking air through a clogged straw. She dropped it on the floor and recovered on the couch, gaining her breath back slowly.

That was close. It couldn't happen again. She couldn't let any of it in. The good or the bad. It would destroy her. So she sealed off her weakened corners and resolved to maintain full emotional distance. Especially from the daughter, whom she'd had the desire to get personal with, not once, not twice, but almost seven times in the last few days.

That could not stand. Must focus on what's important.

Cassie had a feeling Josiah knew about the curse. Why else would he put her father's lockbox in their tree? Did he think she would find it there if she came back? Did he put something in the box, too?

Whenever she thought of Josiah, she pictured the nest, where they'd met. Everything changed after that day in Calypso Woods. Every minute she spent with him strengthened a curse that would never let her go. The pain began, the flowers died, her mother became a monster.

What if the curse was tied to the nest? There was something deep in the water below, something ancient that spoke to her, much like an inner voice, for years when she went there to be alone. She wondered if the daughter had experienced the same phenomenon. And there she went again, willy-nilly wondering about the daughter. It had to stop.

But maybe there were answers in the woods.

TWENTY-FIVE

Cassie crept through the brush carrying the box, careful not to trip over any hidden logs lying under the dead leaves and brambles. She didn't remember it being such a treacherous trip out there before, but she was also forty years younger then. She arrived, sweaty and out of breath, at the top of the hill overlooking the spring. The railroad tie stairs that led down to the nest were still there, and still perilously steep, so she stopped to rest a minute. It was harder for her to breathe out here. She'd hoped it would be the opposite.

The daughter sat at the bottom of the hill with her legs dangling over the edge of the spring like Cassie used to when she came here. She knew the minute she crested the hill this was the daughter's place, too. Almost expected to find her here. The beast lay next to her, sleeping. She seemed peaceful communing with whatever was down there in the water.

Cassie sneaked a little closer, but when she stepped toward the top railroad tie of the staircase, the earth fell out from under her. She struggled to stay upright for a few unnerving seconds as the side of the hill gave way.

"Not again!" she wailed, swaying this way and that without gaining firm footing on the ground. And then, unable to right herself, she tumbled head over tail down the entire hill, mirroring the day she'd met Josiah there. Except this time she was, thank the Lord, fully clothed. Why did this keep happening? And more important, was anything broken?

She landed at the bottom of the hill, moaning, not sure she was still alive. It hurt far more now than it had at seventeen. She'd dropped the box somewhere uphill and lay there, aching and ashamed.

"Oh my god, are you okay?" the daughter asked, rushing over to her. The beast tried to inspect Cassie, but she shooed him away with an unsteady hand. "No Bob, leave it," the daughter commanded. He did as he was told.

Cassie tried to move, but it felt like she'd broken everything. The daughter sat next to her. She hadn't touched her yet, to help her, but Cassie could see she was in that unsure territory of deciding whether it would be okay to.

"I'm fine," Cassie said, waving her off. She was utterly uncertain that was the truth.

"Can you move?"

"In a minute."

"Anything broken?"

"I'd like to let everything settle before I try to find out," she said, not moving. "Sorry to interrupt you."

Sitting there next to Cassie, the daughter erupted in a sudden fit of laughter, pounding her fists on her lap until tears leaked onto her cheeks. After almost a minute of unrestrained joy from the daughter, Cassie took it personally.

"What's so funny?"

"You were like a pinwheel coming down that hill. I don't know how you missed those giant railroad ties with your head. You did, right? Pretty sure I've never seen anyone with less grace and more luck. If we're cursed, it's a lucky one."

"Happy I could entertain you," Cassie said, the farthest thing from happy one could be.

"And the noises. You were Buttercup throwing herself ass

over teakettle down the hill after her sweet Westley."
Another fit of inconsolable laughter struck the daughter.
The mutt seemed worried and tried to lick the tears from
her cheeks.

Though she was the butt of the daughter's joke, Cassie had to
admit hearing her laugh, seeing joy in her eyes, if only for a
moment, had a profound effect. As if one tiny blossom had
unfurled inside her, warming a bit of the cold, distant place that
had become her soul.

And then she began to cough again. When would she learn?

I gained control of myself and stopped laughing at the
ridiculousness of what had just happened. Then it dawned on me
to question what had just happened.

"Why are you here? Did you follow me?"

Cassie ignored me and groped the surrounding ground, filled
with dead leaves. "Where is it? I had it..."

"Where is what?"

"The box. I was holding it when I fell."

"I'm sure it's here somewhere. Can you stand?"

She glared at me like I was a daft child. "Of course I can
stand."

I stood and held my hand out to her. She ignored it and struggled to her feet on her own. Her snub might have offended me
before, but I remembered the feeling I'd had at the Blackwell
house when I'd brushed against her back. Everything made
sense now.

"That's part of it, isn't it?" I asked, still inside my own
thoughts.

"What is part of what?" she asked, searching the leaf and
brush covered hillside for the box. "You ought to learn how to
form a cogent question."

"Noted." Can a person be born arrogant? "Touching you,

that terrible bleak feeling, the burning everywhere. That's all part of the curse, isn't it?"

She stopped with her back to me, panting, but didn't turn around. I stood about three feet down the hill from her.

"You shouldn't say that word in public."

"I think we're okay. Not a lot of foot traffic out here."

"I could use less sass, if you don't mind. It's been a day. Now, what was your question?"

"At the Blackwell house, when I touched you, I felt…"

"Burned and hollowed out all at once," she said, still turned away from me.

"It was like I could feel your sadness, everything you've suffered through. Have I come unbuckled?"

"No," she said, turning toward me, careful not to lose her footing again. "You're quite firmly buckled."

"Does it work both ways?"

"It does."

"Wow." The things I'd experienced in my life nearly drowned me at every turn. It was the Everest I was sure I'd never summit. I'd always be stuck at base camp because I didn't have the proper training to move forward and keep climbing.

When I was younger, I wanted her to know my pain. To feel it and understand what she'd put me through by leaving us. But now that she was here—here, with me, at the nest!—tiny and sick and looking like a lost child, I couldn't imagine wanting her to suffer through that. I wouldn't wish that on anyone.

"Found it!" Cassie shouted, halfway up the hill. She pulled the box out of the underbrush and navigated the path down, much more carefully this time.

"How do you know about this place?" I asked. "Did you follow me?"

"Everyone knows about the nest. No one's brave enough to come here."

"Well, brave or stupid, we're here now."

"Indeed."

"Should we get back, though? We've got a curse to break."

"What did I just say?" She sounded more and more like someone's mother.

"Sorry," I said, not sorry. "Why did you bring the box with you? It's heavy and awkward. Makes for tricky hiking as you were clever enough to discover on your way down the hill."

"To see if it would open here," she said, ignoring my snark. She tried to pry the box open again. Futile effort, as usual.

"Why would it open here and not anywhere else?"

"I think Calypso's spring is related to our...condition somehow."

"You can say curse. Nobody's here but me." I turned to leave and she gasped. When I glanced back, her face had gone pale. She held her hand over her mouth like she was trying to keep herself from screaming. "What—"

She interrupted my question by pointing at the water. The entire pool was glowing like there was some sort of light source, or life source, under it, shining up through the desiccated vines.

"What the hell—"

Bob stood and peeked over the edge, too. He started barking and wouldn't stop.

"Sssshhhh," she admonished, like we were bothering whatever was under the water. I thought for sure Bob was going to make himself sicker with all the barking, so I tried to calm him, but nothing worked.

"It's back," Cassie said, her voice laced with awe.

"So, you have been here before?"

"Shhhhh."

"I will not shhhhh until you explain how you know this place, why you know it's back, and what *it* is."

Cassie kept staring down at the water, mesmerized, like she was saying hello to an old friend. In all my years of coming here, I'd never experienced anything like this.

"What is it?" I asked, not understanding anything.

"I don't know."

"But you've seen it before?"

She nodded. "Once."

"Elaborate please."

We watched the light ebb and flow under the water. It became ultra bright at one point, and I thought it might break through the surface. Then, as quickly as it had appeared, it was gone. Darkness reigned in the water once again. Bob stopped barking.

"I understand nothing," I said, still dazed by what we saw.

Cassie screamed and threw the box down on the ground.

"What's wrong?"

"It...I don't know. It burned me." She stared at the box like it was going to attack her again.

"When did you see that light before?" I asked, pointing down at the water.

She glanced from the box to the water and back to me. "The day I met your father."

TWENTY-SIX

When we got home, I had to carry Bob in from the truck. All the activity at the nest had taken a toll on him and he fell into a deep sleep on the couch as soon as I put him down. I pulled my phone out of my purse to call Jake about the CT scan results and it rang in my hand.

"Are the results in?" I asked.

"They were inconclusive. Didn't give us any more insight than the x-rays. I can send his scans to a specialist for a second opinion, get some fresh eyes on them."

My heart sank. More confirmation Cassie was right.

"Em? You there?"

"Sorry. Yes. Send them, please. Get back to me as soon as you hear anything."

"Of course. How's he doing?"

"He's sleeping right now."

"Okay, good. Sleep heals." He paused, like he was trying to find the right thing to say. "I wish I had more answers for you. Call me if his condition changes."

I took a deep breath. "I will."

"Hang in there."

"Yeah." I ended the call and sat with Bob. What if Cassie was wrong? What if it wasn't the curse? What if I was going to lose Bob no matter what I did? Like I lost Dad.

"We're going to figure it out," Cassie said, standing in the kitchen doorway. I'd almost forgotten she was there. "He's not going to die." Her voice breaking the silence wasn't what surprised me. It was the gentle tone and her effort to comfort me, about Bob no less, that was most shocking.

"How can you be sure?"

"Because I'm not going to die."

She was so confident I needed to believe her.

Everything in the house had felt quiet when we returned from the nest. Like it was trying to hide its own secrets. I wasn't in the mood for any more secrets. Apparently, neither was Cassie.

"Here," she said, standing in front of us on the couch. She held out a yellowed envelope to me.

"Did you break into the attic when I left?" I said, taking the letter from her.

"I'm not a common thief. I found it before you kicked me out."

"You mean when you were snooping around my house in the middle of the night?" Our banter felt lighter than it had in the last few days. Less overtly antagonistic, more passively aggressive. So, progress.

The letter was old, with the Maiden Lake address I didn't recognize. "Is this where you lived before..."

"Yes." She didn't look at me when she answered. Maybe she understood what I was thinking but didn't say. *Before you left us.*

"I think your father may have known about the curse."

"Why?" Yet another thing he kept from me.

"We should read his letters. There might be something there to help us figure this out."

The ease with which she said *us* surprised me, like we were a team now, a dynamic duo. My mother and me. I may have warmed up to the idea.

"What about the box? Why did you think it would open at

the nest?" After the light disappeared there, we could handle the box again without getting burned.

"I would guess that's where the curse started."

"Say more."

"When I was young, my father forbade me from going there. It was the only place in town he made off limits. You only keep something off limits if there's a secret there you don't want found out."

"Maybe he didn't want you drowning in the pool. It is creepy there."

"That was the reason he gave."

"You didn't believe him?"

"My father had good intentions. He did what he thought was right to protect his family."

Isn't that what villains say to justify their behavior? Most bad guys don't think they're bad or wrong. Everybody thinks they're doing the right thing for the right reason...for them. I didn't want to pull at that thread, though. Who knew what dark and twisty road we would have been lost down.

"We need more information," she said.

"You really think Dad knew?"

"One way to find out."

I unlocked the door to the attic, and we carried all the boxes with Dad's letters downstairs to the living room. I didn't want to be two floors away from Bob in case something happened and he needed me.

Cassie grabbed a shoebox full and took them over to Dad's old recliner in the corner, about as far away as she could be.

"Don't sit there." I hadn't meant to sound quite so harsh. "That's his chair."

She didn't resist. Just nodded and stared at the chair, touching the worn armrest with the tips of her fingers. Then she brought her box over and sat on the couch with us.

"Did he have that ratty old thing when you were in Maiden Lake?" I asked. She seemed to recognize it.

"He did," she said from the other side of Bob.

"I've worked in vain for many years trying to make him give it away."

"It's my fault," she said.

"How so?"

"I found it."

"Where? The dump?"

She smiled. As incongruous as that was on her face, given its state of perpetual grimace, it didn't appear to break anything. It was genuine and lovely. Reminded me of the moment Pearl Blackwell had smiled at me, the lightness it brought to her.

"We were walking past a yard sale in Maiden Lake when we first moved into the Lilac Cove apartment. We didn't have any furniture or anything at all, and I jokingly said he should get it because it was the perfect dad chair. That was how I told him I was pregnant with you."

"Wow." I was stunned by that ragged old chair's significance in my life now.

"He bought it on the spot, though I begged him not to. Cripes' sake, look at it."

"I have been all my life," I said, without an ounce of snark.

"It hasn't improved."

"No, it has not."

"I tried to make him get rid of it. He wouldn't budge."

"Now I know why..."

We sat quietly, taking in the chair with new appreciation. At least I did.

"Gosh, we've been so preoccupied with all of this," she said, speaking in short, raspy breaths, gesturing toward the letters, "I forgot we have an entire house to pack."

"I'm not worrying about any of that until we get this curse

settled." In my mind, being a cursed child gave me a quality excuse not to have to pack my life up and leave my home. Of course, I wasn't sure claiming a family curse would be a valid legal excuse, but I'd cross that bridge when I came to it. In nine days.

Bob snored softly between us as we dug into the piles of letters Dad had written. I suppose I should have known reading those letters would affect us. It was impossible to have known how profoundly.

Cassie thought she had fortified her walls enough to read through Josiah's letters. She may have misjudged her powers of detachment.

"You're going to give yourself a blister if you keep that up," Emma said.

"Pardon?"

She motioned to Cassie's hand, twisting her cross between her fingers so vigorously she could have created a spark.

"Right." She let the cross fall onto her chest and pulled another letter from the pile.

"Are you still Catholic?"

Cassie glanced at her, not sure how to respond, or if she should. It might lead to deeper questions she wasn't willing to answer.

"My parents were."

"But not you?"

"It faded."

"Did meeting Dad make it fade?"

"Your father was a very free spirit."

"Did that spirit rub off on you a little?"

"A little."

"Is that why Jack didn't want you to be with Dad?"

"Did Tee tell you that?" Cassie sat up and began twisting her cross again.

"It's in Dad's letters. He's not complimentary about Jack."

"Tee likes to run her mouth about our family."

"Not to me she doesn't," Emma said. She picked up another envelope, but didn't take the letter out to read. "So, can we talk about what that was at the nest today? You said you saw it the day you met Dad. What happened?"

"I don't know what it was. I didn't that day either." Cassie took a breath, hoping she wouldn't be in trouble revisiting this memory. The story was embarrassing, but it wouldn't reveal anything she didn't want Emma to know. Maybe she would stop asking questions if she knew how her parents had met.

"I was seventeen. By then I'd been going to the nest for several years by myself. Might sound strange, but I felt called to it. Something in me, it's hard to explain."

"I understand the pull," Emma said, nodding.

"My mother was in a foul mood that day and I needed to get away. Have some peace and quiet."

"And Dad was there?"

"He was. But I didn't know it until a grossly inappropriate moment."

Cassie let the memory of that day wash over her. The sun blinking down through the trees, dappling the ground with light. The thick, humid air of summer covering her body in a layer of sweat, the dead pine needles and leaves crunching under her feet as she crept to her favorite spot alone.

"I sat on the edge of the spring where you were today, wondering if my parents were headed for a divorce. Maybe praying for it a little, if I'm honest."

"Why?"

"It's clear when two people don't belong together. Everyone knew it. But my father was not the type to get a divorce. And my mother was not the type to give him one. So."

"I'm sorry you grew up like that. It sounds miserable."

Cassie had become so accustomed to Emma's usual sass, she was taken aback by her sincerity.

"It was what it was. My father was a principled man."

"So you've said."

"It was hot that day," Cassie continued. "I'd had a gallon of water and my tiny bladder would not leave me alone. Mind you, I would never do my business in public, but I had no choice. I was bursting at the seams. So I hiked up away from the nest looking for a tree to go behind, in case, God forbid, anyone should come down to the area. It was unlikely, but I didn't want to be dropping my shorts in the wide open wilderness. That would be asking for all kinds of rumors a girl like me could not abide."

"A girl like you?"

"The obedient daughter. My parents would have been mortified if they'd known where I was or what I was doing. Especially with a strange boy. Any rumors about me would have sent them over the edge. There were already enough rumors swirling around town about our family. I never would have been allowed out of the house again if they'd found out."

"My grandparents sound great. Shame I never met them. What were the other rumors?"

"Shush. No more interruptions."

Aggrieved but silent, Emma asked no more questions.

"I found a spot at the top of the hill, away from the railroad ties. You're familiar, behind the great pine tree that's still up there. The minute I began relieving myself I heard the snap of a twig." Cassie heard it in the stillness of the living room too. The crack of that twig breaking was the sound of her life irrevocably changing. A swift rush of adrenaline surged through her.

"I looked up and there he was. This giant of a boy with the wildest, bushiest head of hair I'd ever seen, staring at me from across the hill."

"Dad, you perv."

"Indeed. I was squatting in the bushes with my shorts down around my ankles, and well, you don't need to know every detail, I suppose."

Emma laughed. It was beautiful, like the sound of wind

chimes in a breeze. "Of course I do. I need every single detail." She rested her hand on the mutt's head and gazed at Cassie, waiting for her to continue.

The gentle rustling sound of a million willow leaves floated in through the back screen door. "Fine. When I met your father, he quite literally scared the pants off me."

"Oh my gosh!" Cassie shouted, scrambling to pull up her shorts.

"Damn. Sorry," the boy said, spinning away from her.

She pulled her underwear into place, but in her frantic struggle to reach her shorts, they caught underneath her sandals tripping her. She couldn't recover and crashed to the ground on her side. When she hit, half the hill gave way, probably because of the drought. She tumbled, shorts around her ankles, down the hill, landing near the edge of the nest.

She scrambled to her feet, her head still spinning, and tried to regain a bit of her dignity. Looking up, she spied him watching her from the top of the hill.

"You okay?" he called.

She couldn't have been further from okay if she were dead.

"Stop looking at me!" she shouted. So he did. He stepped away, out of sight, at the top of the hill and good riddance. This was all his fault. She'd find out who he was and get her revenge later, but first, she had more important things to do, like pull up her shorts. Which, again, proved too much for her.

Cassie blamed it on the tumble downhill. Her equilibrium was off and her shorts were still stuck on her sandals. This time, when she tried to pull them up, she fell backward, landing on her bum, and rolled over the edge of the nest. Miraculously, she grabbed hold of a narrow ledge of stone before plummeting into the scary mess of vines and water twenty feet below.

Her legs dangled uselessly under her with the dirty shorts still stuck around her ankles. It was the worst possible scenario. She screamed for help.

Something bubbled down in the water.

Hanging there on the edge of the granite wall, she glanced down to see what it was. Cassie had never heard or seen anything moving under the nest of vines in the water. But there was something there now. A bright light emanated up through the surface of the water and the loose parts of the vines. It flashed from below several times as if saying hello and then disappeared. She was still gripping the edge, terrified, her fingers burning from the strain.

Then, from nowhere, a bushy head of hair popped into view above her. The largest, strongest hands she'd ever felt wrapped around her wrists, pulling her away from danger.

"Hey, stop that. I'm trying to help you." His voice was both irritating and comforting at the same time. In her semi-crazed state, Cassie swatted at him to let her go, even as he lifted her from the edge. Once he got her up on top, above the ledge, he was going to see things he shouldn't and she couldn't allow that.

"You know, this will be easier on both of us if you stop fighting me."

He was right, of course, but she wasn't raised to be all right with some strange boy putting his hands and eyes all over her, so she made sure he understood this was a special, one-time-only kind of circumstance.

"I hope so. For your sake," he said.

He'd somehow secured both of her arms above her head now as he pulled her up.

"Put me down." If her shorts hadn't been wrapped around her ankles, she could have reached a leg up to stand on the edge, but her clothes trapped her.

"I'm a little busy saving your life here. Get back to me in a minute."

"Put me down now." She struggled against him again, all in vain. She'd never encountered such a strong boy before. When she was above the edge, he pulled her a few feet away from it and dropped her to the ground, turning his back on her as soon as he let go.

"Need help with anything? You had a little trouble first and second time. Thought I'd ask, in case."

She wanted to throw dirt in his face. "Oh, you're a comedian," she said, yanking her filthy shorts up around her waist. Her armor in place now, she was ready to give him a piece of her mind.

When Cassie marched around to face him, she stared up into his mischievous blue eyes, and nothing came. She couldn't remember her own name. Or where she was. Or who she was. She was perilously lost in those eyes.

He smiled, and like a rubber band snapping, she came rushing back into herself and gave him her what for. "Who are you? Did you follow me here? Are you some kind of perv? You should be ashamed." She stomped off without giving him a chance to respond.

"Hey, wait," he said, chasing after her. Of course, it only took him a few steps to catch up. "So, back there, the part where I saved you from possible death and/or dismemberment, but definite disfiguration, you think maybe you'd like to thank me for that?"

"Thank you? You're the reason I fell. Thank you for sneaking up on me in the middle of the woods? Thank you for being a perv and trying to see me naked?"

"Wait a minute," he said, grasping her arm to stop her. His touch made her body light up like she'd grabbed a live wire.

"I think you've touched enough!" She broke free from his grasp and ran away, up the stairs and through the woods toward the road. Truth be told, she was more embarrassed than angry. She couldn't believe any of that had happened in front of a boy.

When she arrived at the place she usually hid her bike, she remembered she hadn't ridden it this time because it was in the shop. That boy had discombobulated everything in her head and now she'd have to hike home alone with only the havoc of her own mind to keep her company.

After speed-walking alone for a few minutes on old Kramer

Road, she heard gravel crunching under large feet, coming fast. He didn't say anything and didn't stop.

Was he trying to scare her?

She turned to confront him. "What do you want?"

He didn't look at her. Just kept walking right on past.

"Hey!" She ran to catch him and took two steps for every one of his to keep up. Seemed like he was walking faster now, too. "Why are you following me?" she said, wheezing a little from the pace. Sweat glazed her face. So un-ladylike.

He peered down at her. "Seems more like you're following me now. Stalker."

He'd caught her off guard, and before she could control her response with righteous indignation, she giggled.

They walked in silence for another minute, then she spoke into the space between them.

"Thank you." Ugh. It almost killed her to say that.

"You mean for saving your life? Sure, no problem." He didn't say another word and she absorbed the humiliation of the whole terrible scene.

"So what were you doing out in the woods all alone?" he finally asked, about a mile into their trek.

"That's kind of personal, isn't it?"

"I've seen you with your shorts down. I think we're in that zone now." He already knew how to push her buttons.

"Just because you, because I, because we—"

"Easy. Don't hurt yourself." He smiled. It was flawless.

She couldn't tell him the truth about the nest, and she certainly couldn't tell him what she'd seen there.

"I got lost," she said, without looking at him.

"Yeah. Me too."

"But I enjoy being alone. I mean, I don't have a problem with it like some people."

"Yeah, me too." He smiled and gave her a look that set a thousand hummingbirds loose in her belly. Cassie knew two things

then. This boy was trouble, and neither of them would be alone
again.

TWENTY-SEVEN

"Did you go back to the nest after you met Dad?" I asked. He sounded so alive in Cassie's story. So young and bright and unbroken.

She twisted her cross again. "No. That was the last time before today."

"He was a gentle giant. He saved you."

"He sent me flying down a steep hill unclothed. Then, yes, he saved me. In more ways than one that day."

"Why did your parents get married in the first place if they were so wrong for each other? Was it arranged?"

"It might as well have been."

Cassie spoke with great detachment about her mother, and I wondered if she had any kind of relationship with her now. "Your father is gone, but is your mother still..."

"Yes. Mary is alive," Cassie said.

"Do you talk?"

"Not if we can help it."

"I've never seen her. Are we anything alike?"

"You and she? No. She was petite, pale, and blonde with severe features."

"A pale blonde? That's...interesting."

"Because we're both olive brunettes?"

"Well, yeah."

Cassie shrugged it off.

"You never got close to her?" I asked.

She huffed, like the question was ridiculous.

"That's a shame."

"Why? She taught me the great art of dispassion."

"That doesn't seem like something to strive for."

"Why not? Do you want to be felled by every event in your life that doesn't go your way? Strength requires detachment."

"Strength requires courage. Being afraid and doing it anyway."

"But what if you didn't have the fear in the first place?"

"Everyone has fear."

"Only if you have something to lose."

"I don't want to live a life with nothing to lose. Do you?" My body temperature rose about three degrees in three seconds. I wanted to jump out of my clothes. They felt hot and tight on me. Was that what she thought of Dad and me for all those years? *Nothing to lose?*

"We should get back to reading," she said, picking up another letter. "We've got a lot to get through."

"Last one from 1999," I said, holding the letter up to show Cassie. I was rereading it, trying to figure out who Esther Blum was and why Dad had been looking for her back then.

Cassie didn't respond to my update, just kept reading. A thought popped into my head as I watched her. "Did you ever remarry? Or have more kids?" I regretted the questions as soon as they left my mouth because I wasn't ready to hear the answers. That she'd gone on with her life like we'd never existed.

When you're a child, time has a way of bloating and slowing to a crawl when you're waiting for something important to happen. My early days were long years waiting for her to come back to us. It took its toll on me.

"Remarry?" she asked, surprised as much as I was by my question.

"The ring box in the office. It's empty. I assumed..."

"Did he tell you we were married?"

"No. He said he didn't believe in the institution, but then I found the empty ring box and assumed it was something else he'd lied to me about."

"We were never married." This was clearly a sore subject. Her face had changed shade and was less eggshell now, more burgundy.

"Engaged?"

Cassie stared at the floor, but didn't answer.

"I'm sorry if it's—when I saw the box was empty, I thought you had the ring."

"I didn't know he'd bought a ring. When I saw the box upstairs..." She drifted off again. I hadn't meant to upset her. All those letters and the secrets they held, the ring she'd never known about. What else was this house hiding from us?

"Well," she said, snapping out of her trance, "what's done is done. Can't be undone."

"Maybe it can be redone."

"What does that mean?"

"I don't know where the ring is. It's not in the ring box, but maybe we can find it in the house somewhere in the rest of his things. I want you to have it."

"Why?"

It was a valid question and before that day I wouldn't have had an answer for her. "Because you loved each other. I know that now."

She nodded. "I assume you were told otherwise by Tee."

"Not Tee." I glanced out toward the swaying willow tree in the backyard.

"I see. It would seem you've had an incomplete education

about your parent's history. We'll have to rectify that soon. But first things first," she said.

"The letters."

"No. The box. We need to open that damn box."

"The ring might be in the box!" I said. I put Dad's last letter about Esther in my pocket and grabbed the lockbox off the end table next to the couch.

"Where are you going?" Cassie asked.

"To the only other person who might be able to help us. You're not a fan."

"I'm not talking to him."

"I know," I said, heading for the door. "Stay here with Bob. Do not go anywhere, okay? Eyes on him at all times. When he wakes, give him water. If anything changes, call me. I programmed my number into your phone. I'll be back soon. Hopefully with answers."

When Cassie suggested they read the letters from Josiah, it wasn't only because she thought they'd hold clues about how to break the curse; she was hoping to find out what, if anything, had happened between Tee and Josiah.

Instead, she discovered something else. Her walls began crumbling again, but she couldn't rip herself away as she learned about all of Emma's big events. Everything she should have been there to witness with her as she grew. When she gave birth, Cassie had wanted nothing more than to be part of her daughter's firsts, but she'd missed so much now. She couldn't get them back. And there were no more firsts to witness. It was too late. Their time had passed.

The tears surprised her. She wiped them away, folded the letter about Emma's first steps, and put it in her pocket, grateful Emma wasn't there to witness her breakdown.

Right after she blew her nose, someone knocked at the front

door. Cassie opened it to Tee and a young ginger woman she didn't recognize. She'd seen the younger woman in photos on the walls around the house, so Cassie assumed she was a close friend of Emma's. Tee groaned when she came face to face with Cassie again.

"Is she here? We figured she could use help packing," Tee said.

"Come to spy, Teresa? Don't you have other, more pressing, things to be doing?" She flashed Tee a joyless grin.

"Do we have to start at eleven every time?"

"It's just fascinating to me how some people insinuate themselves into other people's lives."

"It's called being a friend, Cassandra. You might look into it someday."

"She's not here, then? We can come back," the redhead said, putting herself in the line of fire, trying to drag Tee away. A futile effort, for sure, for such a skinny thing. She was as tall as Emma, but wafer thin.

"Where is she?" Tee asked, brushing the wafer off.

"I'm Sam, by the way. Samantha."

"I'm...sure you know who I am by now." Cassie said, still in a staring contest with Tee.

"How's Bob?" Tee pushed her way into the house past Cassie.

"By all means, please, come in."

Samantha followed behind Tee. Clearly, neither of them recognized sarcasm.

Tee sat on the couch next to the mutt. He woke groggy and then fell back asleep. Samantha sat on the other side and scratched his head. It was clear they both cared about him.

"Did you give my regards to your father?" Cassie asked.

Tee appeared unfazed. "I did."

"And?"

"He doesn't keep in touch with any of his old friends. Said they're better left where he last knew them, in the past. I agree with him."

"That's a shame," Cassie said, disappointed by the news that

Raymond would not cooperate and help them find Esther Blum. "Maybe he'd change his mind if a close friend asked him. Someone from his past he might want to bring into his present."

Tee stared at Cassie in disbelief. "You wouldn't."

"He must be lonely here all by himself now. Single and ready to mingle, yes?"

Samantha sat petting the beast, glancing back and forth between Tee and Cassie. "Listen, I know there's some weird history here, so please, you know, say what you want to say already. My life is falling apart and I'm here to help Emma. I don't have time for puzzles. Neither do you. Speak your minds, ladies."

A straight-shooter. That one impressed Cassie.

"I'll ask him again," Tee said, obviously still in shock from Cassie's threat. Cassie even surprised herself by how far she would go to find Esther Blum. She only hoped Mary would cooperate if it came to that. And she prayed like hell it wouldn't.

TWENTY-EIGHT

I t was getting dark when I approached Hopper's house, which meant it had to be after eight o'clock. It surprised me how quickly the day had passed with Cassie. When she first came, every minute I had to spend with her felt like an eternity. Now I wanted more time, even when she was being ridiculous.

Hopper's house was lit up like Christmas. Every light on. I knocked on his front door, holding the lockbox under one arm. No one answered. Peering in through the windows, I found his favorite chair in the living room. Apparently, every old man has one, but he wasn't in it. The downstairs was empty.

Then I heard a torch behind the house and realized he was working in his shop. He liked to rebuild old cars and since he was retired and had nothing else to do most of the time, he'd turned his garage into a body shop.

The door to the garage lay open and the lights inside were bright. Hopper hunched over the bumper of an old cherry red Mustang wearing a large welding mask that reminded me of a medieval jousting helmet. He was in the middle of welding some metal thing onto some other metal thing. I didn't know about welding or cars. Sparks danced and flew off the end where the blowtorch sprayed fire like a dragon.

The minute he saw me, he stopped and flipped the helmet up to speak. "Hello, Em."

I kept moving forward toward him, but he threw a hand up to stop me.

"Careful there, it might be hot," he said. "Here, I'll come to you." He turned the torch off and laid all of his gear on the workbench along the wall of the garage.

"What ya got there under your arm?" he asked as he approached me, wiping his hands on an old, dirty towel. He put his arm around me in a half hug and I felt protected, like I used to when Dad would hug me. They were giant men with giant hearts. But one of them was also a liar.

"I was hoping you'd be able to help me with this. I need to get it open. It won't budge. I've tried everything."

"Let's have a look," he said, holding his hands out to me. I put the box in the vast real estate of his open palms, hoping it wouldn't set itself on fire or anything weird. Hopper inspected it, lifting the latch on the end and digging in between the edges, where it should open, with his fingernails. "Looks like one of them old safe deposit boxes from Calypso One. I 'member seeing these back in the day. Ain't seen one in fifty years, though. Where'd you come across it?"

"My backyard."

"Just layin' there in the grass?"

"The tree guys found it in that old stump by the lake when I had it removed."

"Shouldn't be too hard to..." He tried prying it open with his hands. I thought he'd be able to get anything open with those things. He'd used them all his life for hard manual labor. They were powerful, solid.

"I'll be damned," he said, not able to budge it.

"Yeah, it's a tough one. Do you have any heavy duty tools that could, I don't know, crush it a little to change the shape of the box and break the seal?"

"Heavy duty…let me think for a minute." He wandered off to the corner of the garage, poking around to see what he had.

I stayed fixed in my spot, scanning the tools, waiting for Hopper to rescue us. A small black-and-white photo tucked into the end of the bench caught my eye. There was no frame to keep it safe from the elements or nosy friends, so I pulled it out to look closer. The wrinkled photo paper felt brittle between my fingers.

A young woman, still in her teens, stood holding a bouquet of lilacs, smiling at the camera. She was angular, but beautiful. All pointy features, with wavy blonde hair and light eyes. I didn't recognize her, so I turned it over to see if it had an inscription.

Whatever comes between us, I'll always be your girl and you will always have my heart.
M

When she was alive, Hopper's wife, Tee's mother, was a brunette and her name was Betty. They'd been married for almost sixty years, a lifetime, until her death a few years ago. I put the photo back where I'd found it, almost certain I knew who was in it.

"Well, I ain't got nothin' that's as heavy duty as me, so let's try it and see," Hopper said. He put the box on the bench and searched around for something. Had he spotted me looking at the photo?

"Now, where'd I put that sonofabitch? 'Scuse the language, Em. You ain't spent much time with me in here, but I talk to all my tools like they insulted my wife. Keeps things fresh." He found what he was looking for: a rubber mallet. "Now stand back over there. Don't want nothing come careening forth and taking a eye out."

I stood back behind the open door of the garage, using it as a shield. I had little hope this would work, given that Cassie and I had dropped the box onto pavement from six stories up, but it was worth a try.

Hopper set the box on its side, raised the mallet above his head, and thrashed it. The mallet bounced off the box with each hit but didn't make a dent. The last strike landed so hard, the box sprung up like it was on a trampoline and landed on its side, still closed.

"Boy, I tell ya, Em, doesn't make much sense. No lock on it, but latched tighter'n a clam's ass at high tide," he said, inspecting it.

"Had a few, have you, Hopp?" I asked, hoping he hadn't been drunk-welding.

"Might have."

"Careful there," I said, approaching him and the box. "Don't wanna weld something together you shouldn't."

"I'll be fine."

"I know." I rested my hand on his back.

"Don't make sense, though," he said, moving over to get a closer look at the box. "Who'd put this in a old..." He stopped, stared at the side with the engraved initials.

"What is it?" I asked.

"I don't think you should mess with this, Em."

"Why not?"

"Better let that sleeping dog lie."

"Speak English, Hopp."

"This belonged to somebody you didn't know. Somebody you didn't want to know. Take my word, Em. Nothing in there but old ghosts. I'd bury it again if I's you." Staring at the engraving, he picked the box up and handed it back to me without another word.

"Hopper, I need to get it open. It's really important."

"That woman comes back and all hell breaks loose." After handling the box, he wiped his hands on the same greasy towel like he was wiping away someone's spit.

"That woman...?"

"You know the one."

"I believe I do."

"She brings all these damn ghosts back to life. They should stay where they belong, Em. Like that box. Shoulda stayed where it was buried."

"Maybe, but I need to open it now."

"You know who that belonged to?"

"I do."

"What do you think's in it?" Hopper returned to his bench and started rearranging tools without organizing anything.

"I don't know. But we need to find out."

"We?" He stopped moving his tools and looked at me.

"Yes, we." I took a deep breath. "Did you know my grandmother, Mary?"

He lowered his head and his shoulders followed suit. Everything imploded. "What did she say?" he asked, without looking up.

"What did who say?"

"Your mother."

A few butterflies danced in my stomach at that word. I was still getting used to other people talking about her again. "She didn't say anything, Hopp. I saw this." I picked up the photo and showed him. "Is this Mary?"

He dropped onto the stool next to the bench like he didn't have the strength to hold his oversized body up any longer.

"Hopp, I need answers to questions I don't even understand. I think it's the only way I'm going to save Bob."

"What's any of this got to do with Bob?"

"When I figure it all out, I'll let you know." I put my hand on his shoulder and gave him the photo. He softened under my touch and sat staring at the picture. It took him a minute to speak.

"Mary was the love of my life. The most beautiful girl I'd ever known. Inside and out. Whip smart and funny too. Boy, I tell ya, we were, we were happy. For a minute."

"What happened?"

"Your grandfather happened, that's what. Happened so damn fast I didn't see him coming." Hopper stood, and my hand fell off his shoulder. He paced around the dirty garage, a caged animal, restless and angry. "Thing is, human nature, Em. It don't change."

"I'm learning that."

"Damn it. It's been a long time since I thought about any of that."

"You must have been young when you were together."

"We knew each other in school, everybody knew everybody a little, but we was never close. Had my eye on her for a while though. Got together right before graduation."

"What brought you together?"

"I was a damn shy fool. Too scared to make a move. Night before graduation I happened by her house and saw her pickin' up a bouquet of lilacs off her porch like somebody laid 'em there for her."

"A bouquet of lilacs? Like the one she's holding in the photo?" First love. Flowers left on people's porches seemed to be a thing in our town even back then.

"That's it. Next day, at graduation, she came right up to me and said hello, looking me in the eye like she knew me. I mean, really knew me. Turns out, she did. The important parts anyway. We was inseparable that summer."

"Did you find out who left the flowers for her?"

He hesitated before he spoke, like he was remembering something. "She thought I did, so I let her think that. Couldn't hurt. Plus, I cut her fresh ones from our tree out back after that."

How did flowers play a role in all of this? Cassie and I had our own particular issues with flora, but how did they play into other people's lives in town?

"Did you want to marry her?" I asked.

"Thought I was gonna."

"What happened?"

"Economics, Emma. Some are born with advantage and some ain't. Don't mean you can't or won't make something of yourself, but people judge on what they see in front of 'em in the here and now. They don't see down the road potential. All they see is numbers in a bank account."

"And Jack had good numbers?"

"Jack's daddy had good numbers. Don't get it wrong now. Mary was never like that. That was all her folks. But she let 'em run her into the ground with Jack. Perfect this and perfect that. 'Specially since he was newly single after the Blums got run out of town."

"The Blums?" The letter from Dad about Esther Blum was still tucked snug in my pocket. "You knew them?"

"Ah, damn it, I said too much."

"Who were they, Hopp?"

"Nah. I'll tell you same thing I told Tee, no need to dredge up those ghosts. Sorry I mentioned 'em. Didn't know 'em, but they didn't deserve what happened to 'em."

"Tee asked you about them?" What the fresh hell was going on?

"Bombarded me with questions this morning. Like I said, that woman comes back and all hell breaks loose."

"What does Cassie have to do with the Blums?"

"Don't know, but Tee sure as hell ain't ever mentioned 'em till Cassie showed up."

So they both knew about Esther, whoever she is or was, and didn't tell me. Another lie in the bucket. Heat rose in me at this revelation, so I pulled Dad's letter from my pocket and handed it to Hopper.

"S'this?"

"When Cassie left, Dad wrote her a letter every day. After a few years, he tapered off to once a week. Then once a month. But he wrote to her for twenty years straight. Look at the date. He wrote this one back in 1999. This was the last letter I could find. They stopped after this one."

He read it while I waited.

"Josiah was looking for Esther Blum," Hopper said, almost like he already knew.

"Did he say anything about her to you, Hopp?"

Hopper buried his face in the letter again, continuing to read.

"Did Esther know Cassie?" I asked.

"Couldn't have. The Blums got run out the fall of '58. Cassie wasn't born till the summer of '59. I only 'member that 'cause it hadn't even been a year on after Jack and Mary's wedding when Cassie was born. They didn't waste no time having her." His gaze drifted from the letter and glazed over, staring into the middle distance. This wasn't his puzzle to solve. I felt bad making him relive his past, but I didn't know anyone else who might be able to help me.

"Dad says he's looking for *Jack's Esther*," I said, pointing to the spot in the letter where Dad had written those exact words. "Jack and Esther were a couple, weren't they? Did you know her? Do you know what happened to her?"

"I don't know what happened between them two. I didn't know either of 'em 'cept in name at the time, but I heard rumors o'course. Nobody's got nothing better to do in this town than spread poison about somebody else."

"Don't I know it."

"I know you do, Em. Boy, I tell ya, it's a damn shame too."

"Did you ever see them together?"

"They kept it real secret. Understandable, given Jack's father."

"My great grandfather?"

"That's the one. He was a surly bastard who'd kick his own mother if it could make him a buck. Had a real streak of anti-Semitic running through him too."

"The McCormacks were Catholics."

"That's the truth."

"And the Blums?"

"Guess you can figure it out by the name."

"Oh my god. They were a Catholic and Jewish Romeo and Juliet." I wondered how Esther's father felt about Jack.

"Don't know nothing about that. Listen, I gotta get this done." He picked up his blowtorch and helmet to get back to work. But I couldn't leave yet. I didn't have enough information that meant anything, and the box remained a mystery.

"I'm sorry, Hopp. A couple more questions, please. This is such a quagmire and I'm trying to make sense of it all so I can help Bob."

"Still don't understand what any of it has to do with Bob." He put his equipment back on the bench.

"Why did the Blums leave town?"

"That was the biggest scandal this place had ever seen, till your mama disappeared, taking the whole damn family with her. Same as the Blums did."

He made it sound like Cassie was the mastermind behind leaving and Jack and Mary simply went along for the ride. There was sorrow in his voice that hadn't been there before we began talking about Mary.

"Were you still seeing Mary when they left town?"

"That what Cassie told you?" He got fidgety.

"Nobody told me anything, Hopp. That's the problem. Nobody talks in my family. About anything important. They never have. And I'm including you and Tee in there as well. I've known you all my life, and this is the first real talk I think we've ever had. Tee won't tell me anything, wants me to talk to Cassie. Cassie's been zipped up like a body bag until today. And the two of them, they have their own weird thing going on. Something happened with them before Cassie left. They're both still furious and neither of them will talk to me or each other about it."

I paced back and forth in front of Hopper, wearing a groove into the concrete floor.

"I've been kept in the dark my entire life about so many things, Hopp. I don't know what the hell is real and what's a lie anymore. Scratch that. I do know. Bob's real. He's the most important thing in my life right now, the most honest thing. He's sick and I have to help him. I'm losing my mind a little here."

I leaned up against the wall, exhausted by everything. "I'm sorry, Hopp. I didn't mean to...I shouldn't have burdened you with this. It's not your problem."

The look on his face told me I'd exhausted him talking about it. I reached for the box, ready to be done. It was time to get back and check on the one thing that mattered.

"You packin' the house up?" he asked.

"Little behind on that right now. Been preoccupied with other things."

"Might find something you need in there when you do."

"Right. Thanks, Hopp." I started for the open garage door.

"Two generations of McCormack ghosts there. Bound to give you something."

I spun around to face him. "What?"

"Your house." He stared at me like I was supposed to know what he was talking about.

"What about it?" The heat rose in me again.

"It was Jack's house, and his daddy's before that. Josiah bought it from the bank after they split town."

"And the hits keep on coming," I said, shaking my head, and feeling for a wall to steady myself, or to punch. I'd grown up and lived in the same house my missing mother had and I never knew it. The hairy feet of a million spiders scrabbled around inside me and there was no escape hatch for any of them.

"Damn. Sorry to be the one to let that slip. Thought you knew a long time ago."

"No, Hopp. I didn't."

"Well, Em, everybody's got secrets and reasons why they keep 'em. Half the time it's to protect themselves and half it's to protect you. Maybe sometimes it's both."

TWENTY-NINE

My body vibrated with rage when I saw the extra cars in my driveway, but I gently opened the front door in case Bob was still sleeping on the couch. I crept in and placed the lockbox on the kitchen counter.

He was still on the couch, curled up in the same position, like a furry little cinnamon roll. Had he woken since I'd left? Had he moved? I stood over him, monitoring his chest. It didn't expand for the longest time, and then the slow rise and fall proved he was still breathing. My heart started beating again. It couldn't take much more of this.

Sounds from upstairs beckoned.

Tee, Sam, and Cassie, all little busy bees in the office, packing my life away in boxes without me. Correction, packing my father's life. "What are you doing?" I asked, winded from climbing the stairs two at a time. They spun around to face me all at once, like teens caught doing drugs.

"Don't be upset, Em. We wanted to help," Tee said. "Your deadline is only a week away, and you've got an entire house to pack."

"I'm aware of my business, Tee." The temperature in the room dropped about twenty-five degrees with my tone. "By the way," I said to Cassie, "when I say watch him, I mean watch him. Be with him. Don't leave him downstairs on the couch while you come up here and rifle through my life."

"Em, what's going on?" Sam asked. "You're at eleven right now."

"Yeah, okay. Let's do this. Why not? Since everybody knew except me."

"Oh boy," Sam said. "Did Hopper tell you something?"

"I know *you* knew because you grew up here, right?" I said to Cassie.

"Em, I can—" Tee tried to jump in, but I slammed the door on her.

"But did you know, Sam?"

"Did I know what?"

"That I've been living in her house my entire life and had no idea."

"Em, listen—"

"No, Tee, you don't get to speak right now. You had forty years to speak, and you chose to lie to me the whole time. Now it's my turn. Sam? Did you know?"

"Em, I'm living in confusion right now, but I'm gathering this was *your* house," she turned and pointed to Cassie while she spoke, "before you left."

"I had no idea you didn't know," Cassie said to me. "I never would have given you that letter if I didn't think you knew."

"What letter?"

"The letter from earlier. Isn't that how you...your father wrote to me about buying the house."

"Well, we've been a little busy reading a million other letters, so I haven't read it yet."

"What does it mean, though, Em?" Sam asked. "Josiah bought the house. That's a good thing, right?"

"I don't know, Sam. I know nothing about my own life or my family's history, apparently. Everyone around me has made sure of that. Anything you need to tell me?" I asked, praying she'd say no.

"Well, shit," she said. My stomach lurched.

"Are you kidding me right now?" I didn't think we had secrets.

She sighed and then spit it out. "I only did it because he begged me to."

"Who begged you to do what, Sam?"

"The envelopes. He gave me two of them to give to you after he died."

"The envelopes? You mean the orange ones? From Dad?"

"Yeah."

"He gave you two?"

"Yeah."

"I have a stack of thirty envelopes downstairs. All the same ones. Who gave me those?"

"Not me," Sam said, holding her hands up.

"Anything else?" I asked.

"Nope."

I let silence settle into the room around us. Felt like I might explode if I discovered anything else about my life my friends had kept from me. I glanced at Tee and my heart dove into my shoes. Behind her glasses, tears had formed in her eyes, but hadn't fallen yet. She knew how bad this was.

"I don't even know where to start, Tee. How to understand why you and Dad felt compelled to lie to me about so many things. For so long. To what end? You were my rock. My teacher... mentor...mother. I trusted you without question. That's all gone now."

She closed her eyes and those tears streamed down her cheeks. I think Sam gasped, but it was hard to hear over the sound of my heart pounding. The taste of betrayal was bitter in my mouth. I thought I might throw up, but I held myself together long enough to kick Tee and Sam out.

THIRTY

I checked on Bob to make sure he was okay. He was still sleeping on the couch, even through the chaos. That was worrisome. He woke when I felt his side to confirm he was breathing and then fell back asleep immediately.

Still plagued by extra adrenaline, I considered going out back to let Dad have a piece of my mind, but what good would it do now? He didn't respect me enough when he was alive to tell me the truth, so how would yelling at him now change anything?

Cassie appeared behind me in the kitchen.

"I'm going to bed," she said.

"Fine."

"I take it your mission with the box and Hopper was unsuccessful?"

"Correct."

"I..." She seemed stumped for what to say next. "I read most of the letters."

"And?"

"Nothing jumped out."

"Okay."

"I'm...glad you stood up for yourself."

"Yeah."

"Okay," she said, walking away. *Good talk.*

After Cassie went to bed on the couch with Bob, the house became too quiet. Like the calm before the storm. Not long after I went to bed, the storm found me.

Cassie stumbled into my room panting, like the trip up the stairs had been a major challenge for her. Before I could ask what was wrong, she spoke.

"It's the—it's Bob." That was all she had to say. I jumped from the bed, raced past her, and down the stairs with my heart beating outside my chest. I don't remember taking the stairs, only being at the bottom of them, like maybe I'd learned how to fly.

Bob was still on the couch, but he wasn't sleeping anymore. He was wheezing like he couldn't catch a breath and panting hard. The air-sucking sound of it broke me in two. It was like he was trying to breathe around something in his windpipe, but it kept getting blocked with each inhalation.

"Okay, mister, I've got you. You're going to be okay." I didn't believe it this time. We needed to get him to the vet immediately.

"I'll drive," Cassie said, wheezing too. She grabbed her keys and purse from the end table by the couch and held the front door open for me as I carried Bob through it. I was glad not to have to beg her to drive or argue about whose car to take or if she would stay there or not. It was refreshing for her to offer, for once, to help without complaint. I jumped in the back with Bob on my lap and we were on our way without a hitch.

One hitch. Cassie drove like a night-blind, narcoleptic drunk. She was still wheezing, like she hadn't recovered from her trip up the stairs.

"Are you okay?"

"I'm fine."

"You sure? Do we need to go to the hospital too?"

"I'm fine," she said with finality.

"Okay. Can you put your foot down then? It's going to take us an hour to get there at this rate."

"It's late."

"And?"

"I don't see at night."

"Pull over. Now." No way I was going to deal with that when Bob couldn't breathe.

She crept to the shoulder, but I couldn't wait. I jumped out of the moving car before she put it in park. I think it frightened her. She squealed like a little girl when she realized I'd landed on my feet on the gravel.

"Out," I said, holding her door open so she could switch with me.

"But—"

"I know you hate my dog, but get in the back. Pet his head. It might help both of you feel better. Move, move!"

She climbed in the back seat and I had us at the clinic's door almost before she closed hers.

Cassie sat up on the couch with Bob, each on their respective sides. He still slept, she couldn't get to sleep. Dim light through the kitchen window highlighted the lockbox on the counter. She brought it into the living room and sat with it on her lap.

They'd tried everything to get it open and it wouldn't budge. Maybe they should take a different tack. It was not a normal safe deposit box under normal circumstances, some mystical force had kept it locked. So, instead of using brute force, she tried seducing it to open.

"Please tell us your secrets. We're running out of time," she whispered, gently caressing it.

As she brushed her hands over the sides of the box, it began to heat up. Hopeful, she pulled on the latch to see if it would move. It didn't. The box grew hotter. At first she thought it might be friction or the already warm room making the metal warmer. But when she started gasping for air and the mutt woke beside her doing the same, she dropped the box on the floor and kicked it away from them.

The tightening in her lungs, the heaviness squatting inside her. A building had collapsed on her chest again. She could barely move, but she had to get to Emma upstairs. By the time she reached Emma's doorway, she thought she might pass out.

Emma flew past her, like she didn't exist, to get to Bob. What did she expect? That was her problem. She'd begun to expect things from her daughter.

When Emma tore her from the car on the side of the road and relegated her to the back seat with the mutt, she didn't show her frustration. She even did as Emma asked. Let the beast lay his head in her lap as they both struggled to breathe. Emma drove far too fast for any reasonable person, but it cut down on the time Cassie had to spend with the mutt, so that was a positive.

A minute into the wild ride, something strange and wonderful happened after she began petting the beast. When she put her hand on his head, it loosened the tightness in her chest, letting go of whatever was holding her lungs hostage. As if the disease flowed out of her and into him. She breathed easier, but he got worse.

"What's going on?" Emma asked, looking over her shoulder into the back of the car. She pressed on the gas pedal.

"Eyes on the road!" Cassie said. She didn't want to die in a fiery car crash, but she also didn't want Emma to see what was happening with them in the back seat.

Could this be the answer Cassie had been looking for? This dirty beast was making her better somehow. Maybe he wasn't just another puzzle piece, but the actual key to it all?

She didn't have enough time to discover anything more before the car skidded to a stop in the vet's parking lot. Emma already had him in her arms before Cassie could make a move to help. And then, when she tried to get out, she couldn't. Touching him helped her, but as soon as she took her hand off him, she felt far worse. Cassie wondered, as she watched Emma carry the mutt into the clinic without looking back, if she might die before Emma returned.

"Here, I can take him," Jake said, rushing around the corner from the back of the clinic, trying to pull Bob from me.

"I've got him," I said. I couldn't let go. It might have been the last time I would hold him in my arms.

"What's going on?"

"He can't breathe. He started wheezing and wouldn't stop."

"Mark, bring the large oxygen mask to exam four ASAP," Jake said to the vet tech following us.

He led us into the exam room and I placed Bob on the table so Jake could check his vitals. Bob still wheezed, but at least he was breathing. My bar was very low for positive things by then.

I stood next to him with my hand on his side, my sweet good boy, feeling helpless. Nothing I did could change this. If I couldn't figure out how to break this goddamn curse, he was going to die. I didn't have any doubt in my mind now.

"What happened?" Jake asked, while he listened to Bob's lungs. Mark, the vet tech, raced in carrying the oxygen mask and they placed it over Bob's head. He pawed at the mask, trying to get it off.

"No, no, mister, don't do that. It's going to help you," I said, pulling his paws away. When he realized it was helping him breathe, he stopped batting at it and relaxed. He laid back down, breathing almost normally, and let Jake finish his exam.

"I don't know. He was sleeping all day on the couch and then, out of nowhere, this attack."

"Was there any stimulus around him? Anything to upset or excite him?"

"I was upstairs sleeping when it happened, but as far as I know, nothing out of the ordinary. He was sleeping on the couch with Cassie."

"Realtor moved up? Spending the night on the couch now?"

Shit. I'd forgotten the story I told him about her. How did everyone around me keep so many secrets for so long? I found one lie exhausting. But now was not the time to explain anything. "Long story."

"You said. Maybe you'll tell me sometime." He smiled at me the way he used to, with that mischievous knowing, like he was on to me. Good grief. I smiled back at him and a twinge flared up inside me. It was beginning again.

"Maybe. Maybe not," I said. One fire at a time. His smile disappeared, and he returned to being the consummate professional.

He called Mark over and gave him instructions I couldn't hear. Mark nodded and came straight for us. He put his arms under Bob and scooped him up, but I protested.

"Wait. Jake? Where's he taking him?" Mark stopped and took a step back.

"I'm going to put Bob in the oxygen chamber for a few hours and monitor him overnight."

"Overnight?"

"I'm still waiting to hear from the oncologist, but in the meantime, there are a couple things I want to check and rule out if we can."

"Is an oxygen chamber what it sounds like?"

"Hopefully it'll get him back to breathing regularly on his own. We need to stabilize him before we can figure out what's causing this. Before we take any next steps. Okay?"

"Okay," I said, because what else could I say? I was at the mercy of a curse.

"Can I stay with him?"

"You should go home and get some sleep, Em."

"I don't need sleep. I need to know he's going to be okay."

"I'll be with him all night, or Mark will. I'll call if anything changes, so keep your phone on. But try to get some sleep. You look like you haven't been getting much."

"Thanks."

"I didn't mean—you seem exhausted."

"Got it the first time."

Jake dropped his head and gave up, realizing he wouldn't be able to pry his foot from his mouth.

I massaged Bob's head around the mask while they watched me say goodbye. He didn't focus on me because he was too busy trying to breathe. The sound of his lungs struggling to keep him alive made me ache for my beautiful boy. Why was he being punished?

"I'll be here as soon as I can tomorrow, okay, mister? Please get better." I kissed the pointy spot on top of his head, over the strap of the oxygen mask, then Mark took him away. Jake and I watched them go, and I tried to erase the feeling that it might be the last time I'd ever see Bob alive.

THIRTY-ONE

Cassie and I didn't speak when we left the clinic. She'd waited in the car while I was inside with Jake and stayed in the back seat even after we got home. I didn't expect her to hold my hand through any of this, but it would have been nice to have a little support given the severity of the situation.

"Sure you're all right?" I asked after we got home. I glanced at her in the rearview mirror as we sat in the driveway. She nodded, still pale, but breathing more steadily. "In case you're wondering or care at all, Bob's staying the night in an oxygen chamber so he can breathe." I didn't wait for a response, because I figured I wouldn't get one.

Those spiders were back, wriggling around inside me. I didn't know what to do with myself. Should have followed Jake's suggestion to get some sleep, but I couldn't settle my mind or my body.

Instead of raging out back to give the dad-tree a piece of my inflamed mind, I charged inside to get something done. What? I wasn't sure. I didn't know where to start. Hopper hadn't helped with the box, or Esther, and I was back to square one.

Bob's empty bed by the couch was a gut punch. The only true thing in my life was struggling to live. How the hell was that fair? I couldn't talk to my best friends about any of it because they weren't my best friends anymore. They were lying liars who lied.

The quiet emptiness of the house smothered me. Cassie hadn't come in from the car yet and I had this sneaking and terrible feeling I would be alone for the rest of my life. How could I trust anyone to tell me the truth again? Why would I?

What Hopper had said about the house flashed through my chaotic mind. *You might find something you need in there.* What did he know?

I ran up to the attic because if there was anything else Dad was hiding, it might be there. Box after box, I tore into everything I could get my hands on. Old clothes, some of hers, some of his, some of mine. Piles of old toys, stacks of old children's books. The Giving Tree, my favorite book. It gave and gave until it had nothing left.

I threw it in the corner and kept digging.

"Where is it, Dad?" I had no clue what I was looking for. Just needed to be looking for something, anything, that might tell me what to do to save Bob. I tore around the musty space in such a fit of rage I wasn't seeing anything anymore. When I finished up there with no luck, I raced down to Dad's bedroom and ripped into it.

The room was exactly how he'd left it the last night he slept upstairs. His king bed was made, but not well. The cedar night-stands on each side welcomed me with their clean, woody scent. His scent.

I hadn't been in there since he'd died. I'd left it alone on purpose. Didn't want to disturb any of his things because once I emptied his closet there was no going back. It would be real and he would be gone.

But I needed to find something, anything that might help. So I rifled through the drawers in his nightstand to see what he'd hidden in them. A pack of cigarettes (come on, Dad), a pile of stationery, and a handwritten envelope addressed to Josiah Rosen. The writing was almost illegible, cursive and unsteady, like the writer was quite frail. It didn't have a return address. The envelope was open, so any guilt I might have had for reading a personal letter addressed to Dad dissipated because he'd already seen it.

May 4, 1999

Dear Josiah,

I received your letter. Thank you. How sad and unfortunate that happened to you and your daughter. I'm so sorry. I don't have any information that might help in the search for your beautiful girl, Cassie, but I wish you the very best. She sounds like a Ray of light. I hope you find her. I really do.

Very Sincerely Yours,
Esther Blum

Esther Blum? Dad had found Esther in May of 1999?

"What are you reading?"

I jumped out of my skin at the sound of Cassie's voice. "Jesus! Why don't people ever knock?" I folded the letter and put it back in the envelope.

"I thought you would hear me coming up the stairs." She still wasn't looking good, pale and weak.

"Why won't you go to the hospital?"

"What's that?" She pointed to the envelope in my hand.

Hopper said Tee asked him about Esther. I'd forgotten about that in my anger over the house. Didn't even bring it up to Cassie. She hadn't told me about Esther. What was she hiding?

"Old letter Dad got from someone named Esther Blum."

"What?" Cassie perked up, as I expected. "Let me see." She shot over to me with more energy than I'd seen from her since she'd arrived. I held the envelope out and she grabbed it like a hungry cat.

"Do you know her?" I asked.

"I know of her," she said, opening the letter and reading it.

"Who is she?"

"How did he find her address?" she asked under her breath. "Tee couldn't even—"

"What? Tee couldn't even what?"

She looked caught.

"Tee couldn't even what?" I repeated. I could see the gears spinning in her head, trying to come up with something to say to appease me. "Why not, right? Why should I think you might be different? Everybody lies to me. Why the hell would I expect you not to? Especially you."

"What does that mean?"

"You couldn't be bothered to get out of the damn car tonight to help me. I might lose Bob too and you couldn't care less."

"You're upset about that?"

"Yes. No. I don't know. There are too many things, so that's low on the totem pole, but it's there. Where do you think I should start?"

"I think you should get sleep before you say something you're going to regret."

"I think it's time I said all the things I might regret. Because maybe I won't."

"It's very late. I'm tired. I'm going to sleep." Cassie turned to leave, but I spun her around and snatched the letter out of her hand before she could steal it away.

"You may have reasons for being upset with your friends and your father and me, of course, but don't get confused by thinking no one cares about you," she said.

"You know nothing about me or my life. By choice, I might add."

"Fair enough. Be mad at me. I deserve some of that."

"*Some* of that?"

"Your friends cherish you, otherwise why would they come here to help you pack? Who on earth does that?"

She had a point, but I wasn't anywhere near conceding it to her. "Doesn't excuse the lifelong lying."

"Tee warned me about these high standards of yours. I suppose they're much like mine. You don't forgive. Everyone walks on eggshells around you."

"Eggshells?"

"No one can be fallible, no one can be human or make mistakes."

"No. You gave up the right to an opinion about anything in my life when you left."

"That may be, but I'm going to say what I say, anyway. Give your friends a break. Tee loves harder than anyone I've ever met. You shouldn't throw that away."

"She didn't tell me I was living in a house full of ghosts. Your terrible family's ghosts. She didn't tell me you were alive."

"Why would you think I was otherwise?" she asked, surprised and confused.

"Because Dad told me you were dead." I spit the words out like they were nails and she was drywall. Then regretted it instantly.

She deflated in front of me. I sat on the bed, all my energy drained. She stayed where she was for a long, silent moment, then sat a mile away at the foot of the bed.

"He told you I was...when? When did he say that?"

"Twenty years ago. After he took a trip to California. He cut your tree down after he got back from that trip." I wanted to see if she'd admit to what I already knew. He'd found her on that trip.

"I see." She picked at a loose thread on the comforter and took shallow, raspy breaths.

"So do I." Neither of us spoke. It became a test of wills. A standoff. The bones of the house creaked and settled and the rustling willow leaves whispered outside Dad's window by the bed. I hadn't opened the window and didn't remember it being open before, but I was too exhausted to get up and close it.

We sat in silence on the same bed with a lifetime of lies and distrust taking up the space between us. That woman was made of steel. She would not speak. I finally broke.

"What did you say to him? Why was he angry enough tell me that?"

"It's not a simple answer, Emma." It was the first time she'd said my name since she'd ridiculed it in the boardroom the day we met. Everything sounded different from her now. There was sadness in her voice I hadn't heard before.

"Simple. There was a time I thought everything in my life was simple. Straight forward. I thought I knew who I was. But now I don't know anything. Like my puzzle pieces have been torn apart and thrown into a twister, flung in every direction miles away from me. And I don't know how to put anything back together again."

When she spoke, Cassie's voice was soft, barely there.

"When you were born, you were perfect. So tiny and new." She sighed and took a deep, rattling breath, staring at the wall. "Your grandfather had his reasons. Sometimes you have to stand up for what you know is right, even when it's hard. Even if people disagree with you. Or don't understand."

"Did he take you away from us?"

"He thought he was saving us."

"Why? Why would he think taking you away from your newborn child was saving you? And why didn't you fight him? Why would you go along with it?"

"I did fight him."

"You were an adult. How could he steal you away?"

"Because he told me you both had died."

"What?" That knocked the wind out of me.

"They made me stay for observation after you were born and Josiah went home to get rest. I was medicated, because I'd had complications. Already a bit out of my head when I woke, my father told me it had been a couple days and Josiah had left to take you home. But there had been a spring storm, and you were both in a terrible accident. I remember little after that."

"Why? Why would anyone be so cruel? My God. Did you ever question if he was lying?"

"He was my father. I didn't have any reason not to believe him."

"You didn't want to say goodbye? To be at our funerals?"

"I was in shock for months. Unable to function for a very long time afterward.

"Why would anyone be so cruel?"

"What something seems on the surface isn't always what it is. He had his reasons."

"There is no good reason on earth to steal a mother away from her daughter. Did you ever think about us?"

"Of course I did. I'm not a monster."

"Jury's still out."

The weight of her betrayal had held me prisoner my whole life. To find out now she hadn't abandoned us with malice was overwhelming. I'd always hoped the rumors were true, that they'd abducted her against her will. I needed to believe she would have come back for us if she could have. That something out of her control had kept her away all this time. My mind didn't know how to process this new information, but my body did. It felt like the elephant had stepped off my chest and I could breathe again.

Her father had lied to her. A horrible, unconscionable lie. But I couldn't fault her for that. We both had terrible fathers who lied about every important thing.

"Wait," I said, acknowledging the other elephant in the room. "Dad found you twenty years ago. He went to see you."

"Yes. It was a shock." The lack of emotion in her voice was the shocking thing to me.

"So you knew at that point we were very much alive."

"I did."

"And you still didn't come—"

"I don't want you to hold a poor opinion of my father."

"Too late. But let's return to *my* father and why you didn't—"

"He did what he thought was best."

"We're still on this? How? How and for whom was it best?"

"My father knew things about the curse. About how it might affect us if we'd stayed together."

"Like what? Our heads would explode? I don't understand."

"I don't understand it myself. It's all jumbled in my head. But I think it's what he told me."

"Wait. *How it might affect us if we'd stayed together*? You said he told you we died. When did he tell you about the curse? Did he tell you we were alive?"

Cassie twisted her cross again. "I don't know. I don't remember. I'm tired." She tried to leave, but I blocked the door.

"Stop lying to me!"

She stumbled and fell back onto the bed. Her face was flushed and sweaty and her breathing labored, but I couldn't stop. I needed to know the truth. I stood over her like a wise guy with a pipe waiting for answers.

"Yes, okay?" she whispered.

"Yes, what?"

"He told me about the curse." She paused, and I waited. Afraid if I spoke, my breath would erupt into flames and burn her to a crisp. "And that you were alive."

A swelling cluster of spiders swarmed in my belly.

"When?"

"Before he died."

"When did he die?"

She said nothing at first. The guilt on her face aged her ten years.

"When did your father die, Cassie?"

"We're done talking about this. It shouldn't matter what happened so long ago. You're always trying to live in the past."

"When?"

"Chrissakes," she said, and sighed. "Nineteen-eighty-nine."

She didn't even have the courage to look at me. To own the truth of it.

"Nineteen-eighty-nine. I was ten." The words were lead in my mouth, weighing me down again. "You could have...you knew we were alive thirty years ago, and you did nothing."

My body boiled, like I might spontaneously combust.

"Get. Out. Now."

THIRTY-TWO

Maybe it was better this way. Now Emma knew. Not the full story, of course. That would cause irreparable harm. She would never understand. But she knew most of it. Cassie hadn't lied. Everything from her past was jumbled in her head too, much like the puzzle Emma mentioned. Her pieces blown about in the wind.

Two o'clock in the morning was not an ideal time to be kicked out of your house. But now, armed with essential information, Cassie could break this damn curse on her own and move on with her life.

She threw her things into her suitcases, scoffed at how messy it all looked, and dragged them, along with the lockbox, out to the car. Emma was nowhere to be found. She'd made herself scarce after their confrontation.

Where to go now? There were no hotels or motels available in Calypso Springs, especially at that hour. Also, Cassie was in no condition to go anywhere long distance. She drove the four blocks down Main Street and pulled into the driveway of the only person who might open the door for her that late at night.

She sat in the car with the lights shining into the dark house for a few minutes. She needed time to release her pride, at least enough to knock on the door. Cassie McCormack did not accept help easily and asking for it, especially from Teresa, was a soul-crushing errand. But she didn't have much of a soul left to crush, and it was fading daily, so she did what was necessary.

Cassie pulled her suitcase from the back seat of the car, leaving the lockbox on the floor. Something shiny was stuck between the cushions. A phone. It must have fallen out of Emma's pocket on their way to the vet earlier. She would leave it on the porch for her in the morning.

For now, she stored it in the zippered outer compartment of her luggage and approached the house. The porch light flicked on with attitude and Tee opened the door, groggy and yawning, before Cassie reached it. Not a welcoming sight. Cassie's head-lights had probably woken her. She'd always been a light sleeper.

Holding her head high, Cassie stood as tall as she could, grip-ping the handle of her best suitcase behind her, and spoke to her ex-best friend. "I need another favor."

Tee shook her head, like a parent after their child egged the neighbor's house again, and opened the screen door to Cassie. "Only for tonight."

Cassie nodded and strode past her, rolling her suitcase inside the dark house.

"You'll make do on the couch." Tee said. Cassie figured this wasn't up for negotiation, but she was tired of sleeping like a peasant.

"Is it a pullout? A bed would be lovely, thank you." She smiled at Tee. If looks could strangle, Cassie would have been lying dead on the floor. "I'll help."

Tee stomped down the hall without another word, which gave Cassie a minute alone in the living room to snoop. Few family photos adorned the walls and even fewer perched on side tables for display. She didn't see children, other than Emma, in any of them and only one with Tee's husband, Ted. He was a slight, hairy redhead, with an overgrown mustache and sloped shoulders. Not the man Cassie would have imagined Tee marrying. Not nearly enough Josiah in him.

When Tee returned with the linens, they took the cushions off the couch and pulled the bed out, unfolding it with a loud creak. Cassie appreciated Tee not asking why she was on her porch at—

"She kick you out too?" Tee asked.

Cassie didn't want to give Tee more ammunition, so she turned the tables. "How's Ted?" she asked. Cassie had noticed the heaviness of the room when she first came in. The things unsaid in that place were stifling, and it wasn't only between Cassie and Tee. She sensed a storm cloud of old, untended feelings floating on the stale air in there.

Tee seemed surprised by her question, like she didn't think Cassie would know she was married. "I do my homework," Cassie said.

"You always did."

They made the bed together in silence until Cassie broke it. "You never had children?"

Tee stopped tucking the sheet under the thin mattress and stared at Cassie as she spoke. "I raised yours, so I didn't have time for my own."

Tee's low blow landed. But being in her sad, loveless house, Cassie could only conjure one response. "Aside from a few obvious flaws, you did an adequate job."

Tee looked away and continued making the bed, softer in her movements. She wasn't trying to torture the sheets anymore.

"But that temper. It needs work."

Tee hung her head and let loose one sharp burst of a laugh. "Like mother, like daughter."

"Hardly."

"You *are* kidding."

"I'm cool as a frozen cake."

"Maybe now, Ice Queen, but you used to have the wickedest temper in town. You'd blow your wig off if somebody looked at you wrong."

"I don't recall any—"

"Oh, hogwash. The day you met Josiah, you changed. Before him you had a long, slow fuse. Nothing could ruffle you. When he came into the picture, you burned short and quick."

Cassie considered that. Was she so blinded by her near instant love for Josiah she hadn't noticed how it had changed her? Had that been part of the curse? Was Emma's temper part of it, too?

"I don't recall," Cassie said again.

"Are you a politician now? *I don't recall.* Things change and they stay the same too, don't they?" Tee said.

"Say what you're saying, Teresa."

"Look in a mirror once in a while."

"Why? Is my hair out of shape?" Cassie looked for a mirror.

"No, Cassandra. Your life is."

Cassie let Tee have that one, because if she responded, this would go on for days and she didn't have the energy for it.

"Get some rest. You look like hell," Tee said, turning toward the hallway.

Cassie wasn't taking her bait. Besides, no reason to argue with reality. She lay her suitcase on the floor and unzipped it, pulling out the envelope from Esther. She'd held onto it when Emma kicked her out.

"I found Esther," Cassie said, holding the envelope.

Tee stopped and turned to her. "How?"

"Do you have a pencil? A real one, not one of those mechanical pop out things. Something with an edge," Cassie said.

"Can this wait till morning?"

"Do you want me out?"

Tee glared at her.

"Pencil." Cassie held her hand out.

Tee rummaged through several kitchen drawers and brought Cassie what she needed.

"Do you have a sharpener? There's no lead here."

"Seriously?"

"This is in your best interest."

"Fine." Tee grabbed the pencil from her and rifled through more drawers until she found a small sharpener. She ground away at it while menacing Cassie with her patented death looks. "There, nice and sharp," she said, thrusting it at Cassie pointy end first.

Cassie found the invisible scribblings on the back of the envelope where someone had written on top of it, on another piece of paper, and left an imprint. She shaded over it with the side of the sharpened pencil.

White lines emerged through the shades of gray left by the pencil lead. As Cassie had hoped, it was an address. She could feel it. Everything was coming together. Soon enough, she'd be out of this town for good.

"I'll need directions to this address," Cassie said, holding the envelope up for Tee.

THIRTY-THREE

E arly the next morning, I woke under the dad-tree with Esther's letter on my mind. Something about it nagged at me, but I couldn't put my finger on it last night. I pulled the letter out of my pocket to read it again.

I don't have any information that might help in the search for your beautiful girl, Cassie, but I wish you the very best. She sounds like a Ray of light. I hope you find her. I really do.

Ray of light. Ray with a capital R.

Dew-damp and disheveled, but fully clothed, I peeled myself off the lawn and ran straight to Hopper's house. We had unfinished business.

I knocked on Hopper's door and didn't stop until he hobbled down the stairs to let me in. It was an obnoxious hour in the morning to show up at someone's home, but I wasn't leaving without answers this time. And the truth.

"All right, all right, you're wakin' the dead with all that racket," he said, answering the door. His ratty old robe, tied in haste around his thin waist, and his chaotic mop of hair sticking out at all angles, made him appear unhinged. Granted, I did wake him, but this was the first time I'd seen Hopper looking so unkempt.

"Well, Hopp, maybe the dead need to be awakened. Can we talk?"

"I got a choice?"

I answered him with a stern look. He opened the screen door and held it for me.

"Get ya some whisky or scotch—"

"It's not even six yet, Hopp."

"Beer then."

"I'm good, thanks."

"What's on your mind at this unearthly hour?" He stood next to me, towering still, but a little less so now. Like he'd shrunk a bit since the night before.

"I found this in Dad's bedroom last night." I held the letter out to him. He pulled his glasses from the large sagging pocket of his robe and read it. His poker face was on point.

"So he found her, then? Esther," I said.

"It would seem so." He continued to look at the letter instead of me, like he was inspecting it more than reading it. "This why you woke me up?"

"Anything catch your eye in that letter?"

"Real shaky handwritin'. I'd guess maybe she ain't with us no more."

"It's not the handwriting, Raymond. Or do you prefer Ray this early in the morning?" A spark of recognition lit in his eyes.

"I see," he said. "So you think she was referring to me when she wrote that Ray of light thing there?"

"Wasn't she? Did you know where they went? How would she know you knew? Did you talk to Dad?"

"Take a breath, Em. Why would I know anything about that?"

"Because you were having an affair with Mary."

"I..." He puffed up, stood taller, ready to attack the rumor head on, but then deflated and slipped down into his recliner.

"You never stopped loving her, Hopp. That's obvious. Cassie was so angry when she saw you the other day. Did the McCormacks leave because of you?"

He ran his giant hand up and down his rough cheeks. His fingers sounded like low grit sandpaper on wood over the gray stubble of his face. I thought he might break through his skin he was rubbing so hard.

"Em, I don't see what dredgin' the past up is gonna do. How's it helpin' anybody? Sure as shit ain't helpin' me, I tell ya."

"I'm sorry, Hopp. I don't mean to open old wounds, but I need to understand what happened back then."

"What's done is done. Can't be undone."

Exactly what Cassie had said.

"I'm hoping you're wrong about that because I'm going to lose Bob and my sanity if you aren't. Something happened then that's coming back to me now."

"What?"

"I'm not sure. But I need you to trust me."

"What do you wanna know?"

"I'm trying to figure out the link between Esther and my grandparents, Jack and Mary. Why Dad wrote to Esther about Cassie. Where she fits in."

Hopper fidgeted in his chair. Reliving those memories hurt him. The defeated look in his eyes tore at me, but I knew he was keeping something from me.

"I need the truth, Hopp. Please."

"I didn't see or talk to Esther after they left that summer. Didn't think she was close enough to know what was going on in town."

"Close enough? Was she close? Maiden Lake, maybe?" I felt in my pocket for the envelope the letter had been in to see if there was a postmark on it, but it wasn't there. I must have left it in Dad's bedroom. "What about when they were younger? What happened with Jack? Why did Esther and her family leave town so suddenly?"

Hopper sat forward in his chair, perching on the edge, and looked at me with great compassion. My life had become a game of twister and I didn't know how to untwist it. I hoped what he said would help.

"I don't know if Esther's still with us. Far as I know, she ain't been back to town since they left that night. I ain't heard her name in a whole lotta years till Tee asked yesterday morning. But this might be of use to you."

"I'm all ears."

He took a deep breath and let out a long, deep sigh. "Believe it or not, your grandfather wasn't always an evil man."

"Well, he stole my mother away from me and the love of your life away from you. So, that's pretty bad."

"Ayup, but he was also the one who brought us together."

Newsflash. "You're kidding. How?"

"I saw Jack and Esther sneakin' round town late into the night that summer before she left, the summer me and Mary got together. I had a job pumpin' gas at the station over in Maiden Lake and I'd come home after midnight on occasion. I seen 'em runnin' around town through everybody's backyards. They was always carrying bouquets of flowers."

"Flowers?"

"Ayup."

"So *they* put the lilacs on Mary's porch?"

"Knowin' Jack the way I do now, I'd say you lost your marbles for thinkin' it—"

"But you said—"

"Let me finish."

"Sorry."

"Jack was just like his daddy...*after* the Blums left."

"After? So before they left, he was a good guy?"

"It was more likely Esther than Jack, but yeah, I think maybe he had a good heart in him when he was with her. Few weeks after we got together, Mary told me she seen Jack and Esther put those flowers on her porch."

"If she knew they left the flowers, why would she talk to you like you'd done it?"

"Said something compelled her to after she picked 'em up. Like they was enchanted or somethin'. Minute she picked 'em up, she thought of me. I know that's a load a hooey. Ain't no such thing as enchanted flowers, but somethin' those two did led her to me. And for that, I'm grateful. Even though he ended up stealin' her away in the end."

"There's so much I still don't understand, Hopp. I need to find Esther."

"I only know what I was told when the Blums left and you know better n'anybody rumors take on a life of their own. Ghosts that haunt everybody involved." He hung his head, then looked at me with something big on his mind. "But maybe it's time to set those old ghosts free."

THIRTY-FOUR

Cassie woke to the smell of burned toast. Tee wasn't any more competent in the kitchen than she was. A steaming cup of coffee rested on a coaster on the end table next to her. She sat up and searched the living room and kitchen, but no one was about. It was later than she'd hoped to wake. The sun was already up and assaulting her through the sheer living room curtains.

Tee came bustling down the hall in a hurry. Dressed like a teacher, buttoned up and proper, she opened the front door and turned to Cassie. "I hope you got some sleep. You'll be gone by the time I get home?"

Cassie nodded once. "Thank you for letting me stay."

Tee looked like she was going to say something, but didn't.

"The dog is very sick," Cassie said as Tee turned to leave. "She's going to need support."

"Yes." Tee looked at Cassie. "She needed...she needs her mother."

Tee was halfway out the door when Cassie stopped her with a question. "Why did you do it? Did you want him that desperately?"

Tee stopped and came back to face her, looking her in the eye.

"This may be impossible for you to believe, Cassandra, but not everything in my life was about him. Or you."

Cassie left Tee's house thinking about what she'd said. Instead of turning right to go to Maiden Lake, she turned left and drove down the street to Raymond's house. They had unfinished business she needed to take care of before it was too late.

Ray Potrero was the last person she wanted to talk to, but she needed to be done with this ugliness before she left town for good. She'd never get another chance and neither of them were long for this world. He'd already lived far longer than her father had. One example of the fickle unfairness of life.

She climbed the porch stairs, glanced around the neighborhood to see if anyone was watching her, and knocked on the front door. No one answered. It was still early in the morning, so he might have been sleeping. She knocked again, louder this time.

The house was quiet. Undisturbed. That was it then. There would be no resolution. For the best. The idea of confronting him made her sweat.

She turned to leave, and when she took the last step off the porch, she heard it. The sound of a blowtorch. The fuzzy whir of blasting fire.

Cassie stood in the garage doorway watching Ray weld part of a bumper to the old cherry red Mustang her father used to covet. When she was a child, Jack drove a beige, top of the line Plymouth Satellite. Every time Ray sped by in his Mustang, her father's head would swivel and follow it like it was a magnet and he was steel. Before everything happened, she asked him why he didn't buy one. It was obvious he wanted it and they had enough money. They were one of the wealthiest families in town. They could get a brand new one, not a beat up old junker like Ray's.

"A certain kind of person drives a car like that. I'm not that kind of person, understand me?" her father said with a fierceness in his eyes she'd rarely seen in her eight years.

"Yes, Daddy." She understood nothing.

"And I never will be."

That was the end of the conversation about the car. Years later, she realized the real reason her father always watched Ray drive by. It had nothing to do with his car.

"Holy hell! Didn't see ya standin' there," Ray said, extinguishing the flame in his torch. He dropped it on the floor where he stood and flipped his welding helmet off, holding it under his right arm like a football. He was twitchy around her. "Sorry 'bout that. How can I help?" He took a step toward her, then stopped.

How could he help? What a ridiculous question coming from him. She screwed up her courage. It was now or never.

"He knew," she said. It came out in a whisper. All she could manage. So many nights she lay awake yelling at this man in her head. Why wasn't her voice cooperating now?

"Come again?"

"My father knew what you and Mother were doing."

Ray nodded, like this wasn't news. He bowed his head, staring at his boots.

"One of my earliest memories, we were sitting in the living room. Mother and me on the couch, Father in his chair across the room. Mother was reading a book, and she laughed out loud. I giggled at her laughter. They never fought. People would hear. But Father glared at her with such disdain I understood the saying *if looks could kill.*"

"Ain't nothin' I can say that's gonna make any of it better for you now."

"No, there isn't anything. But I want you to know we both knew about you. All those years of sneaking around behind our backs. Taking what was not yours to take. Ruining everything. We knew. And he wanted to get as far away from you as possible."

"That's not why he took you."

"He took us away from you. To protect us."

"But you know that's not why he took *you*."

Cassie didn't respond. She didn't understand what Ray was insinuating, but didn't want him to know that.

"Who your daddy was, that wasn't nothin' to do with me."

"You're not sorry?"

"Course I am. But what good is it now?" He looked at her for the first time. She could tell he meant it.

"You're sorry for ruining my family or for getting caught?"

"Nobody ruined your family but your daddy."

How dare he say that about Jack? "He took me away to protect me."

"You keep sayin' that, you're gonna keep believin' it. Truth is, he wasn't interested in protecting anything but his fragile ego and the curse of bigotry that ran generations deep. Thought he'd escaped it when he was younger, turns out he didn't."

Cassie's father had told her the curse was about sacrificing love. How was bigotry involved? "You don't know what you're talking about."

"I do, and I think maybe you know it deep down. But if you want to keep livin' in that fantasy, that's your choice."

"Fantasy? This was a mistake." She turned to leave when Ray spoke.

"D'you know Josiah converted after you left? Thought it would bring you back."

Cassie stopped. Breathing grew more difficult as Ray spoke.

"Became a card carryin' Catholic. Went to church and everything for a couple years, but he stopped going after he bought your old house."

She turned to face Ray. He'd moved forward, almost out of the garage onto the driveway where she was. She felt suffocated in the open air.

"I didn't know..."

"Well, now you know. You can whitewash who your daddy was if it helps you sleep at night, but if you ain't willin' to face the truth? You ain't never gonna move on from it."

"The truth? What about your truth? What you did."

"I made peace with my sins long time ago."

"You ruined two families."

"You want to go ahead and think I'm a terrible human, that's your right. I ain't gonna try to convince you otherwise. But you should know I loved Mary like Jack never did or could before they was married. That love didn't stop or go away 'cause he took her from me. The heart don't work like that. But I am sorry for the trouble it caused you."

"He took her from you?"

"You weren't the only one your daddy stole away from somebody else."

"He told me you—"

"Imagine he told you a lot of colorful things about me. Some of 'em may even be true. But I loved your mama more than anyone except my own daughter."

"Your daughter," Cassie said, as a terrible thought popped into her head unbidden. "Oh my god. You were together before and after they were married."

"Now hold on. After they married, we was never physical."

"What?"

"Much as I wanted to, I wouldn't do that. It woulda destroyed her. She was a fragile bird. She couldn't be with two men like that. Sorry to say, your daddy is your daddy."

Fragile bird would not have been the words Cassie used to describe her cold, withholding mother.

"If you weren't physical, what did you—"

"Jack never loved her, Cassie. I think you know that. It was a marriage of convenience from the get go. Hate to say that's what you were born into. But I gave her the love and support she needed. I was there for her the way your daddy never wanted to be."

"You were most certainly there."

"I take it Jack never told you the truth."

"Did Tee?"

"Yes. She did."

"I'll never forgive her. Or you. You both ruined my family."

"You can't be blamin' Tee for things that ain't her fault."

"I blame her for what she did. For protecting you."

"You're blaming her for the wrong thing, then."

"I don't think so."

"Tee didn't do what she did to protect me. She did it to protect her mother."

"How did that protect her?"

"Betty didn't know. All those years, she didn't know. Maybe she didn't want to know, I guess."

"So?"

"You gettin' pregnant with Josiah's baby was Jack's last straw. He made a plan to leave with you and blackmailed Tee to find out when you went into labor that night. She wasn't protecting me, Cassie. He was gonna tell Betty everything about Mary and me if Tee didn't tell him where you were. Betty couldn't handle that kinda news. She was too sad already. Woulda put her under. Course I didn't know any of this till Tee told me years later. She was protecting her mother. Wouldn't you do the same for yours?"

Cassie wouldn't. She'd felt nothing but disdain from and for Mary.

"Hell, you did protect your family. Why else wouldn't you tell your own daddy where you were living that year with Josiah or when you were ready to give birth?"

Cassie's mind was a storm. Why had she and Josiah kept everything a secret from her father? She couldn't remember any of it. She could barely focus on the road in front of her as she drove to Maiden Lake.

All this time she'd blamed Tee for betraying her because she thought Tee wanted to be with Josiah. But her father had blackmailed Tee? Could it be true? Everything jumbled in her head.

She'd left Ray's house with more questions than answers, but she needed to get away because it was becoming harder to breathe.

The envelope rested on the passenger seat with the address, 2219 Avery Way, burned into her mind. She was using Emma's phone for the GPS to get her there. Tee had shown her how. She'd return it to Emma after she found Esther.

When the white-haired woman answered the door, Cassie's hope soared. She was tiny, smaller than Cassie. Her clothes were wrinkled and hung off her petite frame and her skin was nearly translucent, but she had energy in her eyes that belied her advanced years. She smiled at Cassie, her face glowing with warmth.

"Well, hello. Can I help you?" the woman asked.

"I'm looking for Esther. Esther Blum."

"Oh my," she said. "I haven't heard that name in such a long time. Would you like to come in?"

"I'm in a hurry. Are you—"

"Nonsense. You look like you could use a cup of tea."

"Are you Esther?"

"Yes, my name is Esther."

The sharp, high-pitched whistle of a hot tea pot sang from the kitchen at the back of the house.

"Oh my, it's ready." Without another word, the woman shuffled back into the house, leaving Cassie alone on her front porch with the door open.

"I'll pour you a cup," Esther called from the kitchen. "Come in and close the door now. We don't want to send an invitation to the flies. They're aggressive this time of year."

Cassie didn't know if this was the Esther she was looking for. She entered the small house with trepidation, glancing around at the photos of people she didn't know on the walls. It was cozy, with a fireplace in the middle of the living room, and warm, like love had lived there.

She made her way to the bright kitchen and found Esther pouring her tea.

"Milk?" Esther asked.

"Are you Esther Blum?" Cassie asked.

"Well, no." Esther poured milk into the tea.

"You're not?" Cassie's chest tightened and her breathing quickened. She wouldn't find her in time. "Damn it." She spun around and hurried to the front door without another word to the imposter Esther.

"She used to live here before we moved in, my Ralph and I," Esther said, following Cassie into the living room.

Cassie faced the old woman. "When?"

"Oh, let's see. We bought the house from the sisters back in 1999. It's been such a long time! Did you want your tea?" Esther said, holding a cup for Cassie.

"Sisters?"

"Well, yes. The Blum sisters. Esther and Dahlia. I much preferred Esther. Dahlia was a cold cup of tea."

"Did they leave a forwarding address?" Cassie asked, hopeful this Esther would have information to reverse her out of this dead end.

"Oh my, well, we keep all of our records in a safe at the bank, you know, in case we have a fire or something awful like that."

"Can you call the bank to find out? Or go down? We could look through your paperwork."

"That would be fun, I suppose, but I would have to find the paperwork for the safe deposit box. My Ralph took care of all that. Plus, it's Sunday and they don't open till tomorrow, so I wouldn't be able to get down there till then. Are you in a hurry to find her?"

All the hope in Cassie deflated. Her breathing became much more labored, and it took every ounce of her energy to stand up now. "I am," she said, turning to leave.

"Do you want me to call tomorrow?" Esther asked, as Cassie opened the front door to leave.

"Don't bother."

"What about your tea?"

"I'm not thirsty."

Cassie left the house barely able to move. Her body had become unnaturally heavy. They couldn't open the box. The mutt most likely hadn't made it through the night. And Esther was a lost cause.

As she pulled away from the curb, the wrong Esther shouted to her from the porch to stop. She shuffled down the stairs and over to the driver's side of the car. Cassie rolled her window down to see what she needed.

"I almost forgot about this. Thank you for reminding me," Esther said, holding a small white square of paper in her hand. She wheezed with the effort of chasing after Cassie.

A phone rang.

Esther leaned forward toward the open car window and Cassie presented her with a raised forefinger to keep her at arm's length. "Hold that thought," Cassie said as she pulled her purse onto her lap. She'd turned her own phone off, so she knew it was Emma's. Fumbling with the purse zipper, she worried she'd miss the call, but pulled the phone out before it stopped ringing.

The caller ID read Maiden Lake Animal Clinic. Her stomach jumped. She didn't have hope the mutt had made it through the night. *She* almost hadn't.

"Hello?" Cassie said.

"Hi, I'm looking for Emma Rosen?" The girl's voice lacked strength.

"She's not available right now. Is this about the—about Bob?"

"Dr. Benson wanted me to call and let her know he's done and ready for pickup."

That was it then. He was gone.

"They don't want to keep him there for cremation?"

"Cremation?" The girl on the other end of the line sounded flummoxed.

"We will not bury him in the backyard."

"Why would you bury him?"

"You said he was done."

"He's done with his tests and off the oxygen. Geez. Dr. Benson left Emma a message earlier."

"I see." Much better news. "Is he going to make it, then?"

"I think so," the girl said. She knew nothing else about his condition.

"Is Dr. Benson available?"

"He went home for the day. He'll be back tonight if you want to call then."

Cassie hung up. She had no intention of talking to the vet. In fact, it was good news he wasn't at the clinic. She didn't want to do this, but, unfortunately, that beast was part of this mess and she needed him.

She put the car in gear as someone sniffled next to her in the street. She'd forgotten about Esther standing outside her window and almost drove away.

"I'm sorry. What did you want to give me?" Cassie asked.

Esther's eyes were teary. "I do hope Bob gets well soon," she said with a weak smile, and wiped her cheek with the back of her arthritic hand. Esther was a sensitive soul.

With shaky, gnarled fingers, she handed Cassie a small black-and-white photo. "I found it in the back of a kitchen drawer when we moved in all those years ago. I was so busy unpacking and making our home, I forgot all about it till now. If you find Esther, will you please return it for me? I'd be very grateful. Such a lovely photo of them."

Cassie took the picture, and one look sent a jolt of energy through her entire body. Esther. She'd found her.

THIRTY-FIVE

According to Hopper, Jack and his father had spread rumors about the Blums around town after they left sixty years ago. Terrible, nasty things. A false narrative from sick minds.

I was too preoccupied processing everything he'd told me about Jack & Esther to notice what was waiting on my porch. I felt it before I knew what it was under my foot. My cell phone, lying in the middle of the porch. Luckily, I realized I was standing on something fragile before I put my full weight down. She didn't place it against the door, out of harm's way, where no one would step on it. Seemed like Cassie had thrown it and run away. Nice of her to take care of my things. It justified my decision to kick her out even more.

Our old grandfather clock chimed eight times in the corner when I walked in the door. I was still thinking about everything Hopper had told me, but I'd sort through all of that later after I checked on Bob. The clock reminded me I hadn't talked to Jake in hours.

As I dialed the clinic, a dark feeling of unease swept through me.

"Hi, this is Emma Rosen. I'm calling about Bob, the golden—"

"Yep, he's all set," the girl said. I didn't recognize her voice. She must have been new.

"What do you mean, all set?"

"Your mother picked him up about ten minutes ago. He should be home soon."

"My mother? Wait, he's okay? He's breathing okay?"

"Dr. Benson left you a message earlier."

I hadn't seen the notification.

"Did she say where she was—never mind." Of course she didn't tell the daft girl at the front desk where she was going. Why would she do that?

My gut told me something wasn't right.

I raced into the kitchen and checked the counter where I'd left it after I came home from Hopper's the night before. It wasn't there. The living room, upstairs, I even searched the attic. The lockbox was gone.

She must have taken it with her when I kicked her out last night. I'd locked myself in my room before she left, avoiding any more contact. How could I be foolish enough to think she wouldn't take something so important with her.

I didn't know where she was or what she was doing with Bob, but I knew one thing for certain: she wasn't bringing him home to me.

THIRTY-SIX

Cassie pulled into the old leaning garage and turned off her car. It was dark and cool in there, secret. Bob lay on the seat next to her, panting. The closer they were to that ancient house, the harder it was for both of them to breathe. She touched his back and her lungs opened enough for her to catch a good breath. He coughed and wheezed. She wasn't sure how much longer either of them could keep this up.

She took the lockbox and dead carnation she'd stolen from Emma's porch, then struggled to close the decrepit garage door behind them. It was imperative to hide her car from anyone who might come searching for them. She and Bob trudged to the house side by side. They were in this together now.

The porch creaked and groaned when they climbed the steps. The dead vines were still dead. Had she expected things to be different because she knew who really lived in this house?

Cassie knocked, the door opened. Pearl, the white-haired one, stared at her, then tried to close the door on her. As she'd done with Emma, Cassie threw her body in between the door and the frame so Pearl couldn't close it. She stopped short of slamming the door on Cassie. The kitchen was empty. No sign of Fern or the wheelchair. Pearl glanced down at the box under Cassie's arm, the dead pink carnation in her hand, and Bob by her side.

Cassie held up the photo the other Esther had given her. "I believe this belongs to you."

Pearl stared at her, as if she couldn't be bothered to look at a picture, but when she did, her demeanor changed.

"Where'd you get that?" she asked, grabbing it from Cassie.

"Doesn't matter. We don't have a lot of time." Cassie began wheezing and couldn't stop. Sitting beside her, Bob wheezed too.

"Well, come on, then." Pearl let go of the door and shuffled into the kitchen without another word, leaving the path clear for them to move inside the house.

THIRTY-SEVEN

I called Cassie non-stop. Each time it went straight to voicemail. She'd said the curse probably began at the nest, so that's where I needed to go first. I couldn't think about what she might do to Bob there. Everything was about her. She'd made that clear last night. Dad and I didn't figure into her life at all if she knew the truth thirty years ago and didn't come back for us.

My truck wouldn't start. I tried it over and over, but it whined and complained and then gave up the ghost altogether.

"No. Not now. Worst time ever for you to choose unreliable. Please. Please!"

I tried a few more times, but none of my begging worked. I called Hopper to see if I could borrow his truck, but he didn't answer. He must have been welding again. I ran down to his house, panting by the time I got there, but he wasn't around, not even in the garage.

Then I remembered Jake had left me a message. I stood in the doorway of Hopper's garage, listening to it.

"Morning, Em. Great news." His voice was full of optimism. "Bob's improvement is remarkable. We monitored him overnight and by this morning he was breathing on his own with no effort and his energy levels were back to normal." The best news I'd had in a long time.

"Listen, I still don't know what this is, but we'll keep at it till we figure it out. I'll let you know as soon as I hear from the oncologist. In the meantime, he's ready to go home. Sorry for calling so early. I hope you got some rest. Not because you...ugh. Right. Pardon me while I pry my foot from my mouth again. You really look great, Em. Anyway, I'm shutting up now. If you have any questions, or want to talk, this is my cell."

My heart soared. Bob was better, for now at least. And Jake was charming as hell, but every minute mattered. Cassie hadn't let him anywhere near her since she'd been there with us. So why would she steal him away? I couldn't trust her with anything important in my life, couldn't even trust her to be a decent human being.

I swallowed my pride and called Sam. I needed a ride to the nest.

THIRTY-EIGHT

S till wheezing, Cassie dropped the box and carnation on the cluttered kitchen table and sat. Bob rested on the filthy floor next to her. She put her hand on his back for a bit of relief. The burning in her throat dissipated and her chest opened up, like thick fog clearing in a sudden breeze.

Pearl pulled a glass from a dirty cupboard, filled it from the tap, and put it down in front of Cassie.

"Thank you, I'm fine," Cassie said. Coughing wreaked havoc on her throat. It was rough and raw, but nothing was safe to touch in that filthy house.

"Don't sound fine." Pearl tucked the photo into her robe pocket and sat across from Cassie at the table. She'd put her cigarette out when they'd come into the house and hadn't lit another one.

Cassie dragged her hand away from Bob's back when he wheezed. He stopped almost immediately and perked up, while she fell back into the heaviness consuming her.

"'S'this?" Pearl tapped her forefinger against the side of the safe deposit box.

"Can you open it?" Cassie asked.

"Prolly. What's in it?"

"Open it."

"Bossy."

"Please. Open it."

Pearl stared at the box longer than seemed appropriate and then tried to open it. She couldn't. Cassie hadn't been positive which one was Esther, but now she knew for sure.

"Where is Esther?" Cassie asked, pulling the box back over in front of her again.

"Who?"

"I don't have time for games. Where is she?"

The sound of rubber wheels creaking over the broken linoleum startled Cassie. She turned around to find Bob standing next to Fern's wheelchair, wagging his tail and panting.

"It's time, Dahli," Fern said to Pearl.

"No!" Pearl shouted. Her ferocity was alarming.

"She came back to us, Dahli. We talked about this." Fern's voice was confident standing up to Pearl. Different from when Cassie initially met her. "Everything will be okay."

"How can you say that? You don't know that," Pearl said, her voice on the edge of breaking.

"I don't know what's happening here and, frankly, I don't have time for it," Cassie said, on a mission. She rushed the lockbox over to Fern and set it on her frail lap. "Can you open this?" she asked, taking a step back.

Fern stared at the box, then held her gnarled hand over the top of it without touching the metal.

"Please open it," Cassie said.

Fern glanced at Pearl with sadness and determination in her eyes. "It's time," she said, taking the latch between her thumb and forefinger. She pulled, but nothing happened. The box remained closed. Cassie's heart sank. Did she figure this all wrong?

Fern closed her eyes and whispered to the box like she was praying or holding a secret conversation with it. Much like Cassie had done the night before. It hadn't turned out well for her. Maybe this would be different. Fern continued speaking to the box and tried the latch again. The top loosened and lifted like the cover of a tomb opening for the first time in a thousand years.

"Thank you, Esther," Cassie said. Her pulse quickened and her body buzzed with renewed energy, knowing she was one step closer to surviving. "I have questions."

"I imagine you do, dear." Esther sat gazing into the box, transfixed.

Pearl grumbled under her breath at both of them.

THIRTY-NINE

I'd briefed Sam on the phone about the situation with Bob, so when she picked me up in her Jeep we didn't speak until we were almost to the nest. The air grew stale between us. Uncomfortable. Something we'd never experienced before.

I scoured both sides of the road, searching for any sign of Cassie's rental car, or Bob wandering through backyards or fields. Sam kept glancing over at me, like she wanted to make sure I was still there.

"I'm sorry! I'm really, really sorry, Em! Okay?" she blurted out. "He made me promise not to tell you. I hated keeping a secret from you. He said it would be a fun little surprise, not this massive quagmire of shit you're going through. I'm so sorry."

Desperation threaded through her voice. It was reedy and stretched thin. I'd never heard her like that before.

"If I'd known all this was going to happen, I never would have—"

"It's okay," I whispered.

"It is?"

"It's fine."

"Oh. Okay."

"What?"

"I know what that means."

"It means it's fine."

"No, it means you're going to hold on to it for another fifty years and use it against me whenever you need..."

"Whenever I need what?"

"Nevermind."

"Sam."

"Em, I love you, but you don't exactly let things go. Like, ever."

"That's ridiculous. I let things go all the time."

"You're still angry about Jasper Jenkins stealing your lunch box in kindergarten."

"Who does that? Who steals someone else's lunch?" I felt the angst rise in me thinking about it. She smirked like I'd made her point. I sulked for a minute in the truth of what she'd said, not willing to concede.

"The turn's up here," I said. "And you're wrong."

"Em, come on."

"Is this why we've never had an argument?"

"What?"

"We never argue." Cassie said my friends walked on eggshells around me. I thought it was ridiculous. But did she see, in less than a week, something I hadn't in forty years?

"Well, I'd consider that a good thing, wouldn't you?" Sam asked.

"Not if you're tiptoeing around me, afraid to rock the boat or tell me the truth. Afraid I'll hold on to it forever if you do or say something I don't like."

"You know I can't tiptoe. It hurts my bunion. And I don't like boats."

"I'm serious."

"So am I," she said, smiling. But what kind of friendship could we have if we weren't honest with each other? If we couldn't trust one another to tell the truth?

She turned onto the dirt path leading into the woods and we

bumped our way through the field toward the parking area. There was no sign of Cassie, her car, or Bob.

"It's been a hell of a month, Sam. Losing Dad. Then, Cassie. What? I mean seriously, what?"

"Right?" Sam said.

"I can't lose Bob too."

"You're not going to," she said, grabbing my hand and squeezing.

"I'm sorry if I've been...whatever I've been. I feel like I don't know who I am anymore, or who I'm supposed to be. I'm forty years old. I thought I knew everything I needed to know."

"Maybe that's the problem."

"Meaning?"

"You're supposed to be who *you* decide to be, Em. I don't think you've thought about that much, have you? You've always done what other people needed, mostly what your father needed. The map of Emma had already been drawn in ink when you were born, so you made no room for discovery. About yourself or anyone else."

The map of Emma? She was right. My map had been drawn the minute my mother left that hospital, but what could I do about it now?

"Goddamnit!"

"What?" Sam slammed on the brakes. "Did I hit something?" The Jeep skidded to a stop in the middle of the dirt path and we both lurched forward. I wasn't wearing my seatbelt and Sam flung her arm across my chest, holding me back from hitting the windshield. Had my friends been holding themselves back from slamming into the unyielding windshield that was me all this time?

"I hate it when you make sense," I said, looking at her arm still stretched across my chest. I reached up and held it with both hands.

"Shit, Em! Don't do that when I'm driving. Or, you know, have less aggressive epiphanies when we're moving in the Jeep."

"Sorry."

She took a breath, squeezed my hands in hers, and we continued on into the woods.

"Keeping in mind what I said about discovery..."

"What's she doing here?" Tee stood next to her car waiting for us at the dead end of the trail.

"I called her."

"Sam."

"She loves you and wants to help find Bob. You need to listen to her. Only way out is through, Em. Maybe it's time to draw a new map, yeah? Discovery is fun. Yay!"

I wanted to impale Sam with the sharp end of her snarky wit. "Or I could lock myself in the Jeep and never come out."

"Way to adult, Em."

"I hate you."

"Love you, too."

Tee smiled solemnly as we pulled up next to her. I didn't want to be the kind of person others had to walk on eggshells around. Wielding my friendship like a weapon. I'd listen to what she had to say and try to reserve judgment till afterward like a reasonable adult.

I opened the door and climbed out, facing Tee. We stood glancing at one another for a second or two, which felt like a year. She spoke.

"Let's go find Bob."

Exactly what I needed to hear. I'd save adulting for another time.

FORTY

Cassie and Esther sat opposite each other at the kitchen table. Pearl paced behind them, muttering to herself, wearing deeper grooves into the floor.

Esther held the box tight on her lap. Cassie couldn't see what was inside.

"My father said you could help me. Jack McCormack. Do you remember him?"

A sliver of a smile parted Esther's lips, and she glanced at Cassie. Her red-rimmed, glassy eyes answered the question.

"Were you close?" Cassie asked.

"Close, huh," Pearl scoffed from the corner. Her voice grew thorns.

"You're not helping, Dahli," Esther said.

"Why do you call her Dahli?" Cassie asked, frustrated with them.

"I suppose that's a good place to start, dear. My name is Esther Blum, as you cleverly figured out, not Fern Blackwell. And this is my sister, Dahlia Blum, not Pearl."

"Why did you change your names?"

"I loathed having to, of course, but it was necessary when we moved back to Calypso Springs. The rumors had destroyed our good name all those years ago. We worried we wouldn't survive the backlash if people still believed the awful things they'd said about our family," Esther said.

"Starting fresh was easier than trying to explain we weren't some sick sex cult family stealing money from the town. That sonofabitch Jack and his father did a real number on us. They was the ones embezzlin' from the bank," Dahlia said.

"Dahli, please."

"I'm speaking the truth."

"Dahlia possesses specific feelings toward your father I don't share," Esther said to Cassie.

"My father? Why on earth would he spread rumors about you?"

"He was very angry with me. But we'll get to all that." Esther fidgeted in her chair. "What do we have in here?" she said, returning her attention to the lockbox. She pulled a bouquet of dead forget-me-not flowers from the bottom of it and held them to her chest like a lost treasure found. Forget-me-nots. The same flowers that, according to their x-rays, had filled Cassie's and Bob's lungs like invasive kudzu vines.

Cassie felt ridiculous about the question she had to ask because any sensible person would. But if this woman couldn't help her, the terrible truth was simple. She was out of options.

"Are you aware of my family curse?" she asked, sucking all the air out of the room. Esther and Dahlia stared at her, one with affection, one with wariness. "Something very similar to those flowers is growing inside my chest because of it. I'm going to die if I can't figure out how to break it. My father told me to find you and bring you this box. He said you would help me."

"I hope we can, dear," Esther said. It seemed as though she knew what Cassie was there for.

"How do you know my father? Who cursed us? What's in the box?"

"All splendid questions. You are very curious indeed. A wonderful quality. Let's start with the last question first," Esther said. She lifted two letters from the box and placed them on her lap with great care. When she removed the faded pink diary with sunflowers and Cassie's name sketched on the front, Cassie's heart beat double-time.

"I believe this belongs to you," Esther said, handing it to Cassie.

"How did it get in there?"

"Sometimes our lost things find their way back to us," Esther said. She gazed at Cassie as though she wanted to say something important, but then refocused on the letters.

Cassie skimmed through her diary, flooded with memories of Josiah. The pages heated as she fell in love with her mischievous giant all over again. That wicked, irreverent sense of humor he had and the way he made her feel like she was the only person in the world who mattered. His hungry lips, desperate for hers on so many sultry nights that summer. As she kept reading, kept yearning for a love she would never have again, her chest tightened and she gasped for breath. Without another thought, she threw the book across the table away from her.

"What else is in there?" Cassie asked through shallow breaths, praying whatever was there would help save her.

"Are you all right, dear? Goodness, you don't sound well."

"Like I said, I have little time."

"What brings on these attacks?"

"Memories, powerful feelings."

"I see." Esther glanced at the diary on the table with a knowing look.

"Do you? Because I'm not any closer to finding the answers I need."

Esther pulled an old dog collar, a short piece of frayed rope, and a jagged shard of thick red plastic from the box and put them on the table. Cassie didn't understand their significance, but if there wasn't something else in the box, she would have to choose her worst and only recourse.

She leaned down and put her hand on Bob's back again, reassuring herself the dreadful option was still available, and breathed easier knowing it was.

"What does any of that have to do with the curse?" Cassie asked, wagging her hand at the items on the table.

"This letter from your father," Esther said, sliding the yellowed paper across the table to Cassie with her shaky hand, "will help you understand more."

Cassie took the letter from Esther and it felt like fire between her fingers. She threw it on the table too.

"His anger could do that," Esther said. Dahlia grunted from the corner.

"Burn?" Cassie asked.

"Yes, unfortunately."

Cassie moved closer to the table to read the letter where it lay without touching it again.

Esther,

It's been a week since you left and I don't know why I'm writing this. I'm never going to send it to you. We're a lost cause. Everything was a lie. You never loved me. I was a game to you. A silly, stupid boy who fell for the wrong kind of girl.

You wanted to change the world, and I believed you. I'm not the world, but you've changed me. I never thought you were capable of such duplicity, but you proved we never really know anyone. My father was right. Your apple fell at the foot of your father's tree. I'll never look at you people the same way again.

I regret everything. Every minute. Every kiss.

Every word. I never should have talked to you in the first place that day at the spring. I should have made you leave me, let me drown with Bo. Death would have been better than the torture of betrayal you left me with that night.

I blame Calypso too. She put me under your spell. Enchanted me just to break me. All a game for both of you. Don't worry, I won't ever feel that kind of pain again. But you and everyone you love will. Because love is a lie. It will be as foreign to you and your children as I am to you now. I made sure of it that night with Calypso. She owed me.

We said we'd never forget each other, but that was another empty promise. Another lie. How ridiculous it all seems now. Forget-me-nots. It's only been a week and I bet you've already forgotten me. But you're not the only one who's capable of that. In fact, you're fading as I write this. I can't even remember the color of your eyes.

Jack

Tears flowed down Esther's withered face. Cassie wasn't sure what to think of the letter. It created more questions than answers.

"What did you do to make him hate you?" she asked Esther.

"I saved his life."

"Why would he hate you for that? I don't understand."

"Neither did he."

"How does this letter help me break the curse?"

Esther glanced at Dahlia, who had stopped pacing in the corner of the kitchen and stood a statue, listening. "This is what we've been waiting for," Esther said to her.

"I know." Dahlia sighed and crossed her arms, as if resigning herself to whatever decision Esther had made. "I'm here," Dahlia continued.

"I need to explain a few things," Esther said to Cassie.

"Please hurry," Cassie replied.

"My father was a strict disciplinarian. Abusive by modern standards. When I was a child, he injured me and I went deaf." Esther glanced at Dahlia, but Dahlia averted her eyes and wouldn't maintain contact with her. Cassie felt the tension thicken between them.

"That's terrible. I'm sorry..." Cassie said, horrified by the thought.

"He didn't want me to learn sign language because he thought it was the language of the devil, so I found other ways to communicate with people," Esther said.

"How does this pertain to—"

"I fell in love with your father in Calypso's spring. Flowers became our mode of communication because they were enchanting. Magical even."

"Flowers," Cassie repeated. The revelation intrigued her, but she still didn't understand how it fit into her own story.

"When I found Jack that day at the spring, he was exhausted, treading water in the middle of it with his poodle, Bo," Esther said. "Back then, the pool was heavenly, but also very dangerous. The water was higher, only about ten feet from the top edge, but still too far down to get out without help. And there were no vines across the surface to buoy you if you fell in. No ladder or stairs or rope, no way to escape. You were stuck until someone found you, or heaven forbid, no one did. The day I found your father, Bo had fallen in chasing a rabbit through the woods. Jack loved his dog so much, the damn fool jumped in to save him. Of course, I would have done the same thing for my Bailey. Our dogs were our best friends back then. Our only friends."

"What did you do?" Cassie asked.

"I ran home and found a sled and rope," Esther said. She pointed to the piece of red plastic and bit of rope she'd pulled from the lockbox and put on the table. "My sister and I—"

"We saved them. Pulled them out," Dahlia said, interrupting her.

"So where was the betrayal?" Cassie asked.

"That came later. First, there was love. And magic," Esther said.

"Magic?"

"Beautiful magic and dark magic, all from the same source," Esther said. "After Calypso enchanted us with—"

"Enchanted you? Calypso, the water spirit? She's a myth. She's not real. She can't be real. Is she real?" The memory of glowing light under the water at the nest struck Cassie.

"I'll show you the answer if you let me."

Cassie wasn't sure what that meant or whom to believe at this point.

"Calypso gave us a glorious gift. My garden sprang to life with thousands of flowers where none had grown before and they were all enchanted."

"Enchanted," Cassie repeated, not quite on board.

"Yes, the flowers spoke to me and helped me bring true love together. Jack and I didn't want to keep this delightful power to ourselves, so we spread it around town, leaving flowers on doorsteps in the middle of the night. But as happy as we were together, we knew we were loving on borrowed time. Our fathers despised one another and would have done anything to keep us apart."

"Why?"

"Bigotry is a powerful weapon when wielded against love. But love is stronger. Always will be," Esther said to Cassie.

"Is it?" When she was young and foolish, Cassie believed her love for Josiah would prevail against any terrible thing in her life, but she'd spent so many years living the opposite of that notion in order to survive, she knew it wasn't true.

"I believe it is," Esther said with both conviction and sadness in her voice.

"What happened the night you left? The night you betrayed him?"

"I want you to know, dear Cassandra, if I'd known about you before it all happened that night, I never would have allowed my father to—"

"Known what about me? I didn't exist. My father wasn't even married to my mother yet."

"And he never would be," Esther said.

The old woman was making even less sense now, talking in circles. Of course he would be married to Cassie's mother.

"I don't know who you are or what you did to my father, but I think I've heard enough." No closer to understanding how she would survive, Cassie stood to leave but became dizzy and disoriented. She fell back to the chair and Bob rushed to her side. He looked at her as if he knew he was her only choice now, and was a willing participant. That couldn't have been the case, of course. Dogs don't comprehend life at that level, but there seemed to be understanding in those sad, rust-colored eyes.

Something shifted in her. An appreciation for him, for the selflessness of that notion, even if it was only in her mind. But she couldn't let it sway her from what she needed to do.

Cassie lay her hand on Bob's back and life began flowing into her again. And out of him. Her lungs cleared as his filled with muck. He panted louder and grew weaker.

This was it. Her only way out. It would devastate Emma to lose Bob, but Cassie had no choice. She tried to put the last week out of her mind. She'd come back here with a simple goal. Save herself. And now she was all at sea, bobbing and twisting with confusion and an overwhelming sadness for all she'd lost and all she'd given up. Feeling the anguish and guilt she hadn't allowed herself to feel for years.

"What are you doing to that poor dog?" Dahlia asked. She approached Cassie from the corner.

Bob wheezed and coughed and collapsed to the floor. His body went limp under Cassie's hand and she knew in that moment how this would devastate Emma. She couldn't go through with it. She would rather sacrifice herself than make Emma suffer any more.

This was quite a discovery for her, but before she had time to acknowledge what it truly meant, she realized she couldn't pull her hand off Bob's back. It wouldn't release.

"Look at her, the color is back in her face. She's taking life from him," Dahlia said to Esther.

"You can't do that, Cassie," Esther said, frantic now. She tried to get out of her chair, but didn't seem to have the strength. Dahlia rushed to help her. "It'll destroy Emma."

"I'm trying to stop it, but I can't separate myself."

Esther and Dahlia shared a grave look. "I have to. It's the only way," Esther said.

"But we don't know what it'll do to you." Dahlia's concern broke her husky voice.

"No, we don't," Esther said, determined.

Dahlia wheeled Esther over to face Cassie, so close Cassie felt trapped. She still couldn't lift her hand off Bob's back. He was not well. As she approached, Esther wore an expression Cassie didn't understand, both fearful and compassionate at once.

"I'm so sorry, dear. This is going to hurt."

FORTY-ONE

We checked the nest and surrounding area in the woods for Bob and Cassie, but they were nowhere to be found. It shook me thinking she might have done something to him there, but the vines were all still intact. Nothing had broken through them, so I assumed no one had been back there since we left yesterday.

When we returned to the cars, Sam hopped in her Jeep so fast I didn't have time to get in before she pulled away from me and Tee.

"Hey! What are you—"

"You two have things to discuss. I'm going to drive around town now. Look for a sweet golden retriever and a blue Kia Rio. If I find either, I'll call. You do the same. I'll take north and east, you take south and west. Yes?"

"I'm not a fan of you, today."

"Love you, too." Sam winked and drove away, leaving us alone to contend with our mess.

We did not do that. Tee and I drove around the outskirts of town in strained silence, stopping to question anyone who might have seen Bob with Cassie. It all led nowhere. When we'd exhausted our options in Calypso Springs, we drove to Maiden

Lake and Rock Hill, the next towns over, to search the country-side. And still found nothing.

I continued calling Cassie's cell. Each time, straight to voice-mail. Not knowing where Bob was killed me. Every shake of a stranger's head, every "no" we heard, dragged me more and more into deep panic. I didn't know what Cassie was thinking, what he could mean for her, if he was all right, if she'd done something to him, with him. Every second of not knowing became torture.

After being out all day, scouring all three towns, we arrived back at the house around seven that evening. Sam waited with Hopper on the front porch.

I reached for the handle to open the door, but Tee stopped me. "I'm sorry we didn't find him, Em."

"Yet," I said. "We didn't find him yet." My fingers rested on the handle, ready to pull.

"I know we will. We will. Em, can I please—"

"It's late and I'm exhaust—"

"We will not get through this if you don't listen to me."

"Do we need to get through it? We had a good run."

"You don't mean that."

I opened the door and sat there for a minute. I could feel her gaze on me, but didn't have the strength to face her. "We'll talk when we find Bob. Okay? Let's find him first."

I didn't give her the opportunity to respond before I peeled myself off the seat and out of the car. The adrenaline had turned to cement in my veins. My body felt like a sack of stones, every movement difficult and stiff. I greeted Sam and Hopper on the porch with a nod, unlocked the door, and collapsed on the couch.

When I woke a couple hours later, two things surprised me. Thing One: that I could fall asleep at all, and Thing Two: that Tee sat next to me with her hand resting on my leg, wide awake.

"How long was I out? How long have you been sitting there?" I whispered. When I was ten and had the flu, Tee took sick leave for a week to care for me. She only left my side to go to the bath-room and cook.

Hopper snored in Dad's recliner in the corner and Sam slept in the oversized chair next to the couch. She looked like a little girl, all curled up in a ball in it. I was comforted to see my friends had stayed without me asking them to.

Tee motioned toward the back door.

"When we find Bob," I whispered.

"No, Emma. Now." When you're forced to face the truth of your life, how do you handle it? Do you run away or do you stand and meet it head on? I was tired of running. Tired, period.

We slipped off the couch and crept out to the backyard. The sky was losing its light, so it couldn't have been much after nine o'clock. This terrible day would never end.

"Where are you going?" I asked, stopping far short of the canopy of willow branches. Tee headed straight for it.

"We should have done this before, Em. We should have talked about things instead of sidestepping and burying them. It wasn't healthy or right. I know that. He knows it too."

"He?"

"Come on, honey. We're past the secrets now. Let's go." She disappeared behind the curtain of the dad-tree.

"What do you mean by *he*?" I asked, following her inside the canopy, still playing dumb, in case she wasn't referring to what I thought she was referring to.

"Josiah, tell your daughter you're here," Tee said. To. The. Tree. It shook and swayed, branches flying back and forth as if in a strong wind, but there was no wind. "Subtlety not in your vocabulary? Settle down. Jeez," Tee said.

"You know? How did you—"

"I was out here that first night."

News.

"After he died, I came over to talk to him. I needed to talk to him, you know?"

I sighed and nodded. Of course I knew.

"I didn't want to disturb you inside. It was late, so I stayed out here, under the tree. He didn't make a fuss at first, not until I said something about Cassie. He rustled around, fidgeting like he used to whenever her name came up after she left. I don't know how he's this new version of himself, but I knew it was him."

"And how do you feel about that?" I asked.

"Feel about it?"

"How does it...when you realized, did you think, *wow, my mind took a lap without me*?"

"Is that why you didn't tell me about him? It? Him? You thought your deck was one card short?"

"I did until now. I didn't know how it was possible. I thought you'd think..."

"Think what? Less of you? Judge you? Want to commit you?"

"Yes, yes, and possibly yes."

"Emma, you're family. Nothing you say or do will ever change how I feel about you. We're your family. We've got you, no matter what. Me, Sam, even my idiot father. We've tried to show you that over the years and especially the last couple months, but you've shut us out. Quite literally."

"I think I had good reason not to trust you."

"Fair point to an extent, but this was before recent revelations. It's been going on far longer than the last month or two. After Jake, when you came home from Maiden Lake to take care of Josiah, you barricaded yourself off from all of us."

"How so?"

"Honey, it's been an open secret between us forever. You somehow possess strange natural abilities. Right? The flowers? It's unexplainable. And the misery you went through with Jake. But we couldn't help you deal with any of it because you never wanted to talk about it and we didn't know how to approach you without scaring you away."

Scaring me away? There was that eggshell thing again. Everybody worried about how I would react to them.

"I didn't want to burden you. I was trying to work it out myself."

"Why? Why would you choose to go through the heartbreak

of Jake alone? Or the confusion with the flowers? We may not
have been able to understand exactly what you were dealing with,
but we could have been a support system for you. To lean on and
talk it through with."

"How long have you known about the flowers?"

"The same thing that happened to you after Jake, the black
thumb, happened to Cassie after she fell in love with your father.
You both were born preternaturally gifted around flora. If anyone
asked me, I'd deny it, but you both could make flowers bloom just
by touching them. It was baffling, of course, and supremely fascinating. But it all turned after you fell in love. You destroyed everything in your path."

"I knew something had changed after Jake, but I never saw
the truth of it until Cassie came back."

"Well, that's interesting."

"Is that why you never wanted me to help with your garden?"

"Well..."

"Why didn't you say anything before?"

"It wasn't my place. I was waiting for you to come to me. But
you never did. You want us to tell you the truth, rightly so, but
you've kept the truth of yourself from us. And I know, I don't
have a leg to stand on saying this. I've made terrible choices to
protect you over the years, and myself too, but I've watched you
protect yourself from the full experience of being alive. Of being
open and vulnerable and letting people in who want to be close to
you."

She was right. I never trusted any of them with my secrets,
fearing they would all abandon me. I'd sooner kick them out of
my house than reveal my truth to them.

Tee didn't say anything for a long moment, and then she
whispered, like she was reliving a memory. "Did you know this
tree wasn't here when your father bought the house?"

"It's been here forever."

"Actually, it hasn't. You were two when you moved in. He
used to come out here late every night after he'd put you to bed

and sit on the lawn, listening to the lake and the night creatures."

"Waiting for her."

"Yes, always waiting. One night, he opened up to me. Tears slid down his cheeks while we sat talking, and he didn't wipe them away before they fell to the ground. The next morning, the tree appeared, fully grown."

The branches surrounding us rustled and shook.

"You're kidding."

"I never questioned him about it."

"Why not? An entire tree grew overnight. I mean, it makes sense, a weeping willow. But it's also batshit."

"Well, as with you, I figured he would talk to me if he wanted me to know about it, but he never did. We were still dealing with so many unanswered questions about Cassie. I didn't ask him to explain another unexplainable thing to me."

"Like how a mother could abandon her newborn child?"

"No, honey. That needed an explanation, and you never got the real one."

I wasn't ready to share with Tee the conversation Cassie and I had before I kicked her out. I knew more of the truth, but I didn't think I knew everything. Maybe I never would.

"She defended you," I said. "Told me I should give you a break."

"You should listen to your mother."

"How dare you."

"Em, I want to fix this."

"I don't know if it's fixable."

She sighed. "We made a lot of mistakes—"

"Mistakes?"

"Decisions."

"Lies, Tee. Lies."

"We lied, but always with the right intention. But, yes, we still lied, and for that, I'm deeply sorry. If I could go back and do it again—"

"But you can't. Now I question everything you say, looking for the lie in it. Looking for what you're not telling me. It's exhausting. You've knocked me off balance, and it feels like I'm walking a tightrope every time you speak."

Tee sighed and sat on my old swing. "When Cassie left, it broke your father." The branches shivered around us. He never wanted to talk about anything relating to her. "I know, Josiah, but we need to," Tee said to the dad-tree. "He didn't know what to do with himself, Em. Couldn't function. He was a solid mess. He searched for clues about where they'd gone, but nothing came of it. Not till many years later. When she left, he shattered into a thousand pieces and never glued himself back together again."

After today, I understood that helplessness, the terror of not knowing. I'd had hours and hours of it searching for Bob. I couldn't imagine going through that with the love of my life. For years on end. It would crush me. Like it did him.

"You needed him," Tee said. "You were brand new. He didn't know what to do for you or for himself. He had no idea how to take care of you without her in those first few months, so I stepped in and helped."

"You were in love with him." I'd never said those words out loud to her before. It was almost an accusation. But it was obvious from day one to anyone who knew them. All the branches crept toward us at once like they were eavesdropping but trying to be subtle about it.

"Yes."

"And you still are."

"This is news to no one, Em. Of course I am. I will always love your father." The branches drooped. "But that doesn't mean I was living my life for you, so don't get any ideas," she said to him. "I know where I stood in your heart."

"He never got over her, did he?"

"No, honey. He didn't."

The branches swung out and away, like they didn't want to hear any more.

"Why not tell me the truth about her and them? Why lie to me for all these years? I built my life around being the opposite of who I thought she was. Who you both said she was when we still talked about her. When I was young, still hoping she might show up on our doorstep every day, I thought there must have been something good about her. Otherwise, why would he want to be with her in the first place?"

"There was. When we were young, she was, well, she's never been a party, but she was a good person. Loyal. Steadfast. Stubborn to a fault. And they were...magical together."

"Then why would you talk about her like that?"

"Like what? I don't remember ever saying much about her to you. When you were old enough to make memories, we weren't talking about her anymore."

"Christmas Eve. I was six. It was late, and I thought I heard Santa downstairs, so I went to investigate. Imagine my disappointment when I found Dad face down on the floor. He'd been drinking again. Yes, I knew. Even back then. He was pretty far gone and didn't sugarcoat anything."

"What did he say?"

"He was ranting about her, how selfish she was. What a terrible person she was to leave and never come back. What kind of mother does that? Abandons her family. His face was sweaty and red and the veins in his neck popped out like snakes. He held a photo of her and spit on it as he spoke. Anger seethed from him. It terrified me. I'd never seen him like that. I didn't know what he was going to do."

"Oh honey, I'm sorry you saw that."

"He stopped in the middle of his rant, glared at the photo for a long time, and you asked what he was thinking. He said, 'The terrible irony about all of it is how much Emma reminds me of her. She acts like her, especially when she laughs. Every day, a flesh and blood reminder of the worst thing that ever happened to me. Death by a thousand giggles.'"

The tree created a storm around us. It scared me for a minute.

I didn't know what he was going to do. I felt like I was six again, eavesdropping on my own conversation. The branches swooped down and around me, trying to hug me or attack me, I wasn't sure which.

"No!" I said. "I'm not ready for that." They flew away like I'd set them on fire.

"Give her space," Tee said with authority, holding her arms out to protect me like the mama bear she was. "Em, I'm so sorry. We didn't know you were there."

"He was speaking his truth."

"Yes, and he was also a drunken ass, feeling sorry for himself. That man loved you more than anything in this world, including her. He adored you."

"He adored me because I became everything he wanted me to be from that night on. If I could be the opposite of her, it would make him happy, and I'd never have to see him like that again. The opposite of her was—"

"Being here. Taking care of him."

"Yes."

"He didn't want that for you. You have to know that. How many times did he try to send you back to school after he went into remission? You never budged."

"He needed me."

"Yes, but maybe he was a convenient excuse, too."

"What's that mean?"

"He didn't want you to live for him, Emma. Josiah wanted you to go back to school, back to your life. But I think it scared you."

"It didn't scare me. Dad needed me at home."

"Why did you and Jake break up, then? You could have continued to see him. As we've recently discovered, he was still in Maiden Lake."

I imagined what I'd felt with Jake was because of the curse, but I couldn't reveal that to Tee. Not yet. That was unfinished business between Cassie and me.

"Dad didn't complain when I stayed home," I said, deftly changing the subject.

"Actually, he did. I guess you've forgotten the three times he tried to kick you out. He made every effort to get you to leave, short of—"

"Selling the house out from under me?"

The branches rattled.

"Why did you buy this goddamn house in the first place if it had so many ghosts, Dad?" I asked him. The tree continued to shake and flail. It was a difficult and unsatisfying way to communicate.

"Too bad, Josiah. You had the opportunity to talk to her about it and you chose not to. It's enough," Tee said to the tree. She turned to me and spoke. "Your father stubbornly hoped Cassie would return to you for a very long time. Longer than was healthy or reasonable. He bought this house when you were two, hoping when Cassie came back, she'd be thrilled he'd made a home for you all. Her home. He hung on to every shred of her he could."

"I know. He kept the ring box with no ring. All the letters he wrote to her, all of her clothes are still in the attic. Seems like he kept everything."

Tee went quiet. "Not everything," she finally said.

"Say more."

"The ring. He took it to a pawnshop when he was sick the first time."

"So it's gone?"

"Not exactly." Tee pulled something shiny and round from her pocket and put it in my hand. The branches came back in a frenzy, whirling around us.

"Easy, Dad. Did you buy it back for him?"

"Not for him."

"I don't understand."

"I told myself if she ever came back, I would—"

"Give it to her? But why? She said they were never married. She didn't even know he had a ring."

Tee lowered her head and stared at the ground for such a long time I thought she might have fallen asleep there.

"You know what, never mind. We're both exhausted," I said, giving her the ring back. "Let's talk in the—"

"Your grandfather was...a quiet monster," she said, interrupting me. Determination lifted her voice, like what she had to say was essential. "By the time I came to know him, his anger had consumed him, but he wouldn't let it show on the outside. Not in public. He reserved that for his wife and daughter in the privacy of their home."

What Hopper, and now Tee, said about Jack wasn't matching what Cassie had told me. But wouldn't Cassie know her own father better than anyone? Especially given their history and the bias Hopper had against Jack. I wasn't sure which version to believe. Was Tee regurgitating the version her father told her without knowing the truth? That's how rumors spread.

"Cassie said he was stern but principled. She never said he was abusive."

"He was never physically abusive. He wouldn't want to leave any noticeable marks. Mental and emotional scars, those are the ones no one sees, and they rarely heal. Honey, I..." Tee gasped and threw her hand over her mouth. A strangled little chirp escaped her and then she sniffled.

"What? You what, Tee?"

"I told Jack where they were that night," Tee blurted. I took a step back from her. "I regretted it the minute I called him. I swear, I didn't know what he was planning. If I'd known, I never would have called him. But he threatened to tell my mother. To ruin my family. I didn't know what else to do. I didn't have a choice." Tears streamed down her cheeks. I'd never seen Tee so vulnerable.

"Tell your mother what?"

"That Dad was having an affair with Mary."

"So what happened?" My jaw clenched and heavy knots

formed in the pit of my stomach. I didn't understand what she was admitting to yet, but I knew it wasn't good.

"Cassie and Josiah ran away from Jack to Maiden Lake and didn't tell him where they were because he threatened to force her to have an abortion."

"Oh my god. That's...I thought he was Catholic."

"Didn't matter. He wouldn't accept any family member of his having Jewish blood."

Everything clicked into place for me then. I shivered, head to toe, though it wasn't the least bit cold. Felt like my cells were panicking, smashing into one another to free themselves from my body.

"You told Jack they were at the hospital the night I was born," I whispered between my teeth. The tree quaked and swayed around us, mirroring what was happening inside me. I was afraid it might hurt us, so I ran to the back door. Tee chased after me, leaving the tree to self destruct behind us. I gathered from his reaction, Tee hadn't told him either. That she was the reason they took Cassie. To save her own family, Tee had ruined mine.

"Emma, I'm—"

I held the back screen door open, ready to go inside, but I turned to face her one last time.

"I didn't know, Em. I didn't have any idea what he was going to do."

"You said he was a monster. You knew he would do something terrible."

"Not that terrible. I never imagined he would kidnap her. If I could go back...if I could—"

"But you can't, Tee. And neither can I."

FORTY-TWO

Esther pulled Cassie's hand from Bob's back, saving them both from a dire outcome Cassie wasn't able to control. Bob slumped to the floor, exhausted, but breathing easier. Esther grasped Cassie's hands and held them between her own.

The moment they touched, a tidal wave of suffering and sadness overcame Cassie. It was too much to bear, so she jerked her hands away from the old woman. Esther crumpled over in her chair. Dahlia flew to her side to comfort her.

"My lord!" Cassie shouted through labored breath. "What did you do to me? That was far worse than any of the other..." She couldn't finish her thought, too preoccupied with surviving.

"You've felt that before," Esther whispered. Dahlia kneeled next to her, holding her hand. It was the first time Cassie had witnessed a deeper level of affection between the two.

"Nothing so intense," Cassie said. Her breathing deepened as she recovered from the contact.

"No, I imagine not. I haven't either." Esther and Dahlia shared a weighted look.

"You still think it'll work?" Dahlia asked.

"It worked with us," Esther replied.

"It almost didn't."

"We figured it out in the end."

"Are you a witch?" Cassie felt ridiculous asking it, but also, it needed to be asked. "Did you curse my family?"

"I need to show you so you understand," Esther said.

"Why does it hurt so much?"

"Because we're feeling each other's pain on top of our own."

"This has only ever happened with two other people in my family. So who are you?"

"Please let me show you. If we hold on long enough to get through it, you'll understand," Esther said.

"Understand what?"

"What it might take to break the curse."

Cassie would not walk into that all-consuming darkness again. She'd been dragged through enough agony for ten lifetimes already.

"I wouldn't ask you to do this if I didn't think it was what you needed. In my experience, if you lean into it and let it move through you, it will find its way out. Don't let it squat inside you."

"In your experience?"

"Yes." Esther caressed Dahlia's hand, squeezed it between hers, and then let it go. Dahlia gripped Esther's shoulder and stood next to her wheelchair, watching over them.

"Don't fight it. If you fight, it will dig in," Esther said to Cassie. She struggled to free herself from the wheelchair. Dahlia helped her stand and moved to the side to clear the way for Cassie to join her.

Electricity filled the air. Something extraordinary was about to happen.

"Please?" Esther said, extending her arms out to Cassie. "You'll find the answers you've been searching for."

Cassie stood to meet Esther face to face. Only then did she notice the distinctiveness of Esther's eyes, hazel with sunflowers growing around her pupils.

"Who are you?" she whispered. Her stomach twisted with anticipation.

"All your questions will be answered," Esther said.

Cassie had already endured more in her life than she ever imagined she could. She would get through this too. "What do I have to do?"

Without a word, Esther flung her bony arms around Cassie in the tightest hug she'd ever experienced and didn't let go. An explosion tore through her body. It throbbed through every cell.

"Hold on, Cassie. We must stay together for it to work," Esther said when Cassie tried to pull away. "Hold on and breathe through it."

Cassie settled some at the sound of Esther's reassuring voice in her ear. Instead of running from it like she'd done for the last forty years, she leaned into the pain and breathed. At first it felt like cement gumming up her lungs, but the longer she worked to calm herself and breathe as much as she could into it, the easier it became.

Eventually, the storms settled inside her and turned to a dull ache. But she could handle that. Before she knew what was happening, she embraced Esther and concentrated on letting everything flow through her.

And then it happened. She was transported through time, back to a warm summer sunset at the nest in Calypso Woods. But she didn't recognize it. Instead of a dead wood, it was gloriously alive with the scent of pine trees and all the flora and fauna of a thriving forest. The setting sun lit rich clusters of wildflowers around the top of the spring in a warm glow. Instead of thousands of twisted dead morning glory vines covering the surface of the water, the pool was wide open and magnificent. Clear, deep, sublime, as Esther had described it. Cassie felt called to it again. She wanted to jump in and she didn't even know how to swim.

Two teenagers surfaced down in the middle of the spring from deep below, treading water together. The girl had dark hair and large, innocent eyes. Was it Esther or someone else? Cassie couldn't tell. The boy was blonde with a chiseled, tanned face. She recognized her father from old photo albums he'd kept of his early years. The two dipped under water, as if playing tag, and when they resurfaced they drew close, but didn't touch. Fireflies danced in the air, lighting up the space between them like sparks.

Under them, in the depths, the water glowed as it had two times before when Cassie was watching. Someone else surfaced. A beautiful woman with the most glorious red hair Cassie had ever seen. It was braided down her back and splayed out in the water behind her like a river on fire. Her skin was radiant; she was, in all ways, luminescent. Cassie was stunned by her glowing essence.

Calypso, the water spirit, was real.

Without warning, she pulled both teens under the water with her. They didn't resurface for a very long time. Cassie bent over the side of the spring, trying to see where they'd gone, worried they would drown if they didn't come up soon. As the surface settled, a stunning watercolor garden of flowers, lit by Calypso's luminescence, glowed at the bottom of the spring. Cassie watched all three swimming down there.

The two teens resurfaced a few minutes later, breathing normally, not like they'd been trapped under water for an impossible amount of time. The girl's hair had turned bright red like Calypso's. Cassie knew now it had to be Esther.

When Esther shook her head, bright blue forget-me-not flowers appeared everywhere in her hair. The symbol of their love, also the disease invading Cassie's body. Jack caressed Esther's face and kissed her as they treaded water in the dying light of the day.

When their lips touched, a great energy blossomed inside Cassie. It began from her middle and flowed like rushing lava to the far reaches of her body. It was like nothing she'd ever felt before. A chaotic flutter of butterflies set loose in her stomach instead of a writhing mass of spiders. Tranquility and ecstasy all at once. The heat of the sun radiated inside her without burning.

For the first time in her life, Cassie understood how falling in love was supposed to feel. She wanted to bask in the warmth and glow of it, hold on to it forever, but time yanked her away again.

Her world twisted, and she found herself cloaked and disguised, carrying a bassinet through the dark backyards of Calypso Springs. Young Dahlia accompanied her. This time, Cassie wasn't watching things unfold. She was inside them, looking through Esther's eyes.

"Are you sure you want to do this?" Dahlia asked.

"Of course I don't. But I never want to hurt her like that again," Esther said.

She placed the bassinet on the back porch of Cassie's old house. Inside it, next to the swaddled baby girl, was one delicate, blue forget-me-not. Esther bent over her daughter, but didn't touch her. It killed her to be so close and not be able to kiss or hold her. Esther's tears blossomed into an array of pink carnations surrounding the baby.

Cassie was stunned, overwhelmed. Her heart and mind cast into the turmoil of realization. As shocking as this revelation was, it made sense out of how Mary had treated Cassie. Why she never felt loved as a child. Never felt like she had a mother at all.

The despair rushed in waves through Cassie as Esther said goodbye to her as a baby. It consumed her, became her. She felt it all, Esther's consuming grief, her own guilt and anguish over losing Emma, their deep and shared desire to know and love their lost daughters. She didn't think she could survive it.

And then Esther let go.

They both fell back into their chairs, exhausted. Dahlia was by Esther's side the minute she opened her eyes. "Are you all right? Can you move? Can you breathe?" The concern in her voice was clear.

"I'm...okay," Esther said, surprised.

Cassie reeled in her chair, leaning to the side. Bob appeared next to her. He lifted her arm with his nose and held her weight with his head as she regained her equilibrium. It was difficult to form a coherent thought. She felt like a rag doll, full of nothing but cotton stuffing.

The pain had dissipated quickly this time as Esther let go of her. But her mind ricocheted from one thought to the next, so she took a few slow, deep breaths and realized she could do that now. Her chest didn't feel like she was breathing under water anymore. Her body felt lighter, open and free.

She focused on the most important revelation sitting in front of her.

"You're my..."

"Yes," Esther said, smiling at her in a way her father and Mary never had.

"But you gave me up."

"Only to protect you."

"From?"

"Me," Esther said, with deep melancholy in her voice.

"It was the curse," Dahlia said. "She couldn't hold you, touch you, care for you in any meaningful way without you screaming."

"You were brand new to the world, Cassandra," Esther said, seemingly lost in a memory. "A clean slate with no disappointments, no heartaches, or betrayals. You were pure joy. And I loved you with the force of the sun." She smiled at Cassie and the room filled with her warmth.

"Then why..."

"The strength of my love was matched only by the intensity of the pain we both felt every time I touched you. I passed my sorrow on to you with every touch. Of course, we didn't understand that at first. It took months of doctor visits trying to figure out what was wrong with you to realize *I* was what was wrong. Giving you up was the hardest thing I've ever had to do, but I couldn't wound you like that before you'd even begun. I know your childhood with Jack and Mary was desperately lacking in ways I couldn't foresee at the time. Had I known then what I know now, I would have chosen differently. But I did what I

thought would be best. I couldn't bear to damage you like that."
Tears streamed down Esther's face. Cassie knew that sorrow intimately because she'd been through the same terrible loss with Emma.

"I always tried to stay close. Tried to let you know I was there. That you were never alone. We went to all of your recitals. All of your debates, even the out-of-town events."

"You did?"

"I couldn't be with you the way I wanted to be, but I still needed to know you were okay. To witness your life however you were going to live it."

This news was both heartening and devastating all at once. It shocked her to know Esther, her real mother, was always there. And she understood the terrible error of her own decision not to do the same for Emma. To run away, block and numb her heartache instead of facing it head-on. She wasn't strong enough for that.

"The pink carnations. It was you," Cassie said, remembering how the carnations were always there on the porch for her. Every day. Unless Mary threw them away.

"Yes, they were from me." Esther nodded and smiled.

Esther had shown Cassie in her own way she was still with her. The guilt Cassie felt for not doing the same for Emma was crushing.

"Motherly love," Cassie said. "It makes so much sense now. I never felt loved at home. I was always alone. Mary never would have given them to me. In fact, if I wasn't quick enough in the morning, she would sneak out to the porch, steal them, and throw them on our compost heap in the backyard."

"Mary did the best she could, given the circumstances. Try not to blame her for things out of her control," Esther said.

"That's right. Your father deserves the blame for what happened," Dahlia said. "Mary didn't steal your carnations. He did."

"No, I remember her taking them," Cassie said.

"We watched him steal 'em. We'd wait on the other side of the street until you found 'em in the morning or he stole 'em," Dahlia said.

"Why would he...? Why do I remember it so differently?"

"Sometimes our minds fill in the blanks for things our hearts can't let us acknowledge. You needed him to love you, to be your protector, a good and caring father," Esther said. "Before that terrible night, when everything went wrong, he would have been. I realized too late, after we took you to him, that my Jack was gone. He'd become someone else. Someone not fit for the job of being your father. He'd become his own father. I never would have taken you there if I'd known what he would do in the end."

"He never hugged me, never touched me. There was no affection in him for me."

"I'm so sorry, Cassie. It's not what I ever would have wished for you. You deserved so much more. You deserve so much more." Esther's eyes were full of remorse and sorrow, but something else, too. Love.

From the beginning, all Cassie wanted was to be seen and loved by her parents, the one thing neither of them was capable of. For the first time in her life, she knew the truth. She felt and received that love from Esther now.

It caused a profound shift in her sense of the world, her place in it. And what she needed to do for her own daughter.

"Did we break the curse? I feel much lighter now," Cassie said.

"I don't think so, my girl. I believe Emma is our last hope for that. She's the last of our blood."

"Emma," Cassie repeated. Her daughter's name felt familiar now, not foreign like it had when she first arrived in town. She wanted more than anything to see her, but questions still flooded her mind. "How did you figure it out? The curse."

"Well, we haven't fully. Not yet. After the night everything fell apart and we left town, Dahli and I would see sparks flying between us whenever we were close to each other. When I touched her hand, the same thing happened with us. Many years later, we realized we could get past it if we let it move through us instead of trying to stop it. It took more years of working through it, but we eventually got to the point with one another where we could touch and not feel overwhelmed with grief. And that opened up the other magic you were able to see. My memories."

"Which opened up another can o'worms we don't need to get into now," said Dahlia. "We know you wanna know, and someday soon, we'll show you what happened that night."

"If you knew how to handle it, why didn't you come tell me?"

"We didn't figure it out until you were long gone," Dahlia said.

"And even if we had, I question whether you would have believed us. Your father had a powerful hold on you back then, didn't he, dear?"

"I suppose he did," Cassie said, thinking of when she gave birth. She remembered everything she'd buried about that night. And there was only one person she needed to tell.

"I know you've made choices you regret as well," Esther said, handing Cassie the other letter from the box. "This might help open the door for discussion."

Cassie read it and knew what she needed to do.

"Will what we did work with Emma too?"

"It's worth a try," Esther said, smiling. She caressed Cassie's hand. Neither seemed to be affected by the touch like they had been before. As if they'd broken some bond of the curse between them with the truth.

"This is very good. A step in the right direction, my girl. A bit of a reprieve, but after reading Jack's letter, I'm certain the answer to breaking this curse for good lies deep in the spring," Esther said. She squeezed Cassie's hand, then cupped her cheek with great affection in her eyes. How strange and magnificent it was for Cassie to be with her mother and feel her love.

"It's late, sister. You gotta rest. Big day tomorrow," Dahlia said, stepping toward Esther's chair.

"Come back tonight if you need us, dear. We're always here for you. Wherever you land, try to sleep. We're visiting an old friend at dawn."

FORTY-THREE

I sat alone in the middle of the night on the back stoop. Just me, the dad-tree, and my splintering psyche trying to make sense of my life and the people in it. I couldn't sleep if I tried and looking for Bob in the dark was futile, but I needed him to ground me, settle my racing mind.

Tee's revelation of her oldest and worst betrayal threw me, and I wasn't sure I could ever forgive her for it. Or Cassie, for not coming back to us. Learning the truth about my life in the last couple weeks was enough to drive me to drink whisky straight from Bob's water bowl.

They say the truth will set you free, but I'm not so sure. What do we do when it wounds us to the core and shakes our faith in the people we love the most?

Is it the truth that sets us free or how we choose to handle it?

Movement from the right side of the house startled me. The motion sensor light flicked on, revealing Cassie standing with something white in her hand. My blood froze. I didn't hear Bob's tag tinkling against his collar. He wasn't with her.

"What did you do to him? Where is he?" I charged at her, not knowing what I would do if she told me something I couldn't bear to hear.

"He's fine. Bob's safe," she said, holding a piece of paper in her raised hands.

"Where is he then? Where did you take him? Why isn't he with you? Is he back with Jake at the clinic?"

"Emma, he's fine. He's fine," she said, her voice unsteady. Why was her voice shaking if he was fine?

"I don't believe you. Where did you go? Why did you take him?"

"He's in excellent hands. You'll see him tomorrow. Right now, we need to talk without distraction."

"Bob is not a distraction."

"I need to show you something."

"No. I can't...I can't handle any more soul baring truth right now. I'm full up," I said, marching back toward the stoop.

She followed, trying to hand me the paper. "I know that feeling better than you might imagine right now, but it's imperative we do this."

"You don't know anything about how I feel." I brushed the paper away as she held it out in front of me. The light flicked on above us.

"Please read it." Her eyes begged me, which was odd for her.

"Not another goddamn letter."

"It's from your father." The dad-tree rustled and a group of branches tried to insinuate themselves into our conversation.

"Not now, Dad." The branches slumped away. It was strange how comfortable I'd become talking to him in this new form. How normal it all seemed now.

"It's his last letter to me," Cassie said, knowing that would pique my interest.

I sighed and took the letter, reading it while she stood in front of the dad-tree. Almost close enough to touch. The branches swayed side to side in front of her. It reminded me of a toreador waving his red cape at the bull.

May 19, 1999

Cassie,

This will be my last letter. I don't know what to say or why I'm writing it. I probably won't send it to you. What's the point? I suppose I needed to get this down too, since I put everything else in writing over these last twenty years. I had an idea of how our reunion would go and I was wrong on every account. Shame on me for having expectations, right? It made me wonder if the love we had was ever real for you. Maybe it wasn't and I'll have to live with that. But it was for me and that's what I'm taking away as I say goodbye to you. I'm angry. Hell yes, I'm red hot, but I still love you, Cass. Even when you won't come home to meet your daughter. But I will not let her wait one more day for you to come back to her. It's time I set her free from that prison of hope. I don't know or understand your reasons for staying away. Maybe someday you'll explain it and maybe you won't. Either way, as furious as I am, and I am steaming right now, I love you, Cassandra McCormack. Always have, always will.

Josiah

His words opened my wounds again, but they also made clear why he'd lied to me about her. After the day I'd had, I understood on a visceral level what it must have been like for him back then.

Waiting. Hoping. Not knowing what happened to her, where she'd gone, or why.

"I'm lost without Bob and it's only been a day," I said, approaching the canopy of branches. "I can't imagine what it was like for you losing her." I glanced at Cassie. "I never saw hope as a prison, but now I totally understand how you would, especially after so long."

So, how could he still love her after everything she'd put us through? How do hearts work?

"I'm so sorry you suffered all those years, Dad. You didn't deserve it. I tried to fill that void for you, but I couldn't. Nobody could. I shouldn't have spent so much time trying to replace her for you."

Cassie stepped forward, so we both stood in front of him now. She reached her hands out toward the still swaying branches. "Of course it was real," she whispered to him. Being so close to him must have hurt her.

"How are you standing here? Doesn't it hurt?"

She didn't answer. Just kept reaching out toward him. Then she turned to me and smiled. "It's okay now. I know what to do."

I didn't know what she was referring to, and I didn't ask her to elaborate, but as I stood there, talking to the dad-tree, I became more aggravated with Cassie for everything she'd put him through. She should have been the one apologizing.

"I'm glad you understand now," Cassie said to me.

"Understand what? That you didn't give a damn about us? Yes, I understood perfectly well last night and for the last forty years."

"Emma," she said, facing me. The sound of my name coming from her was so different now. There was no detachment in her voice like before. It was unguarded, almost tender. If I didn't know better, I would have thought she was just a wounded soul speaking the name of a long-lost loved one. It nearly knocked me over.

She turned from the dad-tree and approached me, determined

and intense. I'd never seen affection in her eyes. It was the same way Tee looked at me.

"I was hoping we could talk this through, but I think we're going to have to do it the hard way," she said, glancing down at her intertwined hands.

"The hard way?"

She shifted her gaze back up to me and my heart sank when I saw her face. Pure anguish. Her eyes were shiny with tears, and it seemed like she was holding her breath. "The last thing I want to do is hurt you more, Emma. Please believe that. But if you can be strong through the pain, I need to show you something so you understand."

"Pain?"

"We need to stay together. Don't pull away. Let it flow through you. Breathe into it and let it pass. Don't hold on to it."

"Not going to lie. You're freaking me out right now."

"I'm sorry, Emma," she said and then threw her arms around me in the most aggressive hug I'd ever received. I couldn't move, could barely breathe.

It came raging, a blazing inferno of darkness and desperation, with no warning. Instinct kicked in and I tried to pull away, but her will was stronger than mine. And she was ready for it. She kept me with her, wouldn't let go.

"Stay with me, Emma. I know it hurts. Breathe into it," she whispered in my ear. "I'm with you." The sound of her voice had changed. It wasn't harsh or judgmental like before. It was comforting, supportive. "You can do this. You're stubborn like me," she said. "And you're far stronger."

I stopped trying to pull away and let her hold me as the wild blaze burned me up inside. "Breathe, Emma, breathe," she whispered. Had I ever really breathed before this? Filling my lungs, I felt like I'd been holding my breath, waiting for my life to begin, for forty years.

"Why are you doing this to me all over again?" Through the heat I felt something cool against my arms, a tickling sensation.

They were branches, but I couldn't tell if they were trying to free me from her or hug me, too.

"I'm so sorry, but you need to see so you'll understand."

"See what? All I see is—"

The fire suddenly calmed inside me and I was swept away to a time and place I didn't recognize. A bleak hospital room. I was lying in the bed, but I wasn't me. I was Cassie forty years ago.

An imposing man I didn't know flew into the room, squeezing a fedora between his thick fingers. He was dressed in a three-piece tweed suit, followed by a petite blonde in a tailored dress with matching pillbox hat. She didn't enter the room. She stood by the doorway, fidgeting and glancing back and forth down the empty hallway.

"Daddy?" Cassie said. "How did you—"

"Unimportant, Cassandra. Where is Josiah?" His voice was thorny.

"He went home to shower. How did you find us—"

"Listen to me. We don't have time for discussion. You're in danger."

"Did Tee tell you? She's the only one who—"

"Cassandra, did you not hear what I said?"

"Danger? How? What—"

"Did you hold her?"

"Hold who?"

"The baby. Did you hold her?"

"I couldn't. She wasn't breathing well. They had to put her on oxygen right away."

"Good."

"Good? How can you say—why would that be good? I want to hold my daughter."

"Well, you can't."

"What are you talking about? You're not—I'm not under your rules anymore, Daddy. You don't run my life."

"No, I don't. Something else does."

"You're not making sense."

"No, I suppose not. Nothing I say will make you understand, so I'll have to show you." Without warning, he grabbed Cassie's hand and held it tight between both of his. Living through her experience, I knew this was the first time he had ever touched her. Her insides thrashed, electricity bouncing off every nerve. She yanked her hand away from his, shocked by the sudden stab of pain.

"What was that? What did you do to me?"

"I can't explain it now, but every time you touch the baby, the same kind of thing will happen to her."

"Why?"

"Something terrible happened, before you were born, and I don't know how to fix it. So you need to leave. With us. You can't have children. You'll only damage them. I tried to make you understand this before, but you wouldn't listen."

"But I love them, Daddy. They're my family now. I don't want to leave. You can't make me."

"Are you prepared to raise a daughter you can never touch without making her suffer? Why do you think I've never touched you? Hugged you. You are not a monster, Cassandra. You don't want to hurt your child. But you're going to destroy her if you stay. It will tear you apart."

"Why is this happening? What did you do to us?"

"Someday I'll tell you, but right now, you must make a decision. Stay and damage your child and yourself. Or leave with us and save your family. It's up to you."

Every cell in Cassie's body protested this choice. The grief it caused her, even considering it, was unbearable. I saw flashes of my father's boyish face in her mind. The love she had for him was endless. But she also acknowledged that loving him came at a cost. It had always hurt her. She never understood why, but she was beginning to.

A nurse came in to check on her. She felt Cassie's wrist for a pulse, but there was no discomfort in her touch.

"Can I see her? Is she better?" Cassie asked, desperation filling her voice. It broke my heart for her and for me. She seemed so fragile and uncertain.

"She is. She's breathing on her own now."

Relief flooded Cassie. I felt it all happening.

"Can I go see her?"

"I'll bring her to you," the nurse said and left the room.

"Cassandra, this will not end well. Believe me."

"Believe you? I believe I have to take care of my child."

A moment later, the nurse returned with a swaddled baby. As she moved closer, Cassie's heart quickened to a gallop. Every nerve ending stood at attention, waiting to touch her new baby girl. I felt her anticipation, her love. It rushed through her body as the nurse brought me ever closer.

But then.

Cassie took me in her arms. The moment I settled there, against her bare skin, she caressed my face with her forefinger, and a shattering jolt of fiery electricity passed through us. So intense, we both screamed.

"No!" she cried. "No, this can't be happening. What did you do to us, Daddy?"

The nurse, shocked and confused, rushed back into the room, standing dumbfounded next to Jack.

Cassie and I both continued to shriek, but before the nurse could lift me away from her, Cassie whispered in my ear. "I'm so sorry, my baby girl. I'm so sorry. I'll come back to you someday. I promise."

"What happened?" the nurse asked.

"Take her. Please take her!" Cassie pleaded.

She kissed me quickly on the cheek and drank in the sweet smell of my new skin, something for her to hold on to, even though it felt like fire had ignited where we touched.

The nurse pulled us apart, and Cassie screamed in agony as she took me away. The burning pain she'd felt touching me perfectly matched by the emotional storm raging inside her as she lost me.

FORTY-FOUR

Cassie released me and we both sank to the cold ground, exhausted.

"Are you okay?" she asked, catching her breath. The question caught me off guard for its selflessness. That she would be worried about me at all was something I didn't think I'd ever experience after meeting her.

Her concern made me feel something I hadn't for a long time, and never in her presence: a spark of joy.

"I'm...I don't know what I am. How did you...what was that?" I said, trying to catch my breath and wrap my frazzled mind around what had just happened. "How...how was that possible?"

"I don't know," she said, panting next to me.

"You seemed to know something."

"I don't know how any of it is possible, but it's because of the curse."

"Well," I said, breathing easier, "it was amazing. And excruciating. And I never want to do it again."

"Takes walking in another person's shoes to a new level."

"Understatement of the year."

Cassie rolled on her side, facing me, and the light flicked on.

The judgment so alive in her eyes when we met and the tight-lipped glare that had woven her features into a caricature of herself were gone. The severe angles of her nose and high cheek-bones, threatening to impale unsuspecting daughters with their imperiousness, had softened, too. At that moment, I saw the person she was the night she let me go. A terrified new mother in love with a child she couldn't bear to hurt.

But which kind of pain is worse? Physical or emotional? What happens when your body can't tell the difference between the two? When they become so entwined that the emotional becomes the physical and vice versa. Is one worse than the other if they become the same thing? An insurmountable roadblock to joy, to living your life fully.

"What am I supposed to do now?" I said.

"That's up to you. I needed you to know the truth. How I felt about you."

"You leaving us, it..."

"I know."

"But you don't."

"If you'd said that to me yesterday, or even an hour ago, I might have agreed with you. But this," she said, pointing at me and back to herself, "was a two-way street. I can assure you, I am viscerally aware of how you felt. Everything my absence put you through. But...I'm listening. If you want to tell me more."

"Who are you, and what have you done with Cassie?" I said, only somewhat joking.

"Hilarious. Continue."

My whole life I'd wanted to tell her how her leaving had affected every part of me, and now she was a rapt audience. Why did I feel so vulnerable, like an octopus with nowhere to hide in shark-infested waters?

"I always thought there must be something wrong with me growing up. You left and never came back. So in my mind, I wasn't all that great. I wasn't worth coming back for. I've spent my life making up for your absence and trying to prove my worth to the world." Saying it out loud made me sweat.

"And when I came back, all I did was reinforce those feelings of inadequacy for you."

"Yes."

She didn't apologize like I'd hoped she might. Just rolled away from me and laid back on the grass, staring up into the night sky. Had nothing else changed for her?

"You have forty years to make up for. Forty birthdays you didn't celebrate with me. Forty Christmases. Forty Mother's Days. Forty Groundhog's Days, for Christ's sake. Forty everything."

"I can't go back. But we can move forward, if you want to."

I didn't know what I wanted from her. Knowing the truth was a relief, I didn't need to wonder anymore, but did it change anything for me now?

"Why didn't you tell me this last night? Why make up stories, lies?"

"I wasn't lying. I didn't remember the truth. Not until about an hour ago."

She laid back down on the ground, staring up at the starry sky. The dad-tree rustled his branches at her like he was trying to convince her to continue. "I struggled to function when we left Calypso Springs," she said. "I think I may have lost my mind for a time. I couldn't reconcile my decision to leave with my love for you two. So my father created a story I came to believe. I suppose being stolen away was better in my addled mind than making the choice to leave you, no matter what the reason. Knowing what I do now of my father back in those days, I wouldn't have put it past him to steal me away. But he didn't. He told me the truth and let me choose."

"And you chose to leave."

"Because I couldn't bear to hurt you. The sound of you screaming like I'd burned you has haunted me. I couldn't be with you and not touch you, not hold you. Not love you like I wanted to as your mother."

"So you decided not being in my life at all was a better choice? Being present is everything to kids. You missed it. All of it."

Cassie took a breath and held it for the longest time. "I didn't know what else to do. Knowing what I know now, I would have done everything differently, but I can't go back. We can only move forward."

"What do you know now?"

"What we did. That we can move through the pain. But that's still not something I would have put you through as a child. We would have had to wait until you were much older to reconnect."

"How do you even know about this now? What happened today? Where did you go?"

"I'll show you in the morning. We need to go back to the woods to break the curse."

"The nest."

"Yes."

I sat up, realizing something. "You're breathing better. Did you open the box? Are you healed now? Is Bob? Is he really okay?"

"We haven't broken the curse, but yes, we're both better. For now, anyway. He seems to have made big strides last night away from us."

"Where is he?"

"I'll explain everything tomorrow when we're there. I think we should get some rest now. Hopefully, you'll sleep better knowing he's going to be all right."

I was bone tired, but felt like I might never sleep well again. My mind would not behave, couldn't sit still. The stars winked down from the night sky, sending the message that my problems were tiny in the grand scheme of the universe, but they still felt overwhelming to me. The truth was overwhelming.

"I wish you'd come back sooner. For me, yes, but especially for him. Before it was too late." The dad-tree branches gently swayed side to side above us, as if trying to put us to sleep or in a trance.

"So do I," she said, regret cracking her voice. About time. She still hadn't apologized for anything. I didn't know what I was hoping for, but it would have been a good faith gesture to open the door to more.

"Do you? Because it seems to me, in forty years, there would have been an opportunity to try. To see if you could make something work with us. Especially after he flew all the way out to California to find you."

"I wish for so many things to be different in my life, Emma. I thought I was protecting you. If I'd known how much you would suffer anyway, I never would have left. It was the worst mistake of my life. But I didn't think I had a choice."

"Well, you have a choice now. I guess we both do."

FORTY-FIVE

I woke in the wee hours the next morning, curled up facing Cassie under the dad-tree. The willow branches tucked in around us like a leafy quilt, sheltering us from the cool early-morning breeze. I wanted to enjoy it, this quiet moment with both of my parents in the same place for the first time. But Cassie woke, and the branches shook, and the moment passed, as moments always do.

I thought I might find Tee in the living room, but no one was there. The house was dark and empty. Far too quiet for me. Sam and Hopper had disappeared somewhere in the middle of the night, too. Probably when Cassie came back. I thought about calling Sam for moral support at the nest, but this was something I needed to do alone.

Before we left, I caught Cassie whispering on the phone. I wondered who she was talking to, especially that early in the morning. But I didn't press her. I had far more pressing issues on my mind.

A sliver of light formed at the edge of the inky horizon when we parked in the dirt lot leading to the nest. My body vibrated when we entered the woods. Nerves? Something else?

Climbing the dark hill to the railroad tie steps seemed more daunting early in the morning. The ground felt fragile, unpredictable, like it might break apart any minute and swallow me whole. Charged energy ricocheted around us like the agitation in the atmosphere before a powerful lightning storm.

"Who's that?" I said as we crested the hill, looking down on the spring. Several people stood at the bottom by the mouth of the nest, but in the faint light, I couldn't tell who it was. It surprised me that anyone at all would be there, but especially so early in the morning. A crowd was an unexpected and unprecedented affair there.

Cassie didn't answer my question, just made her way down the hill. She hesitated with every step, landing each footfall on solid ground. "Cassie? Hello?" I called. She didn't stop.

Light seeped into the sky, diffusing into the forest to help us conquer the hill on the way down. As we drew closer to the water, the cluster of spiders awakened in my stomach.

"Wait, why are *they* here? And where's Bob?" I asked Cassie or anyone who would listen.

And then the jingle of his tags filled the silent morning air. He sprang out around Tee and charged halfway up the hill, straight to me. Everything felt lighter.

"Mister! Oh my god, you look so good."

I dropped to my knees, petting and scratching and massaging him in all his favorite places. He knocked me over and laid on my chest, trying to lick my cheeks off. I hugged him close and felt his manic puppy energy flowing through me.

Cassie had stopped to watch us at the bottom of the hill. I peeked down at her between the onslaught of love and slobber. Instead of being disgusted by this blatant show of emotion, she seemed delighted. Her eyes even appeared shiny, like maybe she'd gotten dust or some kind of humanity in them.

But Cassie and I had work to do, so I cut my reunion with Bob short and trekked to the bottom of the hill with him following on my heels. Sam stepped forward and hugged me first.

"Why are you guys here?" I asked, hugging her back. Bob sat

next to us, waiting for more attention. His tail swished back and forth, a windshield wiper in the dead leaves. I still had made no contact, eye or otherwise, with Tee. Maybe if I ignored her altogether, she would get the hint and leave.

"We were invited," Sam said.

"Invited?"

"Instructed." She glanced at Cassie.

"I see."

Cassie stood behind us, locked in a staring contest with Tee. Neither of them moved. Or blinked. It was disconcerting.

"We come to be moral support, Em," Hopper said, lumbering over to stand next to me.

"I appreciate that, Hopper." I reached out and touched his arm. "Moral support for what, though?" How much did they know?

"Whatever's gonna happen here, I guess," Hopper said.

He made a good point. What *was* going to happen? Cassie said we needed to come, but she didn't say what we needed to do when we got here.

The genuine surprise of the morning was Fern and Pearl. They stood away from the rest of us at the edge of the nest, watching everything. Fern smiled at me, holding something under her arm, and Pearl scowled at everyone. Business as usual.

"Hi," I said with an awkward wave. Then I recognized what Fern had. "Why do you have the lockbox?" I left Sam and Hopper to chat amongst themselves and stalked over to Fern. She wasn't in her wheelchair. She was standing on solid ground, but she didn't look solid herself. A stiff breeze could have blown her right into the spring.

Cassie, catching up to current events, shuffled over next to me, leaving Tee with Sam and Hopper. They didn't follow us, but Bob did.

"Emma," Cassie said, breathy and winded. "Oh boy. How do I say this?"

She looked at Fern, who looked at Pearl, who looked back at

both of them as if someone there should have the answer. Then Fern pulled her hair back like Cassie had when we first met. Swarms of spiders broke into a frenzy inside me. There was no mistaking those ears.

"We're family," Pearl blurted.

"Well, that's one way," Cassie said, glaring at Pearl.

"Easier than I thought it would be," Pearl said smugly.

"I don't understand what's...Cassie?" I turned to her for an explanation. Nobody spoke for the longest time. The three of them glanced from one to the other again, like they were doing a comedy bit. What was my life? "I mean, how many secrets can one family have?" I said. "Somebody better talk or I'm going to lose it."

"Too many secrets. Time to fix that," Pearl said.

"Emma, dear, I'm Esther, not Fern," the tiny one said. Whoever-the-hell she was. Fern. Esther. Fester.

"Wait. Esther...Blum?" I asked. Chills sprang up all over my body and I felt a little dizzy, so I bent down and scratched Bob's head to steady myself.

"I'm Dahlia, not Pearl."

"But why? Who are you?"

"The Blum name came with too much baggage for this crap little town to handle—"

"Dahlia," Esther scolded.

"Telling the truth, sister."

"Tell it more delicately, dear."

"Ain't nothin' delicate about it."

"Who are you? To me?" I asked through gritted teeth.

Esther sidled up to me and whispered, "I'm your grandmother, dear. Cassie's mother. It feels so good to say it out loud." Her face lit up as she smiled, like it had when we first met in her kitchen.

My grandmother? I'd never had a grandmother before. I didn't know what that was supposed to be like, but this relationship was getting off to a mighty rocky start. Much like the one with the mother I'd never had. I hoped they would both improve.

"What about Mary?" I asked, confused by everything.

"It's a long story, dear," Esther, my grandmother, said.

"I bet."

"We've come to break the curse with you, dear."

I felt self-conscious. How much did my friends already know about the craziness of my life? How much did I want them to know? I checked to see if they were paying attention to our conversation. No one seemed fazed by any of it, so either this was old news or they were sleep-standing like cows and didn't hear a thing. It *was* very early in the morning.

"You're going to break the curse with me? Great. What do we do?" I whispered.

"First, we've got to reconnect with a dear friend," Esther said, turning toward the open mouth of the spring.

"A dear friend?"

"Calypso," Cassie said, sensing my confusion. "The light we saw down there? She's real."

Calypso, the mythical water spirit, was real. Yeah. That tracked.

"So, how do we do that?" I asked.

"Little pieces of the past." Esther set the lockbox down on the dirt by the edge. She was unsteady and weak and I worried she might topple into the spring head first. But then she opened the hermetically sealed, impenetrable box with one arthritic finger and pulled several items from it.

"Okay," I said. Not much surprised me anymore. But it was hard to erase the vision of the same box plunging from the roof of a six story building and bouncing, eternally sealed, on the pavement below.

Tee, Sam, and Hopper stood behind us by the bottom of the hill, gathered in a huddle like spectators at a multi-car pileup. Not sure what to do, but not wanting to leave in case things got weird. Bob, still lying by my side, started panting when Esther opened the box. I tried calming him, scratching his favorite spot, but it didn't work.

An old piece of frayed rope, a shard of red plastic, a weathered leather dog collar, and a dead bouquet of forget-me-not flowers. Those were the items Esther pulled from the box and held out to me like a peace offering.

"What are these?" I said, not taking them.

"Fragments of our history. Where it all began. I believe Calypso will come if you call her with these," Esther said.

I wasn't sure what *I* believed, but even if my strange little grandmother was wrong, what could it hurt? These things were in the box for a reason, a reason I didn't understand, much like the rest of my life and history, so why not try? I took them from her. And immediately felt my energy shift.

Everything vibrated in my hands like the lockbox had when I first held it. Something lived inside these objects, memories needing to be released. They burned my hands like they'd been set on fire. So I did what any sensible person would do when touched by burning objects. I threw them as far away from me as possible. Into the water.

"One way to do it," Dahlia said.

We peeked over into the spring to see if they'd floated or sunk into the water. The pieces of our past popped up between the gnarled vines on the surface, but nothing stirred below. Bob joined us, looking down as if he understood the gravity of the situation. Or maybe he thought they were treats I'd carelessly thrown away. He was still panting, so I kneeled next to him and gave his head and chest a good scratch. It didn't help.

"Can we do something else to get her attention?" I asked Esther, feeling the urgency in Bob's shallow breathing. "I'm gonna fix you, mister. Hold on, okay?"

"She knows we're here, dear. Don't worry."

"Why do you say that?" Cassie asked, like she already knew the answer.

Out of the blue, I heard an unfamiliar female voice.

In. My. Head.

"I've been waiting so long for you all. I hope you're ready," she said in a low, hushed tone. Her voice was soothing, but this was not great. Until that point, I could at least say I'd never heard voices in my head.

Tee and Hopper still stood behind us. They hadn't heard what I had. But Sam had inched her way over to the edge, peeking down at the water with us.

"What're you guys looking at here?" she asked, curious. Didn't give any indication she'd heard a mythical creature speaking in her head though.

Dahlia kept a close eye on Esther, as did Cassie. As if Esther could feel the weight of everyone's gaze on her, she glanced at Cassie and me.

"Are you ready?" Esther asked.

"Ready for what?" Sam said, oblivious.

Cassie and I exchanged a look. I could tell she was nervous about what was to come, too. Whether I was ready didn't seem important to this equation. We were in it till the end, like it or not. Like a proper family, I guess.

"Hey, anybody else seeing this?" Sam asked breathlessly. "Water. Water rising." She pointed down at the water creeping up the stone walls of the spring toward us. I still couldn't see anything underneath the thick layer of vines, but I'd been there enough over the years to know this wasn't normal.

Tee and Hopper joined us at the edge, peeking over the side to watch the water rise.

"Shoulda worn my galoshes," Hopper said. "Looks like we might be gettin' wet."

The water kept rising, more precipitously as it neared the top where we stood. Everyone backed away except for Esther and Dahlia. The water was near the top edge of the spring, and Dahlia whispered something to Esther. They gazed at each other like this might be the last time they'd be able to do that.

Then Dahlia stepped away and left Esther there with her toes inched over the edge. The water stopped rising right below them.

Esther extended both arms out by her sides, palms facing back, like she was waiting for someone to come take her hands. Cassie and I looked at one another and, without a word, followed the cue. We stood, one on each side of her, but didn't grasp her hands in ours yet.

Esther sensed our trepidation. "As long as she's with us, we're safe. We can breathe under the water. I don't know how or why. But you have to trust it."

Cassie and I considered what Esther said for a moment. Trusting in anything or anyone had been especially difficult lately. This was a big ask.

"Uh, what's happening here?" Tee's sudden voice was a shotgun fired into the air of my chaotic thoughts. There was a tightness in her tone I'd seldom heard. Sounded like jealousy. She stood next to me as Cassie and I considered the consequences of touching Esther. Physical connection was not for the faint of heart in this family.

It killed me to not include Tee inside this moment, because she'd been inside all of my moments, big and small, but I couldn't get there with her. I couldn't move past the betrayal. I didn't even acknowledge her.

"Come on, honey," Tee said, a little more urgently. "What's the plan here? Looks like you all might be thinking about doing something really stupid, like...jumping in deep water when you don't know how to swim." Her voice was stretched thin with concern.

It was true. I had the swimming prowess of a two-year-old, but I wouldn't let that stop me if it meant bringing an end to this nightmare of a curse. If we all needed to go down to meet this sea witch, or whatever she was, so be it.

"I don't swim well either," Esther said.

"Makes three of us," Cassie said, almost whimsically. Like it was a fun familial coincidence instead of a probable byproduct of a curse and a grave hazard to our health, considering what we were planning to do.

"Doesn't matter. Once you're with Calypso, she takes over," Esther said. She may have thought this was reassuring to someone.

"Emma, why are you doing this? Please don't." Tee took my hand and my skin burned against hers. She released me like she'd touched a hot stove. "What *was* that?"

"That...is why I'm doing this," I said without looking her in the eyes. And because I was exhausted from trying to hide the truth of my life from the people I loved, I turned to Sam and Hopper to include them.

"In the spirit of full disclosure...truth is, you guys, I'm cursed. We're cursed," I said, including Esther and Cassie. "A real-life, actual curse. I kill flowers with one touch. I can't hug my mother without experiencing every ounce of her considerable trauma in my own bones. Love is a barren wasteland that brings me nothing but suffering. And my father is a tree. Oh, and, up till about five minutes ago, I would have been excited to report that at least I don't hear voices in my head. But I can't say that anymore. So, yeah, sums me up in a nutshell. The real me. And I don't know what my role is in breaking this thing, but I think we've got to figure it out together," I said, motioning to Esther and Cassie. "So that's what we're going to do. I needed you to know that. In case this is the last time..." But I couldn't finish the thought. "I hope the absurdity of my life doesn't scare you away. Like you said, Sam, only way out is through."

Bob panted by my side and I bent down to give him a kiss on the nose and a good scratch behind the ears. "I love you, mister. No more suffering for you. Or for any of us." I stood and glanced at Bob and then at Sam, asking for the favor I couldn't put into words without shattering.

"No, Em," she said. "Because you're coming back. So don't even think about that nonsense. Go kick that curse's ass so we have wild, amazing stories to freak everyone out with."

Tee still stood next to me. I could feel the weight of her gaze, but I couldn't acknowledge her or let her concern cloud my sense of purpose in this mission. I also couldn't bear the idea of never seeing her again and I feared if I looked into her eyes, I would forever regret *that* as our last moment.

Instead, I asked Cassie a question. "Ready?"

"Doesn't matter, does it?"

"Nope."

"Okay then."

We each grasped one of Esther's hands. I'm not clear about what happened after because I was transported into darkness. I woke at the bottom of the spring, floating upright in the deep water like a ghost levitating, still holding Esther's hand. Cassie floated ghostlike on the other side of Esther, holding on too. We hovered over an expansive garden of dead flowers, staring into the otherworldly eyes of Calypso, Keeper of the Spring. She held the pieces of our past in her hands and then revealed how our curse was cast.

FORTY-SIX

It had been sixty years since Esther had last seen Calypso. She didn't imagine time would have been as cruel to a water spirit as it had been to her, but Calypso had withered much like Esther had.

She was smaller, as though living there in the darkness, under the weight of those vines for so long, had diminished her body and spirit. Her long, red hair wandered behind her in a mess of tangles instead of the usual neat braid she used to wear as she swam toward the three of them. Her skin had lost much of its glow, and her enchanting green eyes had faded to gray.

"It's been a lifetime, old friend," Calypso said as she approached them. Esther, Cassie, and Emma were still holding hands, suspended in the middle of the spring without effort. "I've been waiting for you." Calypso smiled. Esther heard her velvety voice in her head, as always. "I hope we all find our freedom today."

The first time Esther met the water spirit, Calypso's touch was pure love. A warmth that circulated through Esther's body and made her feel whole and light, like everything in her life would be wonderful from that moment forward.

It was time to find out how it all went so terribly wrong.

Calypso released each item Emma had thrown from the lockbox into the watery space between them. They floated there, didn't rise to the surface or sink. She reached out for Emma and Cassie to take her hands in theirs to encircle the objects.

As soon as Calypso connected with Cassie and Emma, Esther felt it. The electric jolt shot through them into her and she knew now, with no doubt, where the curse had come from. All those years, she hadn't thought Calypso would have been capable of inflicting such misery because she possessed so much love in her heart, but now Esther knew it had been her.

But why? Esther couldn't imagine what she'd done to encourage Calypso to hurt her. She wasn't allowed time to ponder. They were instantly transported back to the day, sixty years ago, when everything went wrong.

In the fading light of a late summer day, teenage Dahlia stood at the edge of the dazzling spring in full bloom, next to Jack. They were engaged in a heated discussion. Esther's heart beat faster seeing him young again. Despite what he'd done, a quiet yearning for him, for the love they once had, still pulled at her like no time had passed.

"She's not coming, Jack," Dahlia said with delight. "She doesn't love you."

"You don't know what you're talking about."

"That's cute. You thought it was real. Don't you know? It was all a game for her. A big lie."

"She wouldn't do that. Not to me," he said, but doubt had crept into his voice.

"She wanted to see if you were dumb enough to fall for it. And guess what?"

"Esther loves me. We've...we're leaving tonight. We're eloping."

"Then why is she getting engaged to Ben Abrams right now?"

"What? No. She wouldn't..." Jack said. But something had shifted in him. He wasn't standing as tall as he had been a moment before.

"Go see for yourself if you don't believe me. She's with my father and her real fiancé right now, making plans for their wedding," Dahlia said with a wicked grin.

Esther felt heavy living through Calypso's memory. Weighed down by the revelation of what Dahlia had done to set the wheels of that terrible night in motion. The surprise was not that Dahlia had betrayed Esther back then. She remembered every minute of how her sister had helped their father steal them away that night. But Esther didn't imagine Dahlia had been part of the plan from the beginning. No one would ever accuse her sister of being joyful, or even good-humored. But Esther never thought she was capable of such malice against her.

Calypso sent them spinning into another memory of that night. This time, it was Esther's.

The only reason she went to Ben Abrams' house that evening was because her father told her it was mandatory and essentially kidnapped her. But he'd said it was a going-away party for the Abrams' family, not an arranged engagement announcement. If she'd had an inkling of what was to come, she would have run to Jack at the spring and made sure they were long gone before her father knocked on her bedroom door.

After Ben announced their engagement to the room full of strangers, he took Esther's hand without permission and kissed her cheek unbidden. At that terrible moment, she felt the weight of someone's gaze on her through the living room window. She had a sick feeling it was Jack. When she turned to search outside, she found the yard empty, but knew, from that place of instinct inside every woman, he'd been there.

When Esther found the single black dahlia on her pillow later, she was sure Jack had seen her at Ben's and was thinking wild, untrue things. He hadn't seen her tear her hand away from Ben's or wipe her cheek clean of his kiss. He'd only seen what he would assume was her deep betrayal.

She had to fix it, make him understand she loved him and would never betray him like that. And she would not be forced into marrying anyone she didn't love. Not at eighteen or any age. It was 1960, not 1760.

Esther burst out the front door of their house, gripping the keys to the car, but her father confronted her in the driveway. It stopped her cold. She'd made it very clear on the drive home she was not interested in an arranged marriage. But he was unrelenting in his disapproval of Jack and his family. He forbade her to see him again.

Now, standing there in front of her, a sweaty, seething wall on her path to freedom, there was a darkness in her father's eyes she'd never seen before. Even when he'd wounded her as a child. Her body went stiff with fear at the sight of the shotgun in his hands.

"You're not going anywhere!" he yelled. The sky had darkened, which made reading his lips more difficult, but there was no mistaking his intentions. Esther swung around him to get to the car. She was going to elope with Jack tonight, even if she had to go with only the clothes on her back.

The shotgun blast shook the ground under her. Shocked, she spun around to see her father's face glowing with rage. The gun pointed at the sky.

"You will not go with him!"

"I love Jack, Daddy," Esther signed, even though he couldn't, wouldn't read sign language. "I love him," she mouthed.

"You don't know love."

"I won't marry Ben!"

"I'll kill Jack before I let you marry him."

"You wouldn't," she silently screamed.

"Let's find out," he said and stole the keys from her. She tried to pull him away from the car, but he was too strong. He pushed her aside and jumped in the driver's seat, throwing the gun on the seat next to him.

Something primal snapped inside her when he slammed the car door shut. She couldn't hear the sound, but she could feel it. The finality of it. The reality that nothing would be okay again if he drove away. She had to stop him. To save Jack.

The scream came from somewhere so deep inside her she didn't know that place existed. And somehow, she could hear every shocking moment of it. The terror of losing Jack had unleashed a power in her so mighty and overwhelming it opened her ears and healed her old injuries.

"No, Daddy!" she wailed, hanging off the car window. Her sudden voice broke through his murderous frenzy. He stared at her in disbelief. She could barely see his face through her tears.

Finally, he spoke. She wished he hadn't. "If you disobey me now, I will destroy them. His father will go to prison and they'll be left with nothing but disgrace."

"Why? Why would you do that?" Esther felt like she was drowning. Jack's family was so important to him. She couldn't let her father destroy them.

"You're my daughter. It's not your place to question me. You will do as I say. But since I can't trust you now to do anything suitable or proper, go pack your things. We're leaving. Tonight."

"No. No, Daddy!" she cried, clinging to the window. "You can't do this! You can't—"

"Take her inside and pack," her father snapped at someone standing behind them.

Dahlia dragged Esther away from the car as she collapsed in agony and pulled her back into the dark house without a word of comfort.

Esther had never once stopped to wonder why Jack was at Ben Abrams' house that evening instead of waiting for her at the spring where they'd planned to meet. She never questioned why he would leave the black dahlia for her, either. For sixty years, she had assumed the flower was a symbol of what Jack thought was her great betrayal, not someone else's, too.

FORTY-SEVEN

When Cassie had packed her bags for this final trip back to Calypso Springs, she never imagined she'd find herself at the bottom of the spring, partaking in the strangest family therapy session on earth. But there she was. Breathing under water. Holding hands with her long-lost mother and the mythical creature who cursed them all. Reliving the worst moments of their lives. She wondered if they might create something out of the experience to take with them. *I survived a family curse, and all I got was this lousy tee-shirt.*

Perhaps something a bit more meaningful.

She hoped plowing through the weeds of their history to find the truth would set them all free. But she bristled when the memories Calypso wanted to visit next became clear. The clever water spirit was directing their recollections to suit some sort of agenda, but Cassie hadn't planned to share this one with Emma. She was too ashamed.

In a cold, dark room thirty years ago, Cassie sat next to Jack, her father, on his deathbed. He'd had another heart attack and wouldn't survive the night. But she stared into the middle distance with other people on her mind.

"You're thinking about doing something stupid, aren't you,"

Jack said out of the blue. It wasn't a question, and there was no humor behind it.

"Why would you say that?" she asked.

"You've got the look."

"No. I'm...I had another dream about them last night."

"And..."

"It was so real I felt like I could touch them."

"I told you, they're not—"

"Sometimes, in my dreams, they feel real. Like they're still alive."

He inhaled and held his breath. "I'm dying, Cassie."

"Don't say that, Daddy. You're going to pull through this one, too."

"No, Cassandra. I'm not." He coughed and hesitated before he spoke. When he did, it came out in a whisper. "You can't go back," he wheezed.

"Back? What do you mean, back?"

Then Jack did the thing he hadn't done since the hospital that night in Calypso Springs a decade before. The thing she'd forgotten because it hurt too much to remember. He touched her bare arm. Everything about that night came rushing back to her. It took her a minute to breathe and speak.

"They're alive. I knew it. I could feel it. I want to go, Daddy. I have to try."

"You're not strong enough," he said.

"What do you mean? I'll get strong, I'll—"

"You're not strong enough to love through it. It'll destroy you."

"You mean live through it?"

"I meant...what I said."

"I don't know what that means."

"You have to find a way to break it if you're ever going to have a chance there."

"How? How do I break it?"

"I can't tell you. I don't...I don't know. Maybe...a great sacrifice of love."

"What does that mean?"

"Give me a pen and paper," he barked.

She searched his room and found a piece of scrap paper with a pen in his nightstand drawer. He took them feebly from her and wrote a name on the paper before he handed it back.

"When the time is right, find her. She'll help you."

His hand was so unsteady, Cassie could hardly read his writing. "Esther...Blum. Who is she? Where is she? How will I know when the time is right?"

"When you have to go back, you'll know."

"But—"

"Get the box under the floor in your old bedroom." He coughed out each word. "Take it to her."

"You're not making sense, Daddy."

"But stay away from that spring. Only trouble there." He exhaled one last breath and then he was gone.

Cassie didn't cry at the funeral. The moment Jack died, all the lies he'd told her over the years lifted like a ghostly fog and she remembered the truth. All of it from long before they left Calypso Springs. How he'd tried to keep her away from Josiah from the very beginning.

Now, she had a plane ticket in her pocket and determination in her bones to prove her father wrong. She would be strong enough for her family.

Back in Calypso Springs, Cassie stood lurking outside Josiah's house, her house, waiting. When her ten-year-old daughter came bursting through the front door and down the porch steps to pick up her bike, Cassie's heart beat double-time. Her palms sweat and her body prickled with thorny excitement. Her little girl was beautiful. So vibrant and full of life. Cassie's chest opened, and she took a deep, endless breath. It felt like the first one she'd taken since she'd left town that terrible night.

But she wasn't ready to meet her. Not yet. Cassie followed as her girl went on a bike ride with friends to the outskirts of town and then took a wrong turn, winding up on the road leading to the nest. Her little girl sat on the edge of the spring, gazing down into the water, mesmerized. But when Cassie approached her there, her chest filled with fire, the intensity increasing with every step she took forward.

She didn't understand why it was so intense this time without making physical contact, but it was probably because of where they were. Jack had told her to stay away from the spring. She imagined it had something to do with the curse.

When Cassie was close enough to talk, her little girl turned to face her. But by then, the burning was so intense she couldn't speak. Cassie couldn't bear to let her father be right, so she took a few more feeble steps toward the daughter she knew as Flora. With every inch she grew closer, Cassie's body shut down more until she nearly collapsed.

"Are you okay?" Flora said, as Cassie stumbled through the dead pine needles and leaves covering the ground near her. "Should I get help?"

"I'm so sorry," Cassie whispered. "I hate him for it, but he was right." She considered touching Flora's cheek, one last memory of her skin, but knew what it would do to both of them, so she didn't.

Cassie stumbled away from her daughter. Her heart splintered into a thousand pieces she would never put back together because it would hurt too damn much. Leaving that time destroyed her more than the first because she knew, now, how final it was. There was nothing left to hope for. Her father was right. She wasn't strong enough to love through the pain. She'd failed her family again.

No matter how many walls she built, or how much she buried her feelings in the quicksand of counterfeit narcissism, she never forgave herself for that.

FORTY-EIGHT

"One last memory," Calypso said. "This will be difficult, but stay with me."

Jack was out of his mind that night. His jealousy had morphed into rage after seeing Esther with Ben. He tore back to the spring and shouted at Calypso.

"Why? Why did you do this to me?" he screamed as she broke through the surface of the water. "Why did you trick me into loving her?"

"I didn't trick you, Jack. You chose love on your own."

"I didn't choose this."

"Maybe you did."

"Nobody in their right mind would choose to be betrayed."

"But I think you expected it."

"What are you talking about?"

"I had my doubts."

"About what? Her? Well, so did I."

"Exactly. I saw the frayed edges of your heart, Jack. The layers you'd built around it over the years to keep everyone out, they unraveled with her. But it was still there. Still strong enough to hold you back from truly loving her."

"What was still there? You're not making sense."

"Your expectation that she would disappoint you too, like everyone else. Maybe even betray you."

"You don't know what you're talking about."

"The one time you let your guard down..."

"You put a spell on us that day."

"I only encouraged what was already there. For Esther at least."

"You tricked us with magic. The flowers you gave us. They were enchanted."

"Esther gave *me* the flowers, Jack. The bottom of my spring was empty for many, many years. When I brought you both down that day, Esther made them blossom. I simply facilitated what was in her heart."

"So she's a witch like you? Some kind of sorceress?"

"No, Jack. Just a girl in love with a boy."

"Lies."

"I never lie. But the truth is what you make of it, Jack. And the truth is, you were always afraid, weren't you?"

"Afraid of what? Drowning? I wasn't afraid."

"Part of you always believed this would be how it ended."

"You know nothing about me, water witch."

"I know more than you think. But it doesn't matter what I know. What do you know, Jack? Did you talk to her? Ask her what the truth is?"

"Dahlia told me everything. And I saw her with my own eyes. Now they're gone."

"For good?"

"Good riddance. I want her out of my system. My father warned me. I never should have trusted her. Or you. You both tricked me. Now I want you to purge her. Fix what you broke!" Jack threw the dog collar, the piece of sled, the rope, and the forget-me-nots, which were very much alive, at Calypso in the water. He dove in and swam as far down as he could before he had to come back up for air. She wasn't protecting his lungs for this.

Calypso didn't understand what was about to happen. She gathered all the pieces of his history with Esther into her hands and held them, like they were fragile. Which they were. Jack surfaced in front of her and grabbed her hands with his, crushing them so she couldn't let go of him or his things.

"You cursed me with love!"

"Love is not a curse, Jack," she said, trying to calm him.

"Love is a lie. You cursed me with a lie. It's my turn now." His eyes grew dark, and it frightened Calypso. The vicious energy she felt in him. He was changing in front of her into someone she didn't recognize. Someone she didn't want to know.

"I curse you for helping her. For 'facilitating' what was in her duplicitous heart." He let go of Calypso long enough to slap both of his hands back and forth hard against the surface of the water, stirring it up into a frenzy.

"I curse her and everyone she loves for tricking me into loving her. Trusting her. Her children, her children's children, they're all going to know this suffering. Any spark of love for them will feel like the agony of betrayal down to their bones. No one is strong enough to love through that kind of pain." With each proclamation, he riled the water more until it was a churning storm surrounding them.

Jack grabbed Calypso's hands again and squeezed. They were both raised high above the edge of the spring on the furious storm he'd created with his anger, it spiraled them up on a giant water spout, and at its zenith Jack released the most terrifying, soul-shredding scream she'd ever heard. The sort of cry that tears a human spirit to pieces.

And because Calypso accommodated the desires of human hearts, without choice or thought, the curse existed in the world, as quickly as he'd wished for it. The water storm died, and they splashed down into the spring, broken and exhausted. She pulled her hands free from his and unfurled them. The forget-me-not flowers had turned as black and dead as Jack's heart.

And he was a man now, no longer a foolish boy.

A new man. Not a better man. A man just like his father.

All the wild flowers at the edge of the spring died as Jack trudged through them, leaving Calypso without another word. Dead morning glory vines grew from nowhere, a great mass of desiccated weeds blanketing the entire surface of the spring. They buried her under the heavy reminder of what it was like for a troubled soul, ruled by fear, to love in vain.

As the water drained down down down, twenty feet from the top of the spring now, it left Calypso trapped underneath the vines to live in a barren cavern alone. The magnificent garden Esther had grown from the essence of her generous heart lay decaying in the dark at the bottom.

As she rode in the back seat of her family's car that night, stolen away from the life she most wanted to live, Esther heard and felt Jack's cry and it tore her to pieces. In the same moment, a spark flickered inside her belly and she knew her life would never be the same.

Twenty years later, before he left town for good, Jack returned to the spring one last time. As soon as she heard his deep voice beckoning her, Calypso's spirit soared, hopeful he was there to reverse what he'd done, repair what he'd destroyed. The spring water rose twenty feet up to the edge and she surfaced through the thick vines to speak to him.

"Have you come back to heal, Jack? To fix it?" she asked.

"I want my things," he said without looking at her. This was not the response she had hoped for.

"Surely you've discovered the truth?"

"The truth doesn't matter."

"The truth always matters. But what you do with it matters more."

"You think you're so wise, but you know nothing. You're not even human."

"You don't have to be human to know how the human heart works."

"Give me my things." He thrust his hand out to her, expecting her to do as he demanded. She ignored it.

"Have you found peace, Jack?"

"I make a good living. I support my family."

"That's not what I asked."

"I don't know what you want from me."

"Forgive, Jack."

"Forgiveness means nothing. It changes nothing for her."

"It's not for her. She did nothing that needs forgiveness. I think you know that by now."

"Doesn't matter what I know."

"Of course it matters. You have the power to fix this. To heal the past."

"What's done is done."

"Why were you so quick to believe Dahlia that night? The minute she gave you the opportunity to believe the worst of Esther, you took it."

"And?"

"You've never forgiven yourself for it. For ruining her life and your own. For what it's done to your child. What it will keep doing to your family if you let it. You can stop it, Jack. You can break it."

Calypso swam to the edge and gave Jack his things. The same mementos that would find their way into a lockbox to be opened forty years later. She held his hand, enclosing it in hers the way he'd done that terrible night. Searched his steel-gray eyes for signs of softening, any sense that he processed what she was trying to tell him. But he was an empty shell built of impenetrable walls.

"Forgiveness is powerful, Jack. It can change everything."

He stayed with her for a moment, long enough to spark a glimmer of hope. But then he flung her hands away, like they were burning him, and left without another word, stealing that hope with him for good.

FORTY-NINE

W e woke on solid ground, all three of us lying on our backs in a pile of dead leaves and pine needles off to the side of the nest. Everything was different now, yet nothing had changed. Sparks flew between us because we were still holding hands, like the paper people chains kids used to make in grade school. A paper family chain. Had that just happened or had it been some kind of fever dream we'd all experienced together?

We were soaking wet, so it must have been real. But how did we get back there with everyone again? And what were we supposed to do now? We released each other's hands as Tee, Hopper, Sam, and Dahlia helped us to our feet and to breathe the air again.

No one spoke, which was odd for people who always had something to say about everything. But there was so much to say, now. Where to begin?

The shock was still wearing off and I wasn't sure if my voice would work. Living inside those disturbing family memories was such a total body experience, I wasn't sure anything was working yet. My legs were rubbery and weak and it felt like I was still breathing under water. Or breathing in the water.

I wasn't the only one struggling. Cassie and Esther began

wheezing along with me, and Bob lay on his side, gasping for air. I didn't have time to process the things we'd all been through down in the spring because Bob was worse than ever now, like the curse was digging in its heels.

"No, Bob." I couldn't force my wobbly legs to move, so Sam came to my rescue, holding me up as I stumbled over to him. His quick, shallow breaths scared me. His tongue hung limp outside his mouth, turning a terrifying shade of blue.

"What do I do? I don't know what to do." Everyone stood there watching us. No one knew how to fix Bob. "I thought it would be over. I thought we broke it down there, the three of us. We all know what happened now, what Jack did. We know the truth. What are we supposed to do now?" I yelled, hoping Calypso would hear me.

I curled up on my side next to Bob, trying to comfort him and help him breathe easier, but nothing worked. I was ready to start CPR when Calypso's voice came to me again.

"From the beginning comes the end," she whispered in my head. I glanced at Cassie and Esther to see if they'd heard her too, but they didn't acknowledge anything, so maybe it was a personal message to me.

"Jack may have cursed you, but I gave you a gift inside of it," she said.

"A gift?" I asked, silently.

"Your memories are a gift to each other. Use them."

"How do I use them to help Bob?"

"You said, 'whatever it takes.' You would do whatever it took to heal him."

"Yes. Whatever it takes."

"Then you have to do what it takes, Emma."

"Tell me!"

"I've shown you."

"But I don't understand!"

"Bob has never hurt you, never disappointed you," Calypso said. "Loving him is easy. Loving people is difficult. Your grandfather wasn't brave enough to love or forgive. He cursed his own children with hardness because he never understood a vulnerable heart is a courageous heart," Calypso said in my head.

"A vulnerable heart is a courageous heart," Esther said out loud. Calypso had been speaking to all of us. "And courageous hearts love through the pain."

Esther faced Dahlia, who'd rushed to her side when we woke. She flung her frail arms around Dahlia's thin waist with the enthusiasm of a child. Dahlia wasn't expecting it, and it nearly bowled her over. She didn't seem to know what to do with the embrace. She didn't return it, kept her arms straight by her sides with balled fists.

"It wasn't your fault, Dahli," Esther said.

"Calypso showed you then," Dahlia replied through clenched teeth. She seemed to be in every kind of distress. "I was terrified you'd hate me if you knew the truth."

"I could never hate you. I was surprised, yes, but then I felt it."

"Felt it?"

"Your deep sadness," Esther said, tightening her grip. "You were in love with him too. I didn't know. I didn't know, Dahli. We're all capable of treachery when we're hurting, especially at that age. I was too preoccupied to pay attention to you. I'm so sorry."

"It's all my fault," Dahlia whispered, hanging her head. "Everything. If I hadn't..." She seemed defeated, still not embracing Esther. "I don't know how to make it right."

"You've been making it right for the last sixty years, Dahli, taking care of me. No matter what you did that night, this curse was no one's fault but Jack's. He did this, not you. It's well past time you release yourself from that guilt."

Dahlia's fists stayed still for a few long moments and then began to loosen and stretch. Esther didn't move, didn't let go. When Dahlia's arms finally crept around Esther's back to embrace her, the energy around them shifted. They softened into one another and stayed there with no sign of discomfort. Both smiled through their tears.

"Hold on, mister. Please, hold on," I said to Bob, kissing his nose as he continued to struggle.

I knew what I needed to do now, but as soon as I stood and turned toward Cassie, she was already there, throwing her arms around me.

We gripped each other and our connection was fire. The curse wasn't done with us yet.

We'd been through a war down in the spring. So much family history relived. And now I knew how completely wrong I'd been about her this whole time.

"I'm sorry," she said breathlessly, squeezing me tighter to her. "I'm so sorry, Emma."

It was the one thing I'd needed to hear, but it almost felt wrong for her to say it now, knowing what she'd been through too. What we'd both fought through because of Jack. Building fortresses around ourselves, sacrificing love, living in constant pain.

We were working against dark forces sewn into our bones from the beginning. How do you combat that?

"You did what you could. That's all I ever wanted. Just to know you wanted me."

"I was desperate to be your mother, Emma. I'm so sorry I wasn't strong enough to do that. To be here for you."

"You tried. You couldn't see a way around it, but you tried. That means everything."

The blazing heat between us began to cool and the pain eased slowly away. I could even feel the warmth of her arms around me now instead of a rushing firestorm.

We released our grip on each other, thinking, hoping, this was it. We'd done it. Pieced the broken puzzle of our family back together.

Such a strange and foreign thing, my mother gazing at me with love and pride and that hint of mischievousness I was thrilled to see again. We breathed easier, finally out of the storm.

"Oh no," Tee gasped, pulling us back to reality. She ran to Bob lying on his side, not moving. Not breathing.

FIFTY

Tee jumped aside as I crashed to the ground next to Bob. I felt for breath around his nose and mouth and searched his chest for movement, but it was still.

"No. No! We did what you said, Calypso. Please don't take him. What do you want from me?" I screamed, laying over Bob. Everyone stood around us now, unable to help.

Calypso's voice came to me again.

"Emma, your heart is pure and strong. Resilient, much like your mother's and grandmother's. But you've forgotten someone."

"Who?"

"Every heart has a story to tell, including yours. You must decide if you're willing to listen," Calypso said. "Loving is difficult. Complicated. Messy. Especially after someone has hurt you and betrayed your trust," she whispered into me. "Every disappointment hardens your heart a little more. You love and trust a little less. Much like Jack before the curse. But if you have the courage to love them through their faults and let them love you through your own, no matter how big or small, you can break this cycle right now."

We weren't related by blood, so I didn't imagine she would be an integral part of breaking this family curse, but of course, I was wrong. Without another thought, I jumped up and grabbed Tee as I wept for Bob. We held each other so tightly it was difficult for either of us to breathe. But we did, through the storm, and into our history together.

My much younger father was sitting in the middle of a small, dark living room in his tattered recliner cradling a baby. Cradling me. He sat hunched over, like a big man trying to become a small one. Trying to disappear.

His frizzy ginger hair rose, unruly as ever, over his head, like a wild beast. Unkempt, with stains on his flannel shirt, he looked like he hadn't showered in days.

He was feeding me a bottle and crying. Dad, silently weeping. I'd never seen that before. My body ached for him. I was inside his suffering through Tee's eyes now. His excruciating loss and bewilderment about what happened to the love of his life. The panic and fear of having to care for a brand new baby all on his own now. Suddenly not knowing or understanding anything about his own life and feeling irrevocably lost.

A young, timid Tee took me from him as a gentle favor before he imploded and drew me into the black hole he'd become. She fed me and held me, cooing and caressing my head as I drifted off to sleep, unaware of anything that had transpired in my young life. Unaware of all that was to come.

Tee was there from the very beginning, helping, comforting, being a friend. There was love in her heart for my father. I could feel that energy, and maybe there was hope there too, for something that might become more someday between them. But mostly there was a pureness of intention to help her dear friend when he needed it most.

As quickly as we'd come, we were off into a succession of memories. Tee braiding my hair for my seventh-grade recital. Camping by my side when I was sick with the flu days later. Tee in the audience for every single terrible play I did in middle and high school. Taking pictures of me with my prom date, Matt Furlow. Comforting me when Matt Furlow dumped me for Katie Brooks at the prom. Hugging me a little too long when I left for college. Hugging me a little too long when I quit college and came back home to take care of Dad.

Tee there for every big and small event in my life that mattered and didn't.

But it all mattered. Every single moment. As we stood holding each other, something struck me. I couldn't remember the last time I'd told Tee I loved her, or let her know how much I appreciated her being there for me, no matter what. All I did was push her away.

"I'm so sorry," I said. The words rushed out of me and I said it again and again because I was worried they wouldn't land. "I'm so sorry, Tee."

She pulled away and held me by the shoulders. "What are *you* apologizing for? Emma, honey...if I could go back. If I could change anything, I never would have—"

"—I would have. To protect you." I understood that now. "You were protecting your family, Tee."

"But I ruined yours."

"No, you didn't. You are my family." The ache still ricocheting around inside me dissipated as we talked. "For forty years, you've been right here, showing me how much you love me, and I took it for granted. I took you for granted. And I'm so sorry. I've never said this before, but I should have a million times. You're an amazing mom, Tee. You always have been."

Tears streamed down her flushed and sweaty cheeks. "You mean our run isn't over yet?" she asked.

"Not by a long shot, honey," I said, pulling her tight against me again. Then I felt another arm around me.

"I understand why you did it, Tee," Cassie said, wrapping her arms around both of us.

"If I'd known he was going to take you—"

"He didn't."

"What?" Tee asked, pulling back to look at both of us.

"He didn't take me. I left on my own," Cassie said, maintaining eye contact with Tee. She seemed to need to own her truth now.

"Why?"

"I didn't think I had a choice."

"She didn't want to hurt me, Tee," I said. "What you felt touching me, imagine a newborn feeling that. Every touch, nothing but fire and misery. It was the curse."

Tee's understanding came swiftly, lifting forty years of guilt from her spirit. She hugged us both again.

"I'm sorry you've lived with that burden for so long," Cassie said. "My father was responsible for everything that happened back then. But it's not an excuse for the way I treated you. I apologize for being such a terror."

"Well, curse or no curse, I don't expect that to change much." Tee smiled and squeezed us even tighter. The storm subsided little by little with every word we spoke.

And then, to close the circle once more, Esther joined us and brought a sudden jolt of energy with her. It was exhilarating and filled me limb to limb with something I hadn't felt in a very long time.

Hope.

"From the beginning comes the end," she whispered. Instead of grief and pain, her touch now brought much needed comfort and peace, the driving force of life.

Love.

The sky didn't part. Angels didn't sing. No one came down from on high to proclaim we'd broken the curse, but we knew we had. Like demons being exorcised, the darkness in us had fled.

When we pulled apart, electric-blue forget-me-nots blossomed in Esther's hair. A ring of wildflowers grew all around the top of the spring, sprawling and beautiful. And we all seemed twenty years younger, like we'd aged in reverse.

Then it hit me.

Bob.

The most magnificent and unexpected sound erupted next to us. Bob barked, jealous he wasn't getting attention from his favorite people.

I felt like I could fly.

FIFTY-ONE

That afternoon at the house, I stood in the back doorway, not able to move into the yard to find out. Bob behind me, nudging my leg forward, didn't even persuade me to take the first step. The branches of the dad-tree swayed in the breeze the way regular willow branches might on an ordinary tree. One not possessed by the spirit of a much-beloved father anymore. I didn't know if the curse had extended to him as well. If that was how he'd become this *other version of himself*, as Tee had said. And if, in breaking it, we'd broken his spell too.

Cassie and Tee stood on either side of me as we watched the leaves dance and flutter on their branches. They each put one hand on my back, crisscrossing arms behind me. They were being warm and supportive, and annoyingly pushy.

I didn't want to say goodbye to Dad yet. I'd grown fond of the idea that he'd always be there in the backyard, whenever I needed him. Even if I was angry with him, he'd still be there.

"Only way out is through," Tee whispered.

"I don't know. I could just never go into the backyard again. It could be a fun game. Is he or isn't he?"

"It's an option," Tee said.

"It's ridiculous," Cassie chimed in. Breaking the curse hadn't *entirely* transformed her...

"But we're here, and we will be, whether or not he is," she said.

...only in the most important ways.

"Is it silly to hope a little magic stayed with me?" I asked.

"Not at all, honey."

The first step on the journey to truth is the hardest, isn't it? Overcoming that wall of inertia that keeps you from moving toward it, keeps you locked into your current cycle of denial and avoidance.

But when you have love at your back, however that manifests itself, the truth isn't so scary, because, no matter what, you're going to be okay.

"I miss you, Dad," I said, standing under the willow, staring at the trunk. Begging him to stare back at me. But he didn't. I was talking to a once extraordinary, now ordinary tree.

"Everything's changed, but you know that by now. I...I just miss you. I wish you were here." Saying it out loud made it real, made him really gone. And for the first time since he'd died, I allowed myself to mourn him, to feel my sadness, instead of running away from it.

It started in my fingertips and toes. A slow-burning ache filled me as I stood there desperately wanting to hug my father one last time. Tears came and my body folded in on itself. I wasn't sure if I could withstand any more suffering. But this was different. Because I was different. This was normal, and the grief would come and go in waves, maybe for the rest of my life, but I wasn't going to run from it anymore. I let it wash over me and breathed through it.

It felt like a butterfly or some other fluttering thing tickling my back with its wings or leaves, but the tree branches rustled in the wind where they fell naturally, not in my personal space like they had for the last month. My father hadn't come back to hug me, and he never would again.

But my mothers had. They both embraced me, tickling my face with their hair, lifting me up when I didn't feel like I could stand on my own. And I let them because you're never too old or too strong to be loved and supported. What a glorious thing when that connection brings peace.

FIFTY-TWO

That evening, Tee, Cassie, Bob, and I met Esther and Dahlia back at the spring to thank Calypso and say our goodbyes, while Sam and Hopper continued packing up the house for me. I'd sorted out piles of Dad's things for keeping, thrift store, and trash in the attic that day with everyone helping. I was beyond grateful for that help since I had less than a week to leave.

Everything had changed at the spring. I was too much in shock earlier to notice the stunning beauty of it all. Breaking the curse transformed Calypso Woods into a lush, thriving forest. Wildflowers sprouted everywhere.

The nest was no longer an appropriate nickname. The water rested five feet from the top now. A giant pool so deep and clear and inviting, it took every ounce of restraint I had not to dive in head first, even with my lack of swimming skills. The air surrounding the spring had always been cold and devoid of scent. Now it was warm and filled with the fragrances of a thousand different blossoms.

And down at the bottom of the spring, a dazzling garden, a watercolor masterpiece.

We stood at the edge next to one another, close enough to

touch, while we searched for Calypso. I called to her in my mind, but she was being coy.

No one said anything out loud for the longest time. And then a question popped into my head. "Why did it take so long? I mean, for all of this to happen?" My voice felt rusty and out of place in the stillness.

"We watched you from afar, dear," Esther said. "For so long. We always kept track of you."

That felt good. Knowing they were witnessing my life, watching over me, even if I didn't know they existed. Like grumpy guardian angels.

"We needed to get you two together," Dahlia said, pointing to me and Cassie. "But Cassie couldn't be around Josiah, it would hurt her too much, so we had to wait for the right time, when he was gone. That tree situation threw a wrench into things, though."

"Oh my god," I said, seized by a horrifying thought. "You didn't, he didn't...precipitate his own...?"

"Oh, heavens no!" Esther said. "We're not monsters, dear. He was very ill, your father. Such a lovely soul, but very, very ill."

"So, why didn't you tell me the first time I met you? When Bob and I came to your house that night?"

"Were you ready then?" Dahlia asked.

"What do you mean, ready?"

"Would you have been open to it if we'd told you then?"

"Fair point." I definitely wouldn't have been ready for any of this. I still wasn't ready when it came down to it this morning.

"We needed you both to come back to us in your own time, so we knew it was right for you. Can't rush these things, dear. You can't force them like our fathers tried to do," Esther said.

"How long have you known Dad? Did you meet after he sent you the letter?"

"Oh, no, dear. We were still living in Maiden Lake then. It wasn't the right time."

"How did you meet him?"

"Quite by chance, actually. He began delivering our meals about a year ago. Until he couldn't anymore."

"That sneaky sonofa..." I said, shaking my head in disbelief. Tee smiled wistfully at me while she listened. "Did you know he did that?" I asked her.

"Like I said, he didn't tell me *everything*," Tee said, shaking her head.

"Did he know about the curse?" I asked Esther.

"He knew enough. That we had issues to sort out," Esther said. "And he wanted that to happen for all of us. Your father loved you so much, dear." Esther took my hands in hers and squeezed.

"Why did he sell the house? Why make me give away all of his things?"

"He knew you'd stay stuck, trying to dig your way out of the debt he blamed himself for. He wanted more for you than that," Dahlia said.

"He wanted you to soar, dear." Esther's eyes twinkled when she smiled at me, still squeezing my hand.

"About the house." Dahlia pulled an official-looking envelope from her purse and handed it to me. *Cranston and Associates* was printed on it. I read through the brief letter inside, stunned.

"What is it, honey?" Tee whispered in my ear.

"We bought it, dear. And we're signing it over to you. No more debt. It's yours now," Esther said.

My head spun. They bought the house for me. The grandmother I didn't know I had before that morning bought my house for me. How was that possible? "I don't know what to say."

"Thank you is standard," Dahlia said without a hint of good humor. Breaking the curse hadn't changed her personality a bit.

"Thank you," I said, "of course, thank you! I can't believe you did this for me." I hugged Esther, but something didn't feel right. My gut told me I didn't belong there anymore. "I don't know how I can repay this incredible gift."

"That's the thing about gifts, dear. You don't have to."

"Can I pay it forward, then?" I asked, releasing Esther.

"I don't know what that means."

"I'd love for you to give it to Cassie."

Cassie looked dumbfounded. She'd been quiet for so long, I might have forgotten she was there if she hadn't grabbed my hand.

"Dad was right," I said to Cassie, "I need to move out, find my own way. Maybe even do a little soaring." It felt great to say that out loud. "You'll be home. Maybe not the way you imagined back then, but it's something. If you want it."

"Thank you, daughter," she said with tears in her eyes. She pulled me close and I wondered if I'd ever get used to hugging my mother. One thing was certain, I'd never take it for granted.

When we separated, Cassie handed me a small pink diary with hand-drawn sunflowers on the cover. "You wanted to know our story. This was the beginning."

The diary felt substantial, like it consisted of more than just paper and ink. It held the weight and power of love inside. "Thank you," I said, holding my parents' story close to my heart. "I can't wait to read it."

Following Cassie, Esther handed me a worn leather book, too. Filled with hundreds of pages of delicate cursive handwriting and pressed flowers between every page. "In case you'd like to know how everything began," Esther said. "It's all there." She touched my cheek with her warm hand. "Oh my. I've waited such a long time to be able to do that. I don't think I'll ever get used to it."

I flipped through the diary and found several flattened pink camellias pressed between the pages. When I brushed the flowers with my fingertips, searching for the history in them, they came back to life. In fact, everything blossomed at my touch now.

I glanced up to see everyone smiling at me, even Dahlia.

"I think a little magic stayed with you after all." Tee winked and looked down around our feet, delighted. A ring of delicate pink camellias surrounded us. She bent over to pick one and I was concerned it might hurt her achy back, but she moved with the ease and grace of someone suddenly relieved of a lifetime of guilt. She would never need another cortisone shot.

The new camellias expressed everything I felt being there with those women. How our destinies had always been, and would forever be, inextricably linked.

Then it hit me...Esther *Blum*. How had I not put that together before?

Esther held my shoulders and gazed up at me like she couldn't be more proud. It was a strange sensation. She knew so much about my life and I only knew what she'd shared in memories in the spring and the little details of her early life Hopper had told me. "When you get settled wherever you're going to be, would you mind if we came to visit once in a while?" she asked.

"I'd love that," I said, looking forward to her stories. She took me in her arms and the strength of her embrace surprised me.

I glanced at Dahlia, who stood behind Esther, with her arms straight at her sides and a stern look on her face, as usual. She shook her head at me. "Not a hugger."

Dahlia was born knowing who she was and who she was not. It was time I figured that out for myself. I couldn't wait to explore my new superpowers. Maybe I would carry on my grandmother's legacy with flowers. We would have a much happier ending this time around.

Esther plucked a flower and tucked it behind Cassie's ear. A simple act of love, not so simple in the making. It took us sixty years to get there. I tried not to mourn the lost time, but to appreciate whatever time we had left.

Under the best circumstances, navigating relationships is complicated. Allowing someone to wander through your heart can be a daunting proposition. It takes courage to trust, and maybe even a little magic, to open yourself up to real, meaningful connection. One day, one moment of kindness, one act of forgiveness at a time.

Of course, Bob understood all of that, because dogs understand things humans never will. Their capacity for unconditional love proves what's possible for us all, if we'd only follow their lead.

Easier said than done, but we can keep trying.

Calypso never came back to us, that day or any other. I imagine she knew we would take care of each other now.

And she was right.

EPILOGUE

C assie's hands shook as she waited at the airport. It had been years since she was this nervous. Everything had changed, and she hoped she wasn't meddling in something she didn't have a right to. She'd find out soon enough.

Esther had convinced her to do it. Cassie hoped she was right to listen to her mother. Her mother. She was still getting used to that. Like they all were.

"Hello," Mary said, stiff as ever when she greeted Cassie in the small airport terminal. She didn't reach out to hug Cassie, but she never had, so it was business as usual.

"Good flight?" Cassie asked, to avoid the heavy silences that filled their time together.

"It was fine," Mary said with a tight smile.

The ride back to Calypso Springs was much of the same. But when they approached the house, her old home, Mary gasped. Cassie hadn't told her anything yet. There was time for that later, if she would take part in a conversation.

Raymond stepped out onto the porch, hair combed neatly (it was about time and only because Cassie made him), clean shaven, wearing one of Josiah's suits.

Mary stopped when she saw him. "Ray," she whispered,

breathless. They stayed that way, gazing at one another for the longest time. Cassie knew then she'd done the right thing.

But Mary still didn't move forward. Cassie suddenly worried that too much time had passed. That too many years of uncertainty filled the limited space between them now. That Mary wouldn't find the strength to move through it.

Ray pulled a delicate bouquet of magenta lilacs from behind his back and held them out to her.

"I'll let you two catch up," Cassie said and turned to walk away, giving them privacy.

Mary grasped Cassie's arm. With a quizzical look in her eye, she smiled. "I don't understand."

"I didn't either, but I do now," Cassie said.

"All those years. I—"

"We have things to discuss. But right now..." Cassie motioned to Raymond, waiting. Mary glanced at him and back to Cassie. In all the years she'd known her, she'd never seen Mary cry. This was a first.

Then, Mary did something else she'd never done. She embraced Cassie. "Thank you," she whispered, gripping her. "Thank you."

Mary didn't waste another moment. She rushed into Raymond's embrace with the energy of a much younger woman.

All the years apart, marriages to the wrong people, abuse and betrayal, bigotry and heartache. Nothing could stop their love for one another.

Esther was right. Love is stronger. Like life, love will always find a way. Cassie's heart blossomed as she sat under the willow tree in her backyard to share her other mother's story with Josiah.

A few weeks later, we were all gathered in what was now my mother's living room to take care of the will. We'd cleaned the house, especially that thing in the corner. It was homey and habitable again, which Cassie appreciated. And while I stayed there until I found my own place to live, I never woke under the tree again.

After Cranston read Dad's will, Tee gave me her laptop.

"What's this?" I asked. Bob lay curled up next to me on the floor with his head resting on my feet.

"This," she said, tapping the spacebar to bring the computer to life, "is for you."

It was a Go-Fund-Me page with my name on it and a photo of Dad, Bob, and me under the tree.

"You were struggling, honey. The funeral, all your father's bills, and then when Bob got sick, well, we had to help."

"So we started this, Em, and it got a virus," Hopper said.

"Went viral, Hopper," Sam said, correcting him.

"Right. That." Hopper held hands with Mary on the couch. He would never steal another lawnmower or anyone else's lingerie again.

"There are so many numbers here," I said, staring at the screen. "I can't take this." My initial, knee-jerk reaction was Rosen's give help. We don't receive it.

"Oh, you can and you will," Cassie said, smiling. She still loved telling me what to do. That hadn't changed.

It took a minute of deep breathing and a quick conversation with Dad. Then I accepted the gift with tremendous gratitude for the generous people in my life and used it to pay off my outstanding bills.

With the remainder, I bought Fussy's flower shop and, a month later, I opened under a new name. *Carpe Diem*, which, literally translated, means *pluck the flower of the day*.

Minutes after I opened the shop on my first day, the tinkle bell above the door chimed. My heart fluttered when I peeked out from the back arrangement room and saw him. I'd called the day before, hoping he might want to talk.

After my time in the spring with Calypso, other lost memories had resurfaced. I finally knew what had happened between

Jake and me in college. Without warning, as if he didn't matter, I'd cut him out of my life under the weight of the curse. I left school and never spoke to him again. Even when he called and came to my house over and over, searching for answers I wasn't willing or able to give.

Much like Cassie, to ease the guilt for what I'd done, I revised our story in my mind. Convinced myself he'd chosen his family over me. His duty as a son had sent him thousands of miles away, and made it easier to deal with the loss. Our break-up became understandable, inevitable. It was self-preservation at its most basic, but curse or no curse, I had a responsibility to make it right.

He glanced around at the tubs of roses and sunflowers and the chrysanthemums speaking their truths. But he was drawn straight to the bucket of daffodils like I hoped he would be.

"Hi," Jake said, gazing at me like I was the most beautiful thing he'd ever seen. I could get used to that.

"Hi." I wiped my hands on my apron, trying like hell to keep my cool. It felt like the first time we met. I was all jittery and buzzing inside.

"I'd like one of these." He reached into the bucket and pulled out a single yellow daffodil. Its petals glowed in the bright morning sun. The closer he came with it the louder it spoke to me.

"For someone special?" I asked.

"Jury's still out," he said with a cheeky grin. The flower knew what was in his heart. It whispered to me about beginning anew. But I couldn't do that before I atoned for my previous sins.

"Well, if it please the court, this defendant needs to apologize for her past transgressions. Specifically, for the way she shut the plaintiff out, all those years ago, so abruptly, and without explanation. It was cruel, and he most definitely did not deserve that. The defendant would like the court to know she was a very different person then. She didn't understand herself, or how her actions could hurt those she...loved."

"I see. Well, the plaintiff appreciates and hereby accepts the defendant's apology. And in so doing, this court finds her forgiv-en." A shiver raced through me from head to toe and I knew...love was in my future.

"So? How much?" he asked, offering the daffodil to me.

"How much is it worth to you?" I leaned on the counter toward him, smiling as butterflies danced a delightful jig in my belly.

"A date?"

"But I'm so busy with my new business."

"You have stories to tell me," he said, leaning ever closer on the counter.

Wild, amazing stories to freak everyone out with.

"In that case, we may need more than one date," I said, smiling.

"I think we can manage that."

And then we did.

My Dear Reader:

I hope you loved this book and enjoyed living in Calypso Springs with Emma & Bob for a while. In our chaotic world, you chose to spend your time with my story and characters and, to me, that means you're pretty fantastic.

Would you like to tell others what you thought of the story? I'd be so grateful if you could *rate and review it online.*

Just scan the QR code below with your phone's camera and click the webpage button that comes up. It'll take you to *Unbecoming Emma* and you can choose your preferred online retailer.

Or you can type this link into your browser:

https://books2read.com/unbecomingemma

The thing is, ratings and reviews are *magical* for indie authors.

They help us stand out in a congested marketplace by providing social proof for our work, and they also help other readers decide what to buy. *Every. Single. Rating & Review. Helps.*

So, if you do leave one or both, please accept my immense gratitude for taking the time to do that. I've said it before, I'll say it again, *you're pretty fantastic.*

Which also means I'd love to get to know you better. If you *really* enjoyed *Unbecoming Emma* and would like more Kelly Byrne books in your life, sign up to my readers' list with the QR code below.

Or you can type this link into your browser if that's easier:

subscribepage.io/kellybyrnelist

Being on my readers' list is the best way for us to stay connected. I'll send you updates about new releases and projects I'm working on.

I may even ask for suggestions about new stories, which is a fun way for you to be involved in the overall creation process if you want to be.

Whatever you choose, thank you for your time and being a cherished reader. I hope you decide to stick with me on my journey through the wild world of indie publishing. It would be lovely to get to know you better and have you along for the ride.

Till next time,

Kelly Byrne

ACKNOWLEDGMENTS

Thank you, Suzanne Adams, for your brilliant observations and recommendations for the first *and* second draft of this book. Your generosity, honesty, and enthusiasm helped make the story so much better and I'll be forever grateful. Without your nudge, Emma would still be a Scrivener file on my MacBook Air.

My fabulous beta readers: Shawna Littrell, Kristen Newman, Rachael Maltbie, and Chris Adler — your feedback was indispensable. Thank you for reading Emma closely and answering all of my questions. You ladies rock!

Natascha Corrigan Aldridge, my friend, my supporter, my cheerleader. Thank you for being whatever I need, whenever I need it.

And Tony, my love, my positivity warrior, my superhero, thank you for the ridiculous number of hours you spent helping me bring Emma's cover to such vivid life (over and over and over again). For reading Emma and letting me brag about making you cry. And for always, always being my safe place.

ABOUT THE AUTHOR

Kelly Byrne created photography, invented the wheel, and taught Alanis Morissette the meaning of ironic. She has broken the speed of light typing. Twice. In under a year, she's written 1,296 novels. They're all New York Times best sellers with over one billion sales worldwide. On a whim, she discovered the meaning of life and created a crossword puzzle with the answer. No one has solved it. She's never prone to hyperbole, always tells the truth, and loves writing about herself in the third person. Her home is a castle in the sky above Los Angeles. There, you'll find her playing badminton with her superhero boyfriend, snuggling her very silly dog, and breaking the speed of light for the third time on her 1,297th novel while listening to an absurd number of true-crime podcasts. You'll also find her at authorkellybyrne.com.

facebook.com/authorkellybyrne

instagram.com/author_kelly_byrne

goodreads.com/authorkellybyrne